Praise for *New York Times* bestselling author Diana Palmer

"Palmer proves that love and passion can be found even in the most dangerous situations."
—*Publishers Weekly* on *Untamed*

"The popular Palmer has penned another winning novel, a perfect blend of romance and suspense."
—*Booklist* on *Lawman*

"Diana Palmer's characters leap off the page. She captures their emotions and scars beautifully and makes them come alive for readers."
—*RT Book Reviews* on *Lawless*

Praise for author Mona Shroff

"*Matched by Masala* is a mouthwatering book with an easy, funny and fast reading that celebrates Indian culture and cuisine…family values and how facing difficult moments in your life is better when love is around."
—*Harlequin Junkie*

"I am thrilled that Harlequin is featuring more stories about diverse communities. *The Five-Day Reunion*…is a solid book with believable characters, motivations, and evidence of growth that had me totally onboard for Nikhil and Anita to rediscover their love for each other."
—*Dear Author*

"Annika and Daniel's story was sweet and authentic… There is so much love in this story, it's impossible not to get lost in it." —Sera Taíno, author of *A Delicious Dilemma*, on *Then There Was You*

NEW YORK TIMES BESTSELLING AUTHOR

DIANA PALMER

ROGUE STALLION

Special thanks and acknowledgment to Diana Palmer
for her contribution to the Montana Mavericks series.

Recycling programs
for this product may
not exist in your area.

ISBN-13: 978-1-335-66249-1

Rogue Stallion
First published in 1994.
This edition published in 2023.
Copyright © 1994 by Harlequin Enterprises ULC

The Five-Day Reunion
First published in 2022.
This edition published in 2023.
Copyright © 2022 by Mona Shroff

For questions and comments about the quality of this book,
please contact us at CustomerService@Harlequin.com.

Harlequin Enterprises ULC
22 Adelaide St. West, 41st Floor
Toronto, Ontario M5H 4E3, Canada
www.Harlequin.com

Printed in U.S.A.

A prolific author of more than one hundred books,
Diana Palmer got her start as a newspaper reporter.
A *New York Times* bestselling author and voted one of the
top ten romance writers in America, she has a gift for telling
the most sensual tales with charm and humor. Diana lives
with her family in Cornelia, Georgia. Visit her website at
dianapalmer.com.

Visit the Author Profile page
at Harlequin.com for more titles.

ROGUE STALLION

Diana Palmer

Chapter 1

There was a lull in Sheriff Judd Hensley's office, broken only by the soft whir of the fan. It sometimes amused visitors from back East that springtime in Whitehorn, Montana, was every bit as unpredictable as spring in the southeastern part of America, and that the weather could be quite warm. But the man sitting across the desk from Hensley was neither visitor nor was he amused. His dark, handsome face was wearing a brooding scowl, and he was glaring at his superior.

"Why can't the city police investigate? They have two detectives. I'm the only special investigator in the sheriff's department, and I'm overworked as it is," Sterling McCallum said, trying once more.

Hensley toyed with a pen, twirling it on the desk absently while he thought. He was about the same build as McCallum, rugged and quiet. He didn't say much. When he did, the words meant something.

He looked up from the desk. "I know that," he said. "But right now, you're the one who deserves a little aggravation."

McCallum crossed his long legs and leaned back with a rough sigh. His black boots had a flawless shine, a legacy from his years in the U.S. Navy as a career officer. He had an ex-military mind-set that often put him at odds with his boss, especially since he'd mustered out with the rank of captain. He was much more used to giving orders than to taking them.

In the navy, the expected answer to any charge of dereliction of duty, regardless of innocence or guilt, was, "No excuse, sir." It was still hard for McCallum to get used to defending his actions. "I did what the situation called for," he said tersely. "When someone tries to pull a gun on me, I get twitchy."

"That was only bravado," Hensley pointed out, "and you knocked out one of his teeth. The department has to pay for it. The county commission climbed all over me and I didn't like it." He leaned forward with his hands clasped and gave the younger man a steady look. "Now you're the one with the problems. Dugin Kincaid found an abandoned baby on his doorstep."

"Maybe it's his," McCallum said with smiling sarcasm. Dugin was a pale imitation of his rancher father, Jeremiah. The thought of him with a woman amused McCallum.

"As I was saying," the sheriff continued without reacting to the comment, "the baby was found outside the city limits—hence our involvement—and its parents have to be found. You're not working on anything that pressing. You can take this case. I want you to talk with Jessica Larson at the social-welfare office."

McCallum groaned. "Why don't you just shoot me?"

"Now, there's no need to be like that," Hensley said, surprised. "She's a nice woman," he said. "Why, her dad was a fine doctor...."

His voice trailed off abruptly. McCallum remembered that Hensley's son had died in a hunting accident. Jessica's father had tried everything to save the boy, but it had been impossible. Hensley's wife, Tracy, divorced him a year after the funeral. That had happened years ago, long before McCallum left the service.

"Anyway, Jessica is one of the best social workers in the department," Hensley continued.

"She's the head of the department now, and a royal pain in the neck since her promotion," McCallum shot right back. "She's Little Miss Sunshine, spreading smiles of joy wherever she goes." His black eyes, a legacy from a Crow ancestor, glittered angrily. "She can't separate governmental responsibility from bleeding-heart activism."

"I wonder if it's fair to punish her by sticking her with you?" Hensley asked himself aloud. He threw up his hands. "Well, you'll just have to grin and bear it. I can't sit here arguing with you all day. This is my department. I'm the sheriff. See this?" He pointed at the badge on his uniform.

"Needs polishing," McCallum noted.

Hensley's eyes narrowed. He stood up. "Get out of here before I forget you work for me."

McCallum unfolded his six-foot-plus length from the chair and stood up. He was just a hair taller than the sheriff, and he looked casual in his jeans and knit shirt and denim jacket. But when the jacket fell open, the butt of his .45 automatic was revealed, giving bystanders a hint of the sort of work he did. He was a plain-clothes detective, although only outsiders were fooled by his casual attire. Most everyone in Whitehorn knew that McCallum was as conservative and military as the shine on his black boots indicated.

"Don't shoot anybody," Hensley told him. "And next time a man threatens to shoot you, check for a gun and disarm him before you hit him, please?" Hensley's eyes went to the huge silver-and-turquoise ring that McCallum wore on the middle finger of his right hand. "That ring is so heavy it's a miracle you didn't break his jaw."

McCallum held up his left hand, which was ringless. "This is the hand I hit him with."

"He said it felt like a baseball bat."

"I won't tell you where he hit *me* before he started ranting about shooting," the detective replied, turning to the door. "And if I didn't work for you, a loose tooth would have been the least of his complaints."

"Jessica Larson is expecting you over at the social-services office," Hensley called.

McCallum, to his credit, didn't slam the door.

Jessica Larson was fielding paperwork and phone calls with a calmness that she didn't feel at all. She'd become adept at presenting an unflappable appearance while having hysterics. Since her promotion to social-services director, she'd learned that she could eat at her desk during the day and forgo any private life after work at night. She also realized why her predecessor had taken an early retirement. A lot of people came into this office to get help.

Like most of the rest of the country, Montana was having a hard time with the economy. Even though gambling had been legalized, adding a little more money to the state's strained coffers, it was harder and harder for many local citizens to make ends meet. Ranches went under all the time these days, forced into receivership or eaten up by big corporations. Manual labor, once a valuable commodity in the agricultural sector, was now a burden on the system when those workers lost jobs. They were unskilled and unemployable in any of the new, high-tech markets. Even secretaries had to use computers these days. So did policemen.

The perfunctory knock on her office door was emphasized by her secretary's high-pitched, "But she's busy...!"

"It's all right, Candy," Jessica called to the harassed young blonde. "I'm expecting McCallum." She didn't add that she hadn't expected him a half hour early. She tried to think of Sterling McCallum as a force of nature. He was like a wild stallion, a rogue stallion who traveled alone and made his own rules. Secretly, she was awed by him. He made her wish that she was a gorgeous model with curves in all the right places and a beautiful face—maybe with blond hair instead of brown. At least she was able to replace her big-rimmed glasses with contacts, which helped her appearance. But when she had allergies, she had to wear the glasses...like right now.

McCallum didn't wait for her to ask him to sit down. He took the chair beside her desk and crossed one long leg over the other.

"Let's have it," he said without preamble, looking unutterably bored.

Her eyes slid over his thick dark hair, so conventionally cut, down to his equally dark eyebrows and eyes in an olive-tan face. He had big ears and big hands and big feet, although there was nothing remotely clumsy about him. He had a nose with a crook in it, probably from being broken, and a mouth that she dreamed about: very wide and sexy and definite. Broad shoulders tapered to a broad chest and narrow hips like a rodeo rider's. His stomach was flat and he had long, muscular legs. He was so masculine that he made her ache. She was twenty-five, a mature woman and only about ten years younger than he was, but he made her feel childish sometimes, and inadequate—as a professional and as a woman.

"Hero worship again, Jessica?" he chided, amused by her soft blush.

"Don't tease. This is serious," she chided gently in turn.

He shrugged and sighed. "Okay. What have you done with the child?"

"Jennifer," she told him.

He glowered. "The abandoned baby."

She gave up. He wouldn't allow anyone to become personalized in his company. Boys he had to pick up were juvenile delinquents. Abandoned babies were exactly that. No names. No identity. No complications in his ordered, uncluttered life. He let no one close to him. He had no friends, no family, no connections. Jessica felt painfully sorry for him, although she tried not to let it show. He was so alone and so vulnerable under that tough exterior that he must imagine was his best protection from being wounded. His childhood was no secret to anyone in Whitehorn. Everyone knew that his mother had been an alcoholic and that, after her arrest and subsequent death, he had been shunted from foster home to foster home. His only real value had been as an extra hand on one ranch or another, an outsider always looking in through a cloudy window at what home life might have been under other circumstances.

"You're doing it again," he muttered irritably.

Her slender eyebrows lifted over soft brown eyes. "What?" she asked.

"Pigeonholing me," he said. "Poor orphan, tossed from pillar to post…"

"I wish you'd stop reading my mind," she told him. "It's very disconcerting."

"I wish you'd stop bleeding all over me," he returned. "I don't need pity. I'm content with my life, just as it is. I had a rough time. So what? Plenty of people do. I'm here to talk about a case, Jessica, and it isn't mine."

She smiled self-consciously. "All right, McCallum," she said agreeably, reaching for a file. "The baby was taken to Whitehorn Memorial and checked over. She's perfectly healthy, clean and well-cared for, barely two weeks old. They're keeping her for observation overnight and then it will be up to the juvenile authorities to make arrangements about her care until her parents are located. I'm going over to see her in the morning. I'd like you to come with me."

"I don't need to see it—"

"Her," she corrected. "Baby Jennifer."

"—to start searching for its parents," he concluded without missing a beat.

"Her parents," Jessica corrected calmly.

His dark eyes didn't blink. "Was there anything else?"

"I'll leave here about nine," Jessica continued. "You can ride with me."

His eyes widened. "In that glorified yellow tank you drive?"

"It's a pickup truck!" she exclaimed defensively. "And it's very necessary, considering where I live!"

He refused to think about her cabin in the middle of nowhere, across a creek that flooded with every cloud-burst. It wasn't his place to worry about her just because she had no family. In that aspect of their lives they were very much alike. In other ways...

He stood up. "You can ride with me," he said, giving in with noticeable impatience.

"I hate riding around in a patrol car," she muttered.

"It doesn't have a sign on it. It's a plainclothes car."

"Of course it is, with those plain hubcaps, no white sidewalls, fifteen antennas sticking out of it and a spotlight. It doesn't need a sign, does it? Anyone who isn't blind would recognize it as an unmarked patrol car!"

"It beats driving a yellow tank," he pointed out.

She stood up, too, feeling at a disadvantage when she didn't. But he was still much taller than she was. She pushed at a wisp of brown hair that had escaped from the bun on top of her head. Her beige suit emphasized her slender build, devoid as it was of any really noticeable curves.

"Why do you screw your hair up like that?" he asked curiously.

"It falls in my face when I'm trying to work," she said, indicating the stack of files on her desk. "Besides Candy, I only have two caseworkers, and they're trying to take away one of them because of new budget cuts. I'm already working Saturdays trying to catch up, and they've just complained about the amount of overtime I do."

"That sounds familiar."

"I know," she said cheerily. "Everyone has to work

around tight budgets these days. It's one of the joys of public service."

"Why don't you get married and let some strong man support you?" he taunted.

She tilted her chin saucily. "Are you proposing to me, Deputy?" she asked with a wicked smile. "Has someone been tantalizing you with stories of my home-made bread?"

He'd meant it sarcastically, but she'd turned the tables on him neatly. He gave in with a reluctant grin.

"I'm not the marrying kind," he said. "I don't want a wife and kids."

Her bright expression dimmed a little, but remnants of the smile lingered. "Not everyone does," she said agreeably. The loud interruption of the telephone ringing in the outer office caught her attention, followed by the insistent buzz of the intercom. She turned back to her desk. "Thanks for stopping by. I'll see you in the morning, then," she added as she lifted the receiver. "Yes, Candy," she said.

McCallum's eyes slid quietly over her bowed head. After a minute, he turned and walked out, closing the door gently behind him. He did it without a goodbye. Early in his life, he'd learned not to look back.

The house where McCallum lived was at the end of a wide, dead-end street. His neighbors never intruded, but it got back to him that they felt more secure having a law-enforcement officer in the neighborhood. He sat on his front porch sometimes with a beer and looked at the beauty of his surroundings while watching the children ride by on bicycles. He watched as a stranger watches, learning which children belonged at which houses. He saw affection from some parents and amazing indifference from others. He saw sadness and joy. But he saw it from a distance. His own life held no highs or lows. He was answerable to no one, free to do whatever he pleased with no interference.

He'd had the flu last winter. He'd lain in his bed for over twenty-four hours, burning with fever, unable to cook or even get into the kitchen. Not until he missed work did anyone come looking for him. The incident had punctuated how alone he really was.

He hadn't been alone long. Jessica had hotfooted it over to look after him, ignoring his ranting and raving about not wanting any woman cluttering up his house. She'd fed him and cleaned for him in between doing her own job, and only left when he proved to her that he could get out of bed. Because of the experience, he'd been ruder than ever to her. When he'd gone back to work, she'd taken a pot of chicken soup to the office, enough that he could share it with the other men on his shift. It had been uncomfortable when they'd teased him about Jessica's nurturing, and he'd taken out that irritation on her.

He hadn't even thanked her for her trouble, he recalled. No matter how rude he was she kept coming back, like a friendly little elf who only wanted to make him happy. She was his one soft spot, although, thank God, she didn't know it. He was curt with her because he had to keep her from knowing about his weakness for her. He had been doing a good job; when she looked at him these days, she never met his eyes.

He sipped his beer, glowering at the memories. His free hand dropped to the head of his big brown-and-black Doberman. He'd had the dog for almost a year.

He'd found Mack tied in a croker sack, yipping help-lessly in the shallows of a nearby river. Having rescued the dog, he couldn't find anyone who was willing to take it, and he hadn't had the heart to shoot it. There was no agency in Whitehorn to care for abandoned or stray animals. The only alternative was to adopt the pup, and he had.

At first Mack had been a trial to him. But once he housebroke the dog and it began to follow him around the house—and later, to work—he grew reluctantly fond of it. Now Mack was part of his life. They were insepa-rable, especially on hunting and fishing trips. If he had a family at all, McCallum thought, it was Mack.

He sat back, just enjoying the beauty of Whitehorn. The sun set; the children went inside. And still McCal-lum sat, thinking and listening to the hum of the quiet springtime night.

Finally, he got up. It was after eleven. He'd just gone inside and was turning out the lights when the phone rang.

"It's Hensley," the sheriff announced over the phone. "We've got a 10-16 at the Miles place, a real hummer. It's outside the city police's jurisdiction, so it either has to be you or a deputy."

"It won't do any good to go, you know," McCallum said. "Jerry Miles beats Ellen up twice a month, but she never presses charges. Last time he beat up their twelve-year-old son, and even then—"

"I know."

"I'll go anyway," McCallum said. "It's a hell of a shame we can't lock him up without her having to press charges. She's afraid of him. If she left him, he'd prob-ably go after her, and God knows what he'd do. I've seen it happen. So have you. Everybody says leave him. No-

body says they'll take care of her when he comes looking for her with a gun."

"We have to keep hoping that she'll get help."

"Jessica has tried," McCallum admitted, "but nothing changes. You can't help people until they're ready
to accept it, and the consequences of accepting it."

"I heard that."

McCallum drove out to the Miles home. It was three
miles out of Whitehorn, in the rolling, wide-open coun-
tryside.

He didn't put on the siren. He drove up into the yard
and cut the lights. Then he got out, unfastening the loop
that held his pistol in place in the holster on his hip,
just in case. One of Whitehorn's policemen had been
shot and killed trying to break up a domestic dispute
some years ago.

There was no noise coming from inside. The night
was ominously quiet. McCallum's keen eyes scanned
the area and suddenly noticed a yellow truck parked
just behind the house, on a dirt road that ran behind it
and parallel to the main highway.

Jessica was in there!

He quickened his steps, went up on the front porch
and knocked at the door.

"Police," he announced. "Open up!"

There was a pause. His hand went to the pistol and
he stood just to the side of the doorway, waiting.

The main door opened quite suddenly, and a tired-
looking Jessica Larson smiled at him through a torn
screen. "It's all right," she said, opening the screen door
for him. "He's passed out on the bed. Ellen and Chad
are all right."

McCallum walked into the living room, feeling uncomfortable as he looked at the two people whose lives were as much in ruin as the broken, cheap lamp on the floor. The sofa was stained and the rug on the wood floor had frayed edges. There were old, faded curtains at the windows and a small television still blaring out a game show. Ellen sat on the sofa with red-rimmed eyes, her arm around Chad, who was crying. He had a bruise on one cheek.

"How much longer are you going to let the boy suffer like this, Ellen?" McCallum asked quietly.

She stared at him from dull eyes. "Mister, if I send my husband to jail, he says he'll kill me," she announced. "I think he will. Last time I tried to run away, he shot our dog."

"He's sick, Ellen," Jessica added gently. Her glance in the direction of the bedroom had an odd, frightened edge to it. "He's very sick. Alcoholism can destroy his body, you know. It can kill him."

"Yes, ma'am, I know that. He's a big man, though," the woman continued in a lackluster voice, absently smoothing her son's hair. "He loves me. He says so. He's always sorry, after."

"He's not sorry," McCallum said, his voice deep and steady. "He enjoys watching you cry. He likes making you afraid of him. He gets off on it."

"McCallum!" Jessica said sharply.

He ignored her. He knelt in front of Ellen and stared at her levelly. "Listen to me. My mother was an alcoholic. She used a bottle on me once, and laughed when she broke my arm with it. She said she was sorry, too, after she sobered up, but the day she broke my arm, I stopped believing it. I called the police and they locked her up. And the beatings stopped. For good."

Ellen wiped at her eyes. "Weren't you sorry? I mean, she was your mother. You're supposed to love your mother."

"You don't beat the hell out of people you love," he said coldly. "And you know that. Are you going to keep making excuses for him until he kills your son?"

She gasped, clasping the boy close. "But he won't!" she said huskily. "Oh, no, I know he won't! He loves Chad. He loves me, too. He just drinks so much that he forgets he loves us, that's all."

"If he hurts the child, you'll go to jail as an accessory," McCallum told her. He said it without feeling, without remorse. He said it deliberately. "I swear to God you will. I'll arrest you myself."

Ellen paled. The hands holding her son contracted. "Chad doesn't want to see his daddy go to jail," she said firmly. "Do you, son?"

Chad lifted his head from her shoulder and looked straight at McCallum. "Yes, sir, I do," he said in a choked voice. "I don't want him to hit my mama anymore. I tried to stop him and he did this." He pointed to his eye.

McCallum looked back at Ellen. There was accusation and cold anger in his dark eyes. They seemed to see right through her.

She shivered. "He'll hurt us if I let you take him to jail," she said, admitting the truth at last. "I'm scared of him. I'm so scared!"

Jessica stepped forward. "There's a shelter for battered women," she replied. "I'll make sure you get there. You'll be protected. He won't come after you or Chad, and even if he tries, he can be arrested for that, too."

Ellen bit her lower lip. "He's my *husband,*" she said with emphasis. "The good book says that when you take a vow, you don't ever break it."

McCallum's chin lifted. "The same book says that when a man marries a woman, he cherishes her. It doesn't say one damned thing about being permitted to beat her, does it?"

She hesitated, but only for a minute. "I have an aunt in Lexington, Kentucky. She'd let me and Chad live with her, I know she would. I could go there. He doesn't know about my aunt. He'd never find us."

"Is that what you want?" Jessica asked.

The woman hesitated. Her weary eyes glanced around the room, taking measure of the destruction. She felt as abused as the broken lamp, as the sagging sofa with its torn fabric. Her gaze rested finally on her son and she looked, really looked, at him. No child of twelve should have eyes like that. She'd been thinking only of her own safety, of her vows to her husband, not of the one person whose future should have mattered to her. She touched Chad's hair gently.

"It's all right, son," she said. "It's gonna be all right. I'll get you out of here." She glanced away from his wet eyes to McCallum. Her head jerked toward the bedroom. "I have to get away. I can't press charges against him...."

"Don't worry about it," McCallum said. "He'll sleep for a long time and then he won't know where to look for you. By the time he thinks about trying, he'll be drunk again. The minute he gets behind a wheel, I'll have him before a judge. With three prior DWI convictions, he'll spend some time in jail."

"All right." She got uneasily to her feet. "I'll have to get my things...." Her eyes darted nervously to the bedroom.

McCallum walked to the doorway and stood there. He didn't say a word, but she knew what his actions meant. If her husband woke up while she was packing, McCallum would deal with him.

She smiled gratefully and went hesitantly into the dimly lit bedroom, where her husband was passed out on the bed. Jessica didn't offer to go with her. She sat very still on the sofa, looking around her with a kind of subdued fear that piqued McCallum's curiosity.

Jessica drove her own truck to the bus station, parking it next to the unmarked car in which McCallum had put Chad and his mother. It was acting up again, and she tried to recrank it but it refused to start.

They saw the mother and son onto the bus and stood together until it vanished into the distance.

McCallum glanced at his watch. It was after midnight, but he was wound up and not at all sleepy.

Jessica mistook the obvious gesture for an indication that he wanted to get going. "Thanks for your help," she told him. "I'd better get back home. Could you take me? My truck's on the blink again."

"Sure. I'll send someone over in the morning to fix the truck and deliver it to your office. I'm sure you can get a ride to work."

"Yes, I can. Thanks," she said, relieved.

He caught her arm and shepherded her into the depot, which was open all night. There was a small coffee concession, where an old man sold coffee and doughnuts and soft drinks.

Jessica was dumbfounded. Usually McCallum couldn't wait to get away from her. His wanting to have coffee with her was an historic occasion, and she didn't quite know what to expect.

Chapter 2

McCallum helped her into a small booth and came back with two mugs of steaming coffee.

"What if I didn't drink coffee?" she asked.

He smiled faintly. "I've never seen you without a cup at your elbow," he remarked. "No cream, either. Sugar?"

She shook her head. "I live on the caffeine, not the taste." She cupped her hands around the hot cup and looked at him across the table. "You don't like my company enough to take me out for coffee unless you want something. What is it?"

He was shocked. Did she really have such a low self-image? His dark eyes narrowed on her face, and he couldn't decide why she looked so different. She wasn't wearing makeup—probably she'd been in too big a hurry to get to Ellen's house to bother. And her infrequently worn, big-lensed glasses were perched jauntily on her nose. But it was more than that. Then he realized what the difference was. Her hair—her long, glorious, sable-colored hair—was falling in thick waves around her shoulders and halfway down her back. His fingers itched to bury themselves in it, and the very idea made his eyebrows fly up in surprise.

"I don't read minds," she said politely.

"What?" He frowned, then remembered her question. "I wanted to ask you something."

She nodded resignedly and sipped at her coffee.

He leaned back against the dark red vinyl of the booth, studying her oval face and her big brown eyes behind the round lenses for longer than he meant to. "How is it you wound up in that house during a domestic dispute?"

"Oh. That."

He glared at her. "Don't make light of it," he said shortly. "More cops have been hurt during family quarrels than in shoot-outs."

"Yes, I know, I do read statistics. Ellen called me and I went. That's all."

One eye narrowed. "Next time," he said slowly, "you phone me first, before you walk into something like that. Do you understand me?"

"But I was in no danger," she began.

"The man weighs two-fifty if he weighs a pound," he said shortly. "You're what—a hundred and twenty sopping wet?"

"I'm not helpless!" She laughed nervously. It wouldn't do to let him know the terror she'd felt when Ellen had called her, crying hysterically, begging her to come. It had taken all her courage to walk into that house.

"Do you have martial-arts training?"

She hesitated and then shook her head irritably.

"Do you carry a piece?"

"What would I do with a loaded gun?" she exclaimed. "I'd shoot my leg off!"

The scowl got worse. "Then how did you expect to handle a drunken man who outweighs you by over a hundred pounds and was bent on proving his strength to anyone who came within swinging range?"

She nibbled her lower lip and stared into her coffee. "Because Ellen begged me to. It's my job."

"No, it's not," he said firmly. "Your job is to help people who are down on their luck and to rescue kids from abusive environments. It doesn't include trying to do a policeman's work."

His eyes were unblinking. He had a stare that made her want to back up two steps. She imagined it worked very well on lawbreakers.

She let out a weary breath. "Okay," she said, holding up a slender, ringless hand. "I let my emotions get the best of me. I did something stupid and, fortunately, I didn't get hurt."

"Big of you to admit it," he drawled.

"You're a pain, McCallum," she told him bluntly.

"Funny you should mention it," he replied. "I made the same complaint about you to Hensley only this morning."

"Oh, I know you don't approve of me," she agreed. "You think social workers should be like you—all-business, treating people as though they were statistics, not getting emotionally involved—"

"Bingo!" he said immediately.

She put her coffee cup down gently. "A hundred years ago, most of the country south of here belonged to the Crow," she said, looking pointedly at him, because she knew about his ancestry. "They had a social system that was one of the most efficient ever devised. No one valued personal property above the needs of the group. Gifts were given annually among the whole tribe. When a man killed a deer, regardless of his own need, the meat was given away. To claim it for himself was unthinkable. Arguments were settled by gift giving. Each person cared about every other person in the village, and people were accepted for what they were. And no one was so solitary that he or she didn't belong, in some way, to every family."

He leaned forward. "With the pointed exception of Crazy Horse, who kept to himself almost exclusively."

She nodded. "With his exception."

"Someone told you that I had a Crow ancestor," he guessed accurately.

She shrugged. "In Whitehorn, everyone knows everyone else's business. Well, mostly, anyway," she added, because she was pretty sure that he didn't know about her own emotional scars. The incident had been hushed up because of the nature of the crime, and because there'd been a minor involved. It was just as well. Jessica couldn't have a permanent relationship with a man, even if she would have given most of a leg to have one with McCallum. He was perfect for her in every way.

"I'm more French Canadian in my ancestry than Crow." He studied her own face with quiet curiosity. She had a pretty mouth, like a little bow, and her nose was straight. Her big, dark eyes with their long, curly lashes were her finest feature. Even glasses didn't disguise their beauty.

"Are you nearsighted or farsighted?" he asked abruptly.

"Nearsighted." She adjusted her glasses self-consciously. "I usually wear contacts, but my eyes itch lately from all the grass cuttings. I'm blind as a bat without these. I couldn't even cross a street if I lost them."

His eyes fell to her hands. They were slightly tanned, long-fingered, with oval nails. Very pretty.

"Are you going to arrest Ellen's husband?" she asked suddenly.

He pursed his lips. "Now what do you think?"

"We didn't get Ellen to press charges," she reminded him.

"We couldn't have. If she had, she'd have to come back and face him in court. She's afraid that he might kill her. He's threatened to," he reminded her. "But as it is, he won't know where to look for her, and even if he did, it won't matter."

"What do you mean?" she asked curiously.

His eyes took on a faint glitter, like a stormy night sky. "He gets drunk every night. He's got three previous convictions on DWI and he likes to mix it up in taverns. He'll step over the line and I'll have him behind bars, without Ellen's help. This time I'll make sure the charges stick. Drunkenness is no excuse for brutality."

She was remembering what he'd said to Ellen about his own mother breaking his arm with a bottle when he was a little boy.

She reached out without thinking and gently touched the long sleeve of his blue-patterned Western shirt. "Which arm was it?" she asked quietly.

The compassion in her voice hurt him. He'd never known it in his youth. Even now, he wasn't used to people caring about him in any way. Jessica did, and he didn't want her to. He didn't trust anyone close to him. Years of abuse had made him suspicious of any overture, no matter how well meant.

He jerked his arm away. "What you heard wasn't something you were meant to hear," he said icily. "You had no business being in the house in the first place."

She cupped her mug in her hands and smiled. The words didn't sting her. She'd learned long ago not to take verbal abuse personally. Most children who'd been hurt reacted that way to kindness. They couldn't trust anymore, because the people they loved most had betrayed them in one way or another. His was the same story she'd heard a hundred times before. It never got easier to listen to.

But there was a big difference between anger and hostility. Anger was normal, healthy. Hostility was more habit than anything else, and it stemmed from low esteem, feelings of inadequacy. It was impersonal, unlike aggression, which was intended to hurt. A good social worker quickly learned the difference, and how not to take verbal outpourings seriously. McCallum was something of a psychologist himself. He probably understood himself very well by now.

"I didn't mean to snap," he said curtly.

She only smiled at him, her eyes warm and gentle. "I know. I've spent the past three years working with abused children."

He cursed under his breath. He was overly defensive with her because she knew too much about people like him, and it made him feel naked. He knew that he must hurt her sometimes with his roughness, but damn it, she never fought back or made sarcastic comments. She just sat there with that serene expression on her face.

He wondered if she ever gave way to blazing temper or passion. Both were part and parcel of his tempestuous nature, although he usually managed to control them. Years of self-discipline had helped.

"You don't like being touched, do you?" she asked suddenly.

"Don't presume, ever, to psychoanalyze me," he replied bluntly. "I'm not one of your clients."

"Wasn't there any social worker who tried to help you?" she asked.

"They helped me," he retorted. "I had homes. Several of them, in fact, mostly on ranches."

Her hands tightened on the cup. "Weren't you loved?"

His eyes flashed like glowing coals. "If you mean have I had women, yes," he said with deliberate cruelty. "Plenty of them!"

Jessica surrendered the field. She should have known better than to pry. She didn't want to hear anything about his intimate conquests. The thought of him... like that...was too disturbing. She finished her coffee and dragged a dollar bill out of her pocket to pay for it.

"I'll take care of it," he said carelessly.

She looked at him. "No, you won't," she said quietly. "I pay my own way. Always."

She got up and paid the old man behind the counter, and walked out of the concession ahead of McCallum.

She was already unlocking her pickup truck when he got outside. Even if it wouldn't start, she needed her sweater. She got it out and locked it up again.

"You actually lock that thing?" he asked sarcastically. "My God, anyone who stole it would be doing you a favor."

"I can't afford theft insurance," she said simply. "Keeping my family home takes all my spare cash."

He remembered where she lived, across the creek on the outskirts of town, with a huge tract of land—hundreds of acres. She played at raising cattle on it, and she had a hired hand who looked after things for her. Jessica loved cattle, although she knew nothing about raising them. But prices were down and it wasn't easy. He knew that she was fighting a losing battle, trying to keep the place.

"Why not just sell out and move into one of the new apartment complexes?"

She turned and looked up at him. He was taller up close. "Why, because it's my home. My heritage," she said. "It was one of the first homes built in Whitehorn, over a hundred years ago. I can't sell it."

"Heritage is right here," he said abruptly, placing his hand against her shoulder and collarbone, in the general area of her heart.

The contact shocked her. She moved back, but the truck was in the way.

He smiled quizzically. "What are you so nervous about?" he asked lazily. "This isn't intimate."

She was flushed. The dark eyes that looked up into his were a little frightened.

He stared at her until images began to suggest themselves, and still he didn't move his hand. "You've had to go a lot of places alone, to interview people who wanted assistance," he began. "At least one or two of those places must have had men very much like Ellen's husband—men who were drunk or who thought that a woman coming into a house alone must be asking for it. And when you were younger, you wouldn't have expected…" She caught her breath and his chin lifted. "Yes," he said slowly, almost to himself. "That's it. That's why you're so jumpy around men. I noticed it at Ellen's house. You were concerned for her, but that wasn't altogether why you kept staring so nervously toward the bedroom."

She bit her lower lip and looked at his chest instead of his eyes. His pearl-button shirt was open down past his collarbone, and she could see a thick, black mat of curling hair inside. He was the most aggressively masculine man she'd ever known, and God only knew why she wasn't afraid of him when most men frightened her.

"You won't talk, will you?" he asked above her head.

"McCallum…" She caught his big hand, feeling its strength and warmth. She told herself to push it away, but her fingers couldn't seem to do what her brain was telling them.

His breathing changed, suddenly and audibly. His warm breath stirred the hair at her temple. "But despite whatever happened to you," he continued as if she hadn't spoken, "you're not afraid of me."

"You must let me go now." She spoke quietly. Her hand went flat against his shirtfront. She knew at once that it was a mistake when she felt the warm strength of his body and the cushy softness of the thick hair under the shirt. The feel of him shocked her. "My…goodness, you're—you're furry," she said with a nervous laugh.

"Furry." He deliberately unsnapped two pearly buttons and drew the fabric from under her flattened hand. He guided her cold fingers over the thick pelt that covered him from his collarbone down, and pressed them over the hard nipple.

She opened her mouth to protest, but his body fascinated her. She'd never seen a man like this at close range, much less touched one. He smelled of soap and faint cologne. He drowned her in images, in sensations, in smells. Her fascinated eyes widened as she gave way to her curiosity and began to stroke him hesitantly.

He shivered. Her gaze shot up to his hard face, but his expression was unreadable—except for the faint, unnerving glitter of his eyes.

"A man's nipple is as sensitive as a woman's," he explained quietly. "It excites me when you trace it like that."

The soft words brought her abruptly to her senses. She was making love to a man on a public street in front of the bus depot. With a soft groan, she dragged her hand away from him and bit her lower lip until she tasted blood.

"What a horrified expression," he murmured as he refastened his shirt. "Does it shock you that you can feel like a woman? Or don't you think I know that you hide your own emotions in the job? All this empathy you pour out on your clients is no more than a shield behind which you hide your own needs, your own desires."

Her face tightened. "Don't *you* psychoanalyze *me!*" she gasped, throwing his earlier words right back at him.

"If I'm locked up inside, so are you, honey," he drawled, watching her react to the blunt remark.

"My personal life is my own business, and don't you call me honey!"

She started to turn, but he caught her by the upper arms and turned her back around. His eyes were merciless, predatory.

"Were you raped?" he asked bluntly.

"No!" she said angrily, glaring at him. "And that's all you need to know, McCallum!"

His hands on her arms relaxed, became caressing. He scowled down at her, searching for the right words.

"Let me go!"

"No."

He reached around her and relocked the truck. He helped her into his car without asking if she was ready to come with him, started it and drove straight to his house.

She was numb with surprise. But she came out of her stupor when he pulled the car into his driveway and turned off the engine and lights. "Oh, I can't," she began quickly. "I have to go home!"

Ignoring her protest, he got out and opened the door for her. She let him extricate her and lead her up onto his porch. Mack barked from inside, but once Sterling let them in and turned on the lights, he calmed the big dog easily.

"You know Mack," he told Jessica. "While you're getting reacquainted, I'll make another pot of coffee. If you need to wash your face, bathroom's there," he added, gesturing toward a room between the living room and the kitchen.

Mack growled at Jessica. She would try becoming his friend later, but right now she wanted to bathe her hot face. She couldn't really imagine why she'd allowed McCallum to bring her here, when it was certainly going to destroy her reputation if anyone saw her alone with him after midnight.

By the time she got back to the living room, he had hot coffee on the coffee table, in fairly disreputable black mugs with faded emblems on them.

"I don't have china," he said when she tried to read the writing on hers.

"Neither do I," she confessed. "Except, I do have two place settings of Havilland, but they're cracked. They

were my great-aunt's." She looked at him over her coffee cup. "I shouldn't be here."

"Because it's late and we're alone?"

She nodded.

"I'm a cop."

"Well…yes."

"Your reputation won't suffer," he said, leaning back
to cross his long legs. "If there's one thing I'm not,
it's a womanizer, and everyone knows it. I don't have
women."

"You said you did," she muttered.

He looked toward her with wise, amused eyes. "*Did,*
yes. Not since I came back here. Small towns are hot-
beds of gossip, and I've been the subject of it enough in
my life. I won't risk becoming a household word again
just to satisfy an infrequent ache."

She drank her coffee quickly, trying to hide how
much his words embarrassed her, as well as the refer-
ence to gossip. She had her own skeletons, about which
he apparently knew nothing. It had been a long time
ago, after all, and most of the people who knew about
Jessica's past had moved away or died. Sheriff Judd
Hensley knew, but he wasn't likely to volunteer information to McCallum. Judd was tight-lipped, and he'd
been Jessica's foremost ally at a time when she'd needed
one desperately.

After a minute, Sterling put down his coffee cup
and took hers away from her, setting it neatly in line
with his. He leaned back on the sofa, his body turned
toward hers.

"Tell me."

She clasped her hands tightly in her lap. "I've never

talked about it," she said shortly. "He's dead, anyway, so what good would it do now?"

"I want to know."

"Why?"

His broad shoulders rose and fell. "Who else is there? You don't have any family, Jessica, and I know for a fact you don't have even one friend. Who do you talk to?"

"I talk to God!"

He smiled. "Well, He's probably pretty busy right now, so why don't you tell me?"

She pushed back her long hair. Her eyes sought the framed print of a stag in an autumn forest on the opposite wall. "I can't."

"Have you told anyone?"

Her slender shoulders hunched forward and she dropped her face into her hands with a heavy sigh. "I told my supervisor. My parents were dead by then, and I was living alone."

"Come on," he coaxed. "I may not be your idea of the perfect confidant, but I'll never repeat a word of it. Talking is therapeutic, or so they tell me."

His tone was unexpectedly tender. She glanced at him, grimaced at the patience she saw there—as if he were willing to wait all night if he had to. She might as well tell him a little of what had happened, she supposed.

"I was twenty," she said. "Grass green and sheltered. I knew nothing about men. I was sent out as a case-worker to a house where a man had badly beaten his wife and little daughter. I was going to question his wife one more time after she suddenly withdrew the charges. I went there to find out why, but she wasn't at home and he blamed me for his having been accused. I'd encouraged his wife and daughter to report what happened. He hit me until I couldn't stand up, and then he stripped me...." She paused, then forced the rest of it out. "He didn't rape me, although I suppose he would have if his brother-in-law hadn't driven up. He was arrested and charged, but he plea-bargained his way to a reduced sentence."

"He wasn't charged with attempted rape?"

"One of the more powerful city councilmen was his brother," she told him. She left out the black torment of those weeks. "He was killed in a car wreck after being paroled, and the councilman moved away."

"So he got away with it," McCallum murmured angrily. He smoothed his hand over his hair and stared out the dark window. "I thought you'd led a sheltered, pampered life."

"I did. Up to a point. My best friend had parents who drank too much. There were never any charges, and she hid her bruises really well. She's the reason I went into social work." She smiled bitterly. "It's amazing how much damage liquor does in our society, isn't it?"

He couldn't deny that. "Does your friend live here?"

She shook her head. "She lives in England with her husband. We lost touch years ago."

"Why in God's name didn't you give up your job when you were attacked?"

"Because I do a lot of good," she replied quietly. "After it happened, I thought about quitting. It was only when the man's wife came to me and apologized for what he'd done, and thanked me for trying to help, that I realized I had at least accomplished something. She took her daughter and went to live with her mother.

"I cared too much about the children to quit. I still

do. It taught me a lesson. Now, when I send caseworkers out, I always send them in pairs, even if it takes
more time to work cases. Some children have no ad-
vocates except us."

"God knows, someone needs to care about them," he
replied quietly. "Kids get a rough shake in this world."

She nodded and finished her coffee. Her eyes were
curious, roaming around the room. There were hunting
prints on the walls, but no photographs, no mementos.
Everything that was personal had something military
or work-related stamped on it. Like the mugs with the
police insignias.

"What are you looking for? Sentiment?" he chided.
"You won't find it here. I'm not a sentimental man."

"You're a caring one, in your way," she returned.
"You were kind to Ellen and Chad."

"Taking care of emotionally wounded people goes
with the job," he reminded her. He picked up his coffee
cup and sipped the black liquid. His dark eyes searched
hers. "I'll remind you again that I don't need hero worship from a social worker with a stunted libido."

"Why, McCallum, I didn't know you knew such big
words," she murmured demurely. "Do you read diction-
aries in your spare time? I thought you spent it polishing your pistol."

He chuckled with reserved pleasure. His deep voice
sounded different when he laughed, probably because
the sound was so rare, she mused.

"What do you do with yours?" he asked.

"I do housework," she said. "And read over case files.
I can't sit around and do nothing. I have to stay busy."

He finished his coffee and got up. "Want another
cup?" he asked.

She shook her head and stood up, too. "I have to get home. Tomorrow's another workday."

"Let me open the latch for Mack so that he has access to the backyard and I'll take you over there."

"Won't he run off?" she asked.

"He's got a fenced-in area and his own entrance," he replied. "I keep it latched to make sure the neighbor's damned cat stays out of the house. It walks in and helps itself to his dog food when I'm not home. It climbs right over the fence!"

Jessica had to smother a laugh, he sounded so disgusted. She moved toward the dog, who suddenly growled up at her.

She stopped dead. He was a big dog, and pretty menacing at close range.

"Sorry," McCallum said, tugging Mack toward his exit in the door. "He's not used to women."

"He's big, isn't he?" she asked, avoiding any further comment.

"Big enough. He eats like a horse." He took his keys out of his pocket and locked up behind her while she got into the car.

They drove back toward her place. The night sky was dark, but full of stars. The sky went on forever in this part of the country, and Jessica could understand how McCallum would return here. She herself could never really leave. Her heart would always yearn for home in Montana.

When they got to her cabin, there was a single lighted window, and her big tomcat was outlined in it.

"That's Meriwether," she told him. "He wandered up here a couple of years ago and I let him stay. He's an orange tabby with battle-scarred ears."

"I hate cats," he murmured as he stopped the car at her front door.

"That doesn't surprise me, McCallum. What surprises me is that you have a pet at all—and that you even allow a stray cat on your property."

"Sarcasm is not your style, Miss Larson," he chided.

"How do you know? Other than the time you were sick, you only see me at work."

He pursed his lips and smiled faintly. "It's safer that way. You lonely spinsters are dangerous."

"Not me. I intend to be a lonely spinster for life," she said firmly. "Marriage isn't in my plans."

He scowled. "Don't you want kids?"

She opened her purse and took out her house key. "I like my life exactly as it is. Thanks for the lift. And the shoulder." She glanced at him a little selfconsciously.

"I'm a clam," he said. "I don't broadcast secrets; my own or anyone else's."

"That must be why you're still working for Judd Hensley. He's the same way."

"He knew about your problem, I gather?"

She nodded. "He's been sheriff here for a long time. He and his wife were good friends of my parents. I'm sorry about their divorce. He's a lonely man these days."

"Loneliness isn't a disease," he muttered. "Despite the fact that you women like to treat it like one."

"Still upset about my bringing you that pot of soup, aren't you?" she asked him. "Well, you were sick and nobody else was going to feed and look after you. I'm a social worker. I like taking care of the underprivileged."

"I am *not* underprivileged."

"You were sick and alone."

"I wouldn't have starved."

"You didn't have any food in the house," she countered. "What did you plan to do, eat your dog?"

He made a face. "Considering some of the things *he* eats, God forbid!"

"Well, I wouldn't eat Meriwether even if I really were starving."

He glanced at the cat in the window. "I don't blame you. Anything that ugly should be buried, not eaten."

She made a sound deep in her throat and opened the car door.

"Go ahead," he invited. "Tell me he's not ugly."

"I wouldn't give you the satisfaction of arguing," she said smugly. "Good night."

"Lock that door."

She glowered at him. "I'm twenty-five years old." She pointed at her head. "This works."

"No kidding!"

She made a dismissive gesture with her hand and walked up onto the porch. She didn't look back, even when he beeped the horn as he drove away.

Chapter 3

Jessica unlocked her front door and walked into the familiar confines of the big cabin. A long hall led to the kitchen, past a spare bedroom. The floor, heart of pine, was scattered with worn throw rugs. The living and dining areas were in one room at the front. At the end of the hall near the kitchen was an elegant old bathroom. The plumbing drove her crazy in the winters—which were almost unsurvivable in this house—and the summers were hotter than blazes. She had no air-conditioning and the heating system was unreliable. She had to supplement it with fireplaces and scattered kerosene heaters. Probably one day she'd burn the whole place down around her ears trying to keep warm, but except for the infrequent cold, she remained healthy. She dreamed of a house that was livable year-round.

A soft meow came from the parlor, and Meriwether

came trotting out to greet her. The huge tabby was marmalade colored. He'd been a stray when she found him, a pitiful half-grown scrap of fur with fleas and a stubby tail. She'd cleaned him up and brought him in, and they'd been inseparable ever since. But he hated men. He was a particularly big cat, with sharp claws, and he had to be locked up when the infrequent repairman was called to the house. He spat and hissed at them, and he'd even attacked the man who read the water meter. Now the poor fellow wouldn't come into the yard unless he knew Meriwether was safely locked in the house.

"Well, hello," she said, smiling as he wrapped himself around her ankle. "Want to hear all about the time I had?"

He made a soft sound. She scooped him up under one arm and started up the staircase. "Let me tell you, I've had better nights."

Later, with Meriwether curled up beside her, his big head on her shoulder, she slept, but the old nightmare came back, resurrected probably by the violence she'd seen and heard. She woke in a cold sweat, crying out in the darkness. It was a relief to find herself safe, here in her own house. Meriwether opened his eyes and looked at her when she turned on the light.

"Never mind. Go back to sleep," she told him gently. "I think I'll just read for a while."

She picked up a favorite romance novel from her shelf and settled back to read it. She liked these old ones best, the ones that belonged to a different world and always delivered a happy ending. Soon she was caught up in the novel and reality thankfully vanished for a little while.

* * *

At nine o'clock sharp the next morning, McCallum showed up in Jessica's office. He was wearing beige jeans and a sports jacket over his short-sleeved shirt this morning. No tie. He seemed to hate them; at least, Jessica had yet to see him dressed in one.

She was wearing a gray suit with a loose jacket. Her hair was severely confined on top of her head and she had on just a light touch of makeup. Watching her gather her briefcase, McCallum thought absently that he much preferred the tired woman of the night before, with her glorious hair loose around her shoulders.

"We'll go in my car," he said when they reached the parking lot, putting his sunglasses over his eyes. They gave him an even more threatening demeanor.

"I have to go on to another appointment, so I'll take my truck, now that it's been fixed, thanks to you...."

He opened the passenger door of the patrol car and stood there without saying a word.

She hesitated for a minute, then let him help her into the car. "Are you deliberately intimidating, or does it just come naturally?" she asked when they were on the way to the hospital.

"I spent years ordering noncoms around," he said easily. "Old habits are hard to break. Plays hell at work sometimes. I keep forgetting that Hensley outranks me."

That sounded like humor, but she'd had no sleep to speak of and she felt out of sorts. She clasped her briefcase closer, glancing out the window at the landscape. Montana was beautiful in spring. The area around Whitehorn was uncluttered, with rolling hills that ran forever to the horizon and that later in the year would be rich with grain crops. Occasional herds of cattle dotted the horizon. There were cottonwood and willow trees along the streams, but mostly the country was wide open. It was home. She loved it.

She especially loved Whitehorn. With its wide streets and multitude of trees, the town reminded her of Billings—which had quiet neighborhoods and a spread-out city center, with a refinery right within the city limits. The railroad cut through Billings, just as it did here in Whitehorn. It was necessary for transportation, because mining was big business in southern Montana.

The Whitehorn hospital was surrounded by cottonwood trees. Its grounds were nicely landscaped and there was a statue of Lewis and Clark out front. William Clark's autograph in stone at Pompey's Pillar, near Hardin, Montana, still drew photographers. The Lewis and Clark expedition had come right through Whitehorn.

Jessica introduced herself and McCallum to the ward nurse, and they were taken to the nursery.

Baby Jennifer, or Jenny as she was called, was in a crib there. She looked very pretty, with big blue eyes and a tiny tuft of blond hair on top of her head. She looked up at her visitors without a change of expression, although her eyes were alert and intelligent.

Jessica looked at her hungrily. She put down her briefcase and with a questioning glance at the nurse, who nodded, she picked the baby up and held her close.

"Little angel," she whispered, smiling so sadly that the man at her side scowled. She touched the tiny hand and felt it curl around her finger. She blinked back tears. She would never have a baby. She would never know the joy of feeling it grow in her body, watching its birth, nourishing it at her breast....

She made a sound and McCallum moved between her

and the nurse with magnificent carelessness. "I want to see any articles of clothing that were found on or with the child," he said courteously.

The nurse, diverted, produced a small bundle. He unfastened it. There was one blanket, a worn pink one—probably homemade, judging by the hand-sewn border—with no label. There was a tiny gown, a pretty lacy thing with a foreign label, the sort that might be found at a fancy garage sale. There were some hand-knitted booties and a bottle. The bottle was a common plastic one with nothing outstanding about it. He sighed angrily. No clues here.

"Oh, yes, there's one more thing, Detective," the nurse said suddenly. She produced a small brooch, a pink cameo. "This was attached to the gown. Odd, isn't it, to put something so valuable on a baby? This looks like real gold."

McCallum touched it, turned it over. It was gold, all right, and very old. That was someone's heirloom. It might be the very clue he needed to track down the baby's parents.

He fished out a plastic bag and dropped the cameo into it, fastening it and sticking it in his inside jacket pocket. It was too small to search for prints, and it had been handled by too many people to be of value in that respect. Hensley had checked all these things yesterday when the baby was found. The bottle had been wiped clean of prints, although not by anybody at the Kincaid home. Apparently the child's parents weren't anxious to be found. The puzzling thing was that brooch. Why wipe fingerprints off and then include a probably identifiable piece of heirloom jewelry?

He was still frowning when he turned back to Jessica. She was just putting the child into its crib and straightening. The look on her face was all too easy to read, but she quickly concealed her thoughts with a businesslike expression.

"We'll have to settle her with a child-care provider until the court determines placement," Jessica told the nurse. "I'll take care of that immediately when I get back to the office. I'll need to speak to the attending physician, as well."

"Of course, Miss Larson. If you'll come with me?"

McCallum fell into step beside her, down the long hall to Dr. Henderson's office. They spoke with him about the child's condition and were satisfied that she could be released the next morning.

"I'll send over the necessary forms," Jessica assured him, shaking hands.

"Pity, isn't it?" the doctor said sadly. "Throwing away a baby, like a used paper plate."

"She wasn't exactly thrown away," Jessica reminded him. "At least she was left where people would find her. We've had babies who weren't so fortunate."

McCallum pursed his lips. "Has anyone called to check on the baby?" he asked suddenly.

"Why, yes," the doctor replied curiously. "As a matter of fact, a woman from the *Whitehorn Journal* office called. She wanted to do a story, but I said she must first check with you."

McCallum lifted an eyebrow. "The *Whitehorn Journal* doesn't have a woman reporter."

He frowned. "I understood her to say the *Journal*. I may have been mistaken."

"I doubt it," McCallum said thoughtfully. "It was

probably the child's mother, making sure the baby had been found."

"If she calls again, I'll get in touch with you."

"Thanks," McCallum said.

He and Jessica walked back down the hall toward the hospital exit. He glanced down at her. "How old are you?"

She started. "I'm twenty-five," she said. "Why?"

He looked ahead instead of at her, his hands stuck deep in his jean pockets. "These modern attitudes may work for some women, but they won't work for you. Why don't you get married and have babies of your own, instead of mooning over someone else's?"

She didn't answer him. Rage boiled up inside her, quickening her steps as she made her way out the door toward his car.

He held the door open for her. She didn't even bother to comment on the courtesy or question it, she was so angry. He had no right to make such remarks to her. Her private life was none of his business!

He got in beside her, but he didn't start the engine. He turned toward her, his keen eyes cutting into her face. "You cried," he said shortly.

She grasped her briefcase like a lifeline, staring straight ahead, ignoring him.

He hit the steering wheel with his hand in impotent anger. He shouldn't let her get to him this way.

"How can you be in law enforcement with a temper like that?" she demanded icily.

He stared at her levelly. "I don't hit people."

"You do, too!" she raged. "You hit that man who threatened to pull a gun on you. I heard all about it!"

"Did you hear that *he* kicked me in the… Well, never

mind, but he damned near unmanned me before I laid a finger on him!" he said harshly.

She clutched the briefcase like a shield. "McCallum, you are crude! Crude and absolutely insensitive!"

"Crude? Insensitive?" he exclaimed shortly. He glared at her. "If you think that's crude, suppose I give you the slang term for it then?" he added with a cold smile, and he told her, graphically, what the man had done.

She was breathing through her nostrils. Her eyes were like brown coals, and she was livid.

"Your hand is itching, isn't it?" he taunted. "You want to slap me, but you can't quite work up the nerve."

"You have no right to talk to me like this!"

"How did you ever get into this line of work?" he demanded. "You're a bleeding-heart liberal with more pity than purpose in your life. If you'd take down that hair—" he pulled some pins from her bun "—and keep on those contact lenses, you might even find a man who'd marry you. Then you wouldn't have to spend your life burying your own needs in a job that's little more than a substitute for an adult relationship with a man!"

"You…!" The impact of the briefcase hitting his shoulder shocked him speechless. She hit him again before he could recover. The leather briefcase was heavy, but it was the shock of the attack that left him frozen in his seat when she tumbled out of the car and slammed the door furiously behind her.

She started off down the street with her hair hanging in unruly strands from its once-neat bun and her jacket askew. She looked dignified even in her pathetic state, and she didn't look back once.

Chapter 4

She made it two blocks before her feet gave out. Thank goodness for the Chamber of Commerce, she thought, taking advantage of the strategically placed bench near the curb bearing that agency's compliments. The late April sun was hot, and her suit, though light, was smothering her. The high heels she was wearing with it were killing her. She took off the right one, grimaced and rubbed her hose-clad foot.

She was suddenly aware of the unmarked patrol car that cruised to the curb and stopped.

McCallum got out without any rush and sat down beside her on the bench.

"You are the most difficult man I've ever met," she told him bluntly. "I don't understand why you feel compelled to make me so miserable, when all I've ever wanted to do was be kind to you!"

He leaned back, his eyes hidden behind dark sunglasses, and crossed his long legs. "I don't need kindness and I don't like your kind of woman."

"I know that," she said. "It shows. But I haven't done a thing to you."

He took off his sunglasses and turned his face toward her. It was as unreadable as stone, and about that warm. How could he tell her that her nurturing attitude made him want to scream? He needed a woman and she had a delectable body, but despite her response to him that night in front of the bus station, she backed away from him the minute he came too close. He wasn't conceited, yet he knew he was a physically dynamic, handsome man. Women usually ran after him, not the reverse. Jessica was the exception, and perhaps it was just as well. He wasn't a man with commitment on his mind.

"We're supposed to be working on a case together," he reminded her.

"I don't work on cases with men who talk to me as if I were a hooker," she shot back with cold dark eyes. "I don't have to take that sort of language from you. And I'll remind you that you're supposed to be upholding the law, not verbally breaking it. Or is using foul language in front of a woman no longer on the books as a misdemeanor in Whitehorn?"

He moved uncomfortably on the bench, because it *was* a misdemeanor. She'd knocked him off balance and he'd reacted like an idiot. He didn't like admitting it. "It wasn't foul language. It was explicit," he defended himself.

"Splitting hairs!"

"All right, I was out of line!" He shifted his long legs.

"You get under my skin," he said irritably. "Haven't you noticed?"

"It's hard to miss," she conceded. "If I'm such a trial to you, Detective, there are other caseworkers in my office...."

He turned his head toward her. "Hensley said I work with you. So I work with you."

She reached down and put her shoe back on, unwittingly calling his attention to her long, elegant legs in silky hose.

"That doesn't mean we have to hang out together," she informed him. "We can talk over the phone when necessary."

"I don't like telephones."

Her eyes met his, exasperated. "Have you ever thought of making a list of your dislikes and just handing it to people?" she asked. "Better yet, you might consider a list of things you *do* like. It would be shorter."

He glowered at her. "I never planned to wind up being a hick cop in a hick town working with a woman who thinks a meaningful relationship has something to do with owning a cat."

"I can't imagine why you don't go back into the service, where you felt at home!"

"Made too many enemies." He bit off the words. "I don't fit in there, either, anymore. Everything's changing. New regulations, policies..."

"Did you ever think of becoming a diplomat?" she said with veiled sarcasm.

"No chance of that," he murmured heavily, then sighed. "I should have studied anthropology, I guess."

Her bad temper dissipated like clouds in sunlight. She could picture it. She laughed.

"Oh, hell, don't do that," he said shortly. "I didn't mean to be funny."

"I don't imagine so. Is your lack of diplomacy why you're not in the service anymore?"

He shook his head. "It didn't help my career. But the real problem was the new political climate. I'm no bigot, but I'm not politically correct when it comes to bending over backwards to please special-interest groups. If I don't like something, I can't pretend that I do. I didn't want to end up stationed in a microwavable room in Moscow, listening to people's conversations."

She frowned. "I thought you were in the navy? You know…sailing around in ships and stuff."

His dark eyes narrowed. "I didn't serve on a ship. I was in Naval Intelligence."

"Oh." She hadn't realized that. His past took on a whole new dimension in her eyes. "Then how in the world did you end up here?"

"I had to live someplace. I hate cities, and this is as close to a home as I've ever known," he said simply. "The last place I lived was with an elderly couple over near the county line. They're dead now, but they left me a little property in the Bighorn Mountains. Who knows, I may build a house there one day. Just for me and Mack."

"I don't think I like dogs."

"And I hate cats," he said at once.

"Why doesn't that surprise me?"

His eyebrow jumped. He put his sunglasses back on and got to his feet. He looked marvelously fit, all muscular strength and height, a man in the prime of his life. "I'll run you back to your office. I want to go out to the Kincaid place and have a talk with Jeremiah."

She stood up, holding her briefcase beside her. "I can walk. It's only another block or so."

"Five blocks, and it's midday," he reminded her. "Come on. I won't make any more questionable remarks."

"I'd like that sworn to," she muttered as she let him open the door for her.

"You're a hot-tempered little thing, aren't you?" he asked abruptly.

"I defend myself," she conceded. "I don't know about the 'little' part."

He got in beside her and started the engine. Five minutes later she was back in the parking lot at her office. She was strangely reluctant to get out of the car, though. It was as though something had shifted between them, after weeks of working fairly comfortably with each other. He'd said "the last place he lived," and he'd mentioned an elderly couple, not parents.

"May I ask you something personal?" she said.

He looked straight at her, without removing his sunglasses. "No."

She was used to abruptness and even verbal abuse from clients, but McCallum set new records for it. He was the touchiest man she'd ever met.

"Okay," she said, clutching her briefcase as she opened the door. She looked over her shoulder. "Oh, I'm, uh, sorry about hitting you with this thing. I didn't hurt you, did I?"

"I've been shot a couple of times," he mentioned, just to make sure she got the idea that a bash with a briefcase wasn't going to do much damage.

"Poor old bullets," she muttered.

His face went clean of all expression, but his chest convulsed a time or two.

She got out of the car and slammed the door. She walked around to the driver's side and bent down. "I accept your apology."

"I didn't make any damned apology," he shot right back.

"I'm sure you meant to. I expect you were raised to be a gentleman, it's just that you've forgotten how."

The sunglasses glittered. She moved back a little.

"Don't you have anything to do? What the hell do they pay you for, and don't tell me it's for stand-up comedy."

"Actually, I'm doing a brain-surgery-by-mail course," she said pertly. "You're first on my list of potential patients."

"God forbid." He slipped the car into gear.

"Wait a minute," she said. "Are you going to tell anyone about the brooch you found?"

"No," he replied impatiently. "That brooch is my ace in the hole. I don't want it publicized in case someone comes to claim the baby. I'll mention it to selected people when it comes in useful."

"Oh, I see," she said at once. "You can rule out impostors. If they don't know about the brooch, they're not the baby's mother."

"Smart lady. Don't mention it to anyone."

"I wouldn't think of it. You'll let me know what you find out at the Kincaids', won't you?" she asked.

"Sure. But don't expect miracles. I don't think Dugin's the father, and I don't think we're going to find the baby's mother or any other relatives."

"The baby is blond," she said thoughtfully. "And so is Dugin."

"A lot of men in this community are blond. Besides, have you forgotten that Dugin is engaged to Mary Jo

Plummer? With a dish like that wearing his ring, he isn't likely to be running around making other women pregnant."

"And he could afford to send it away if it was his, or have it adopted," she agreed. "Funny, though, isn't it, for someone to leave a baby on his doorstep? What did his father say?"

"Jeremiah wasn't there, according to Hensley. He'd been away and so Dugin called the law."

"That isn't like the Jeremiah Kincaid I know," she mused. "It would be more in character for him to start yelling his head off and accusing Dugin of fathering it."

"So I've heard."

He didn't say another word. Under that rough exterior, there had to be a heart somewhere. She kept thinking she might excavate it one day, but he was a hard case.

He gave her a curt nod, his mind already on the chore ahead. Dismissing her from his mind, he picked up the mike from his police radio and gave his position and his call letters and signed off. Without even a wave, he sped out of the parking lot.

She watched him until he was out of sight. She was feeling oddly vulnerable. There was a curious warm glow inside her as she went back into the office. She wished she understood her own reactions to the man. McCallum confused and delighted her. Of course, he also made her homicidal.

McCallum went out to the Kincaid ranch the next day, with the brooch in hand. He had some suspicions about that brooch, and it would be just as well to find out if anyone at the ranch recognized it.

When he drove up, the door was opened by Jeremiah himself. He was tall and silver haired, a handsome man in his late sixties. His son was nothing like him, in temperament or looks. Jeremiah had a face that a movie star would have envied.

"Come on in, McCallum, I've been expecting you," Jeremiah said cordially. "Can I pour you a whiskey?"

Characteristically, the man thought everyone shared his own fondness for Old Grandad. McCallum, when he drank, which was rarely, liked the smoothness of scotch whiskey.

"No, thanks. I'm working," McCallum replied.

"You cops." Jeremiah shook his head and poured himself a drink. "Now," he said, when they were seated on the elegant living room furniture, "how can I help you?"

McCallum pulled the brooch, in its plastic bag, out of his pocket and tossed it to the older man. Jeremiah stared at it for a long moment, one finger touching it lightly, reflectively. Then his head lifted.

"Nope," he told McCallum without any expression. "Never saw this before. If it was something that belonged to anyone in this family, you'd better believe I'd recognize it," he added.

He tossed it back to McCallum and lifted his glass to his lips. "What else can I tell you?"

"Was there anything on the baby that wasn't turned in when Sheriff Hensley came?" McCallum persisted.

"Not that I'm aware of," the other man said pleasantly. "Of course, I wasn't home at the time, you know. I didn't find out what had happened until the baby had been taken away. Hell of a thing, isn't it, for a mother to desert her child like that!"

"I didn't say it was deserted by its mother," McCallum replied slowly.

Jeremiah laughed, a little too loudly. "Well, it's hardly likely that the baby's father would have custody, is it? Even in these modern times, most men don't know what to do with a baby!"

"Apparently, some men still don't know how to prevent one, either."

Jeremiah grunted. "Maybe so." He glanced at the younger man. "It isn't Dugin's. I know there's been talk, but I asked the boy straight out. He said that since he got engaged to Mary Jo last year, there hasn't been any other woman."

"And you believe him?"

Jeremiah cleared his throat. "Dugin's sort of slow in that department. Takes a real woman to, uh, help him. That's why he's waited so late in life to marry. Mary Jo's a sweet little thing, but she's a firecracker, too. Caught her kissing him one afternoon out in the barn, and by God if they didn't almost go at it right there, standing up, in front of the whole world! She's something, isn't she, for a children's librarian."

McCallum's eyes were on the lean hands holding the glass of whiskey. They were restless, nervous. Jeremiah was edgy. He hid it well, but not with complete success.

"It sounds as though they'll have a good marriage."

"I think so. She's close to his age, and they sure enjoy being together. Pity about your boss's marriage," he added with a shrug, "but his wife always was too brainy for a man like that. I mean, after all, a cop isn't exactly an Ivy League boy." He noticed the look on McCallum's face and cleared his throat. "Sorry. No offense meant."

"None taken," Sterling replied. He got to his feet.

"If you think of anything that might help us, don't hesitate to call."

"Sure, sure. Look, that crack I made about cops not having much education…"

"I took my baccalaureate degree in science while I was in the navy," he told Jeremiah evenly. "The last few years before I mustered out, I worked in Naval Intelligence."

Jeremiah was surprised. "With that sort of background, why are you working for the sheriff's department?"

"Maybe I just like small towns. And I did grow up here."

"But, man, you could starve on what you make in law enforcement!"

"Do you think so?" McCallum asked with a smile. "Thanks for your time, Mr. Kincaid."

He shook hands with the man and left, thinking privately that he'd rather work for peanuts in law enforcement than live the sort of aimless existence that Jeremiah Kincaid did. The man might have silver hair, but he was a playboy of the first order. He was hardly ever at home, and Dugin certainly wasn't up to the chore of taking care of a spread that size.

Speaking of Dugin… McCallum spotted him near the toolshed, talking to a younger man, and walked toward him.

Dugin shaded his eyes against the sun. He was tall and fair, in his forties, and he was mild-mannered and unassuming. He'd always seemed younger than he was. Perhaps it was because his father had always overshadowed him. Dugin still lived at home and did most everything his father told him to. He smiled and held out his hand when McCallum reached him.

"Nice day, isn't it?" Dugin asked. "What can I do for you, Deputy? And how's the kid?"

"She's fine. They're placing her in care until the case comes up. Listen, do you know anything that you haven't told the sheriff? Was there anything else with the baby that wasn't turned in?"

Dugin thought for a minute and shook his head. "Not a thing. It isn't my kid," he added solemnly. "I hear there's been some talk around Whitehorn about my being the father, but I'm telling you, I don't know anything. I wouldn't risk losing Mary Jo for any other woman, Deputy. Just between us," he added wryly, "I wouldn't have the energy."

McCallum chuckled. "Okay. Thanks."

"Keep in touch with us about the case, will you?" Dugin asked. "Even though it's not my child, I'd still like to know how things come out."

"Sure."

McCallum walked slowly back to his patrol car, wondering all the way why the baby had been left here, and with Dugin. There had to be a clue. He should have shown that cameo to Dugin, but if Jeremiah didn't recognize it, there was little point in showing it to his son. As Jeremiah had suggested, if it were a family heirloom, he would have recognized it immediately.

It was a lazy day, after that. McCallum was drinking coffee in the Hip Hop Café with his mind only vaguely on baby Jennifer and her missing parents. He was aware of faint interest from some of the other diners when his portable walkie-talkie made static as it picked up a call.

Even though most people in Whitehorn knew him, he still drew some curiosity from tourists passing through. He was a good-looking man with a solid, muscular physique that wasn't overdone or exaggerated. He looked powerful, especially with the gun in its holster visible under his lightweight summer jacket.

The call that came over the radio made him scowl. He'd had enough of Jessica Larson the day before, but here she was after him again. Apparently there was a domestic disturbance at the Colson home, where a young boy lived with his father and grandmother.

Sterling went out to the car to answer the call, muttering all the way as he sat down and jerked up the mike.

"Why is Miss Larson going?" he demanded.

"I don't know, K-236," the dispatcher drawled, using his call letters instead of his name. "And even if I did, I wouldn't tell you on an open channel."

"I'll see that you get a Christmas present for being such a good boy," McCallum drawled back.

There was an unidentified laugh as McCallum hung up and drove to the small cottagelike Colson house on a dirt road just out of town.

He got there before Jessica did. If there was a fight going on here, it wasn't anything obvious. Terrance Colson was sitting on the porch cleaning his rifle while his mother fed her chickens out back in the fenced-in compound. The boy, Keith, was nowhere in sight. Terrance was red-faced and seemed to have trouble holding the rifle still.

"Afternoon, McCallum!" Terrance called pleasantly. "What can I do for you?"

McCallum walked up on the porch, shook hands with the man and sat down on one of the chairs. "We had a report, but it must have been some crank," he said, looking around.

"Report of what?" Terrance asked curiously.

Before McCallum could answer, Jessica came driving up in her rickety yellow truck. She shut it off, but it kept running for a few seconds, knocking like crazy. That fan belt sounded as if it were still slipping, too. He'd noticed it the night at the bus station.

She got out, almost dropping her shoulder bag in the dirt, and approached the house. McCallum wondered just how many of those shapeless suits she owned. This one was green, and just as unnoticeable as the others. Her hair was up in a bun again. She looked the soul of business.

"Well, hello, Miss Larson," Terrance called. "We seem to be having a party today!"

She stopped at the steps and glanced around, frowning. "We had a call at the office—" she faltered for a moment "—about a terrible fight going on out here. I was requested to come and talk to you."

Terrance looked around pointedly, calling her attention to the peaceful surroundings. "What fight?"

She sighed. "An unnecessary call, I suppose," she said with a smile. "I'm sorry. But as I'm here already, do you think I might talk to Keith for a minute? He told his counselor at school that he'd like to talk to me when I had time."

Terrance stared at her without blinking. "Funny, he never said anything to me about it. And he's not here right now. He's out fishing."

"Do you think I could find him?" she asked persistently.

"He goes way back in the woods," he said quickly.

"It's not a good time. He came home in a real bad mood. Best to leave him alone until he cools down."

She shrugged. "As you wish. But do tell him that I'll be glad to listen anytime he wants to talk about those school problems." She didn't add that she wondered why he couldn't tell them to the counselor, who was a good psychologist.

"I'll tell him," Terrance said curtly.

"Good day then." She smiled at Terrance, nodded at McCallum and went to climb back into her truck.

McCallum said his own goodbye, wondering why Mrs. Colson never came out of the chicken pen to say hello the whole time he was there. And Terrance's expression had hardened when he'd mentioned the boy. Odd.

He climbed into the patrol car and gave his call sign and location, announcing that he was back in service again. He followed after Jessica's sluggish truck and wondered if she was going to make it back into town.

When she parked her car at the office, he drove in behind her. The squealing of her fan belt was louder than ever. She really would have to do something about it when she had time.

"Your fan belt is loose," he told her firmly. "It's going to break one day and you'll be stranded."

"I know. I'm not totally stupid."

He got out of the car and walked with her to the office, not making a comment back, as he usually did. He seemed deep in thought. "Something funny's going on out at that place," he said suddenly. "Old Mrs. Colson hiding out with the chickens, Keith nowhere in sight, Terrance cleaning his gun, but without any gun oil…."

"You have a very suspicious mind," she accused gently. "For heaven's sake, do you always go looking for trouble? I'm delighted that there wasn't anything to it. I know the family, and they're good people. It's Keith who gives them fits. He's been into one bout of trouble after another at school since he was in the fifth grade. He's a junior now, and still getting into fights and breaking rules. He was picked up with another boy for shoplifting, although Keith swore he was innocent and the officers involved believed him. I've been trying to help the family as much as possible. Terrance lost his job at the manufacturing company that shut down last fall, and Milly is trying to make a little money by taking in ironing and doing alterations for the dry cleaners. The Colsons are hurting, but they're too proud to let me help much."

He frowned thoughtfully. "Isn't that the way of it?" he asked quietly. "The people who need help most never ask for it. On the other hand, plenty who don't deserve it get it."

She glowered up at him. "You're so cynical, McCallum! Don't you believe anybody can be basically good?"

"No."

She laughed and shook her head. "I give up. You're a hopeless case."

"I'm in law enforcement," he pointed out. "What we see doesn't lead us to look for the best in people."

"Neither does what I see, but I still try to believe in basic goodness," she replied.

He looked down at her for a long moment, letting his eyes linger on her soft mouth and straight nose before they lifted to catch her eyes.

"No, you don't," he said abruptly. "How can you still believe? What happens is that you just close your eyes to the ugliness. That's what most people do. They don't want to know that human beings can do such hideous things. Murder and robbery and beatings are so unthinkable that people pretend it can't occur. Then some terrible crime happens to them personally, and they have to believe it."

"You don't close your eyes to it," she said earnestly. "In fact, you look for it everywhere, even when you have to dig to find it. You have to try to rise above the ugliness."

His eyes darkened. He turned away. "I work for a living," he said lazily. "I haven't got time to stand around here socializing with you. Get that fan belt seen to."

She looked after him. "My goodness, do I really need a big, strong man to tell me how to take care of myself?"

"Yes."

He got into his car, leaving her aghast, and drove off.

Chapter 5

For several days, McCallum scoured the area for any clues as to the identity of the baby called Jennifer. He checked at every clinic and doctor's office in the area, as well as the local hospital and those in the surrounding counties. But every child's parents were accounted for. There were no leftover babies at any of the medical facilities. Which meant that the baby had probably been born at home, and a midwife had attended the birth. There were plenty of old women in the community who knew how to deliver a baby, and McCallum knew that he could spend years searching for the right person. Prospects looked dismal.

He was just leaving the office for lunch when Jessica Larson walked up to him on the street.

"I need to get your opinion on something," she said, and without preamble, caught his big, lean hand in hers and began to drag him off toward a parked car nearby.

"Now, hold it," he growled, hating and loving the feel of her soft hand in his.

"Don't grumble," she chided. "It won't hurt a bit. I just want you to talk to these young people for me before they make a big mistake." She paused at the beat-up old Chevy, where two teenagers sat guiltily in the front seat. They didn't look old enough to be out of school.

"This is Deputy McCallum," Jessica told the teens. "Ben and Amy want to get married," she explained to him. "Their parents are against it. Ben is seventeen and Amy is sixteen. I've told them that any marriage they make can be legally annulled by her parents because she's under age. Will you tell them that, too?"

He wasn't sure about the statutes on marriageable age in Montana, having never had occasion or reason to look them up. But he was pretty sure the girl was under the age of consent, and he knew what Jessica wanted him to say. He could bluff when he had to.

"She's absolutely right," he told them. "A minor can't legally marry without written permission from a parent. It would be terrible for you to have to—"

"She's pregnant," Ben mumbled, red-faced, and looked away. "I tried to get her to have it… Well, to not have it, really. She won't listen. She says we have to get married or her folks'll kill her."

Jessica hadn't counted on that complication. She stood there, stunned.

McCallum squatted down beside the car and looked at Amy, who was obviously upset. "Why don't we start at the beginning?" he asked her gently. "These are big decisions that need thought."

While Jessica looked on, stunned by the tenderness in McCallum's deep voice, Amy began to warm to him.

"I don't know if I'm pregnant, really," she confessed slowly. "I think I am."

"Shouldn't you find out for sure, before you wind up in a marriage neither of you is ready for?" he asked evenly.

"Yes, sir."

"Then the obvious next step is to see a doctor, isn't it?"

She grimaced. "My dad'll kill me."

"I'll speak to your parents," Jessica promised her. "They won't kill you. They're good people, and they love you. You're their only child."

"I'd just love to have a baby," Amy said dreamily, looking at Ben with fantasy-filled eyes that didn't even see his desperation, his fear. "We can have a house of our own, and I can get a job...."

McCallum looked hard at Jessica.

"Let's go over to your parents' house, Amy," she said. She had McCallum firmly by the hand again, and she wasn't about to let go. "I'm sure Deputy McCallum won't mind coming with us," she added, daring him to say no.

He gave up plans for a hamburger and fries and told his stomach to shut up. Resignedly, he helped Jessica into his car, and they followed the teens to Amy's house.

"It wasn't so bad, was it?" Jessica commented after the ordeal was finally over. "She'll see a doctor and then get counseling if she needs it. And there won't be a rushed marriage with no hope of success. They didn't even blame Ben too much."

"Why should they?" he muttered as he negotiated a right turn. "She's the one with dreams of babies and happy ever after, not him. He just wants to finish high school and go on to veterinary college."

"Ah, the man's eternal argument. 'Eve tempted me with the apple.'"

He glanced at her musingly. "Most women can lead a man straight to bed with very little conscious effort. Especially a young man."

She lifted her eyebrows. "Don't look at me. I've never led anyone to my bed with conscious effort or without it." She stemmed the memories that thoughts of intimacy resurrected.

"Have you wanted to?"

The question, coming from such an impersonal sort of man, surprised her. "Why...no."

"Have you let the opportunity present itself?" he persisted.

She straightened her skirt unnecessarily. "I'm sorry I made you miss your lunch."

He let the subject go. "How do you know you did?"

"Oh, you always go to lunch at eleven-thirty," she remarked. "I see you crossing over to the café from my office."

He chuckled softly, and it wasn't until she saw the speculation on his face that she realized why.

"I wasn't...watching you, for God's sake!" she blurted out, reddening.

"Really?" he teased. "You mean I've mistaken that hero worship in your eyes all this time?"

Her dark eyes glared at him. "You are very conceited."

"Made so by a very expressive young face," he countered. He glanced at her while they paused at a stop sign. "Don't build a pedestal under me, Jessie," he said, using a nickname for her for the first time. "I'm not tame enough for a woman like you."

She gaped at him. "If you think that I…!"

Incredibly, he caught the back of her head with a steely hand and leaned over her with slow, quiet intent. His dark eyes fell to her shocked mouth and he tugged gently until her mouth was a fraction below his. She could taste his minty breath, feel the heat of his mouth threatening her lips. She could feel the restrained passion in his long, fit body as it loomed over hers.

"You're afraid of me," he whispered into her mouth. "And it has nothing to do with that bad experience you had. It isn't the kind of fear that causes nightmares. It's the kind that makes your body swell hard with desire."

While she was absorbing the muted shock the words produced, his mouth lowered to touch and tease her soft lips in tender, biting kisses that made her muscles go rigid with sensation. Her hand caught at his shirt, searching for something to hold on to while she spun out of reality altogether. Her nails bit into his chest.

He groaned under his breath. "You'd be a handful," he whispered. "And if you were a different sort of woman, I'd accept with open arms the invitation you're making me right now."

"What…invitation?"

His nose rubbed against hers. "This one."

He brought his mouth down over her parted lips with real intent, feeling them open and shiver convulsively as he deepened the pressure. She whimpered, and the sound shot through him like fire. He abruptly drew back.

His breathing was a little quick, but his expression

showed none of the turmoil that kissing her had aroused in him.

She was slower to recover. Her face was flushed, and her mouth was red, swollen from the hard pressure of his lips. She looked at him with wide-eyed surprise.

"You're like a little violet under a doorstep," he commented quietly. "A lovely surprise waiting to be discovered."

She couldn't find the words to express what she felt.

He touched her soft mouth. "Don't worry about it. Someday the right man will come along. I'm not him."

"Why did you do that?" she whispered in a choked voice.

"Because you wanted me to, Jessica," he drawled. "You've watched me for months, wondering how it would feel if I kissed you. Okay. Now you know."

Her eyes darkened with something like pain. She averted them.

"What did you expect?" he mused, pulling the car back out into the road. "I'm not a teenager on his first date. I know exactly what to do with a woman. But you're off-limits, sweetheart. I don't make promises I can't keep."

"I haven't asked you to marry me, have I?" she asked, bouncing back.

He smiled appreciatively. "Not yet."

"And you can hold your breath until I do." She pushed back a disheveled strand of hair. "I'm not getting mixed up with you."

"You like kissing me."

She glared at him. "I like kissing my cat, too, McCallum," she said maliciously.

"Ouch!"

She nodded her head curtly. "Now how arrogant do you feel?"

He chuckled. "Well, as one of my history professors was fond of saying, 'I've always felt that arrogance was a very admirable quality in a man.'"

She rolled her eyes.

He drove back into town, but he didn't stop at her office. He kept going until he reached the Hip Hop Café, a small restaurant on the southeast corner of Amity Lane and Center.

She glanced at him uncertainly.

"If I haven't eaten, I know you haven't," he explained.

"All right. But I pay for my own food."

His eyes slowly wandered over her face. "I like independence," he said unexpectedly.

"Do I care?" she asked with mock surprise.

He smiled. "Fix your lipstick before we go inside, or everyone's going to know what we've been doing."

She wouldn't blush, she wouldn't blush, she wouldn't…!

All the same, her cheeks were pink in the compact mirror she used as she reapplied her lipstick and powdered her nose.

McCallum had taken the time to wipe the traces of pink off his own firm mouth with his handkerchief.

"Next time, I'll get rid of that lipstick before I start," he murmured.

"Oh, you'd be so lucky!" she hissed.

He lifted an eyebrow over wise, soft eyes. "Or you would. It gets better, the deeper you go. You cried out, and I hadn't even touched you. Imagine, Jessica, how it would feel if I did."

She was out of the car before he finished speaking.

She should go back to her office and leave him standing there. He was wicked to tease her about something she couldn't control. It didn't occur to her that he might be overcompensating for the desire he'd felt with her. Experienced he might be, but it had been a while since he'd had a woman and Jessica went right to his head. He hadn't realized it was going to be so fulfilling to kiss her. And it seemed to be addictive, because it was all he could think about.

"I won't let you torment me," she said, walking ahead of him to the door. "And before we go any farther, you'd better remember that Whitehorn isn't that big. Everybody knows everybody else's business. If I go in there with you, people are going to talk about us."

He had one hand in his pocket, the other on the door handle. He searched her eyes. "I know," he said quietly. He opened the door deliberately.

It was a quiet, companionable lunch. There were a few interested looks, including a sad one from a young waitress who had a hopeless crush on McCallum. But people were discreet enough not to stare at them.

"After all, we could be talking over a case," Jessica said.

He frowned at her. "Does it really matter?" he asked. "You're very sensitive to gossip. Why?"

She shrugged, averting her eyes. "Nobody likes being talked about."

"I don't know that I ever have been since I've come back," he said idly. He sipped his coffee. "And with your spotless reputation, it's hardly likely to think that you have," he added with a chuckle.

She picked up her coffee cup, steadying it with her

other hand. "Thank you for helping me with Amy and Ben."

"Did I have a choice? I wonder if there isn't a law against deputy sheriffs being kidnapped by overconscientious social workers. And while we're on the subject of laws, that one about underage marriages is one I'll have to look up or ask Hensley about. I've never had cause to use it before."

"You may again. We've had several cases like Amy and Ben over the years."

"What if she is pregnant?" he asked.

"Then she'll have choices and people to help her make them."

He glared at her.

"I know that look," she said softly. "I even understand it. But you have to consider that sometimes what's best for a young girl isn't necessarily what you feel is right."

"What if I lost my head one dark night and got you pregnant, Jessica?" He leaned back, his eyes narrowed. "What would you do in Amy's place?"

The color that rushed into her face was a revelation. She spilled a bit of coffee onto the table.

"Well, well," he murmured softly.

She put the cup down and mopped up the coffee with napkins. "You love shocking me, don't you?"

"Never mind the shock. Answer me. What would you do?"

She bit her lower lip. "The correct thing…"

He caught her hand and held it tight in his. "Not the correct thing, or the sensible thing, or even the decent thing. What would *you* do?" he asked evenly.

"Oh, I'd keep it," she said, angry at being pushed

into answering a question that would not, could not, ever arise. It hurt her to remember how barren she was. "I'm just brimming over with motherly instincts, old-fashioned morality and an overworked sense of duty. But what I'm trying to make you see is that regardless of my opinion, I have no right to force my personal sense of right and wrong on the rest of the world!"

He forgot the social issue in the heat of the moment, as he allowed himself to wonder how it would feel to create a child with Jessica. It made him feel…odd.

Jessica saw the speculation in his eyes and all her old inadequacies came rushing back. "McCallum," she began, wondering whether or not to tell him about her condition.

His fingers linked with hers, his thumb smoothing over them. "You're twenty-five, aren't you? I'm ten years older."

"Yes, I know. McCallum…"

His eyes lifted to catch hers. "My first name is Sterling," he said.

"That's an unusual name. Was it in your family?"

He shrugged. "My mother never said." Memories of his mother filled his mind. He withdrew, mentally and physically. He pulled his hand slowly away from Jessica's. "Maybe it was the name of her favorite brand of gin, who knows?"

She grimaced, hating that pain in his eyes. She wanted to soothe him, to comfort him.

He looked up and saw the expression on her face. It made him furious.

"I don't need pity," he said through gritted teeth.

"Is that how I looked? I'm sorry. It disturbs me to see how badly your past has affected you, that's all."

She smiled. "I know. I'm a hopeless do-gooder. But think, McCallum—if you'd had someone who really cared what happened to you, wouldn't it have changed your whole life?"

He averted his eyes. "Facts are facts. We can't go back and change the past."

"I know that. If we could, think how many people would leap at the chance."

"True," he agreed.

She studied him over her cup. "This town must hold some bad memories for you. Why did you come back after all these years?"

"I got tired of my job," he replied. "I can't even talk about it, do you know? It was all classified. Let's just say that I got into a situation I couldn't handle for the first time in my life, and I got out. I don't regret it. I manage better here than I ever dreamed I would. I'm not rich, but I'm comfortable, and I like my job and the people I work with. Besides," he added, "the memories weren't all bad. I have a few good ones tucked away. They keep me going when I need them."

"And was there ever a special woman?" she asked, deliberately not looking at him.

He cocked an eyebrow. "*Women,* plural," he replied. "Not just one woman. They all knew the score. I made sure of it and I'm a loner. I don't want to change."

Jessica felt a vague disappointment.

"Were you hoping?" he taunted.

She glared at him. "For what? You, with a bow around your neck on Christmas morning? It's a long time until Christmas, McCallum, and you'd look silly in gift wrapping."

"Probably so." He studied her. "I wonder how you'd look in a long red stocking?"

"Dead, because that's the only way I'd ever end up in one. Heavens, look at the time! I've got my desk stacked halfway to the ceiling. I have to go!"

"So do I," he agreed. "The days are never long enough to cope with all the paperwork, even in my job."

"In everyone's job. God knows how many trees die every day to satisfy bureaucrats. Know what I think they do with all those triplicate copies? I think they make confetti and store it for parades."

"I wouldn't doubt it." He pushed away his empty cup, stood up, laid a bill on the table, picked up the check and walked to the counter with it.

Jessica dug out a five dollar bill and paid her share.

"Late lunch, huh, McCallum?" the waitress asked with an inviting smile.

"Yeah." He smiled back at her. "Thanks, Daisy."

She colored prettily. She was barely twenty, red-headed, cute and totally infatuated with McCallum.

He opened the door for Jessica and walked her back to his car.

"Thanks for your help," she told him with genuine appreciation. "Those kids needed more of a talking to than I could give them. There's something about a uniform…" she added with a gleam in her eyes. Of course she was kidding; McCallum, a plainclothesman, wasn't wearing a uniform.

"Tell me about it." He'd already discovered that uniforms attracted women. It was something most career law-enforcement officers learned how to deal with early.

"Have you found out anything about Jennifer?" she asked on the way back to her office.

He detailed the bits and pieces he'd been following up. "But with no luck. Do you know any midwives around the community?" he asked. "Someone who would be able to deliver a child and could do it without telling half the world?"

Jessica pursed her lips. "One or two women come to mind. I'll look into it."

"Thanks."

He stopped at her office and waited, with the car idling, for her to get out.

"I'll let you know how things go with Amy," she offered.

He looked at her with an expression that bordered on dislike. It had flattered him that she kept asking for his help, and she seemed to like his company. But he liked kissing her too much, and that made him irritable. He didn't want a social worker to move into his life. He was weakening toward her, and he couldn't afford that. "I don't remember asking for a follow-up report," he said, deliberately being difficult.

It didn't faze Jessica, who was used to him. His bad humor bounced off her. That kiss hadn't, of course, but she had to remember that he was a loner and keep things in perspective. She could mark that lapse down to experience. She knew she wouldn't forget it anytime soon, but she had to keep her eyes off McCallum.

"You're so cynical, McCallum," she said heavily. "Haven't you ever heard that old saying about no man being an island?"

"I read John Donne in college," he replied. "I can be an island if I please."

She pursed her lips again, surveying him with marked interest. "If you really were an island, you'd have barbed wire strung around the trees and land mines on the beaches."

She went inside, aware of the deep masculine laughter she left behind her.

The abandoned baby, Jennifer, had been placed in care, and Jessica couldn't help going to see her. She was living temporarily as a ward of the court with a local family that seemed to thrive on anyone's needful children.

"We can't have any of our own, you see," Mabel Darren said with a grin. She was in her mid-thirties, dark and bubbly, and it didn't take a clairvoyant to know that she loved children. She had six of them, all from broken homes or orphaned, ranging in age from a toddler to a teen.

The house was littered, but clean. The social-services office had to check it out periodically to comply with various regulations, but there had never been any question of the Darrens' ability to provide for their charges. And if ever children were loved, these underprivileged ones were.

"Isn't she a little angel?" Mabel asked when Jessica had the sweet-smelling infant in her arms.

"Oh, yes," Jessica said, feeling a terrible pain as she cuddled the child. She would never know the joy of childbirth, much less that of watching a baby grow to adulthood. She would be alone all her life.

Mabel would have understood, but Jessica could never bring herself to discuss her anguish with anyone. She carried Jennifer to the rocking chair and sat down with her, oblivious to the many other duties that were supposed to be demanding her attention.

The older woman just smiled. "It's time for her bottle. Would you like to feed her while you're here? Then I could get on with my dirty dishes," she added. She knew already that if she could make Jessica think she was helping, the social worker was much more likely to do what she really wanted to.

"If it would help," Jessica said. Her soft, dark eyes were on the baby's face and she touched the tiny head, the hands, the face with fingers that trembled. She'd never known such a profound hunger in her life, and tears stung her eyes.

As if the baby sensed her pain, her big eyes opened and she stared up at Jessica, unblinking. She made a soft gurgling noise in her throat. With a muffled cry, Jessica cuddled Jennifer close and started the chair rocking. At that moment, she would have given anything—anything!—for this tiny precious thing to be her very own.

Mabel's footsteps signaled her approach. Jessica composed herself just before the other woman reappeared with a bottle. She managed to feed the baby and carry on a pleasant conversation with Mabel, apparently unruffled by the experience. But deep inside, she was devastated. Something about Jennifer accentuated all the terrible feelings of inadequacy and made her child hungry. She'd never wanted anything as much as she wanted the abandoned infant.

After she fed the baby, she went back to the office, where she was broody and quiet for the rest of the day. She was so silent that Bess, who worked in the outer office, stuck her auburn head in the door to inquire if her boss was sick.

"No, I'm all right, but thanks," Jessica said dully. "It's been a long day, that's all."

"Well, you got to have lunch with Sterling McCallum," Bess mused. "I wouldn't call that tedious. I dress up, I wear sexy perfume, but he never gives me a second look. Is he really that formidable and businesslike *all* the time?" she asked with a keen stare.

Jessica's well-schooled features gave nothing away. She smiled serenely. "If I ever find out, you'll be the first to know. It was a business lunch, Bess, not a date," she added.

"Oh, you stick-in-the-mud," she muttered. "A gorgeous man like that, and all you want to talk about is work! I'd have him on his back in the front seat so fast…!"

Shocking images presented themselves, but with Jessica, not Bess, imprisoning Sterling McCallum on the seat of his car. She had to stop thinking of him in those terms! "Really, Bess!" she muttered.

"Jessica, you do know what century this is?" Bess asked gently. "You know, women's liberation, uninhibited sex?"

"AIDS? STDs?" Jessica added.

Bess made a soft sound. "Well, I didn't mean that you don't have to be careful. But McCallum strikes me as the sort of man who would be. I'll bet he's always properly equipped."

Jessica's face had gone scarlet and she stood up abruptly.

"I'm just leaving for home!" Bess said quickly, all too aware that she'd overstepped the mark. "See you tomorrow!"

She closed the door and ran for it. Jessica was even-tempered most of the time, but she, too, could be formidable when she lost her cool.

Jessica restrained a laugh at the speed with which Bess took to her heels. It was just as well not to let employees get too complacent, she decided, as she opened another file and went back to work.

It was after dark and pouring rain when she decided to go home. Meriwether would be wanting his supper, and she was hungry enough herself. The work would still be here, waiting, in the morning. But it had taken her mind off Baby Jennifer, which was a good thing.

She locked up the office and got into her yellow pickup as quickly as possible. Her umbrella, as usual, was at home. She had one in the office, too, but she'd forgotten it. She was wet enough without trying to go back and get it. She fumbled the key into the ignition, locked her door and started the vehicle.

The engine made the most ghastly squealing noise. It didn't help to remember McCallum's grim warning about trouble ahead if she didn't get it seen to.

But the mechanic's shop was closed, and so were all the service stations. The convenience store was open, and it had self-service gas pumps, but nobody who worked inside would know how to replace a fan belt. In fact, Tammie Jane was working the counter tonight, and the most complicated thing she knew how to do was change her nail polish.

With a long sigh, Jessica pulled the truck out onto the highway and said a silent prayer that she would be able to make it home before the belt broke. The squeal that usually vanished when she went faster only got worse tonight.

The windshield wipers were inadequate, too. A big leaf had gotten caught in the one on the driver's side, smearing the water rather than removing it. Jessica groaned out loud at her bad luck. It had been a horrible day altogether, and not just because of the predicament she was in now.

She pulled onto the dirt road that led to her home. The rain was coming down harder. She had no idea how long it had been pouring, because she'd been so engrossed in her work. Now she saw the creek ahead and wondered if she'd even be able to get across it. The water was very high. This was an old and worrying problem.

She gunned the engine and shot across, barely missing another struggling motorist, her elderly CB-radio-fanatic neighbor. He waved to her as he went past, but she was too occupied with trying to see ahead to really look at him. She almost made it up the hill, but at that very moment, the fan belt decided to give up the ghost. It snapped and the engine raced, but nothing happened. The truck slid back to the bottom of the hill beside the wide, rising creek, and the engine went dead.

Chapter 6

Jessica sat in the truck without moving, muttering under her breath. She hoped that her eccentric neighbor had noticed her plight and alerted someone in town on his CB radio, but whether or not he'd seen her slide back down the hill was anyone's guess.

She decided after a few minutes that she was going to be stranded unless she did something. The creek was rising steadily. She was terrified of floods. If she didn't get up that hill, God only knew what might happen to her when the water rose higher. The rain showed no sign of slackening.

She opened the door and got out, becoming soaked within the first couple of minutes. She made a rough sound in her throat and let out an equally rough word to go with it. Stupid old truck! She should have listened to McCallum.

She managed to get the hood up, but it did no good. There was no source of light except the few patches of sky on the horizon that weren't black as thunder. She didn't even have a flashlight. Well, she had one—but the battery was dead. She'd meant to replace it....

The deep drone of an engine caught her attention. She turned, blinded by headlights, hoping against hope that it was her elderly neighbor. He could give her a ride home, at least.

A huge red-and-black Bronco with antennas all over it and a bar of lights on top swept up beside her and stopped. She recognized it from McCallum's house. It had been sitting in the garage next to the patrol car he used when he was on call at night. He got out of it, wearing a yellow rain slicker. The rain seemed to slacken as he approached her.

"Nice wheels," she commented.

"I like it," he replied. "Fan belt broke, huh?"

She glowered, shivering in the rain. "Terrific guess."

"No help here, until I can get a new belt and put it on for you. Nothing's open this late." He closed the hood and marched her around to the passenger side of the Bronco. "Climb in."

He helped her into the big vehicle and she sat, shivering, on the vinyl seat while, with the four-wheel drive in operation, he drove effortlessly up the muddy hill and on to her cabin.

"What were you doing out at this time of night anyway?" he asked.

"Trying to get stranded in the rain," she told him.

He glared at her.

"I was working late." She sneezed.

"Get in there and take a bath."

"I had planned to. Have you…had supper?" she added, without looking at him.

"Not yet."

She touched the door handle. "I have a pot of soup in the refrigerator. I could make some corn bread to go with it."

"If you could make some coffee, I'd be delighted to join you. I'd just got off duty when I monitored a call about a stranded motorist."

She grinned, because she knew which motorist he meant. "Done." She got out and left him to follow.

The minute he walked in the door, Meriwether, having come to meet his mistress, bristled and began spitting viciously at the newcomer.

"I like you, too, pal," McCallum muttered as he and the cat had a glaring contest.

"Meri, behave yourself!" Jessica fussed.

"If you'll show me what the soup's in, I'll start heating it while you're in the shower," he offered.

She led him into the kitchen, dripping everywhere, and got out the big pot of soup while he hung up his drenched slicker.

"I'll make the corn bread when I get back. You could preheat the oven," she added, and told him what temperature to set it.

"Okay. Where's the coffee?"

She showed him the filters and coffee and how to work the pot. Then she rushed down the hall to the bathroom.

Ten minutes later, clean and presentable in a sweatshirt and jeans, with her hair hanging in damp strands down her back, she joined him in the kitchen.

"You'll catch a cold," he murmured, glancing at her

from his seat at the table with a steaming cup of black coffee. "Sit down for a minute and I'll pour you a cup."

"I'll make the corn bread first," she said. "It won't take a minute."

And it didn't. She put it in the preheated oven to bake and then sat down across from McCallum to sip her coffee. He was wearing a brown plaid shirt, with jeans and boots. He always looked clean and neat, even when he was drenched, she thought, and wondered if his military training had a lot to do with it.

"Do you always keep your house this hot?" he asked, unfastening the top buttons of his shirt.

"I don't have air-conditioning," she explained apologetically. "But I can turn on the fan."

"Are you cool?"

She shook her head. "I'm rather cold-blooded, I'm afraid. But if you're too hot…"

"Leave it. It's probably the coffee." He leaned back. The action pulled his shirt away from his chest and she got a glimpse of the thick mat of curling black hair that covered it.

She averted her eyes in the direction of the stove and watched it fanatically, not daring to look at him again. He was devastating like that, so attractive physically that he made her toes curl.

He saw the look he was getting. It made his heart race. She was certainly less sophisticated than most women he knew, but she still made him hungry in a new and odd sort of way.

"You said you monitored a stranded motorist's call?" she asked curiously.

"Yes. Your neighbor called the office on his mobile unit, and when I heard where the stranded motorist was,

I told Dispatch that I'd respond." He grinned at her. "I knew who it was and what was wrong before I got here."

She took an audible breath. "Well, it might have been something besides the fan belt," she said.

"You're stubborn."

"I meant to have it checked," she defended herself. "I got busy."

"Next time you'll know better, won't you?"

"I hate it when you use that tone," she muttered. "I'm not brain dead just because I'm a woman!"

His eyebrows raised. "Did I imply that you were?"

"You have an attitude...."

"So do you," he shot back. "Defensive and standoffish. I'd have told a man no differently than I told you that your fan belt needed replacing. The difference is that a man would have listened."

She put her coffee cup down hard and opened her mouth to speak just as the beeper on the oven's timer went off.

He got up with her and took the soup off the burner while she checked the corn bread in the oven. It was nicely browned, just right.

She was silent while she dished up the abbreviated meal, and while they ate it.

"You're a good cook, Jessie," he commented when he'd finished his second helping. "Who taught you?"

"My grandmother," she said. "My mother was not a good cook. She tried, God bless her, but we never gained weight around here." She pushed back her bowl. "You're handy enough in a kitchen yourself."

"Had to be," he said simply. "My mother was never sober enough to cook. If I hadn't learned, we'd both have starved. Not that she ate much. She drank most of her meals."

"You sound so bitter," she said gently.

"I *am* bitter," he shot back. He crossed his long legs, brushing at a smudge of mud on one polished black boot. "She robbed me of my childhood." His eyes sought her. "Isn't that what most victims of child abuse tell you—that what they mourn most is the loss of childhood?"

She nodded. "That's the worst of it. The pain and bitterness go on for a long time, even after therapy. You can't remake the past, McCallum. The scars don't go away, even if the patient can be made to restructure the way he or she thinks about the experience."

He turned his coffee cup around, his eyes on the white china soup bowl, now empty. "I never did what young boys usually get to do—play sports, join the Boy Scouts, go on trips, go to parties... From the time I was old enough, I did nothing except look after my mother, night after drunken night." His lean hand contacted absently on the bowl. "I used to hope she'd die."

"That's very normal," she assured him.

His broad shoulders rose and fell. "She did die, though in jail. I had her arrested when it all got too much after she attacked me one night. She was convicted of child abuse, sent to jail, and she died there when I was in my early teens. I was put to work as a hired hand for any family that would take me in. I had a room in a bunkhouse or in the barn, never with the family. I spent most of my life as an outsider looking in, until I was old enough to join the service. The uniform gave me a little self-esteem. As I grew older, I learned that my situation wasn't all that rare."

"Sadly, it isn't," she told him. "Sterling, what about your father?"

Her use of his first name made him feel warm inside. He smiled at her. "What about him?"

"Did he die?"

"Beats me," he said quietly. "I never found out who he was. I'm not sure she knew."

The implications of that statement were devastating. She winced.

"Feeling sorry for me all over again?" he murmured gently. "I don't need pity, Jessie. I've come to grips with it over the years. Plenty of people had it worse."

She traced the rim of her coffee cup soberly. "I'm sorry that it was that way for you."

"Different from your childhood, I imagine."

"Oh, yes. I was loved and wanted, and petted. I don't suppose I had a single bad experience in my whole childhood."

"They say we carry our childhood around with us, like luggage. I'll have to worry about not being too rough on my kids. You'll be just the opposite."

She felt sick inside, and tried not to show it. "Have you managed to find out anything else about little Jenny?" she asked, changing the subject.

"Nothing except dead ends," he had to admit. "I did find one new lead, but it didn't work out. How about you? Anything on the midwives?"

"I've spoken to two, but they say they don't know anything." She twirled her spoon on the tablecloth. "I'm not sure they'd tell me if they did," she added, looking up. "Sometimes they get in trouble for helping with deliveries, especially if something goes wrong. What if the mother died giving birth, Sterling?"

"That's a thought." His lips pursed. "I might check into any recent deaths involving childbirth."

"It might not lead to anything at all, but someone has to know about her. I mean, she didn't come from under a cabbage leaf."

He chuckled. "I don't think so."

She liked the sound of his laughter. She smiled as she got up to put the dishes in the sink.

"No dishwasher?" he teased as he helped.

"Of course I have a dishwasher—myself." She smiled at him. "I'll put these in to soak and do them later."

"Do them now, while I'm here to help you."

She did, because it would keep him here that much longer. She enjoyed his company far too much. She filled the sink with soapy water, while outside the rain continued steadily, broken occasionally by a rumble of thunder. "Were you always so bossy?" she asked as she washed a plate and handed it to him to be rinsed.

"I suppose so," he confessed. "That's force of habit. I was the highest-ranking officer in my group."

"What did you do in Naval Intelligence?"

He put the plate in the dish drainer and leaned toward her. "That's classified," he whispered.

"Well, excuse me for asking!" she teased.

His dark eyes searched hers. "I like the way you look when you smile," he commented absently. "It lights up your whole face."

"You hardly ever smile."

"I do when I'm with you. Haven't you noticed?"

She laughed self-consciously. "Yes, but I thought it was because you find me tedious." She washed another few dishes and passed them to him.

He rinsed them and then began drying, because there

were none left to be washed. "I find you disturbing," he corrected quietly.

She let the water out of the sink and took a second cloth, helping to dry the few dishes. "Because I'm forever dragging you into awkward situations?"

"Not quite."

They finished drying the dishes and Jessica put them away. She hung up the kitchen towels. Lightning flashed outside the window, followed by a renewal of pelting rain and a deep, vibrating rumble of thunder.

"Are you afraid of thunderstorms?" he asked her.

"A little."

He moved closer, his face filling her whole line of vision. "Are you afraid of me?" he continued.

Her eyes slid over his face, lingering on his firm mouth and chin. "That would depend on what you wanted from me," she countered bluntly.

"That's forthright enough," he said. "All right, cards on the table. Suppose I want you sexually?"

She didn't drop her eyes. "I don't want sex."

His gaze narrowed. "Because of what happened to you?" he guessed.

"Not entirely." She stared at the opening in his shirt, feeling her heartbeat increase as the clean cologne-and-soap scent of his body drifted into her nostrils. "It's mainly a matter of morality, I guess. And I'm not equipped for casual affairs, either. This is a small town. I...don't like gossip. I've always tried to live in such a way that people wouldn't think less of me."

"I see," he said slowly.

She shifted her shoulders. "No, you don't. You've been away so long maybe you've forgotten what it's really like." Her eyes were faintly pleading. "I like my life the way it is. I don't want to complicate it. I'm sorry."

His lean hands caught her waist gently and brought her against the length of his body. He stopped her instinctive withdrawal.

"Hush," he whispered. "Be still."

"What are...you doing?"

"I'm showing you that it's too late," he replied. His big hands smoothed her back up to her shoulder blades. "You want me. I want you. We can slow it down, but we can't stop it. Deep inside, you don't want to stop me." His gaze dropped to her soft mouth, and he watched her lips part. "You've been handled brutally. But you've never been touched with tenderness. I'm going to show you how it feels."

"I'm not sure that I want to know," she whispered.

He bent toward her. "Let's see."

Her fingers went up to touch his lips, staying their downward movement. Her eyes were wide and soft and faintly pleading. "Don't...hurt me," she said.

He moved her hand to his shirtfront and scowled. "Do you think I want to?"

"No, I don't mean physically. I mean..." She searched for words. "Sterling, I can't play games. I'm much too intense. It would be better if we were just friends."

He tilted her chin up and held her eyes. "Think about what you're saying," he said gently. "I know about your past. I know that you've assaulted, that you don't date anyone. I even know that you're half-afraid of me. Considering all that, do you think I'm the sort of man who would tease you?"

She looked perplexed. Her hand had moved somehow into the opening where the buttons were unfastened. She felt the curly tangle of thick chest hair over warm, hard muscle. It was difficult to concentrate when all she wanted to do was touch him, test his maleness.

"Well, no," she confessed.

"I don't play games with women," he said flatly. "I'm straightforward. Sometimes too much so. I want you, but I'd never force you or put you in a position where you couldn't say no." He laughed mirthlessly. "Or don't you realize that I've been in that position myself?"

Her brows jerked together as she tried to puzzle out what he was saying.

"When one of my foster mothers got drunk enough," he said slowly, bitterly, "anything male would do. She tried to seduce me one night."

Her heart ached for him. What a distasteful, sickening experience it would have been for a young boy. "Oh, Sterling!" she said sadly.

The distaste dominated his expression. "I knocked her out of the bed and left the house. The next morning, we had it out. I told her exactly what would happen if she ever tried it again. I was almost as big then as I am now, you see. She couldn't force me." His hands let her go and he moved away.

She'd come across the same situation so many times, with so many families. It was amazing how many children suffered such traumas and never told, because of the shock and shame.

She moved closer to him, but she didn't touch him. She knew very well that abused children had real problems about being touched by other people sometimes—especially when something reminded them of the episodes—unless it was through their own choice. The scars were long lasting.

"You never told anyone," she guessed.

He wouldn't look at her. "No."

"Not even your caseworker?"

He shrugged. "He was the sort who wouldn't have believed me. And I had too much pride to beg for credibility."

She mourned the help he could have gotten from someone with a little more compassion.

"I've never told anyone," he continued, glancing down at her. "Amazing that I could tell you."

"Not really," she said, smiling. "I think you could tell me anything."

His face tautened. It was true. He would never balk at divulging his darkest secrets to this woman, because she had an open, loving heart. She wouldn't ridicule or judge, and she wouldn't repeat anything he said.

"I think I must have that sort of face," she continued, tongue-in-cheek, "because total strangers come up and talk to me about the most shocking things. I actually had a man ask me what to do about impotence."

He chuckled, his bad memories temporarily driven away. "And what did you tell him?"

"That a doctor would be a more sensible choice for asking advice," she returned. Her eyes searched his dark, hard face. "Sex was really hard for you the first time, wasn't it?" she asked bluntly.

Again his face tautened. "Yes."

She glanced away, folding her arms over her breasts. "I wasn't a child when I had my bad experience, but it made the thought of intimacy frightening to me. I'm realistic enough to know that it would be different with someone I cared about, but all I can see is the way he was. He reminded me of an animal."

"Do I?"

She turned quickly. "Don't be absurd!"

One eyebrow quirked. "Well, that's something."

She went back to him, looking up solemnly into his face. "I find *you* very disturbing," she confessed. "Physically, I mean. I guess that's why I shy away from you sometimes."

He traced her smooth cheek with a steely forefinger. "I don't think I've ever known anyone as honest as you."

"I hate lies. Don't you?"

"I hear enough of them. Nobody I've ever arrested has been guilty. It was a frame-up, or they didn't mean to, or somebody talked them into it."

"I know what you mean."

The exploring finger reached her mouth and traced its soft bow shape gently. His jaw tightened. She could hear the heavy breath that passed through his nostrils as his eyes began to darken and narrow.

"Why don't you unfasten my shirt and put your hands on me?" he asked huskily.

Her face colored vividly. "I don't know if that would be a good idea."

"It's the best one I've had tonight," he assured her. "No games. Honest. I want to make love to you a little, that's all. I won't let it get too far."

She put her hands against his shirtfront, torn between what she wanted to do and what was sensible.

"It's hard for me, with women," he said roughly. "Does that reassure you any?"

She smiled gently. "Will it make you angry if I confess that it does?"

He bent and his smiling mouth brushed against hers. "Probably. Open your mouth."

She obeyed him like a sleepwalker, but he soon brought every single nerve she had singing to life. Her hands slid under the shirt and over the thick tangle of hair that covered him, past male nipples that hardened at her touch. He moaned softly and pulled her closer. She sighed into his mouth as he deepened the kiss and made her knees go weak with the passion he kindled in her slender body.

"It isn't enough," he said in a strained tone. He bent and lifted her, his gaze reassuring as she opened startled eyes. "I want to lie down with you," he whispered as he carried her to the sofa. "I have to get closer, Jessie. Closer than this."

"It's dangerous," she managed through swollen lips.

"Life is dangerous." He put her down on the sofa, full length, and stretched out alongside her. "I won't hurt you. I swear to God, I won't. All it will take is one word, when you want me to stop."

His mouth traced hers. "And what…if I can't say it?" she whispered brokenly.

"I'll say it for you…."

He kissed her until she trembled, but even then he didn't touch her intimately or attempt to carry their lovemaking to greater depths. He lifted his head and looked down at her with tenderness and bridled passion. With her long hair loose around her face and her lips swollen from his kisses, her dark eyes wide and soft and dazed, he thought he'd never seen anything so beautiful in all his life.

"Are you stopping?" she whispered unsteadily.

"I think I should," he mused, managing to project a self-assurance he didn't really feel. His lower body ached.

"But we haven't done anything except kiss each other...." She stopped abruptly when she realized what she was saying.

He chuckled wickedly. "Jessie, if I push up that sweatshirt, we're both going to be in trouble. Because, frankly, it shows that you aren't wearing anything under it."

She followed his interested gaze and saw two hard peaks outlined vividly against the soft material. Scarlet faced, she got to her feet. "Well!"

He sat back on the sofa, watching her with smug, delighted eyes. She aroused an odd protectiveness in him that he'd never felt with another woman. She was unique in his shattered life. He wanted her, but it went far beyond desire.

"Don't be embarrassed," he said gently. "I didn't say it with any cruel intent. It delights me that you can want me, Jessie." He hesitated. "It delights me that I can want you. I wasn't sure..."

She searched his hard face. "Yes?" she prompted gently.

He got up and went to her slowly, secrets in his eyes.

She pushed back the glorious cloud of her hair and then reached up to touch his sculptured cheek. "Tell me," she coaxed.

He brought her hand to his lips. "I exaggerated when I told you there had been a parade of women through my bed," he said quietly.

Her eyes were solemn, steady, questioning.

His shoulders moved restlessly. He looked tormented. He tried to tell her, but the words wouldn't come.

Her fingers traced his hard mouth. "It's all right." She pulled his head down and kissed his eyes closed. He shivered. "My dear," she whispered. Her mouth traced his and softly kissed his lips, feeling them open and press down, responding with a sudden feverish need. He pulled her close and increased the pressure, groaning as she gave in to him without a single protest.

He let her go slowly, his tall, fit body taut with desire and need as he looked down at her hungrily.

"I've never been with anyone like you," he said flatly. "Because of the way I grew up, I always equated sex with a certain kind of woman," he said huskily. "So that's where I went, when I had to have it." He sighed heavily. "Not that I was ever careless, Jessie."

She bit her lip, trying not to remember Bess's taunt.

"What is it?" he asked suspiciously.

"I can't tell you. You'll get conceited."

His eyebrows arched. He cocked his head. "Come on."

"A girl I know made the comment that she thought you'd be absolute heaven to make love with, and that she'd bet you were always prepared."

He chuckled softly. "Did she? Who?"

"I'll never tell!"

He pursed his lips, amused. "As it happens, she was right." He bent and brushed her mouth with his. "On both counts," he whispered and nipped her lower lip.

She smiled under his lips. "I know. About the first count, anyway."

"You can take my word for the other. How about supper tomorrow night?"

She stared at him blankly. "What?"

"I want to take you out on a date," he explained. "One of those things where a man and woman spend time together, and at the end of the evening, do what we've already done."

"Oh."

His eyebrow lifted as he fastened his shirt. "Well?"

Her face lit up. "I'd love to!"

He smiled. "So would I. Thanks for supper." He moved to the door and glanced back. She was ruffled and flustered. He liked knowing that he'd made her that way. "I'll send the mechanic over first thing in the morning to see about that fan belt. And I'll come and drive you to work."

"You don't have to," she declared breathlessly.

"I want to." The way he said it projected other images, exciting ones. She laughed inanely, captivated by the look on his dark face.

"I'd better go," he murmured dryly. "Good night, Jessie."

"Good night."

He closed the door gently behind him. "Lock it!" he added from outside.

She rushed forward and threw the lock into place. A minute later she heard deep laughter and the sound of his booted feet going down the steps.

Chapter 7

The restaurant was crowded, and heads turned from all directions when Jessica, in a neat-fitting burgundy dress with her hair loose around her shoulders, walked in with McCallum, who was wearing slacks and a sports coat.

"I told you people would notice that we're together," she said under her breath as they were seated.

"I didn't mind the last time, and I don't mind now," he murmured, smiling. "Do you?"

She smiled back. "Not at all."

The waitress brought menus, poured water into glasses and went away to give them time to decide what to order.

"Why... Miss Larson!"

Jessica looked up. Bess, one of her caseworkers, and a good-looking young man who worked in the bank had paused by their table.

"Hello, Bess," Jessica said, smiling. "How are you?"

"Fine! Don't you look nice? Hi, McCallum," she added, letting her blue eyes sweep over him in pure flirtation. "You look nice, too!"

"Thanks."

"Bess, the waitress is gesturing to us," the young man prompted. He was giving McCallum a nervous look. Probably it was the fact that McCallum was in law enforcement that disturbed him. Lawmen were set apart from the rest of the world, Jessica had discovered over the years. But it could have been the way Bess was looking at the older man. Jessica had to admit that McCallum was sensuous and handsome enough to fit any woman's dream. Compared to him, Bess's date seemed very young, and he was undoubtedly jealous.

"Oh, sure, Steve. Good to see you both!" she said breezily, leading him away.

"She thinks you're a hunk," Jessica said without thinking, then bit her lip.

His eyebrows lifted. "So?" Now he knew who'd made the comment she'd related at her cabin.

"She's very young, of course," she added mischievously.

"No, she isn't," he countered. "In fact, she's only a year younger than you. Nice figure, too."

Jessica fought down an unfamiliar twinge of jealousy. She fumbled with her silverware. Nobody disturbed her like McCallum did.

He reached across the table and caught her hand in his, sending thrills of pleasure up her arm that made her heart race. "I didn't mean it like that. Jessie, if I were interested in your co-worker, why would I spend half my free time thinking about you?"

She smiled at him, thrown off balance by the look in his dark eyes. "Do you?" she asked. Her hand slipped and almost overturned her water glass. He righted it quickly, smiling patiently at her clumsiness. It wasn't like her to do such things.

"Hold tight, and I'll protect you from overturning things," he said, clasping her cold fingers in his. "We'll muddle through together. In my own way, I've got as many hang-ups and inhibitions as you have. But if we try, we can sort it out."

"Sort what out?" she echoed curiously.

He frowned. "Do you think I make a habit of taking women out? I'm thirty-five years old, and since I've been back here, I've lived like a hermit. I'm hungry for a woman...."

This time the glass went over. He called the waitress, who managed to clear away the water with no effort at all. She smiled indulgently at an embarrassed Jessica, who was abjectly apologetic.

She took their order and left. Across the restaurant, Bess was giggling. Jessica looked at Sterling McCallum and knew in that moment that she loved him. She also knew that she could never marry him. He might not realize it now, but he'd want children one day. He was the sort of man who needed children to love and take care of. He'd make a good husband. Of course, marriage was obviously the last thing on his mind at the moment.

"Good God, woman," he muttered, shaking his head with indulgent amusement. "Will you just let me finish a sentence before you react like that? I don't have plans to ravish you. Okay? Now, move that glass aside before we have another mishap."

"I'm sorry. I'm just all thumbs."

"And I keep putting my foot in my mouth," he said ruefully. "What I was going to say, before the great water glass flood," he added with a grin at her flush, "was that it's time I started going out more. I like you. We'll keep it low-key."

She looked at the big, lean hand holding hers so gently. Her fingers moved over the back of it, tracing, savoring its strength and masculinity. "I like your hands," she said absently. "They're very sensitive, for such masculine ones." She thought about how they might feel on bare, soft skin and her lips parted as she exhaled with unexpected force.

His thumb eased into the damp palm of her hand and began to caress it, making her heart race all over again. "Yours are beautiful," he said, and the memory of how her hands felt on his chest was still in his gaze when he looked up.

She was holding her breath. She looked into his eyes, and neither of them smiled. It was like lightning striking. She could see what he was thinking. It was all there in his dark gaze—the need and the hunger and the ardent passion he felt for her.

"Uh, excuse me?"

They both looked up blankly as the waitress, smiling wryly, waited for them to move their hands so she could put the plates down.

"Sorry," Sterling mumbled.

The waitress didn't say a word, but her expression spoke volumes.

"I think we're becoming obvious," he remarked to Jessica as he picked up his fork, trying not to look around at the interested glances they were getting from Bess and Steve.

"Yes." She sounded pained, and looked even more uncomfortable.

"Jessie?"

"Hmm?" She looked up.

He leaned forward. "I'm dying of frustrated passion here. Eat fast, could you?"

She burst out laughing. It broke the tension and got them through the rest of the meal.

But once he paid the check and they went out to the parking lot and got into the Bronco, he didn't take her straight home. He drove a little way past the cabin and pulled down a long, dark trail into the woods.

He locked his door, unfastened his seat belt and then reached across her wordlessly to lock her own door and release her seat belt, as well.

His eyes in the darkness held a faint glitter. She could feel the quick, harsh rush of his breath on her forehead. She didn't protest. Her arms reached around his neck as he pulled her across his lap. When his mouth lowered, hers was ready, waiting.

They melted together, so hungry for each other that nothing else seemed to matter.

She'd never experienced kisses that weren't complete in themselves. He made her want more, much more. Every soft stroke of his hands against her back was arousing, even through the layers of fabric. The brush of his lips on hers didn't satisfy, it taunted and teased. He nibbled at the outside curves of her mouth with brief little touches that made her heart run wild. She clung to him, hoping that he might deepen the kiss on his own account, but he seemed to be waiting.

She reached up, finally, driven to the outskirts of

desperation by the teasing that went on and on until she was taut as drawn rope with unsatisfied needs.

"Please!" she whispered brokenly, trying to pull his head down.

"It isn't enough, is it?" he asked calmly. "I hoped it might not be. Open your mouth, Jessica," he whispered against her lips as he shifted her even closer to his broad, warm chest. "And I'll show you just how hungry a kiss can make you feel."

It was devastating. She felt her breath become suspended, like her mind, as his lips fitted themselves to hers and began to move in slow, teasing touches that quickly grew harder and rougher and deeper. By the time his tongue probed at her lips, they opened eagerly for him. When his tongue went deep into her mouth, she arched up against him and groaned out loud.

Her response kindled a growing hunger in him. It had been a long time for him, and the helpless twisting motions of her breasts against him made him want to rip open her dress and take them in his hands and his mouth.

Without thinking of consequences, he made her open her mouth even farther under the crush of his, and his lean hand dropped to her bodice, teasing her breasts through the cloth until he felt the nipples become hard. Only then did he smooth the firm warmth of one and begin to caress it with his fingertips. When he caught the nipple deliberately in his thumb and forefinger, she cried out. He lifted his head to see why. As he'd suspected, it wasn't out of fear or pain.

She lay there, just watching him as he caressed her. He increased the gentle pressure of his fingers and she gasped as she looked into his eyes. A slow flush spread over her high cheekbones in the dimly lit interior.

He didn't say a word. He simply sat there, holding her and looking down into her shadowed eyes. It was hard to breathe. Her body was soft in his arms and that pretty burgundy dress had buttons down the front. His eyes went past the hand that now lay possessively on her breast and he calculated how easy it would be to open the buttons and bare her breasts to his hungry mouth. But she was trembling, and his body was getting quickly out of control. Besides that, it was too soon for that sort of intimacy. He had to give her time to get used to the idea before he tried to further their relationship. It was important not to frighten her so that she backed away from him.

He moved his hand up and pushed back her disheveled hair with a soft smile. "Sorry," he murmured dryly. "I guess I let it go a little too far."

"It was my fault, too. You're…you're very potent," she said after a minute, feeling the swelling of her mouth from his hard kisses and the tingling of her breast where his hand had toyed with it. She still couldn't imagine that she'd really let him do that. But, oddly, she didn't feel embarrassed about it. It seemed somehow proper for McCallum to touch her like that, as if she belonged to him already.

He grinned at her expression. "You're potent yourself. And that being the case, I think I'd better get you home."

She fingered his collar. "Okay." Her hands traced down to his tie and the top button of his shirt.

"No," he said gently, staying her fingers. "I like having you touch me there too much," he murmured dryly. "Let's not tempt fate twice in one night."

She was a little disappointed, even though she knew he was right. It *was* too soon. But her eyes mirrored more than one emotion.

He watched those expressions chase across her face, his eyes tender, full of secrets. "How did you get under my skin?" he wondered absently.

She glowed with pleasure. "Have I?"

"Right down to the bone, when I wasn't looking. I don't know if I like it." He studied her for a long moment. "Trust comes hard to me. Don't ever lie to me, Jessica," he said unexpectedly. "I can forgive anything except that. I've been sold out once too often in the past. The scars go deep and they came from painful lessons. I can't bear lies."

She thought about being barren, and wondered if this would be the right time to tell him. But it wasn't a lie, was it? It was a secret, one she would get around to, if it ever became necessary to tell him. But right now they were just dating, just friends. She was over-reacting. She smiled. "Okay. I promise that I'll never deliberately lie to you." That got her around the diffi-cult hurdle of her condition. She wasn't lying. She just wasn't confessing. It was middle ground, and not really dishonest. Of course it wasn't.

He let go of her hand and started the vehicle, turning on the lights. He glanced sideways at her as he pulled the Bronco out into the road and drove back to her cabin. She might be afraid, but there was desire in her, as well. She wanted him. He had to keep that in mind and not give up hope.

He stopped at her front steps. "I want to take you out

from time to time," he said firmly. "We can go out to eat—as my budget allows," he added with a grin, "and to movies. And I'd like to take you fishing and deer tracking with me this fall."

"Oh, I'd enjoy that." She looked surprised and delighted. The radiance of her face made her so stunning that he lost his train of thought for a minute.

He frowned. "Just don't go shopping for wedding bands and putting announcements in the local paper," he said firmly. He held up a hand when she started, flustered, to protest. "There's no use arguing about it, my mind's made up. I do know that you make wonderful homemade bread, and that's a point in your favor, but you mustn't rush me."

Her eyes brightened with wicked pleasure. "Oh, I wouldn't dream of it," she said, entering into the spirit of the thing. "I never try to rush men into marriage."

He chuckled. "Okay. Now you stick to that. I don't like most people," he mused. "But I like you."

"I like you, too."

"In between hero-worshipping me," he added outrageously.

She looked him over with a long sigh. "Can I help it if you're the stuff dreams are made of?"

"Pull the other one. I'll see you tomorrow."

"That reminds me, there's a young man in juvenile detention that I'd like you to talk to for me," she said. "He's on a rocky path. Maybe you can turn him around."

He rolled his eyes upward. "Not again!"

"You know you don't mind," she chided. "I'll phone you from the office tomorrow."

"All right." He watched her get out of the Bronco. "Lock your doors."

His concern made her tingle. She grinned at him over her shoulder. "I always do. Thanks for supper."

"I enjoyed it."

"So did I." She wanted to, but she didn't look back as she unlocked the door. She was inside before she heard him drive off. She was sure that her feet didn't touch the floor for the rest of the night. And her dreams were sweet.

In the days and weeks that followed, Jessica and Mc-Callum saw a lot of one another. He kissed her, but it was always absently, tenderly. He'd drawn back from the intensity of the kisses they'd shared the first night he took her out. Now, they talked about things. They discovered much that they had in common, and life took on a new beauty for Jessica.

Just when she thought things couldn't get any better, she walked into the Hip Hop Café and came face-to-face with a nightmare—Sam Jackson.

The sandy-haired man turned and looked at her with cold, contemptuous eyes. He was the brother of the man who'd attacked her and who had later been killed. He was shorter and stockier, but the heavy facial features and small eyes were much the same.

"Hello, Jessica Larson," he said, blocking her path so that she was trapped between the wall and him. "I was passing through and thought I might look you up while I was in town. I wanted to see how my brother's murderer was getting along."

She clutched her purse in hands that trembled. She knew her face was white. Her eyes were huge as she looked at him with terror. He had been the most vocal person in court during the trial, making remarks about her and to her that still hurt.

"I didn't kill your brother. It wasn't my fault," she insisted.

"If you hadn't gone out there and meddled, it never would have happened," he accused. His voice, like his eyes, was full of hate. "You killed him, all right."

"He died in a car wreck," she reminded him with as much poise as she could manage. "It was not my fault that he attacked me!" She carefully kept her voice down so that she wouldn't be overheard.

"You went out there alone, knowing he'd be on his own because you'd tried to get his wife to leave him," he returned. "A woman who goes to a man's house by herself when he's alone is asking for it."

"I didn't know that he was alone!"

"You wanted him. That's why you convinced his wife to leave him."

The man's attitude hadn't changed, it had only intensified. He'd been unable from the beginning to believe his brother could have beaten not only his wife, but his little girl, as well. To keep from accepting the truth, he'd blamed it all on Jessica. His brother had been the most repulsive human being she'd ever known. She looked at him levelly. "That's not true," she corrected. "And you know it. You won't admit it, but you know that your brother was on drugs and you know what he did because of it. You also know that I had nothing to do with his death."

"Like hell you didn't," he said with venom. "You had him arrested! That damned trial destroyed my family, humiliated us beyond belief. Then you just walked away. You walked off and forgot the tragedy you'd caused!"

Her whole body clenched at the remembered agony. "I felt for all of you," she argued. "I didn't want to hurt you, but nothing I did was strictly on my own behalf. I wanted to help his daughter, your niece! Didn't any of you think about her?"

He couldn't speak for a minute. "He never meant to hurt her. He said so. Anyway, she's all right," he muttered. "Kids get over things."

Her eyes looked straight into his. "No, they don't get over things like that. Even I never got over what your brother did to me. I paid and I'm still paying."

"Women like you are trash," he said scornfully. "And before I'm through, everyone around here is going to know it."

"What do you mean?"

He smiled. "I mean I'm going to stick around for a few days and let people know just what sort of social worker they've got here. Maybe during the last few years, some of them have forgotten...."

"If you try to start trouble—" she began.

"You'll what?" he asked smugly. "Sue me for defamation of character? Go ahead. It took everything we had in legal fees to defend my brother. I don't have any money. Sue me. You can't get blood out of a rock."

She tried to breathe normally, but couldn't. "How is Clarisse?" she asked, mentioning the daughter of the man who'd assaulted her so many years before.

"She's in college," he said, "working her way through."

"Is she all right?"

He shifted irritably. "I guess. We hear about her

through a mutual cousin. She and her mother washed their hands of us years ago."

Jessica didn't say another word. She'd been planning to eat, but her appetite was gone.

"Excuse me, I have to get back to work," she said. She turned around and left the café. She hardly felt anything all the way to her office. She'd honestly thought the past was dead. Now here it was again, staring her in the face. She'd done nothing wrong, but it seemed that she was doomed to pay over and over again for a crime that had been committed against her, not by her.

It was a cruel wind that had blown Sam Jackson into town, she thought bitterly. But if he was only passing through, perhaps he wouldn't stay long. She'd stick close to the office for a couple of days, she decided, and not make a target of herself.

But that was easier said than done. Apparently Sam had found out where her office was, because he passed by it three times that day. The next morning, when Jessica went into work, it was to find him sitting in the Hip Hop Café where she usually had coffee. She went on to the office and asked Bess if she'd mind bringing her a coffee when she went across the street.

"Who is that fat man?" Bess asked when she came back. "Does he really know you?"

Jessica's heart stopped. "Did he ask you about me?"

"Oh, no," Bess said carelessly. She put a plastic cup of coffee in front of Jessica. "He didn't say anything to me, but he was talking to some other people about you." She hesitated, wondering if she should continue.

"Some people?" Jessica prompted.

"Sterling McCallum was one of them," the case-worker added slowly.

Jessica didn't have to ask if what the man had said was derogatory. It was obvious from the expression on her face that it was.

"He said his brother died because of you," Bess continued reluctantly. "That you led him on and then threw him over after you'd gotten his wife out of the way."

Jessica sat down heavily. "I see. So I'm a femme fatale."

"Nobody who knows you would believe such a thing!" Bess scoffed. "He was a client, wasn't he? Or rather, his brother was. Honest to God, Jessica, I knew there had to be some reason why you always insist that Candy and Brenda go out on cases together instead of alone. His brother was the reason, wasn't he?"

Jessica nodded. "But that isn't how he's telling it. New people in the community might believe him, though," she added, trying not to remember that several old-timers still believed that Jessica had been running after the man, too.

"Tell him to get lost," the other woman said. "Or threaten to have him arrested for slander. I'll bet McCallum would do it for you. After all, you two are looking cozy these days."

"We're just friends," Jessica said with emphasis. "Nothing more. And Sterling might believe him. He's been away from Whitehorn for a long time, and he doesn't really know me very well." She didn't add that McCallum had such bad experiences in the past that it might be all too easy for him to believe what Sam Jackson was telling him. She was afraid of the damage that might be done to their fragile relationship.

"Don't worry," Bess was saying. "McCallum will give him his walking papers."

"Do you think so?" Jessica took a sip of her coffee. "We'd better get to work."

She half expected McCallum to come storming into the office demanding explanations. But he didn't. Nothing was said at all, by him or by anyone else. Life went on as usual, and by the end of the day, she'd relaxed. She'd overreacted to Sam's presence in Whitehorn. It would be all right. He was probably on his way out of town even now.

McCallum was drinking a beer. He hardly ever had anything even slightly alcoholic. His mother had taught him well what alcohol could do. Therefore, he was always on guard against overindulgence.

That being the case, it was only one beer. He was off duty and not on call. Before he'd met the newcomer in the café that morning, he might have taken Jessica to a movie. Now he felt sick inside. She'd never told him the things he'd learned from Sam Jackson.

Jessica was a pretty woman when she dressed up. She'd been interning at the social-services office, Sam Jackson had told him, when she'd gone out to see his brother Fred. Fred's wife had become jealous of the way Jessica was out there all the time, and she'd left him. Jessica teased and flirted with him, and then, when things got out of hand and the poor man was maddened with passion, she'd yelled rape and had him arrested. The man had hardly touched her. He'd gone to jail for attempted rape, got out on parole six months later and was killed in a horrible car wreck. His wife and child had been lost to him, he was disgraced and it was all Jessica's fault. Everybody believed her wild lies.

Sam Jackson was no fly-by-night con man. He'd been a respected councilman in Whitehorn for many years and was still known locally. McCallum had asked another old-timer, who'd verified that Jessica had had Jackson's brother arrested for sexual assault. It had been a closed hearing, very hushed up, and a bit of gossip was all that managed to escape the tight-lipped sheriff, Judd Hensley, and the attorneys and judge in the case. But people knew it was Jessica who had been involved, and the rumors had flown for weeks, even after Fred Jackson's family left town and he was sent to jail for attempted rape.

The old man had shaken his head as he recalled the incident. Women always said no when they meant yes, he assured McCallum, and several people thought that Jessica had only gotten what she'd asked for, going out to a man's house alone. Women had too goldarned much freedom, the old-timer said. If they'd never gotten the vote, life would have been better all around.

McCallum didn't hear the sexism in the remark; he was too outraged over what he'd learned about Jessica. So that shy, retiring pose was just that—an act. She'd played him for an absolute fool. No woman could be trusted. Hadn't he learned from his mother how treacherous they could be? His mother had smiled so sweetly when people came, infrequently, to the house. She'd lied with a straight face when a neighbor had asked questions about all the yelling and smashing of glass the night before. Nothing had happened except that she'd dropped a vase, she'd insisted, and she'd cried out because it startled her.

Actually, she'd been raving mad from too much alcohol and had been chasing her son around the house with an empty gin bottle. That was the night she'd broken his arm. She'd managed to convince the local doctor, the elderly practitioner who'd preceeded Jessica's father, that he'd slipped and fallen on a rain-wet porch. She'd tried to coax him to set it and say nothing out of loyalty to the family. But Sterling had told. His mother had hurt him. She'd lied deliberately about their home life. She'd pretended to love him, until she drank. And then she was like another person, a brutal and unfeeling one who only wanted to hurt him. He'd never trusted another woman since.

Until Jessica. She was the one exception. He'd grown close to her during their meetings, and he wanted her in every way there was. He valued her friendship, her company. But she'd lied to him, by omission. She hadn't told him the truth about her past.

There was one other truth Sam Jackson had imparted to him, an even worse one. In the course of the trial, it had come out that the doctor who had examined Jessica found a blockage in her fallopian tubes that would make it difficult, if not impossible, for her to get pregnant.

She knew that Sterling was interested in her, that he would probably want children. Yet she'd made sure that she never told him that one terrible fact about herself. She could not give him a child. Yet she'd never stopped going out with him, and she knew that he was growing involved with her. It was a lie by omission, but still a lie. It was the one thing, he confessed to himself, that he could never forgive.

He was only grateful that he'd found her out in time, before he'd made an utter fool of himself.

Chapter 8

Unfortunately, it was impossible for Jessica not to notice that McCallum's attitude toward her had changed since Sam Jackson's advent into town. He didn't call her that evening or the next day. And when she was contacted by the sheriff's office because the child of one of her client families—Keith Colson—was picked up for shoplifting, she wondered if he would have.

She went to the sheriff's office as quickly as she could. McCallum was there as arresting officer. He was polite and not hateful, but he was so distant that Jessica hardly knew what to say to him.

She sat down in a chair beside the lanky boy in the interrogation room and laid her purse on the table.

"Why did you do it, Keith?" she asked gently.

He shrugged and averted his eyes. "I don't know."

"You were caught in the act," she pressed, aware of

McCallum standing quietly behind her, waiting. "The store owner saw you pick up several packages of cigarettes and stick them in your pockets. He said you even looked into the camera while you were doing it. You didn't try to hide what you were doing."

Keith moved restlessly in the chair. "I did it, okay? How about locking me up now?" he added to McCallum. "This time I wasn't an accomplice. This time I'm the—what do you call it?—the perpetrator. That means I do time, right? When are you going to lock me up?"

McCallum was scowling. Something wasn't right here. The boy looked hunted, afraid, but not because he'd been caught shoplifting. He'd waited patiently for McCallum to show up and arrest him, and he'd climbed into the back of the patrol car almost eagerly. There was one other disturbing thing: a fading bruise, a big one, was visible beside his eye.

"I can't do that yet," McCallum said. "We've called the juvenile authorities. You're underage, so you'll have to be turned over to them."

"Juvenile? Not *again!* But I wasn't an accomplice, you know I did it. I did it all by myself! I shouldn't have to go back home this time!"

McCallum hitched up his slacks and sat down on the edge of the table, facing the boy. "Why don't you tell me the truth?" he invited quietly. "I can't help you if I don't know what's going on."

Keith looked as if he wanted to say something, as if it was eating him up inside not to. But at the last minute, his eyes lowered and he shrugged.

"Nothing to tell," he said gruffly. He glanced at McCallum. "There's a chance that they might keep me, isn't there? At the juvenile hall, I mean?"

McCallum scowled. "No. You'll be sent home after they've done the paperwork and your hearing's scheduled."

Keith's face fell. He sighed and wouldn't say another word. McCallum could remember seeing that particular expression on a youngster's face only once before. It had been on his own face, the night the doctor set the arm his mother had broken. He had to get to the bottom of Keith's situation, and he knew he couldn't do that by talking to Keith or any of his family. There had to be another way, a better way. Perhaps he could talk to some people at Keith's school. Someone there might know more than he did and be able to shed some light on the situation for him.

Jessica went out to see Keith's father and grandmother. She'd hoped McCallum might offer to go with her, but he left as soon as Keith was delivered to the juvenile officer. It was all too obvious that he found Jessica's company distasteful, probably because Sam Jackson had been filling his head full of half-truths. If he'd only come out and accuse her of something, she could defend herself. But how could she make any sort of defense against words that were left unspoken?

Terrance Colson was not surprised to hear that his son was in trouble with the law.

"I knew the boy was up to no good," he told Jessica blithely. "Takes after his mother, you know. She ran off with a salesman and dumped him on me and his grandmother years ago. Never wanted him in the first place." He sounded as if he felt the same way. "God knows I've done my best for him, but he never appreciates anything at all. He's always talking back, making trouble. I'm not surprised that he stole things, no, sir."

"Did you know that he smoked?" Jessica asked deliberately, curious because the boy's grandmother stayed conspicuously out of sight and never even came out to the porch, when Jessica knew she'd heard the truck drive up.

"Sure I knew he smoked," Terrance said evenly. "I won't give him money to throw away on cigarettes. That's probably why he stole them."

That was a lie. Jessica knew it was, because McCallum had offered the boy a cigarette in the sheriff's office and he'd refused it with a grimace. He'd said that he didn't like cigarettes, although he quickly corrected that and said that he just didn't want one at the moment. But there were no nicotine stains on his fingers, and he certainly didn't smell of tobacco.

"You tell them to send him home, now, as soon as they get finished with him," Terrance told Jessica firmly. "I got work to do around here and he's needed. They can't lock him up."

"They won't," she assured him. "But he won't tell us anything. Not even why he did it."

"Because he needed cigarettes, that's why," the man said unconvincingly.

Jessica understood why McCallum had been suspicious. The longer she talked to the boy's father, the more curious she became about the situation. She asked a few more questions, but he was as unforthcoming as Keith himself had been. Eventually, she got up to leave.

"I'd like to say hello to Mrs. Colson," she began.

"Oh, she's too busy to come out," he said with careful indifference. "I'll give her your regards, though."

"Yes. You do that." Jessica smiled and held out her hand deliberately. As Terrance reluctantly took it, she saw small bruises on his knuckles. He was righthanded. If he hit someone, it would be with the hand she was holding.

She didn't remark on the bruises. She left the porch, forming a theory that was very disturbing. She wished that she and McCallum were on better terms, because she was going to need his help. She was sorry she hadn't listened to him sooner. If she had, perhaps Keith wouldn't have another shoplifting charge on his record.

When she got back to her office, she called the sheriff's office and asked them to have McCallum drop by. Once, he would have stopped in the middle of whatever he was doing to oblige her. But today it was almost quitting time before he put in a belated appearance. And he didn't look happy about being summoned, either.

She had to pretend that it didn't matter, that she wasn't bothered that he was staring holes through her with those angry dark eyes. She forced a cool smile to her lips and invited him to sit down.

"I've had a long talk with Keith's father," she said at once. "He says that Keith smokes and that's why he took the cigarettes."

"Bull," he said curtly.

"I know. I didn't notice any nicotine stains on Keith's fingers. But I did notice some bruises on Terrance's knuckles and a fading bruise near Keith's eye," she added.

He lifted an eyebrow. "Observant, aren't you?" he asked with thinly veiled sarcasm. "You were the one who said there was nothing wrong at Keith's home, as I recall."

She sat back heavily in her chair. "Yes, I was. I should have listened to you. The thing is, what can we do about it? His father isn't going to admit that he's hitting him, and Keith is too loyal to tell anyone about it. I even thought about talking to old Mrs. Colson, but Terrance won't let me near her."

"Unless Keith volunteers the information, we have no case," McCallum replied. "The district attorney isn't likely to ask a judge to issue an arrest warrant on anyone's hunch."

She grimaced. "I know." She laced her fingers together. "Meanwhile, Keith's desperate to get away from home, even to the extent of landing himself in jail to accomplish it. He won't stop until he does."

"I know that."

"Then do something!" she insisted.

"What do you have in mind?"

She threw up her hands. "How do I know? I'm not in law enforcement."

His dark eyes narrowed accusingly on her face. "No. You're in social work. And you take your job very seriously, don't you?"

It was a pointed remark, unmistakable. She sat up straight, with her hands locked together on her cluttered desk, and stared at him levelly. "Go ahead," she invited. "Get it off your chest."

"All right," he said without raising his voice. "You can't have a child of your own."

She'd expected to be confronted with some of the old gossip, with anything except this. Her face paled. She couldn't even explain it to him. Her eyes fell.

The guilt told him all he needed to know. "Did you

ever plan to tell me?" he asked icily. "Or wasn't it any of my business?"

She stared at the small print on a bottle of correction fluid until she had it memorized. "I thought...we weren't serious about each other, so it...wasn't necessary to tell you."

He didn't want her to know how serious he'd started to feel about her. It made him too vulnerable. He crossed one long leg over the other.

"And how about the court trial?" he added. "Weren't you going to mention anything about it, either?"

Her weary eyes lifted to his. "You must surely realize that Sam Jackson isn't anyone's idea of an unbiased observer. It was his brother. Naturally, he'd think it was all my fault."

"Wasn't it?" he asked coldly. "You did go out to the man's house all alone, didn't you?"

That remark was a slap in the face. She got to her feet, her eyes glittering. "I don't have to defend a decision I made years ago to you," she said coolly. "You have no right to accuse me of anything."

"I wasn't aware that I had," he returned. "Do you feel guilty about what happened to Jackson's brother?"

Her expression hardened to steel. "I have nothing to feel guilty about," she said with as much pride as she could manage. "Given the same circumstances, I'd do exactly what I did again and I'd take the consequences."

He scowled at her. "Including costing a man his family, subjecting him to public humiliation and eventually to what amounted to suicide?"

So that was what Sam had been telling people. That Jessica had driven the man to his death.

She sat back down. "If you care about people," she

said quietly, "you believe them. If you don't, all the words in the world won't change anything. Sam should have been a lawyer. He really has a gift for influencing opinion. He's certainly tarred and feathered me in only two days."

"The truth usually comes out, doesn't it?" he countered.

She didn't flinch. "You don't know the truth. Not that it matters anymore." She was heartsick. She pulled her files toward her. "If you'll excuse me, Deputy McCallum, I've already got a day's work left to finish. I'll have another talk with Keith when the juvenile officers bring him back to the sheriff's office."

"You do that." He got up, furious because she wouldn't offer him any explanation, any apology for keeping him in the dark. "You might have told me the truth in the beginning," he added angrily.

She opened a file. "We all have our scars. Mine are such that it hurts to take them out and look at them." She lifted wounded dark eyes to his. "I can't ever have babies," she said stiffly. "Now you know. Ordinarily, you wouldn't have, because I never had any intention of letting our relationship go that far. You were the one who kept pushing your way into my life. If you had just let me alone…!" She stopped, biting her lower lip to stifle the painful words. She turned a sheet of paper over deftly. "Sam Jackson's brother got what he deserved, McCallum. And that's the last thing I'll ever say about it."

He stood watching her for a minute before he finally turned and went out. He walked aimlessly into the outer office. She was right. He was the one who'd pursued her, not the reverse. All the same, she might have told him the truth.

"Hi, McCallum," Bess called to him from her desk, smiling sweetly.

He paused on his way out and smiled back. "Hi, yourself."

She gave him a look that could have melted ice. "I guess you and Jessica are too thick for me to try my luck, hmm?" she asked with a mock sigh.

He lifted his chin and his dark eyes shimmered as he looked at her. "Jessica and I are friends," he said, refusing to admit that they were hardly even that anymore. "That's all."

"Well, in that case, why don't you come over for supper tonight and I'll feed you some of my homemade spaghetti?" she asked softly. "Then we can watch that new movie on cable. You know, the one with all the warnings on it?" she added suggestively.

She was pretty and young and obviously had no hang-ups about being a woman. He pursed his lips. It had been a long, dry spell, although something in him resisted dating a woman so close to Jessica. On the other hand, he told himself, Jessica had lied to him, and what was it to her if he dated one of her employees?

"What time?" he asked gruffly.

She brightened. "Six sharp. I live next door to Truman Haynes. You know where his house is, don't you?" He nodded. "Well, I rent his furnished cottage. It's very cozy, and old Truman goes to bed real early."

"Does he, now?" he mused.

She grinned. "Yes, indeed!"

"Then I'll see you at six." He winked and walked out, still feeling a twinge of guilt.

Bess stuck her head into Jessica's office just before she left. "McCallum said that you and he were just good friends, and you keep saying the same thing," she began, "so is it all right if I try my luck with him?"

Jessica was dumbfounded, but she was adept at hiding her deepest feelings. She forced a smile. "Why, of course."

Bess let out a sigh of relief. "Thank goodness! I invited him over for supper. I didn't want to step on your toes, but he is so sexy! Thanks, Jessica! See you tomorrow!"

She closed the door quickly, and a minute later, Jessica heard her go out. It was like a door closing on life itself. She hesitated just briefly before she turned her eyes back to the file she was working on. The print was so blurred that she could hardly read it.

Whitehorn was small and, as in most small towns, everyone knew immediately about McCallum's supper with Bess. They didn't know that nothing had happened, however, because Bess made enough innuendos to suggest that it had been the hottest date of her life. Jessica was hard-pressed not to snap at her employee, but she couldn't let anyone know how humiliating and painful the experience was to her. She had her pride, if nothing else.

Sam Jackson heard about the date and laughed heartily. Originally he'd planned to spend only one night in Whitehorn, but he was enjoying himself too much to leave in a rush. A week later, he was still in residence at the small motel and having breakfast every morning at the café across from Jessica's office.

Jessica was near breaking point. People were gossip-

ing about her all over again. She became impatient with
her caseworkers and even with clients, which was unlike her. She couldn't do anything about Sam Jackson,
and certainly McCallum wasn't going to. He seemed to
like the man. And he seemed to like Bess as well, because he began to stop by the office every day to take
her to lunch.

"I'm leaving now," Bess said at noon on Friday. She
hesitated, and from the corner of her eye, Jessica saw
her looking at her in concern. No wonder since even to
her own eyes she looked pale and drawn. In fact, she
was hardly eating anything and was on the verge of
moving out of town. Desperation had cost her the cool
reason she'd always prided herself on.

"Have a nice lunch," she told Bess, refusing to look
up because she knew Sterling McCallum was standing
in the outer office, waiting.

Bess still hesitated. She felt so guilty she couldn't
stand herself lately. It was painfully obvious how her
boss felt about Sterling McCallum. It was even more
obvious now that McCallum was taking Bess out. She
hated being caught between the two of them, and it was
shocking to see how Jessica was being affected by it.
Bess had a few bad moments remembering how she'd
embroidered those dates with McCallum to make everyone in the office think they had a hot relationship going.

Jessica was unfailingly polite, but she treated Bess
like a stranger now. It was painful to have the old, pleasant friendliness apparently gone for good. Jessica never
looked into her eyes. She treated her like a piece of furniture, and it really hurt. Bess couldn't even blame her.
She asked for permission to go out with McCallum, but
she'd known even when Jessica gave it that the other

woman cared deeply about him. She was ashamed of herself for putting her own infatuation with McCallum over Jessica's feelings. Not that it had done her any good. McCallum was fine company, and once he'd kissed her with absent affection, but he couldn't have made it more obvious that he enjoyed being with her only in a casual way. On the other hand, when he looked at Jessica there was real pain in his eyes.

"Can't I bring you back something?" Bess asked abruptly. "Jessica, you look so—"

"I'm fine," Jessica said shortly. "I have a virus and I've lost my appetite, that's all. Please go ahead."

Bess grimaced as she closed the door, and the concern was still on her face when she joined McCallum.

He'd seen Jessica, too, in that brief time while her office door was open. He'd wanted to show her that he didn't care, that he could date other women with complete indifference to her feelings. But it was backfiring on him. He felt sick as he realized how humiliated she must be, to have him dating one of her own coworkers. It wasn't her fault that she couldn't bear a child, after all, and she was right—he'd never acted as if he had any kind of permanent relationship in mind for the two of them. He was still trying to find reasons to keep her at arm's length, he admitted finally. He was afraid to trust her, afraid of being hurt if he gave his heart completely. He'd believed Sam Jackson because he'd wanted to. But now, as he thought about it rationally, he wondered at his own gullibility. Was he really so desperate to have Jessica out of his life that he'd believe a total stranger, a biased total stranger, before he'd even ask Jessica for her version of what had happened?

Sam Jackson had been having lunch in the café, too,

and stopped by McCallum's table to exchange pleas-
antries with him and Bess. Sheriff Hensley drove by
in the patrol car and saw them in the window. Later
that afternoon, he invited McCallum into his office and
closed the door.

"I heard Sam Jackson's been in town six days," he
said quietly. "What's his business here?"

"He's just passing through," McCallum said.

"And...?"

McCallum was puzzled. It wasn't like his boss to be
so interested in strangers who visited town. "And he's
just passing the time of day as well, I guess."

Hensley folded his hands together on his desk
and toyed with a paper clip. "He's the sort who holds
grudges." He looked up. "I've heard some talk I don't
like. It was a closed trial, but a lot of gossip got out
anyway. Fred's wife and daughter left town as soon as
the verdict was read, but Jessica had nowhere to go except here. Fred, of course, gave her a rough time of it."

"Maybe he had reason to," McCallum ventured
curtly.

Hensley put the paper clip down deliberately. "You
listen to me," he said coldly. "Jessica did nothing except
try to help his wife and child. Fred was a cocaine addict.
He liked to bring his friends home at night while his
wife was working at the hospital. One night he was so
high that he beat his daughter and she ran away. It was
Jessica who took her in and comforted her. It was Jessica
who made her mother face the fact that she was married to an addict and that she had to get help for them.
Jessica was told—probably by your buddy Sam—that
Fred had forced Clarisse, his daughter, to go back home

with him. That's why she went out there that day. He attacked Jessica instead, and she barely got away in time."

McCallum didn't say a word. His complexion paled, just a little.

"For her pains, because the court trial was in the judge's chambers, and not publicized for Clarisse's sake, Jessica took the brunt of the gossip. All anyone heard was that Jessica had almost gotten raped. It was the talk of the town. Everywhere she went, thanks to Sam Jackson, she was pointed out and ridiculed as the girl who'd led poor Fred on and then yelled rape. She took it, for Clarisse's sake, until her mother could get another job and they could leave town while Fred was safely in jail."

"He didn't tell me that," McCallum said dully.

"Sam Jackson hated Jessica. He was on the city council. He had influence and he used it. But time passed and Sam left town. It didn't end there, however. Fred got out of jail in six months and came after Jessica. He was killed in a wreck, all right," the sheriff stated. "He was out for vengeance the day he was paroled and was chasing Jessica in his car, high as a March kite, until he ran off a cliff in the process. He would have killed her if he hadn't."

McCallum felt cold chills down his spine. He could picture the scene all too easily.

"Jessica survived," Hensley continued curtly, and McCallum barely registered the odd phrasing. "She held her head up, and those of us who knew the truth couldn't have admired her more. She's suffered enough. I didn't realize Sam Jackson was even in town until I happened to see him this morning, but he won't be here any longer. I'm going to give him a personal escort to the county line right now." He stood up, grabbing his hat. "And for what it's worth, I think you're petty to start dating Bess right under Jessica's nose, on top of everything else. She doesn't deserve that."

McCallum got to his feet, too. "I'd like a word with Jackson before you boot him out of town."

Hensley recognized the deputy's expression too well to agree to what McCallum was really suggesting.

"You believed him without questioning what he said," Hensley reminded him. "If there's fault, it's as much yours as his. You aren't to go near him."

McCallum's thin lips pressed together angrily. "He had no business coming here to spread more lies about her."

"You had no business listening to them," came the merciless reply. "Learn from the experience. There are always two sides to every story. You've got enough work to do. Why don't you go out there and act like a deputy sheriff?"

McCallum reached for his own hat. "I don't feel much like one right now," he said. "I've been a fool."

"Hard times teach hard lessons, but they stay with us. Jessica isn't judgmental, even if you are."

McCallum didn't say another word, but he had his reservations. He'd hurt her too much. He knew before he even asked that she might forgive him, but that she'd never forget the things he'd said to her.

Chapter 9

Sam Jackson left town with the sheriff's car following him every inch of the way to the county line. He'd had to do some fast talking just to keep an irritated Hensley from arresting him for vagrancy. But his bitter hatred of Jessica hadn't abated, and he hoped he'd done her some damage. His poor brother, he told himself, had deserved some sort of revenge. Perhaps now he could rest in peace.

McCallum didn't go near Jessica's office, for fear that Bess might make another play for him and complicate things all over again. He did go to Jessica's house the next afternoon, hat in hand, to apologize.

She met him at the door in a pair of worn jeans and a T-shirt, her hair in a ponytail and her glasses perched on her nose. It was a beautiful day, and the Montana air sparkled. The world was in bloom, and the Whitehorn area had never been more beautiful under the wide blue sky.

"Yes?" Jessica asked politely, as if he were a stranger.

He felt uncomfortable. He wasn't used to making apologies. "I suppose you know why I'm here," he said stiffly.

She stripped off her gardening gloves. "It's about Keith, I guess," she replied matter-of-factly, without any attempt at dissembling.

He frowned. "No. We persuaded the authorities to keep Keith for a few days at the juvenile hall while we did some investigating. I haven't come about that."

"Oh." Her eyes held no expression at all. "Then what do you want?"

He propped one foot on the lowest step and stared at the spotless shine of his black boot. "I came to apologize."

"I can't imagine why."

He looked up in time to catch the bitterness that touched her face just for an instant. "What?"

"I'm a liar and a temptress and a murderess, according to Sam Jackson," she said heavily. "From what everyone says, you were hanging on to every word he said. So why should you want to apologize to me?"

He drew in a breath and shifted his hat from one hand to the other. "Hensley told me all of it."

"And that's why you're here." She sounded weary, resigned. "I might have known it wasn't because you came to your senses," she said without inflection in her voice. "You preferred Sam Jackson's version of the truth, even after I reminded you that he was biased."

"You told me a half-truth from the beginning!"

"Don't you raise your voice to me!" she said angrily, punching her glasses up onto her nose when they started to slip down. "I didn't want to remember it, can't you understand? I hate having to remember. Clarisse was the real victim, a lot more than I was. I just happened to be stupid enough to go out there alone, trying to protect her. And believe me, it wasn't to tempt Fred! The only thing I was thinking about was how to spare Clarisse any more anguish!"

"I know that now." He groaned silently. "Why didn't you tell me?"

"Why should you have expected me to?" she replied, puzzled. "I don't know very much about you, except that your mother drank and was cruel to you and that you had a very nasty time of it in foster care."

He hesitated, searching her eyes.

"You've told me very little about yourself," she said. "I only know bits and pieces, mostly what I've heard from other people. But you expected me to tell you things I haven't told anyone my whole life. Why should you expect something from me that you're not willing to give in return?"

That gave him food for thought. He ran a hand through his hair. "I don't suppose I should have."

"And it's all past history now," she added. "You're dating Bess. I don't trespass on other women's territory. Not ever. Bess even asked if I had anything going with you before she invited you to supper. I told her no," she added firmly.

There was a sudden faint flush high on his cheekbones, because he remembered telling Bess the same thing. But it wasn't true, then or now. "Listen—" he began.

"No, you listen. I appreciate the meals we had together and the help you gave me on cases. I hope we can work together amicably in the future. But as you have reason to know, I have nothing to offer a man on any permanent basis."

He moved closer, his eyes narrowed with concern. "Being barren isn't the end of the world," he said quietly.

She moved back and folded her arms over her chest, stopping him where he stood. "You thought so. You even said so," she reminded him.

His teeth ground together. "I was half out of my mind! It upset me that you could keep something so important to yourself. That was why I got uptight. It isn't that I couldn't learn to live with it...."

"But you don't have to. Nobody has to live with it except me," she said quietly. "I'm sure that Bess has no such drawbacks, and she has the advantage of being completely without inhibitions. She's sweet and young, and she adores you," she said through tight lips. "You're a very lucky man."

"Lucky," he echoed with growing bitterness.

"Now, if you'll excuse me," she said with a bright smile, pulling her gloves back on, "I have to finish weeding my garden. Thanks for stopping by."

"Just like that?" he burst out angrily. "I hadn't finished."

She brushed dirt off the palm of one glove. "What is there left to say?" she asked with calm curiosity.

He studied her impassive face. She had her emotions under impeccable control, but beneath the surface, he perceived pain and a deep wounding that wasn't likely to be assuaged by any apology, however well meant. He was going to have to win back her trust and respect. That wasn't going to happen overnight. And he didn't expect her to make it easy for him.

He rammed his hat back onto his head. "Nothing,

I guess," he agreed, nodding. "I said it all, one way or another, when I jumped down your throat without knowing the truth."

"Sam can be very convincing," she replied. She averted her face. "He turned the whole town against me for a while. You can't imagine how vicious the gossip was," she added involuntarily. "I still hate being talked about."

Jessica didn't add that he'd helped gossip along by dating Bess, so that his rejection of her was made public. But he knew that already. It must have added insult to injury to have his new romantic interest and Sam's renewed accusations being discussed at every lunch counter in town. He understood now, as he hadn't before, why she'd worried so much about being seen in public with him.

"How about Jennifer?" she added suddenly, interrupting his gloomy thoughts. "Any news on her parents?"

"No luck yet," he replied. "But I think I may be on to something with Keith."

"I hope so," she said. "I feel terrible that I didn't suspect something before this."

"None of us is perfect, Jessica," he said, his voice deep and slow and full of regret. His dark eyes searched hers in silence, until she averted her own to ward off the flash of electricity that persisted between the two of them. "I'll let you know what I find out."

She nodded, but didn't reply. She just walked away from him.

He talked to a school official about Keith, and discovered that the boy had been an excellent student until about the time his father lost his job.

"He was never a problem," the counselor told him. "But he let slip something once about his father liking liquor a little too much when he was upset. Things seemed to go badly for Terrance after his wife left, you know. Losing his job must be the last straw."

"I'm sure it's unpleasant for him to have to depend on public assistance," McCallum agreed. "But taking it out on his child isn't the answer."

"People drink and lose control," the counselor said. "More and more of them, in these pressured economic times. They're usually sorry, too late. I'll try to talk to Keith again, if you like. But I can't promise anything. He's very loyal to his father."

"Most kids are," McCallum said curtly. He was remembering how he'd protected his brutal mother, right up until the night she'd broken his arm with the bottle. He'd made excuse after excuse for her behavior, just as Keith was probably doing now.

He contacted the juvenile officer and had a long conversation with him, but the man couldn't tell him any more than he already knew. Keith hadn't reached the end of his rope yet, and until he did, there was little anyone could do for him.

McCallum did get a break, a small one, in the abandoned-baby case. It seemed that a local midwife did remember hearing an old woman from out of town talk about delivering a child in a clandestine manner for a frightened young woman. It wasn't much to go on, but anything would help.

McCallum decided that it might be a good idea to share that tidbit with Jessica. He dreaded having to see Bess again, after the way he'd led her on.

But it turned out not to be the ordeal he'd expected.

Bess was just coming back from the small kitchen with a cup of coffee when he walked into the office. She moved closer and grinned at him.

"Hi, stranger!" she said with a friendly smile. "How about some coffee?"

"Not just now, thanks." He smiled ruefully. "Bess, there's something I need to tell you."

"No, there isn't," she said with a sigh. "I'd already figured it all out, you know. I never meant to step on Jessica's toes, but I had a major crush on you that I had to get out of my system." She gave him a sheepish glance. "I didn't realize how painful it was going to be, trying to work here after I'd all but stabbed Jessica in the back. No one in the office will speak to me, and Jessica's very polite, but she isn't friendly like she used to be. Nothing is the same anymore."

"I'm sorry about that," he said, knowing it was as much his fault as hers.

She shrugged and moved a little closer. "Still friends?" she asked hesitantly.

"Of course," he replied gently. He bent and kissed her lightly on the cheek.

Jessica, who'd come into the outer office to ask Bess to make a phone call for her, got an eyeful of what looked like a tender scene and froze in place.

"Jessica," McCallum said roughly as he lifted his head and saw her.

Bess turned in time to watch her boss disappear back into her own office, her back straight and dignified.

"Well, that was probably the last straw," Bess groaned. "I was going to talk to her today and apologize."

"So was I," he replied. "She didn't deserve to be hurt any more, after what Sam Jackson did to her."

"I hope it's not too late to undo the damage," Bess added. Then she realized how false a picture she'd given everyone about her dates with McCallum, and she felt even worse. She'd embroidered them to make herself look like a femme fatale, because McCallum hadn't been at all loverlike. But her wild stories had backfired in the worst way. In admitting that she'd lied, she'd make herself look like a conceited idiot. Jessica was cool enough to her already. She hated the thought of compounding the problem with confessions of guilt.

"There's nothing to undo," McCallum replied innocently. "I did enjoy your cooking," he added gently.

"I'm glad." She hesitated nervously. She might as well tell him how she'd blown up their friendship, while there was still time. "McCallum, there's just one little thing—"

"Later," he said, patting her absently on the shoulder. "I've got to talk to Jessica about a case."

"Okay." She was glad of the reprieve. Not that she didn't still have to confess her half-truths to Jessica.

He knocked briefly on Jessica's door and walked in. She looked up from her paperwork. Nothing of her inner torment showed on her unlined face, and she even smiled pleasantly at him.

"Come in, Deputy," she invited. "What can I do for you?"

He closed the door and sat down across from her. "You can tell me that I haven't ruined everything between us," he said bluntly.

She looked at him with studied curiosity. "We're still friends," she assured him. "I don't hold grudges."

His jaw clenched. "You know that wasn't what I meant."

She put down the file she'd been reading and crossed

her hands on it. "What can I do for you?" she asked pleasantly.

Her bland expression told him that he couldn't force his way back into her life. He couldn't make her want him, as she might have before things went wrong between them. She was going to draw back into her shell for protection, and it would take dynamite to get her out of it this time. He doubted if he could even get her to go out for a meal with him ever again, because she wouldn't want gossip about them to start up a second time. He'd never felt so helpless. Trust, once sacrificed, was hard to regain.

"What about Keith?" she asked. "I presume that's why you came?"

"Yes," he confirmed untruthfully. He sat back in the chair and told her about the talk he'd had with the school counselor. "But there's nothing we can do until I have some concrete reason to bring his father in for questioning. And Keith is holding out. The juvenile authorities can't dig anything out of him." He crossed his long legs. "On the other hand, we may have a break in the Baby Jennifer case."

She started. It wasn't pleasant to hear him say that. She'd become so involved with the tiny infant that a part of her hoped the mother would never be found. She was shocked at her own wild thoughts.

"Have you?" she asked numbly.

"A midwife knows of an old woman who helped a frightened young woman give birth. I'm trying to track her down. It may be our first real lead to the mother."

"And if you find her, then what?" she asked intently. "She deserted her own little baby. What sort of mother would do that? Surely to God the courts won't want to give the child back to her!"

He'd never seen Jessica so visibly upset. He knew she'd allowed herself to become attached to the infant, but he hadn't realized to what extent until now.

"I'm sure it won't come to that," he said slowly. "Jessica, you aren't having any ideas about taking the baby yourself?" he added abruptly.

She glared at him. "What if I do? What can a court-appointed guardian do that I can't? I can manage free time to devote to a child, I make a good salary—"

"You can't offer her a settled, secure home with two parents," he said curtly. "This isn't the big city. Here in Whitehorn the judge will give prior consideration to a married couple, not a single parent."

"That's unfair!"

"I'm not arguing with that," he said. "I'm just telling you what to expect. You know the judges around here as well as I do—probably better, because you have more dealings with them. Most of them have pretty fixed ideas about family life."

"The world is changing."

"Not here, it isn't," he reminded her. "Here we're in a time capsule and nothing very much changes."

She started to argue again and stopped on a held breath. He was right. She might not like it, but she had to accept it. A single woman wasn't going to get custody of an abandoned baby in Whitehorn, Montana, no matter how great a character she had.

She faced the loss of little Jennifer with quiet desperation. Fate was unfair, she was thinking. Her whole life seemed to be one tragedy after another. She put her head in her hands and sighed wearily.

"She'll be better off in a settled home," he mumbled. He hated seeing her suffer. "You know she will."

She sat up again after a minute, resignation in her demeanor. "Well, I won't stop seeing her until they place her," she said doggedly.

"No one's asked you to."

She glared at him. "She wouldn't get to you, would she, Deputy?" she asked with bitter anger. "You can walk away from anyone and never look back. No one touches you."

"You did," he said gruffly.

"Oh, I'm sure Bess got a lot further than I did," she said, her jealousy rising to the surface. "After all, she doesn't have any hang-ups and she thinks you're God's gift to women."

"You don't understand."

"I understand everything," she said bluntly. "You wanted to make sure that no one in town connected you with the object of so much scandal. Didn't you tell me once that you hated gossip because people talked about you so much when you were a boy? That's really why you started taking Bess out, isn't it? The fact that she was infatuated with you was just a bonus."

He scowled. "That wasn't why—"

She stood up, looking totally unapproachable. "Everyone knows now that Bess is your girlfriend. You're safe, McCallum," she added proudly. "No one is going to pair you off with me ever again. So let well enough alone, please."

He stood up, too, feeling frustrated and half-mad with restrained anger. "I'd been lied to one time too many," he said harshly. "Trust comes hard to me."

"It does to me, too," she replied in a restrained tone.

"You betrayed mine by turning your back on me the first chance you got. You believed Sam instead of me. You wouldn't even come to me for an explanation."

His face tautened to steel. He had no defense. There simply was none.

"You needn't look so torn, McCallum. It doesn't matter anyway. We both know it was a flash in the pan and nothing more. You can't trust women and I'm not casual enough for affairs. Neither of us would have considered marriage. What was left?"

His dark eyes swept over her with quiet appreciation of her slender, graceful body. "I might have shown you, if you'd given me half a chance."

She lifted her chin. "I told you, I'm not the type for casual affairs."

"It wouldn't have been casual, or an affair," he returned. "I'm not a loner by choice. I'm by myself because I never found a woman I liked. Wanted, sure. But there has to be more to a relationship than a few nights in bed. I felt...more than desire for you."

"But not enough," she said, almost choking on the words. "Not nearly enough to make up for what I...am."

His face contracted. "For God's sake, you're a woman! Being barren doesn't change anything!"

She turned away. The pain was almost physical. "Please go," she said in a choked tone. She sat back down behind her desk with the air of an exhausted runner. She looked older, totally drained. "Please, just go."

He rammed his hands into his pockets and glared at her. "You won't give an inch. How do you expect to go through life in that sewn-up mental state? I made a mistake, okay? I'm not perfect. I don't walk around with a halo above my head. Why can't you forget?"

Her eyes were vulnerable for just an instant. "Because it hurt so much to have you turn away from me," she confessed huskily. "I'm not going to let you hurt me again."

His firm lips parted. "Jessica, we learn from our mistakes. That's what life is all about."

"Mistakes are what *my* life is all about," she said, laughing harshly. She rubbed her hand over her forehead. "And there are still things you don't know. I was a fool, McCallum, and it was your fault because you wouldn't take no for an answer. Why did you have to interfere? I was happy alone, I was resigned to it...."

"Why did you keep trying to take care of me?" he shot back.

She had to admit she'd gone out of her way in that respect. She glanced up and then quickly back down to her desk. "Temporary insanity," she pleaded. "You had no one, and neither did I. I wanted to be your friend."

"Friends forgive each other."

She gnawed her lower lip. She couldn't tell him that it was far more than friendship she'd wanted from him. But she had secrets, still, that she could never share with him. She couldn't tell him the rest, even now. His fling with Bess had spared her the fatal weakness of giving in to him, of yielding to a hopeless affair. If it had gone that far, she corrected. Because it was highly doubtful that it would have.

"What are you keeping back?" he asked. "What other dark skeletons are hiding in your closet?"

She pushed her hair back from her wan face. "None that you need to know about, McCallum," she said, leaning back. She forced a smile. "Why don't you take Bess to lunch?"

"Bess and I are friends," he said. "That's all. And I've caused enough trouble around here. I understand that you're barely speaking to her. That's my fault, not hers."

She glared at him. "Bess is a professional who reports to me, and how I treat her is my business."

"I know that," he replied. "But she's feeling guilty enough. So am I."

Her eyebrows lifted. "About what?"

"Neither of us made your life any easier," he said. "I didn't know what happened to you. But even if you'd been all that Sam Jackson accused you of being, I had no right to subject you to even more gossip. Bess knows why I took her out. I could have caused her as much pain as I caused you. I have to live with that, too. Fortunately, she was no more serious than I was."

"That isn't what she told us," Jessica said through her teeth.

He stared at her with dawning horror. What stories had Bess told to produce such antagonism from Jessica, to make her look so outraged?

He scowled. "Jessica, nothing happened. We had a few meals together and I kissed her, once. That's all."

"It's gentlemanly of you to defend her," she said, stone faced. "But I'm not a child. You don't have to lie to protect her."

"I'm not lying!"

She pulled the file open and spread out the papers in it. "I'd like to know what you find out about that midwife," she said. "And about Keith, if the juvenile authorities get any results."

He stared at her for a long moment. "Tit for tat, Jessica?" he asked quietly. "I wouldn't believe you, so now you won't believe me?"

She met his eyes evenly. "That has nothing to do with it. I think you're being gallant, for Bess's sake," she replied. "It's kind of you, but unnecessary. Nothing you do with Bess or anyone else is my business."

He wouldn't have touched that line with a gloved hand. He stared at her for a long moment, searching for the right words. But he couldn't find any that would fit the situation.

He found plenty, however, when he closed Jessica's door and stood over Bess, who'd been waiting for him to finish.

"What did you tell her?" he asked bluntly.

She grimaced. "I embroidered it a little, to save face," she protested. "I thought we were going to be a hot item and it hurt my feelings that you didn't even want to kiss me. I'm sorry! I didn't know how hard Jessica was going to take it, or I'd never have made up those terrible lies about us."

He grimaced. "How terrible?"

She flushed. She couldn't, she just couldn't, admit that! "I'll tell her the truth," she promised. "I'll tell her all of it, honest I will. Please don't be mad."

"Mad." He shook his head, walking toward the door. "I must be mad," he said to himself, "to have painted myself into this sort of corner. Or maybe I just have a talent for creating my own selfdestruction."

He kept walking.

Chapter 10

The last words McCallum spoke to Bess might have been prophetic. He was thinking about Jessica when he shouldn't have been, and he walked into a convenience store outside town not noticing the ominous silence in the place and the frightened look on the young female clerk's face.

It seemed to happen in slow motion. A man in a faded denim jacket turned with a revolver in his hand. As McCallum reached for his own gun, the man fired. There was an impact, as if he'd been hit with a fist on his upper arm. It spun him backwards. A fraction of a second later, he heard the loud pop, like a firecracker going off. In that one long minute while he tried to react, the perpetrator forgot his quarry—Tammie Jane, the terrified young clerk—and ran out the door like a wild man.

"You've been shot! Oh, my goodness, what shall I do?" Tammie Jane burst out. She ran to McCallum, her own danger forgotten in her concern for him.

"It's not so bad," he said, gritting his teeth as he pulled out a handkerchief to stem the surging, rhythmic flow of blood. "Nothing broken, at least, but it looks as if the bullet may have…clipped an artery." He wound the handkerchief tighter and put pressure over the wound despite the pain it caused. "Are you all right?"

"Sure! He came in and asked for some cigarettes, and when I turned to get them, he pulled out that gun. Gosh, I was scared! He'd just told me to empty the cash register when you walked in."

"I walked in on it like a raw recruit," he added ruefully. "My God, I don't know where my mind was. I didn't even get off a shot."

"You're losing a lot of blood. I'd better call for an ambulance—"

"No need. I'll call the dispatcher on my radio." He made his way out to his patrol car, weaving a little. He was losing blood at a rapid rate and his head was spinning. He raised the dispatcher, gave his location and succinctly outlined the situation, adding a terse description of the suspect and asking for an all-points bulletin.

"Stay put. We'll send the ambulance," the dispatcher said, and signed off. The radio blared with sudden activity as she first called an ambulance and then broadcast a BOLO—a "be on the lookout for" bulletin—on the municipal frequency.

The clerk came out of the store with a hand towel and passed it to McCallum. His handkerchief was already soaked.

"I don't know how to make a tourniquet, but I'll try if you'll tell me how," Tammie Jane volunteered worriedly. Blood from his wound was pooling on the pavement, as McCallum was holding his arm outside the car.

He leaned back against the seat, his hand still pressing hard on the wound. "Thanks, but the ambulance will be here any minute. I can hear the siren."

It was fortunate that Whitehorn was a small town. Barely two minutes later, the ambulance sped up and two paramedics got out, assessed the situation and efficiently loaded a dazed McCallum onto a stretcher and into the ambulance.

He was still conscious when they got to the hospital, but weak from loss of blood. They had him stabilized and the blood flow stemmed before they pulled up at the emergency-room entrance.

He grinned sheepishly as they unloaded him and rolled him into the hospital. "Hell of a thing to happen to a law-enforcement officer. I got caught with my eyes closed, I guess."

"Thank your lucky stars he was a bad shot," one of them said with an answering smile. "That's only a flesh wound, but it hit an artery. You'd have bled to death if you'd taken your time about calling us."

"I'm beginning to believe it."

They wheeled him into a cubicle and called for the resident physician who was covering the emergency room.

Jessica had had a long morning, and her calendar was full of return calls to make. McCallum had shaken her pretty badly about Baby Jennifer. She hadn't been facing facts at all while she was spinning cozy daydreams about herself and the baby together in her cozy cottage.

Now she was looking into a cold, lonely future with nothing except old age at the end of it. From the bright, flaming promise of her good times with McCallum, all that was left were ashes.

She took off her glasses and rubbed her tired eyes. She'd just about given up wearing the contact lenses now that she wasn't seeing McCallum anymore. She didn't care how she looked, except in a business sense. She dressed for the job, but there was no reason to dress up for a man now. She couldn't remember ever in her life feeling so low, and there had been plenty of heartaches before this one. It seemed as if nothing would go right for her.

The telephone in the outer office rang noisily, but Jessica paid it very little attention. She was halfheartedly going through her calendar when Bess suddenly opened Jessica's office door and came in, pale and unsettled.

"Sterling McCallum's been shot," she blurted out, and was immediately sorry when she saw the impact the words had on Jessica, who stumbled to her feet, aghast.

"Shot?" she echoed helplessly. "McCallum? Is he all right?"

"That was Sandy. She's a friend of mine who works at the hospital. She just went on duty. She said he was in the recovery room when she got to the hospital. Apparently it happened a couple of hours ago. Goodness, wouldn't you think *someone* would have called us before now? Or that it would have been on the radio? Oh, what am I saying? We don't even listen to the local station."

"Does Sandy know how bad he is?" Jessica asked, shaken.

"She didn't take time to find out. She called me first." She didn't add that it was because Sandy thought, like most people did, that McCallum and Bess were a couple. "All she knew was that he'd been shot and had just come out of emergency surgery."

"Cancel my afternoon appointments," Jessica said as she gathered up her purse. "I'll finish this paperwork when I get back, but I don't know when that will be."

"Do you want me to drive you?" Bess offered.

Jessica was fumbling in her purse for the keys to her truck. "No. I can drive myself."

Bess got in front of her in time to prevent her from rushing out the door. "I lied about Sterling and me," she said bluntly, flushing. "It wasn't true. He didn't want anything to do with me and I was piqued, so I made up a lot of stuff. Don't blame him. He didn't even know I did it."

Jessica hesitated. She wanted to believe it, oh, so much! But did she dare?

"Honest," Bess said, and her eyes met Jessica's evenly, with no trace of subterfuge. "Nothing happened."

"Thanks," Jessica said, and forced a smile. Then she was out the door, running. If he died… But she wouldn't think about that. She had to remember that to stay calm, and that they hadn't said he was in critical condition. She had to believe that he would be all right.

It seemed to take forever to get to the hospital, and when she did, she couldn't find a parking space. She had to drive around, wasting precious time, until someone left the small parking area reserved for visitors. There had been a flu outbreak and the hospital was unusually crowded.

She ran, breathless, into the emergency room. She paused at the desk to ask the clerk where McCallum was.

"Deputy McCallum is in the recovery room three doors down," the clerk told her. "Wait, you can't go in there…!"

Jessica got past a nurse who tried to stop her and pushed into the room, stopping at the sight of a pale, drawn McCallum lying flat on his back, his chest bare and a thick bandage wrapped around his upper arm. There were tubes leading to both forearms, blood being pumped through one and some sort of clear liquid through the other.

The medical team looked up, surprised at Jessica's sudden entrance and white face.

"Are you a relative?" one of them—probably the doctor—asked.

"No," McCallum said drowsily.

"Yes," Jessica said, at the same time.

The man blinked.

"He hasn't got anyone else to look after him," Jessica said stubbornly, moving to McCallum's side. She put her hand over one of his on the table.

"I don't need looking after," he muttered, hating having Jessica see him in such a vulnerable position. He was groggy from the aftereffects of the anesthetic they'd given him while they removed the bullet and repaired the damage it had done.

"Well, actually, you do, for twenty-four hours at least," the doctor replied with a grin. "We're going to admit him overnight," he told Jessica. "He's lost a lot of blood and he's weak. We want to pump some antibiotics into him, too, to prevent infection in that wound. He's going to have a sore arm and some fever for a few days."

"And he can't work, right?" she prompted.

McCallum muttered something.

"Right," the doctor agreed.

"I'll stay with him tonight in case he needs anything," Jessica volunteered.

McCallum turned his head and looked up at her with narrow, drowsy dark eyes. "Sackcloth and ashes, is it?" he asked in a rough approximation of his usual forceful tones.

"I'm not doing penance," she countered. "I'm helping out a friend."

For the first time, his eyes focused enough to allow him to see her face clearly. She was shaken, and there was genuine fear in her eyes when she looked at him. Probably someone had mentioned the shooting without telling her that it was relatively minor. She looked as if she'd expected to find him dead or shot to pieces.

"I'm all right," he told her. "I've been shot before, and worse than this. It's nothing."

"Nothing!" she scoffed.

"A little bitty flesh wound," he agreed.

"Torn ligament, severed artery that we had to sew up, extensive loss of blood..." the doctor was saying.

"Compared to the last time I was shot, it's nothing," McCallum insisted drowsily. "God, what did you give me? I can't keep my eyes open."

"No need to," the doctor agreed, patting him gently on his good shoulder. "You rest now, Deputy. You'll sleep for a while and then you'll have the great-grandfather of a painful arm. But we can give you something to counteract that."

"Don't need any more...painkillers." He yawned and his eyes closed. "Go home, Jessica. I don't need you, either."

"Yes, you do," she said stubbornly. She looked around her, realizing how crazy she'd been to push her way in. She flushed. "Sorry about this," she said, backing toward the door. "I didn't know how badly he was hurt. I was afraid it was a lot worse than this."

"It's all right," the doctor said gently. He smiled. "We'll take him to his room and you can sit with him there, if you like. He'll be fine."

She nodded gratefully, clutching her purse like a life jacket. She slipped out of the room and went to sit down heavily in a chair in the waiting room. Her heart was still racing and she felt sick. Just that quickly, McCallum could have been dead. She'd forgotten how uncertain life was, how risky his job was. Now she was face-to-face with her own insecurities and she was handling them badly.

When they wheeled him to a semiprivate room, she went along. The other half of the room was temporarily empty, so she wouldn't have to contend with another patient and a roomful of visitors. That was a relief.

She noticed that there was a telephone, and when McCallum had been settled properly and the medical team had left, she dialed her office and told Candy his condition and that she wouldn't be back, before asking to be transferred to Bess.

"Can I bring you anything?" Bess offered.

"No, thank you. I'm fine." She didn't want Bess here. She wanted McCallum all to herself, with no intrusions.

It was selfish, but she'd had a bad fright. She wanted time to reassure herself that he was all right, that he wasn't going to die.

"Then call us if you need us," Bess said. "I talked to Sandy again and told her the truth, so she won't, well, say anything to you about me and Sterling McCallum. I'm glad he's going to be okay, Jessica."

"So am I," she agreed. She hung up and pulled a chair near the bed. She'd noticed a strange look from one of the nurses earlier. That had probably been Bess's friend.

McCallum was sleeping now, his expression clear of its usual scowl. He looked younger, vulnerable. She grimaced as she looked at his poor arm and thought how painful it must have been. She didn't even know if they'd caught the man who'd shot him. Presumably they were combing the area for him.

A few minutes later, Sheriff Hensley and one of the other deputies stopped by the room to see him. Hensley had gone by McCallum's house to feed Mack and get McCallum a change of clothing. The shirt he'd been wearing earlier was torn and covered in blood. McCallum was still sleeping off the anesthesia.

"Have you caught the man who did it?" Jessica asked.

Hensley shook his head irritably. "Not yet. But we will," he said gruffly. "I wouldn't have had this happen for the world. McCallum's a good man. On the salary the job pays, we don't get a lot of men of his caliber."

Jessica had never questioned a man of McCallum's education and background working in such a notoriously low-paying job. "I wonder why he does a lot of things," she mused, watching the still, quiet face of the unconscious man. "He's very secretive."

"So are you."

She grimaced. "Well, everyone's entitled to a skeleton or two," she reminded him.

He shrugged. "Plenty of us have them. Tell him I fed his dog, and brought those things by for him. I'll be back tomorrow. Are they going to try to keep him overnight?"

"Yes," she said definitely. "I'll stay with him. He won't leave unless he knocks me out."

"Harris here can stay with you if you think you'll need him," Hensley said with a rare smile.

Jessica glanced at the pleasant young deputy. "Thanks, but the doctor has this big hypodermic syringe...."

"Good point." Hensley took another look at McCallum, who was sleeping peacefully. "Tell him we're on the trail of his assailant. We're pretty sure who it is, from the description. We're watching the suspect's grandmother's house. It's the one place he's sure to run when he thinks it's safe."

Jessica nodded. "That's one advantage of small towns, isn't it?" she mused. "At least we generally know who the scoundrels are and where to find them."

"It makes police work a little easier. The police are helping us. McCallum's well liked."

"Yes." She looked up. "Thanks for getting Sam Jackson off my back."

He smiled. "Neighbors help each other. Maybe you'll do me a favor one day."

"You just ask."

"Well, a loaf of that homemade raisin bread wouldn't exactly insult me," he volunteered.

"When I get McCallum out of here, raisin bread will be my first priority," she promised him.

The way she worded it amused him, but it shocked her that she should feel proprietorial about McCallum, who'd given her no rights over him at all. She'd simply walked in and taken charge, and he wasn't going to like it. But she knew what he'd do if she left—go home this very night and back to work in the morning. He didn't believe in mollycoddling himself. No, she couldn't leave. She had to keep him here overnight and then make sure that he rested as the doctor had told him to. But how was she going to accomplish that?

She was still worrying about the problem when he woke up, after dark, and winced when he tried to stretch. They had a hospital gown on him, and the touch of the soft cotton fabric seemed to irritate him. He tried to pull it off.

Jessica got up and restrained his hand. They still had tubes in him, the steady drips going at a lazy speed.

"No, you mustn't," she said gently, bending over him.

His eyes opened. He stared at her and then looked around and frowned. "I'm still here?"

She nodded. "They want you to stay until tomorrow. You're very weak and they haven't finished the transfusion."

He let out a long, drowsy breath. "I feel terrible. What have they done to me?"

"They stitched you up, I think," she said. "Then they gave you something to make you rest."

He looked up at her again, puzzled. "What are you doing here? It's dark."

"I'm staying tonight, too," she said flatly. Her eyes dared him to argue with her.

"What for?"

"In case you need anything. Especially in case you try to leave," she added. "You're staying right there, McCallum. If you make one move to get up, I'll call the nurse and she'll call the doctor, and they'll fill you so full of painkillers that you'll sleep until Sunday."

He glared at her. "Threats," he said, "will not affect me."

"These aren't threats," she replied calmly. "I asked the doctor, and he said he'd be glad to knock you out anytime I asked him to if you tried to leave."

"Damn!" He lifted both hands and glared at the needles. "How did I get into this mess?"

"You let a man shoot you," she reminded him.

"I didn't let him," he said gruffly. "I walked in without looking while he was trying to rob the store. I didn't even see the gun until the bullet hit me. A police special, no less!" he added furiously. "It was a .38. No wonder it did so much damage!"

"I'm very glad he can't shoot straight," she said.

"Yes. So am I. He was scared—that's probably why he missed any vital areas. He fired wildly." His eyes closed and his face tightened as he moved. "I hope I get five minutes alone with him when they catch him. Have you heard from Hensley?"

"He and Deputy Harris came by to see you while you were asleep. They think they know who it was. They're staking out one of his relative's houses."

"Good."

"Didn't you know the place was being robbed? Wasn't that why you went in?" she persisted.

"I went in because I wanted a cup of coffee," he said

with a rueful smile. "I don't think I'll ever want another one after this. Or if I do, I'll make it at home."

"I could ask the nurse if you can have one now," she offered.

"No, thanks. I'll manage." He hesitated. "Do they have a male nurse on this floor?"

"Yes."

"Could you ask him to step in here, please?"

She didn't have to ask why. She went out to find the nurse and sent him in. She waited until she saw him come out again before she rejoined McCallum.

"Damned tubes and poles and machines," he was muttering. He looked exhausted, lying there among the paraphernalia around the bed. He turned his head and looked at her, seeing the lines in her face, the lack of makeup, the pallor. "Go home."

"I won't," she said firmly. She sat back down in the chair beside his bed. "I'll leave the hospital when you do. Not before."

His eyebrows lifted. "Have I asked you to be responsible for me?" he asked irritably.

"Somebody has to," she told him. "You don't have anybody else."

"Hensley would sit with me if I asked him, or any of the deputies."

"But you wouldn't ask them," she replied. "And the minute I walk out the door, you'll discharge yourself and go home."

"I need to go home. What about Mack?" He groaned. "He'll have to go without his supper."

"Sheriff Hensley has already fed him. He also brought you a change of clothing."

That seemed to relax him. "Nice of him," he commented. "Who'll feed Mack tomorrow morning and let him out?"

"I guess we'll have to ask the sheriff to go again. I'd offer, but that dog doesn't like women. I don't really want to go into your house when you aren't there. He growls at me."

"Your cat growls at me. It didn't stop me from going to your house."

"Meriwether couldn't do too much damage to you. But Mack is a big dog with very sharp teeth."

His eyes searched hers. "Afraid of him?"

"I guess maybe I'm afraid of being chewed up," she said evasively.

"Okay. Hand me the phone."

She did, and helped him push the right buttons. He phoned Hensley and thanked him, then asked him about feeding Mack in the morning. Hensley already knew McCallum kept a spare key in his desk and had used it once already. He readily agreed to take care of Mack.

"That's a load off my mind," McCallum said when he finished and lay back against the pillows. He flexed his shoulder and then frowned. "Do I smell something?"

As he said that, the door opened and a nurse came in bearing two trays. "Dinnertime," she said cheerfully, arranging them on the table. "I brought one for you, too, Miss Larson," she added. "You haven't even had coffee since you've been here."

"That's so nice of you!" Jessica said. "Thank you!"

"It's our pleasure. Make sure he eats," she added to Jessica on her way out. "He'll need all the protein he can get to help replenish that lost blood."

"I'll do that," Jessica promised.

She lifted the tops off the dishes on one tray while McCallum made terrible faces.

"I hate liver," he told her. "I'm not eating it."

She didn't answer him. She cut the meat into small, bite-size pieces and proceeded to present them at his lips. He glared at her, but after a minute of stubborn resistance, opened his mouth and let her put the morsels in, one at a time.

"Outrageous, treating a grown man like this," he muttered. But she noticed that he didn't refuse to eat, as he easily could have. In fact, he didn't lodge a single protest even when she followed the liver with vegetables and, finally, vanilla pudding.

It was intimate, doing this for him. She hadn't considered her actions at all, but now she realized that they could be misconstrued by a large number of people, starting with McCallum. She was acting like a lovesick idiot. What must he have thought when she came bursting into the recovery room where he was lying, forcing her way into his life like this?

She fed him the last of the pudding and, with a worried look, moved the tray to the other table.

"Now eat your own dinner before it gets cold," he insisted. "If you're determined to stay here all night, you need something to keep you going."

"I'm not really hungry...."

"Neither was I," he said with a cutting smile. "But *I* didn't have any choice. Now do you pick up that fork, or do I climb out of this bed and pick it up for you?"

His hand went to the sheet. With a resigned sigh, she uncovered her own plate and took it, and her fork, back to her chair. She didn't like liver any more than he did, but she ate it. At least it was filling.

He watched her until she cleared her plate and finished the last drop of her coffee. "Wasn't that good?" he taunted.

"I hate liver," she muttered.

"So do I, but that didn't save me." He grinned at her. "Turnabout is fair play."

She sighed, standing to replace her plate on the tray. She hadn't touched her pudding.

"Aren't you going to eat that?" he asked.

"I like chocolate," she muttered. "I hate vanilla."

"I don't." His eyes twinkled. "Want to feed it to me?"

Her blush was caused more by the silky soft tone of his voice than by the words. She couldn't help it.

"If you like," she said hesitantly.

"Come on, then."

She got the pudding and approached the bed. But when she started to open the lid, he caught her hand and tugged until she bent forward.

"Sterling!" she protested weakly.

"Humor me," he whispered, reaching up to cup her chin in his lean hand and pull her face down. "I'm a sick man. I need pampering."

"But—"

"I want to kiss you," he whispered at her lips. "You can't imagine how much. Just a little closer, Jessie. Just another inch…"

She sighed against his hard mouth as she moved that tiny distance and let her lips cover his. He made a soft sound and, despite the tubes attached to his arm, his hand snaked behind her head to increase the pressure of his mouth. She stiffened, but it was already too late to save herself. The warm insistence of the kiss worked its way through all her doubts, fears and reservations and touched her very soul. She sighed and gave in to the need to reassure herself that he was alive. Her own mouth opened without coyness and she felt the shock that ran through him before he groaned and deepened the kiss.

The sound of a tray rattling outside the room brought her head up. He looked somber and his eyes were narrow and hot.

"Coward," he taunted.

Her lips felt swollen. She pulled gently back from him and stood up, her knees threatening to give way. He had an effect on her body that no other man ever had. There were so many reasons why she shouldn't allow this feeling between them to grow. But other than disappointment, there was no other emotion left in her at the moment. That, and a raging pleasure that turned quickly to frustration.

Chapter 11

The nurse came in to remove the dishes, and some-how Jessica managed to look calm and pleasant. But inside, her whole being was churning with sensation. She looked at Sterling and her mouth tingled in memory.

She was wondering how she was going to manage the situation, but then the doctor came in on his rounds and ordered a sedative for the patient. It was administered at once, and McCallum glowered as the nurse finished checking his vital signs and the technicians came back to get some samples they needed for the lab. It was fifteen minutes before they left him alone with Jessica. And by then, the shot was beginning to take effect.

"Hell of a thing, the way they treat people here," he murmured as his eyelids began to droop. "I wanted to talk to you."

"You can talk tomorrow. Now go to sleep. You'll feel better in the morning."

"Think so?" he asked drowsily. "I'm not sure about that."

He shifted and a long sigh passed his lips. Only seconds later, he was dozing. Jessica settled in her chair with a new paperback she'd tucked into her purse after a brief stop at the bookstore on her way to lunch. She must have had some sort of premonition, she mused. And unlike McCallum, she didn't have to worry about her pet. Meriwether had plenty of water and cat food waiting for him, and a litter box when he needed it. He might be lonely, but he wouldn't need looking after. She opened the book.

But the book wasn't half as interesting as McCallum. She finally put it aside and sat looking at him, wishing that her life had been different, that she had something to offer such a man. He was a delight to her eyes, to her mind, her heart, her body. She couldn't have imagined anyone more perfect. He liked her, that was obvious, and he was attracted to her. But for his own sake, she had to stop things from progressing any further than liking. Her own weakness was going to be her worst enemy, especially while he was briefly vulnerable and needed her. She had to be sure that she didn't let his depleted state go to her head. Above all, she had to keep her longings under control.

Eventually, she tried to sleep. But the night was long and uncomfortable as she tried to curl up in the padded chair. In the morning, McCallum was awake before she was, and she opened her eyes to find him propped up in bed watching her.

"You don't snore," he commented with a gentle smile.

"Neither do you," she returned.

"Fortunate for us both, isn't it?"

She sat up, winced and stretched. Her hair had come down in the night and it fell around her shoulders in a thick cloud. She pushed it back from her face and re-adjusted her glasses.

"Why don't you wear your contact lenses?" he asked curiously. "And before you fly at me, I don't mean you look better with them or anything. I just wondered why you'd stopped putting them in."

She stood up. "It didn't seem worth the effort any-more," she said. "And they're not as comfortable as these." She touched the big frames with her forefinger. She smiled. "And they're a lot of trouble. Maybe I'm just lazy."

He smiled. "Not you, Jessie."

"How do you feel?"

"Sore." He moved his shoulder with a groan. "It's going to be a few days before I feel like much, I guess."

"Good! That means you won't try to go back to work!"

He glowered at her. "I didn't say that."

"But you meant it, didn't you?" she pressed with a wicked grin.

He laid his head back against the pillow. "I guess so." He studied her possessively. "Are you coming home with me?"

Her heart jumped up into her throat. "What?"

"How do you expect to keep me at home if you don't?" he asked persuasively. "Left on my own, I'm sure I'd go right back to the office."

There was a hint of cunning in his eyes, and she didn't trust the innocent expression on his face. He had something in mind, and she didn't want to explore any possibilities just now.

"You could promise not to," she offered.

"I could lie, too."

"I have a job," she protested.

"Today is Friday. Tomorrow is Saturday. What do you do that someone else can't do as well for one day?"

"Well, nothing, really," she said. She hesitated. "People might talk...."

"Who gives a damn?" he said flatly. "We've both weathered our share of gossip. To hell with it. Come home with me. I need you."

Those three words made her whole body tingle with delight. She stared at him with darkening eyes, with a faint flush on her cheekbones that betrayed how much the statement affected her.

"I need you," he repeated quietly.

"All right."

"Just like that?"

She smiled. "Just like that. But only for today," she added.

His eyebrows rose. "Why, Jessica, did you think I was inviting you to spend the night with me?"

She glowered back. "You stop that. I'm just going to take care of you."

He beamed. "What a delightful prospect."

Her jaws tightened. "You know what I mean, and it isn't that!"

"I know what I wish you meant," he teased softly.

"You're going to be a handful, aren't you?" she asked with resignation.

"I'll try not to cause you a lot of trouble." He studied her long and intently. "Besides, how difficult can it be?" He indicated his shoulder. "I'm not in any shape for what you're most concerned about. Long, intimate sessions on my sofa will have to wait until I'm properly fit again, Jessica," he added in a soft, wicked tone. "Sorry if that disappoints you."

She turned away to keep him from seeing the flush on her cheeks. "Well, if you're going to leave today, I'd better see if the doctor agrees that you can. I'll go and check at the nurses' station."

"You tell them that even if he says I can't, I'm going home," he informed her.

She didn't argue. It wouldn't really do any good.

By noon, they'd discharged him, and Jessica, after stopping by her house to change clothes and feed her cat, drove him to his house. It disturbed her a little to have her pickup truck sitting in his driveway, but there wasn't a lot she could do about it. He wasn't able to cook or clean, and there was no one else she could ask to do it—except possibly Bess, and that was out of the question.

She hesitated when he unlocked the door and Mack growled at the sight of her.

"Stop that," McCallum snapped at the dog.

Mack stopped at once, eagerly greeting his master.

McCallum petted him and motioned Jessica into the house before he dropped heavily into his favorite armchair.

"It's good to be home," he remarked.

"How about something to eat?" she asked. "You didn't stay long enough to have lunch."

"I wasn't hungry then. There's a pizza in the freezer and some bacon and eggs in the fridge."

"Any flour?"

He glared at her. "What the hell would I want with flour?"

She threw up her hands. It wasn't a question she should have asked a bachelor who liked frozen pizza.

"So much for hopes of quiche," she said half to herself as she put down her purse and walked toward the kitchen.

"Real men don't eat quiche," he called after her.

"You would if you had any flour," she muttered. "But I guess it's going to be bacon and eggs."

"We could order a pizza from the place downtown."

"I don't want pizza. And you need something healthy."

"I won't eat tofu and bean sprouts."

She was searching through the refrigerator and vegetable bins. There were three potatoes and a frozen pizza, four eggs of doubtful age, a slice of moldy bacon and a loaf of green bread.

"Don't you ever clean things out in here?" she called.

He shrugged, then winced as the movement hurt his shoulder. "When I get time," he told her.

She came back and reached for her purse. "Please don't try to go to work while I'm gone."

"Where, exactly, are you going?"

"To get some provisions," she said. "Some *edible* provisions. You couldn't feed a dedicated buzzard on what's in your kitchen."

He chuckled and reached for his wallet. He handed her a twenty-dollar bill. "All right. If you're determined, go spend that."

"I'll need to stop by my office, too."

"Whatever."

She hesitated in the doorway, indecision on her face. "If you'd rather I sent Bess over—"

"Bess was a pleasant companion," he replied. "She

was never anything more, regardless of what she might have told you."

"Okay." She went out and closed the door behind her.

She stopped by the office just long enough to delegate some chores and answer everyone's concerns about McCallum. Bess was interested, but not overly so, and she smiled reassuringly at Jessica before she told her to wish him well.

After that, Jessica went shopping. When she got back to McCallum's house, he was sprawled on the sofa in his sock feet with a can of beer in his hand, watching a movie.

"What did you buy?" he asked as she carried two plastic sacks into the kitchen.

"Everything you were out of." She handed him back two dollars and some change.

He glanced at the grocery bags. "What are you going to cook me?"

"Country-fried cubed steak, gravy, biscuits and mashed potatoes."

"Feel my pulse. I think I've just died and gone to heaven. Did I hear you right? I haven't had that since it was a special at the café last month."

"I hope it's something you like."

"'Like' doesn't begin to describe how I feel about it. Try 'overwhelmed with delight.' But to answer your question, yes, I like it."

"It's loaded with cholesterol and calories," she added, "but I can cut down on the grease."

"Not on my account." He chuckled. "I love unwholesome food."

She prepared the meal in between glimpses of the movie he was watching. It was a thriller, an old police drama set back in the thirties, and she enjoyed it as much as he did. Later, they ate in front of the television and watched a nature special about the rain forest.

"That's a good omen," he said when they'd finished and she was collecting the plates.

"What is?"

"We like the same television programs. Not to mention the same food."

"Most people like nature specials."

"One woman I dated only watched wrestling," he commented.

She stacked the plates and picked them up. "I don't want to hear about your other dates."

"Why not?" he asked calculatingly. "I thought you only wanted to be friends with me."

She stopped, searching for words. But she couldn't quite find the right ones, so she beat it back to the kitchen and busied herself washing dishes. Mack sat near her on the floor, watching her without hostility. It was the first time since she'd been in the house that he didn't growl at her.

She put away the dishcloth and cleaned up the kitchen. There was enough food left for McCallum to have for supper. She put it on a platter and covered it, so that he could heat it up later.

He'd turned off the television when she came back into the living room. He was lying full length on the sofa with his eyes closed, but he opened them when he heard her step. His dark eyes slid up and down her body, over the simple blue dress that clung to her slender body. The expression in them made her pulse race.

"I should…go home." Her voice faltered.

He didn't say a word. His hand went to his shirt and

slowly, sensually, unfastened it. He moved it aside, giving her a provocative view of his broad, hair-roughened chest.

"I have things to do," she continued. She couldn't quite drag her eyes away from those hard, bronzed muscles.

He held out his good arm, watching her in a silence that promised pleasures beyond description.

She knew the risks. She'd known them from the first time she saw him. Up until now, they'd weighed against her. But the realization of how close he'd come to death shifted the scales.

She went to him, letting him draw her down against him, so that she was stretched out beside him on the long sofa, pressed close against his hard, warm body.

"Relax," he said gently, easing her onto her back and grimacing as he moved to loom over her. "I'm not stupid enough to start something I can't finish."

"Are you sure?" she asked a little worriedly, because the minute her hips tilted into his, she felt the instant response of his body.

"Not really." He groaned and laughed softly in the same breath, shifting her away slightly. "But let's pretend that I am. I like you in this dress, Jessie. It fits in all the right places. But I don't like the way it fastens. Too damned many buttons and hooks in back.... Ah, that's better."

"McCallum!" she cried as the bodice began to slip. She made a grab for it, but his fingers intercepted the wild movement.

"What are you afraid of?" he murmured softly, smiling down at her. "It won't hurt."

She bit her lower lip. "I...can't let you look at me,"

she said, lowering her eyes to the hard throbbing of his pulse in his neck.

He frowned. "Now, or ever?" he asked with a patience he didn't feel.

"E-ever," she clarified. She pulled the bodice closer. "Let me up, please, I want to... McCallum!"

Even with a bullet wound, he was stronger and quicker than she was. The dress was suddenly around her waist, and he was looking at her body in the wispy nylon bra with its strategically placed lace. But it wasn't her breasts that had his attention.

She closed her eyes and shivered with pain. "I tried to stop you," she said harshly, biting back tears. "Now, will you let me go!"

"My God." The way he spoke was reverent. But there was no revulsion, either in the words or in his face. There was only pain, for what she must have suffered.

"Oh, please," she whispered, humiliated.

"There's no need to look like that," he said quietly. "Lie still. I'm going to take you out of this dress."

"No...!"

He caught her flailing hand and brought it to his mouth, kissing the palm gently. His dark eyes met her wild ones. "You need to be made love to," he said softly. "More than you realize. You're not hideous, Jessica. The scars aren't that bad."

She fought tears and lost. They fell, hot and profuse, pouring down her cheeks. Her hand relaxed its hold on her dress and she lay still, letting him smooth away it and her half-slip and panty hose until she lay there in only her briefs and bra.

He bent and she felt with wonder the touch of his mouth as it traced the thin white lines from her breasts down her belly to where they intersected just below her naval.

His big, lean hand held her hip while he caressed her with his mouth, his thumb edging under the lace of the briefs to touch her almost, but not quite, intimately. She caught her breath at the sensations he was teaching her and arched involuntarily toward the pleasure.

"You crazy woman," he breathed as he lifted his head and looked down into her dazed, hungry eyes. "Why didn't you tell me?"

"I thought… They're so ugly."

He only smiled. He bent and his mouth brushed lazily over hers, parting her lips, teasing, tasting. And while he held her in thrall, his hand went behind her to find the single catch. He freed it and lazily tugged the bra away from her firm, high breasts.

She didn't protest. His eyes on her gave her the purest delight she'd ever known. She gazed up at him with rapt wonder while he looked and looked until her nipples grew hard and began to ache.

Then, finally, he began to touch them, and she shivered with sensations she'd never known. Her lips parted as she tried to catch her breath.

He chuckled with appreciation and triumph. "All that time wasted," he murmured. "They're very sensitive, aren't they?" he added when she jerked at the faint brush of his fingertips. He took the hardness between his thumb and forefinger and pressed it gently, and she cried out. But it wasn't because he was hurting her. She was responsive to a shocking degree. That embarrassed her, because he was watching her like a hawk, and she tried to push his hand away.

"Shh," he whispered gently. "Don't fight it. This is

for you. But when you're a little more confident, I'm going to let you do the same thing to me and watch how it excites me. I'm just as susceptible as you are, just as hungry."

"You're...watching me," she got out.

"Oh, yes," he agreed quietly. "Can you imagine how it makes me feel, to see the pleasure my touch gives you?" His fingers contracted and she shivered. "My God, I couldn't get my head through a doorway right now, do you know that? You make me feel like ten times the man I am."

He bent and put his mouth where his fingers had been. She whimpered at first and pushed against him frantically.

He lifted his head and looked into her eyes, seeing the fear.

"Tell me," he said softly.

"He...bit me there," she managed hoarsely.

He scowled. His eyes went to her body and found the tiny scars. His expression hardened to steel as he touched them lightly.

"I won't bite you," he said deeply. "I promise you, it won't hurt. Can you trust me enough to let me put my mouth on you here?"

She searched his face. He wasn't a cruel man. She knew already that he was protective toward her. She let herself relax into the soft cushions of the sofa and her hands dropped to his shoulders, lingering there, tremulous.

"Good," he whispered. He bent again, slowly. This time it was his tongue she felt, soothing and warm, and then the whispery press of his lips moving on soft skin. The sensations were a little frightening, because they seemed to come out of nowhere and cause reactions not only in her breasts, but much lower.

His hand slid down her body and slowly trespassed under the elastic.

She should protest this, she should tell him to...stop!

He felt her nails bite into him, heard her moans grow, felt her body tauten almost to pain.

He lifted his head and stopped. Her face was gloriously flushed, her eyes shy and hungry and frustrated. She looked at him with wonder.

"Your body is capable of more pleasure than you know," he said gently. "I won't hurt you."

She arched back faintly, involuntarily asking for more, but he moved away. He wasn't touching her now. He was propped just over her, watching her face, her body.

"Why did you stop?" she whispered helplessly.

"Because it's like shooting fish in a barrel," he said simply. "You've just discovered passion for the first time in your life. I want to be sure that it's me, and not just new sensations, that are motivating you. The next step isn't so easy to pull back from, Jessie," he added solemnly. "And I don't know if I can make love completely with my shoulder in this fix."

She blinked, as if she hadn't actually realized how involved they were becoming.

His eyes dropped to her taut breasts and down her long, elegant legs before they moved back up to meet her shy gaze. He didn't smile even then. "I didn't really understand before," he said. "You were involved in the crash that killed Fred, weren't you? You were damaged internally in the wreck."

She nodded. "Fred was released because of a technicality six months after he went to prison. He blamed me for all his trouble, so he got drunk and laid in wait for me one night when I was working late. He chased me and ran me off the road. I was hurt. But he was killed." She shivered, remembering that nightmare ride. "They had to remove an ovary and one of my fallopian tubes. Even before the accident the doctors thought I'd be unlikely to get pregnant, and now... Well, it would be a long shot."

His face didn't change, his expression didn't waver. He didn't say a word.

She grimaced. "You need children, Sterling," she said in a raw whisper, her eyes mirroring the pain in the words. "A wife who loves you, and a home." Her gaze fell to his broad, bare chest and her hands itched to touch him.

"And you think that puts you out of the running?" he asked.

"Doesn't it?"

His fingers pressed down gently over her belly, and his hand was so big that it almost covered her stomach completely. "You're empty here," he said, holding her gaze. "But I'm empty here."

His hand moved to his chest, where his heart was, before it dropped back down beside her to support him. "I've never been loved," he said flatly. "I've been wanted, for various reasons. But my life has been conspicuously lacking in anyone who wanted to look after me."

"Bess did," Jessica recalled painfully.

He touched her mouth with his fingertips. "Bess is young and unsettled and looking for something that she hasn't found yet. I'm fond of her. But I never felt desire for her. It's hard to explain," he added with a humorless laugh, "but for me, desire and friendship don't usually go together."

She searched his face. "They didn't, with Bess?"

"That's right. Not with *Bess*."

He emphasized the name, looking at her with more than idle curiosity.

"With…anyone else?"

He nodded.

Obviously, she was going to have to drag it out of him, but she had to know. "With…me?" she asked, throwing caution to the winds.

"Yes," he said quietly. "With you."

She didn't know how to answer him. Her body felt hot all over at the look he was giving her. She'd never known passion until now, and it was overwhelming her. She wanted him, desired him, ached for him. She wanted to solve all the mysteries with him. The inhibitions she'd always felt before were conspicuously absent.

She felt her breasts tightening as she stared at the hair-matted expanse of his muscular chest.

"Are you surprised that you can feel desire, after all you've been through?" he asked gently.

"Yes."

"But then, strong emotions can overcome fear, can't they?" He bent, nuzzling his face against her bare breasts, savoring the softness of her skin against his. "Jessie, if my arm didn't throb like blazing hell, I'd have you right here," he breathed. "I ache all over from wanting you."

"So do I," she confessed. She slid her arms around his neck and pressed her body completely against his, shivering a little when she felt the extent of his arousal.

He felt her stiffen and his hands were gentle at her

back. "Lie still," he whispered. "It's all right. You're in no danger at all."

"I never dreamed that I could feel like this," she whispered into his throat, where her face was pressed. "That I could want like this." Her breasts moved against the thick hair that covered his chest and she moaned at the sensations she felt.

His lean hand slipped to the base of her spine and one long leg moved, so that he could draw her intimately close, letting her feel him in an embrace they'd never shared.

Her intake of breath was audible and she moaned harshly. So did he, pushing against her roughly for one long, exquisite minute until he came to his senses and rolled away from her. He got unsteadily to his feet with a rough groan.

"Good God, I'm losing it!" he growled. He made it to the window and stared out, gripping the sash. He fought to breathe, straining against the throbbing pain of his need for her.

She lay still for a minute, catching her own breath, before she sat up and quickly got back into her clothes. Her long hair fell all around her shoulders in tangles, but she couldn't find the pins he'd removed that had held it in place.

He turned finally and stared at her with his hands deep in his pockets. He was pale and his shoulder hurt.

"They're in my pocket," he told her, smiling gently at her flush. "Embarrassed, now that we've come to our senses?"

She lifted her eyes to his. "No," she said. "I don't really think I can be embarrassed with you. I—" she smiled gently "—I loved what you did to me."

Chapter 12

For a minute, he didn't seem to breathe at all. Then his eyes began to soften and a faint smile tugged at the corners of his mouth.

"In that case," he said, "we might do it again from time to time."

She smiled, too. "Yes."

He couldn't remember when he'd felt so warm and safe and happy. Just looking at Jessica produced those feelings. Touching her made him feel whole.

"I should go," she said reluctantly. "Meriwether will need his food and water changed, and I have other chores to do."

He thought about how the house was going to feel when she left, and it wasn't very pleasant. He'd been alone all his life and he was used to it. It had never bothered him before, but suddenly, it did. He frowned as he studied her, wondering at the depth of his feelings, at his need to be near her all the time. Once he would have fought that, but something had rearranged his priorities…perhaps getting shot.

"Okay," he said after a minute. "Let me feed Mack and we'll go."

Her heart flew up. "*We'll* go…. You're coming home with me?"

He nodded.

Her lips parted as she looked at him and realized that he didn't want to be separated from her any more than she wanted to be apart from him.

"Did you think it was one-sided?" he asked, moving toward her. "Didn't it occur to you that in order for something to be this explosive, it has to be shared?"

Her expression mirrored her sense of wonder. So did his. He pulled her against him, wincing a little when the movement tugged at his stitches, and bent his head. He kissed her with slow, aching hunger, feeling her instant response with delight.

"If I go home with you, people will really talk about us," he whispered against her mouth. "Aren't you worried?"

"No," she said with a smile. "Kiss me…."

He did, thoroughly, and she returned it with the same hunger. After a minute, he had to step back from her. His chest rose and fell heavily as he searched her eyes.

"Do you have a double bed?" he asked.

"Yes." She flushed and then laughed at her own embarrassment. That part of their relationship was something she'd have to adjust to, but she wasn't too worried about being able to accomplish it.

He touched her mouth with aching tenderness. "I was teasing," he chided. "I can't stay, as much as I want to. But I'll stay until bedtime."

"You could sleep on the sofa," she offered.

"I know that. I'll have one of the guys pick me up and drive me home. I don't want you alone on the roads late at night." He gently touched her cheek, which was flushed at his concern for her. "It's going to be rough. I don't want to be apart from you anymore, even at night. Especially at night," he said with a rough laugh.

"Yes, I know. I feel the same way." With her finger-tips, she traced his thick eyebrows and then his closed eyelids, his cheeks, his mouth. "It's…unexpected. What are we going to do now?"

"Get married as soon as we can," he said simply. He smiled reluctantly at her expression. "Don't faint on me, Jessie."

"But you don't want to get married," she protested. "You said you never wanted to."

"Honey, do you think we could live together in Whitehorn without raising eyebrows?" he asked gently. He smiled. "Besides that, when my shoulder heals, I'm going to have you. It's inevitable. We want each other too badly to abstain for much longer. Let's do this thing properly, by the book."

She traced a pattern in the thick tangle of hair on his broad chest. All her dreams hadn't prepared her for the reality of this. She could hardly believe it. "Marriage," she whispered with aching hunger. She lifted her eyes to his lean, hard face. "Someone of my own," she added involuntarily.

"There's that, too. Belonging to another person." He brought her hand to his lips. His teeth nipped the soft palm and she laughed. The glitter in his eyes grew. "You've never had a man, have you? Except for that one bad experience, you're untouched."

"Not anymore," she murmured demurely. "I've been all but ravished today."

He chuckled. "If you think that was ravishment, you've got a lot to learn."

She searched his eyes and sadness overlaid her joy. "It's a lovely dream. But it isn't realistic. It will matter to you one day, not being able to have a child of your own."

He touched her mouth and his face became as serious as hers. "Jessie, if you could have a child with another man, but not with me, would you marry him?"

She looked confused for a minute. "Well, no," she said. "Why?"

"Because I lo...because I care for you," she corrected.

He pulled her close. "You're not getting away with that," he said. "Tell me. Say the words."

She gnawed at her lower lip, hesitating.

"All the way, Jessie," he coaxed. "Say it."

"You won't," she said accusingly.

"I don't need to," he asserted. "If sex was all I wanted from you, I could have seduced you long ago. If it isn't just for the sake of sex, what other reason would I have for wanting to marry you?"

He hadn't said it, but she looked at him and realized with a start that he was telling her he loved her with everything except words. He couldn't bear to be parted from her, he wanted to marry her even though she couldn't give him a child....

"Of course I love you," she whispered softly. "I've loved you from the first time I saw you, but I never dared to hope—"

The last of the sentence was lost under the soft, slow crush of his mouth on her lips. He drew her close and kissed her with tenderness and passion, savoring her mouth until he had to lift his head to breathe. Yes, it was there, in her eyes, in her face; she loved him, all right. He began to smile and couldn't stop.

"You're surprisingly conventional," she mused, staring at him with loving eyes.

"Depressingly so, in some ways. I want the trimmings. I've never had much tradition in my life, but it starts now. We get engaged, then we get married, in church, and you wear a white gown and a veil for me to lift up when I kiss you."

She sighed. "It sounds lovely."

"It's probably Victorian." He chuckled. "Abstinence until the event and all. But a little tradition can be beautiful. All that separates people from animals, I read once, is a sense of nobility and honor. These days people want instant satisfaction. They don't believe in self-denial or self-sacrifice, or patience. I do. Those old virtues had worth."

"Indeed they did. I'm just as old-fashioned at heart as you are," she said gently. "I believe in forever, Sterling."

He drew her close and held her, hard. "So do I. We'll have differences, but if we compromise and work at it, we can have a long and happy life together." He kissed her forehead with breathless tenderness, grimacing, because holding her pulled the stitches and made his arm throb. But it was a sweet pain, for all that.

"My job…" she began.

He smoothed her hair away from her face. "I work. You work. We won't have to worry about someone staying home with a child."

Her face contorted.

"Don't," he said gently. He scowled with concern.

"Don't. We'll be happy together, I promise you we will. It's all right."

She had to fight down the tears. She pressed against him and closed her eyes. She would never stop regretting her condition. But perhaps Sterling was right. There would be compensations. First and foremost would be having this man love her as she loved him.

It took several weeks for McCallum's arm to heal completely, but they announced their wedding plans almost immediately. No one was really surprised, especially not Bess.

"When I saw how you looked at him that day, it didn't surprise me when I heard the news," Bess said with a grin. "I'm happy for both of you, honestly. I hope I get that lucky someday."

"Thanks," Jessica said warmly.

The office staff gave her an engagement party, complete with necessary household goods to start out—even though she'd accumulated a lot of her own. It was the thought that counted, and theirs were warm and pleasant.

An invitation to the wedding of Mary Jo and Dugin was forthcoming. It would take place in late June, about a month before Jessica and Sterling's. They decided to go together.

Meanwhile, another problem cropped up quite unexpectedly.

Keith Colson had finally done something that landed him in the purview of the county sheriff and not the juvenile authorities. He held up a small car dealership out in the country.

The pistol he used was not loaded, and he didn't

even run. They picked him up not far away, walking down a lonely highway with his sack of money. He even smiled at the sheriff's deputy—not McCallum— who arrested him.

He was brought into the sheriff's office for questioning, with new marks on his face.

This time McCallum wasn't willing to listen to evasions. He sat Keith down in the interrogation room and leaned forward intently.

"I've been too involved in my own life lately to see what was going on around me," he told Keith. "I meant to check on you again when the juvenile authorities released you, but I got shot and I've been pretty well slowed down. Now, however, I'm going to get to the root of this problem before you end up in federal prison." He looked the boy straight in the eye. "Your father is beating you." He watched Keith's eyes dilate. "And probably hitting your grandmother, too. You're going to tell me right now exactly what he's done to you."

Keith gaped at him. He couldn't find words. He shifted nervously in the chair. "Listen, it's not that—"

"Loyalty is stupid after a certain point," McCallum said shortly. "I was loyal to my mother, but when she broke my arm, I decided that my own survival was more important than the family's dark secret."

Keith's expression changed. "Your mother broke your arm?"

McCallum nodded curtly. "She was an alcoholic. She couldn't admit that she had a problem and she couldn't stop. It just got worse, until finally I realized that if she really cared about me, she'd have done something to help herself. She wouldn't, so I had to. I had her arrested. It was painful and there was a lot of gossip. Afterwards, I had no place to go, so I got shuffled around the county, to whichever farm needed an extra hand in exchange for bed and board. She died of a heart attack in jail when I was in my early teens. I had a hell of a life. But even then it was better than having to fend her off when she came at me with bottles or knives or whatever weapon she could lay her hand on."

Keith seemed to grow taller. He let out a long sigh and rubbed the arms of the old wooden chair. "You know all about it then."

"Living with an alcoholic, you mean? Yes, I know all about it. So you won't fool me anymore. You might as well come clean. Protecting your father isn't worth getting a criminal record that will follow you all your life. You can't run away from the problem by getting thrown in jail, son. In fact, you'll find people worse than your father there."

Keith leaned forward and dangled his hands between his knees. "He says it's because he lost his job and nobody else will hire him, at his age. But I don't believe it anymore. He hits my grandma, you see. Mostly he hits her, and I can't stand that, so I try to stop him. But he hits me when I interfere. Last time I landed a couple of shots, but he's bigger than I am. Whenever he sobers up, he says he'll quit. He always says he'll quit, that it will get better." He shook his head and smiled with a cynicism beyond his years. "Only it doesn't. And I'm scared he'll really hurt Grandma one day. But if I left, she could, too. She only stays to try and make some sort of home for me, and cook and clean for us. She can't talk to him. Neither can I. He just doesn't hear us."

"He'll hear me," McCallum said, rising.

"What will you do?" Keith asked miserably.

"I'll pick him up for assault and battery, and you'll sign a warrant," he told the boy. "He may go to jail, but they'll help him and he'll dry out. Meanwhile, we'll place you in a foster home. Your grandmother is too old to look out for you, and she's got a sister in Montana who'd enjoy her company."

"Miss Larson told you, I guess," he mused, smiling sheepishly.

"Yes. Jessica and I are getting married."

"I heard. She's a nice lady."

"I think so."

"You won't hurt my dad?"

"Of course not."

The boy got to his feet. "There's this robbery charge...."

"I'll talk to Bill Murray," McCallum said. "When he knows the circumstances, he won't press charges. The money was all recovered and he knows the gun wasn't loaded. He's a kind man, and not vindictive."

"I'll write him a note and tell him how sorry I am. I didn't want to do it, but I couldn't turn Dad in," he added, pleading for understanding.

McCallum clapped him on the back. "Son, life is full of things we can't do that we have to do. You'll learn that the hard part is living with them afterward. Come on. Let's go see the magistrate."

A warrant was sworn out and signed, and McCallum went to serve it. He felt sorry for Terrance Colson, but sorrier for the boy and his grandmother, who were practically being held hostage by the man.

He found Terrance sitting on his front porch, and obviously not expecting company, since he had a bottle of whiskey in one hand.

"What the hell do you want?" he demanded belligerently. "If it's that damned boy again, you can lock him up and throw away the key. I've had it with him!"

"He's had it with you, too, Terrance," McCallum replied, coming up onto the porch. "This is a warrant for your arrest, for assault and battery. Keith signed it."

"A...what?"

He stumbled to his feet, only to have McCallum grab him and whirl him around to face the wall, pinning him there while he cuffed him efficiently.

"You can't do this to me," Terrance yelled, adding a few choice profanities to emphasize his anger.

The door opened timidly and little Mrs. Colson peered out. Her eyes were red and there were bad bruises on one cheek and around her mouth.

"Are you...gonna take him off?" she asked McCallum.

He had to fight for control at the sight of the bruises on that small, withered face. "Yes, ma'am," he said quietly. "He won't be home for a while. The very least that will happen to him is that he'll be sent off to dry out."

She slumped against the door facing. "Oh, thank God," she breathed, her voice choked. Tears streamed down her face. "Oh, thank God. I've always been too weak and afraid to fight back, and Terrance takes after his daddy—"

Terrance glared at her. "You shut your mouth...!"

McCallum jerked him forward. "Let's go," he said tersely. "Mrs. Colson, Jessica will be out this afternoon to talk to you when I tell her what's happened. I have an idea about where we can place Keith, but we'll talk about that later. Are you all right? Do you need me to take you to the doctor?"

"No, thank you, sir," she replied. "If you'll just carry him off, that's all I need. That's all I need, yes, sir."

Terrance yelled wild, drunken threats at her, which made McCallum even angrier. But he was a trained law-enforcement officer, and didn't allow his fury to show. He was polite to Terrance, easing him into the patrol car with a minimum of fuss. He called goodbye to Mrs. Colson and took Terrance off to jail.

Later, Jessica went with Sterling and Keith to talk to Mrs. Colson.

"This is short notice, but I called Maris Wyler before I came out here. She needs a good hand out at her ranch, and when I explained the circumstances, she said she'd be happy to have Keith if he wanted to come."

"Do I ever!" Keith interjected. "Imagine, Gram, a real ranch! I'll learn cowboying!"

"If that's what you want, son," Mrs. Colson said gently. "Heaven knows, it's about time you had some pleasure in life. I know how you love animals. I reckon you'll fit right in on a ranch. It's very nice of Maris to let you come."

"She's a good woman. She'll take care of Keith, and he'll be somewhere he's really needed," McCallum told the old woman. "He and I have had a long talk about it. The judge has offered to let him plead to a lesser charge in exchange for a probationary sentence in Maris's custody. He'll have a chance to change his whole life and get back on the right track. She's even going to arrange for the homebound teacher to come out and give him his lessons so he won't have to go to school and face the inevitable taunting of the other students."

Mrs. Colson just nodded. "That would be best, Keith," she told her grandson. "I tried to help you as much as I could, but I couldn't fight your father when he was drinking."

"It's all right, Gram," Keith said gently. "You did all you could. I wish you could stay."

"I do, too, but this is your father's house and I could never stay here again."

"Yeah, neither could I," Keith replied. "It wouldn't ever be the same again, even if he does dry out. He talked about moving, and maybe he will. But I won't go with him. The way he's gotten, I'm not sure he wants to change. I'm not sure he can."

"The state will give him the opportunity to try," McCallum told them. "But the rest is up to him. If you want to see him, I can arrange it."

Keith actually shivered. "No, thanks," he said with a laugh. "When can I go and see this lady who says she'll take me in?"

"Right now, I guess," McCallum said with a grin. "We'll take Jessica with us, in case we need backup."

Keith frowned. "This sounds serious."

"Maris is a character," he replied. "But she's fair and she has a kind heart. You'll do fine. Just don't get on the wrong side of her."

"What he means," Jessica said, with a pointed glance at McCallum, "is that Maris is a strong and capable woman who can run a ranch all by herself."

McCallum started to open his mouth.

"You can shut up," Jessica interrupted him deftly. "And you'd better not swagger in front of Maris, or she'll cut you off at the ankles. She isn't the forgiving, long-suffering angel of mercy that I am."

"And not half as modest." McCallum grinned.

Jessica made a face at him, but love gleamed out of her soft brown eyes—and his, too. They had a hard time separating work from their private lives, but they

managed it. They lived in each others' pockets, except
at night. The whole town looked at them with kind indulgence, because they were so obviously in love that
it touched people's hearts.

Even old Mrs. Colson smiled at the way they played.
It took her back fifty years to her own girlhood and her
late husband.

"Well, we'd better be on our way. I'll drive you to
the bus station when you're packed and ready to leave,"
McCallum told her. "And if there's anything we can do,
please let us know."

"All I need is to leave here," she replied, touching
her swollen cheek gingerly. "Thank you for trying to
help me, son," she told Keith. "You were the only reason I stayed at all. I was scared of what he'd do to you
if I left."

"I kept trying to find ways to get out," Keith confessed, "so that you could leave. But they kept sending
me home again."

"Well, nobody's perfect, not even the criminal-justice
system," McCallum said, tongue-in-cheek.

They left Mrs. Colson with an ice bag on her cheek
and drove to the No Bull Ranch. Maris Wyler came
out to meet them.

She was tall and lean, very tan from working out-
doors, her long golden hair pulled back into a ponytail.
She wore jeans and boots and a faded long-sleeved shirt,
but she looked oddly elegant even in that rig.

"You're Keith. I'm Maris," she said forthrightly, introducing herself to the boy with a smile and a firm
handshake. "Ever work with cattle?"

"No, ma'am," Keith shook his head.

"Well, you'll learn quickly. I can sure use a hand out here. I hope you like the work."

"I think I will," he said.

"That's good, 'cause there's plenty of it." Maris replied with a grin.

"He'll be fine here," Maris assured Jessica.

"I knew that already," Jessica replied. "Thanks, Maris. I hope someone does something as kind for you one day."

"No problem. Come on, Keith, grab your gear and let's get you settled. So long, McCallum, Jessica. Feel free to come out and see him whenever you like. Just call first and make sure we're home."

"I will," Jessica replied.

She watched the two walk off toward the neat, new bunkhouse. The ranch, originally called the Circle W, had been in Maris's husband's family for years. Ray hadn't been the sort of man a woman like Maris deserved. He was a heavy drinker like Keith's father, as well as a gambler and womanizer. Nobody had been surprised when he'd recently come to a bad end—running his pickup into a cement bunker on the highway in a drunken state one night. Maris had been doing all the work on the ranch for years while her lazy husband spent money on foolish schemes and chased the rodeo. It was poetic justice that she ended up with the ranch.

"Hensley's always been a little sweet on her, you know," McCallum confided to Jessica as he drove them back to her place. "It was hard for him to tell her about Ray's death."

"Really? My goodness, she's nothing like his ex-wife."

"Men don't always fall for the same type of woman," he teased. "He called her for me when I approached him about someplace for Keith to go, besides into foster care."

"I'm glad Maris was willing," she said quietly. "Keith's not a bad boy, but he could have ended up in prison so easily, trying to get away from his father."

"It's a hell of a world for kids sometimes," he said.

She straightened the long denim skirt she was wearing with a plaid shirt and boots. "Yes."

He reached over and clasped her hand tightly in his. "I've been thinking."

"Have you? Did it hurt?" she teased.

He chuckled. "Not nice."

"Sorry. I'll behave. What were you thinking?"

His grip eased and he slipped his fingers in between hers. "That Baby Jennifer needs a home and we need a baby."

Chapter 13

Jessica had thought about that a lot—that Baby Jennifer needed someone to love her and take care of her. McCallum had been firm about the improbability of a court awarding the baby's care to a single woman. But that situation had changed. She and McCallum were engaged, soon to be married. There was every reason in the world to believe that, under the circumstances, a judge might be willing to let them have custody.

She caught her breath audibly. Bubbles of joy burst inside her. "Oh, Sterling, do you think…!"

His hand grasped hers. "I don't know, but it's worth a try. She's a pretty, sweet baby. And I agree with you—I think our lives would be enriched by having a child to love and raise. There's more to being a mother and father than just biology. It takes love and sacrifice and day-to-day living to manage that." He glanced at her gently. "You aren't the sort of woman who will ever be happy without a baby."

She smiled sadly. "I would have loved to have yours."

"So would I," he replied, his tone as tender as his eyes, which briefly searched hers. "But this is the next best thing. What do you think? Do you want to petition the court for permission to adopt her?"

"Yes!"

He chuckled. "That didn't take much thought."

"Oh, yes, it did. I've thought of nothing else since she was found."

"The judge may say no," he cautioned.

"He may say yes."

He just shook his head. That unshakable optimism touched him, especially in view of all the tragedy Jessica had had in her life. She was amazing. A miracle. He loved her more every day.

"All right, then," he replied. "We'll get a lawyer and fill out the papers."

"Today," she added.

He smiled. "Today."

Their wedding took place just a few weeks later, in July. They were married in the Whitehorn Methodist Church, with a small group of friends as witnesses. Jessica wore a simple white wedding dress. It had a lace bodice and a veil, and it was street length. After their vows, Sterling lifted the veil to kiss her. The love they shared was the end of the rainbow for her. When his lips touched hers, she laid her hand against his hard, lean cheek and felt tears sliding down her face. Tears of joy, of utter happiness.

Their reception was simplicity itself—the women

at the office had baked cookies and a friend had made them a wedding cake. There was coffee and punch at the local community hall, and plenty of people showed up to wish them well.

Finally, the socializing was over. They drove to Jessica's house, where they would have complete privacy, to spend their wedding night. Later, they planned to live at McCallum's more modern place.

"Your knees are shaking," he teased when they were inside, with the door locked. It had just become dark, and the house was quiet—even with Meriwether's vocal welcome—and cozy in its nest of forestland.

"I know," she confessed with a shy smile. "I have a few scars left, I guess, and even now it's all unfamiliar territory. You've been…very patient," she added, recalling his restraint while they were dating. Things had been very circumspect between them, considering the explosive passion they kindled in each other.

"I think we're going to find that this is very addictive," he explained as he drew her gently to him. "And I wanted us to be married before we did a lot of heavy experimenting. We've both suffered enough gossip for one lifetime."

"Indeed we have," she agreed. She reached up to loop her arms around his neck. Her eyes searched his. "And now it's all signed and sealed—all legal." She smiled a little nervously. "I can hardly wait!"

He chuckled softly as he bent is head. "I hope I can manage to live up to all those expectations. What if I can't?"

"Oh, I'll make allowances," she promised as his mouth settled on hers.

The teasing had made her fears recede. She relaxed

as he drew her intimately close. When his tongue gently penetrated the line of her lips, she stiffened slightly, but he lifted his head and softly stroked her mouth, studying her in the intense silence.

"It's strange right now, isn't it, because we haven't done much of this sort of kissing. But you'll get used to it," he said in a tender tone. "Try not to think about anything except the way it feels."

He bent again, brushing his lips lazily against hers for a long time, until the pressure wasn't enough. When he heard her breathing change and felt her mouth start to follow his when he lifted it, he knew she was more than ready for something deeper.

It was like the first time they'd been intimate. She clung to him, loving his strength and the exquisite penetration of his tongue in her mouth. It made her think of what lay ahead, and her body reacted with pleasure and eagerness.

He coaxed her hands to his shirt while he worked on the buttons that held her lacy bodice together. Catches were undone. Fabric was shifted. Before she registered the fact mentally, his hair-roughened chest was rubbing gently across her bare breasts and she was encouraging him shamelessly.

He picked her up, still kissing her, and barely made it to the sofa before he fell onto it with her. The passion was already red-hot. She gave him back kiss for kiss, touch for touch, in a silence that magnified the harsh quickness of their breathing.

When he sat up, she moaned, but it didn't take long to get the rest of the irritating obstacles out of the way. When he came back to her, there was nothing to separate them.

Her body was so attuned to his, so hungry for him, that she took him at once, without pain or difficulty, and was shocked enough to cry out.

His body stilled immediately. His ragged breathing was audible as he lifted his head and looked into her eyes, stark need vying with concern.

"It didn't hurt," she assured him in a choked voice.

"Of course...it didn't hurt," he gasped, pushing down again. "You want me so badly that pain wouldn't register now... God!"

She felt the exquisite stab of pleasure just as he cried out, and her mouth flattened against his shoulder as he began to move feverishly against her taut body.

"I love you," he groaned as the rhythm grew reckless and rough. "Jessie, I love you...!"

Her mouth, opened in a soundless scream as she felt the most incredible sensation she'd ever experienced in her life. It was like a throbbing wave of searing heat that suddenly became unbearable, pleasure beyond pleasure. Her body shuddered convulsively and she arched, gasping. He stilled just a minute later, and his hoarse cry whispered endlessly against her ear.

He collapsed then, and she felt the full weight of him with satisfied indulgence. She was damp with sweat. So was he. She stroked his dark hair, and it was damp, too. Wonder wrapped her up like a blanket and she began to laugh softly.

He managed to lift his head, frowning as he met her dancing eyes.

"You passed," she whispered impishly.

He began to laugh, too, at the absurdity of the remark. "Lucky me."

"Oh, no," she murmured, lifting to him slightly but deliberately. "Lucky *me!*"

He groaned. "I can't yet!"

"I have plenty of time," she assured him, and kissed him softly on the chin. "I can wait. Don't let me rush you."

"Remind me to have a long talk with you about men."

She locked her arms around his neck with a deep sigh. "Later," she said. "Right now I just want to lie here and look at my husband. He's a dish."

"So is my wife." He nuzzled her nose with his, smiling tenderly. "Jessie, I hope we have a hundred more years together."

"I love you," she told him reverently. Her eyes closed and she began to drift to sleep. She wondered how anything so delicious could be so exhausting.

The next morning, she awoke to the smell of bacon. She was in her bedroom, in her gown, with the covers pulled up. The pillow next to hers was dented in and the sheet had been disturbed. She smiled. He must have put her to bed. Now it smelled as if he was busy with breakfast.

She put on her jeans and T-shirt and went downstairs in her stocking feet to find him slaving over a hot stove.

"I haven't burned it," he said before she could ask. "And I have scrambled eggs and toast warming in the oven. Coffee's in the pot. Help yourself."

"You're going to be a very handy husband," she said enthusiastically. She moved closer to him, frowning. "But can you do laundry?"

He looked affronted. "Lady, I can iron. Haven't you noticed my uniform shirts?"

"Well, yes, I thought the dry cleaners—"

"Dry cleaners, hell," he scoffed. "As if I'd trust my uniforms to amateurs!"

She laughed and hugged him warmly. "Mr. McCallum, you're just unbelievable."

"So are you." He hugged her back. "Now get out of the way, will you? Burned bacon would be a terrible blot on my perfect record as a new husband."

"You fed Meriwether!" she gasped, glancing at her cat, who was busy with his own breakfast.

"He stopped hissing at me the second I picked up the can opener," Sterling said smugly. "Now he's putty in my hands. He even likes Mack!"

"Wonderful! It isn't enough that you've got me trained," she complained to the orange cat lying on the floor beside the big dog. Mack was already his friend. "Now you're starting on other people!"

"Wait until Jenny is old enough to use the can opener," he said. "Then he'll start on her!"

Jessica looked at him with her heart in her eyes. She wanted the baby so much.

"What if the judge won't let us have her?" she asked with faint sadness.

He took up the bacon and turned off the burner, placing the platter on the table.

"The judge *will* let us have her," he corrected. He tilted up her chin. "You have to start realizing that good times follow bad. You've paid your dues, haven't you noticed? You've had one tragedy after another. But life has a way of balancing the books, honey. You're about due for a refund. And it's just beginning. Wait and see."

"How in the world did a cynic like you learn to look

for a silver lining in storm clouds?" she asked with mock surprise.

He drew her close. "I started being pestered by this overly optimistic little social worker who got me by the heart and refused to let me go. She taught me to look for miracles. Now I can't seem to stop."

"I hope you find them all the time now," she said. "And I hope we get Jennifer, too. That one little miracle would do me for the rest of my life. With Jennifer and you, I'd have the very world."

"We'll see how it goes. But you have to have faith," he reminded her.

"I have plenty of that," she agreed, looking at him with quiet, hungry eyes. "I've lived on it since the first time I looked at you. It must have worked. Here you are."

"Here I stay, too," he replied, bending his head to kiss her.

Chapter 14

The petition was drawn up by their attorney. It was filed in the county clerk's office. A hearing was scheduled and placed on the docket. Then there was nothing else to do except wait.

Jessica went to work as usual, but she was a different person now that she was married. Her delight in her new husband spilled over into every aspect of her work. She felt whole, for the first time.

They both went out to the No Bull Ranch to see Maris Wyler and Keith Colson. The young man was settled in very nicely now, and was working hard. The homebound teacher who had been working with him since the summer recess was proud of the way he'd pulled up his grades. He was learning the trade of being a cowboy, too, and he'd gone crazy on the subject of wildlife conservation. He wanted to be a forest ranger, and Maris encouraged him. He was already talking about college.

"I couldn't be more delighted," Jessica told McCallum when they were driving back to town. "He's so different, isn't he? He isn't surly or uncooperative or scowling all the time. I hardly knew him."

"Unhappy people don't make good impressions. If you only knew how many children go to prison for lack of love and attention and even discipline.... Some people have no business raising kids."

"I think you and I would be good at it," she said.

He caught the note of sadness in her voice. "Cut that out," he told her. "You're the last person on earth I'd ever suspect of being a closet pessimist."

"I'm trying not to be discouraged. It's just that I want to adopt Jennifer so much," she said. "I'm afraid to want anything that badly."

"You wanted me that badly," he reminded her, "and look what happened."

She looked at him with her heart in her eyes and grinned. "Well, yes. You were unexpected."

"So were you. I'd resigned myself to living alone."

"I suppose we were both blessed."

"Yes. And the blessings are still coming. Wait and see."

She leaned back against the seat with a sigh, complacent but still unconvinced.

They went to court that fall. Kate Randall was the presiding judge. Jessica knew and liked her but couldn't control her nerves. Witness after witness gave positive character readings about both Jessica and McCallum. The juvenile authorities mentioned their fine record with helping young offenders, most recently Keith Colson. And through it all Jessica sat gripping McCallum's hand under the table and chewing the skin off her lower lip with fear and apprehension.

The judge was watching her surreptitiously. When the witnesses had all been called and the recommendations—good ones—given by the juvenile authorities, she spoke directly to Jessica.

"You're very nervous, Mrs. McCallum," Kate said with teasing kindness and a judicial formality. "Do I look like an ogre to you?"

She gasped. "Oh, no, your honor!" she cried, reddening.

"Well, judging by the painful look on your face, you must think I am one. Your joy in that child, and your own background, would make it difficult for even a hanging judge to deny you. And I'm hardly that." She smiled at Jessica. "The petition to adopt the abandoned Baby Jennifer is hereby approved without reservation. Case dismissed." She banged the gavel and stood up.

Jessica burst into tears, and it took McCallum a long time to calm and comfort her.

"She said yes," he kept repeating, laughing with considerable joy of his own. "Stop crying! She may change her mind!"

"No, she won't," the judge assured them, standing patiently by their table.

Jessica wiped her eyes, got up and hugged the judge, too.

"There, there," she comforted. "I've seen a lot of kids go through this court, but I've seen few who ended up with better parents. In the end it doesn't matter that your child is adopted. You'll raise her and be Jennifer's parents. That's the real test of love, I think. It's the bringing up that matters."

She agreed wholeheartedly. "You can't imagine how I felt, how afraid I was," she blurted out.

Kate patted her shoulder. "Yes, I can. I've had a steady stream of people come through my office this past week, all pleading on your behalf. You might be shocked at who some of them were. Your own boss," she said to McCallum, shaking her head. "Who'd have thought it."

"Hensley?" McCallum asked in surprise.

"The very same. And even old Jeremiah Kincaid," she added with a chuckle. "I thought my eyes would fly right out of my head on that one." Kate checked her watch. "I've got another case coming up. You'd better go and see about your baby, Jessica." She dropped the formal address since the court had adjourned. "I expect you new parents will have plenty of things to do now."

"Oh, yes!" she exclaimed. "We'll need to buy formula and diapers and toys and a playpen—"

"We already have the crib," McCallum said smugly, laughing at Jessica's startled reaction. "Well, I was confident, even if you weren't. I ordered it from the furniture store."

"I love you!" She hugged him.

He held her close, shaking hands with the judge.

From the courthouse they went around town, making a number of purchases, and Jessica was in a frenzy of joy as they gathered up all the things they'd need to start life with a new baby.

But the most exciting thing was collecting Baby Jennifer from a delighted Mabel Darren, the woman who'd been keeping her, and taking her home.

Even Meriwether was a perfect gentleman, sniffing the infant, but keeping a respectful distance. Jessica and McCallum sat on the sofa with their precious treasure, and didn't turn on the television at all that night.

Instead they watched the baby. She cooed and stared at them with her big blue eyes and never cried once.

Later, as Jessica and McCallum lay together in bed—with the baby's bed right next to theirs instead of in another room—they both lay watching Jennifer sleep in the soft glow of the night-light.

"I never realized just how it would feel to be a parent," McCallum said quietly. "She's ours. She's all ours."

She inched closer to him. "Sterling, what if her mother ever comes back?"

His arms contracted around her. "If her mother had wanted and been able to keep her, we wouldn't have her," he said. "You have to put that thought out of your mind. Sometimes there are things we never find out about in life—and then there are mysteries that are waiting to be solved just around the corner. We may solve it, we may not. But we've legally adopted Jennifer. She belongs to us, and we to her. That's all there is to it."

Jessica let out her breath in a long sigh. After a minute she nodded. "Okay. Then that's how it will be."

He turned her to face him and kissed her tenderly. "Happy?" he whispered.

"So happy that I could die of it," she whispered back. She pushed her way into his arms and was held tight and close. As her eyes closed, she thought ahead to first steps and birthday parties and school. She'd thought she'd never know those things, but life had been kind. She remembered what McCallum had said to her—that bad times were like dues paid for all the good times that followed. And perhaps they were. God knew, her good times had only just begun!

* * * * *

To Shakuntalaben and Vasantbhai Shroff,
whose love made sure I never had in-laws,
but instead, blessed me with a second set of parents.

Acknowledgments

This is my first Harlequin Special Edition book, but actually the fourth book that I have written. And like the other three, it's never a solitary effort.

First, I'd like to thank editor Susan Litman for reaching out and offering me this incredible opportunity. Anytime someone comes to you and says they enjoy your writing enough to ask you to do more is fabulous. As always, my incredible agent, Rachel Brooks, has been encouraging and supportive and protective and wonderful, and I truly appreciate her for all of that and more!

Ishara Deen and Shaila Patel helped me flesh out Nikhil and Anita's characters and their growth, which is always such a wonderful thing. You both are incredible! Thanks also to Angelina M. Lopez, who gave me the quickest turnaround ever on a first draft with helpful notes and thoughts. Christi Barth is a fabulous mentor and brainstormer and answered my cry of "What comes next?" in addition to giving me invaluable advice as I started writing my first series. These are all amazing writers and their support is priceless.

Thanks to my daughter and son for dealing with Deadline Mom even while they were visiting! My extended family and friends have not yet tired of me saying, "I can't, I'm on deadline!" and for that I love them!

And last but never least, love and thanks to my personal romantic hero, Deven, for patiently waiting for me to turn in my manuscripts and being equally excited every single time.

DAY ONE

MEHNDI PATTERNS

Things that are hidden....

Chapter 1

Nikhil Joshi slipped the cream silk jabho top over his head. The soft material floated over his body. He fastened two of three buttons, leaving the topmost one on the collar undone, then ran a hand through his thick hair and proclaimed himself ready. His younger sister, Tina, was getting married, and today was the first of the five days of festivities. The rhythmic beating of the tabla and the fabulous aroma of contemporary Indian street food wafted up to his room from the kitchen downstairs.

The sounds of laughter and wedding music filled him with a mixture of anticipation and dread. His entire family had congregated in DC from India and various states for Tina's big week. He had to at least appear to be over Anita. Three years was long enough. He inhaled deeply and exhaled slowly.

His phone dinged, alerting him to a text from his

agent. His third book was to be released next week and his agent and publicist were plotting to fill every free moment he had to promote it. He needed to be available; there was no resting on the laurels of bestseller lists. Sure, that reputation helped, but each book was unique. Each book had the power to make or break him.

He would not be broken.

His agent, Chantelle Ellis, had just scheduled a livestream interview for him for tomorrow afternoon. She was sorry that it was so last-minute, yada yada, but he should do it. Could he sneak away from the festivities for an hour, hour and a half, max?

Nikhil hadn't even thought twice about taking the meeting. Work was work. If he was going to be successful, sacrifices needed to be made. How many times had he heard that from his mother over the years?

He glanced at the small picture of him and his father that he kept here on the nightstand. His dad would have loved all this. House full, people partying. At least Nikhil thought so, but it was getting harder and harder to remember him sometimes.

He tossed his phone on the bed and focused on getting ready to face the family and all their questions about his divorce.

The toughest interrogation would be from his recently widowed, elderly grandfather. Nikhil hadn't seen the patriarch of their family since his own wedding close to five years ago. Somehow, every time he'd tried to go to India to visit him, something else had always come up, and he'd been unable to make the trip. There was no way around that conversation. Just through.

He checked his phone again and sure enough there was an email from his publicist, confirming next week's tour schedule, which started on Monday, with a launch party at a local bookstore. This was what he'd been waiting for his whole life. He was finally reaching the level of success he needed to prove to his family that he wasn't a complete screwup. That he was worthy of the Joshi name.

And he'd done it on his own.

Without Joshi Family Law.

Nikhil slipped his phone into his pocket and left his childhood bedroom suite. It was time to allow the festive spirit to fill him as he joined the mass of people in the Joshi house. His sister's wedding was a time for elation and looking to new beginnings. No more reliving his past.

His mother's house was wall-to-wall people enjoying sumptuous food, with musicians playing the tabla and harmonium, a fabulous soundtrack for the event. Maybe it wouldn't be so bad.

Suddenly, he was smothered in hugs by his cousins Hiral and Sangeeta, who had just arrived from Delhi that afternoon. "Nikhil! Where have you been? We've been hanging out for over an hour!"

"I had a couple emails I needed to answer." He returned their hugs. It had been too long since he'd seen them.

Hiral clapped him on the back. "That's what it takes to get a bestseller, huh? We haven't seen you since your wedding, I think."

Nikhil froze. Why would they so casually mention his wedding? "What?"

"Like five years—"

"Well, Tina finally found someone who would put up with her, so..." Nikhil tried a smile.

His cousins looked behind him and around the crowded room. "We thought we just saw Anita-bhabhi, but she looked busy. We'll catch up with her later."

Nikhil furrowed his brow. How was that possible? There was no way they could have seen their former sister-in-law. Why were they even looking for her? He and Anita were divorced. Before he could question them about it, more cousins approached and Nikhil was lost in a sea of greetings and hugs and someone pushed a shot of tequila into his hands. They took turns toasting Tina and her fiancé, Jake, and tossed back the shots.

After another round, Nikhil broke free. "I want to see my sister while I can still walk."

Nikhil made his way through the large house, grabbing a spinach pakora from a tuxedoed waitress and popping it into his mouth. If appetizers were still being served, at least he hadn't missed dinner.

Tina was wearing a simple cotton blue chaniya choli as she had her mehndi done. She was seated in a chair in their largest living room, the mehndi artist beside her. The artist's hand was almost a blur as she applied the mehndi paste in an intricate pattern, using Tina's hands and feet as a canvas for her intricate art.

His sister's besties were seated on the ground around her as if she was a queen holding court, as opposed to a bride having her wedding mehndi applied. Maybe it was the same thing.

Joy filled and lightened him. His baby sister was a force to be reckoned with, and she'd found her equal in Jake. She quite literally glowed with happiness. He grabbed a tray of prosecco from a waiter and approached the circle of women, most of whom he'd known all their lives. They all laughed and accepted the drinks.

His mother was not among the women in the circle. Hmm. That was odd.

Nikhil made his way through to his sister.

She looked up at him, panic in her gray eyes. The mehndi certainly looked beautiful, but didn't seem to be relieving his sister's stress as it was purported to do. He grinned. "Hey, Teen." He put down the near-empty tray and squeezed her shoulder. "What do you look so worried about? Everything'll be fine."

She shook her head. "I'm sorry. I had no idea. I thought you'd be here earlier and I wanted to talk to you."

"I had to finish emails. And I know why you wanted to talk to me."

"You do?" Her already big gray eyes bugged out.

He nodded. "It's just now hitting you what a production a wedding can be." He shrugged. "I told you to try going to city hall like I did." He laughed and held a glass of prosecco out for her to sip. Not that his had lasted.

She looked at it longingly and then down at her mehndi-covered hands. "That's not it."

Nikhil chuckled. "Such a princess." But he held the glass to her mouth so she could take a sip.

She gulped at it like it was water and she was in a desert.

"Easy there, Butthead. You have five days to go."

Tears filled her eyes. "You have to believe me, Nikhil. I didn't know they were going to do this."

Small pricks of panic went through his body. "Who? Do what?"

She bent her head down. He knelt down close to her. "What are you talking about? And why are you crying?"

"*She's* here."

Nikhil had no idea what she was talking about. But the look on her face, the alarm in her eyes unsettled him. "Who is—"

"There you are, beta!" Seema Joshi's voice cut through the din. She was the mother of the bride, and her outfit reflected that to perfection. Her peach-colored sari was exquisitely wrapped, her hair was up and her delicate jewelry sparkled. Nikhil looked away from his sister to see his mother grinning too widely, her eyes too sparkly.

His stomach roiled. Something was clearly up. This was not good.

"Come and say hello to your grandfather. He just got here," his mother called.

Nikhil glanced at Tina. Her eyes were wide, and she bit her bottom lip. His entire being went into high alert as he approached his mother. As he reached her, his heart nearly fell into his stomach.

Standing behind his mother, looking drop-dead gorgeous in a simple peacock blue sari, her black hair in a high, sleek ponytail, amber eyes wide, was none other than Anita Virani.

His ex-wife.

From the look on Nikhil's face, it was clear that he had not expected to see her here. Anita widened her eyes at her former mother-in-law, shocked that she hadn't told her son about the ruse. She hadn't intended to bombard Nikhil with her presence.

She met Nikhil's eyes, trying to communicate intuitively that she hadn't intended to surprise him in this way, at the same time willing him to play along as she smiled as big as she could. "Sweetheart! I've been look-ing all over for you. Dada—" she paused for emphasis, hoping Nikhil would see the light "—has just arrived from the airport and has been asking to see us, and I didn't want to go without you."

There was nothing of the kindness she had come to love in his face. Instead, she was met with hard, cold eyes, lips pressed together in muted anger and a clenched jaw. Much the same expression she'd seen on his face frequently in their last days and months as a married couple.

Her hands shook and heat flushed her face as she reached for his arm. He flinched at her touch, inexpli-cably sinking her heart into her belly. She should not care about his reaction. After all, she had been the one who left.

No matter. She gently threaded her arm through his, continuing her silent, eye-based communication that did not really seem to be working.

"Dada wants to see us," she repeated, squeezing his bicep to steady her hand. Which was worse? Nikhil knowing she was shaking, or squeezing an arm that was so familiar yet foreign it broke her heart? Didn't matter. She'd made her choice three years ago and she made her choice now. *"Together."* She tilted her head toward his mother and tightened her lips. Help would be great right now, since she clearly had avoided this conversation as well.

Seema-auntie used one of her powerful move-it-mom looks, which worked no matter the age of the child. Anita hoped it worked on her children like that someday. Should she ever have any. She and Nikhil had talked about children, but that seemed very far away now.

Nikhil looked down at Anita, his eyes narrowed. He smelled exactly like she remembered. Same cologne, same underlying masculine scent that had given her comfort so many times. She nudged him forward, hand still squeezing his bicep. Was it bigger than she remembered? Well, no matter now. Actual explanations would have to wait.

Right now, they were on. The happily married couple.

As they followed his mother through the small mansion, the party continued around them. Aromas of Indian street food made her stomach growl. Loud voices and laughter competed with the tabla and harmonium. Nikhil grabbed a cocktail from a passing waiter.

Anita eyed his drink with envy. Alcohol would be fabulous right about now. There had been a time when he would have grabbed a drink for her as well, but clearly, that time was behind them. The flash of sadness that swept through her was fleeting, but familiar. It happened whenever she thought about Nikhil, which was more often than she should.

Anita remembered Dada from her own wedding. He had been a strong force, full of vibrant energy and opinions. He had stood a solid six feet, had always maintained fitness in his body as well as in his mind. His laugh had been infectious, wrinkling his dark brown skin, and rumbling from deep within. He'd had a full head of white hair which had strongly resembled Nikhil's in its unruliness.

As they approached him, the toll of his sickness and grief became apparent. Dada had lost some weight, making him appear frail and weak just as her former mother-in-law had told her. Anita sighed with relief when the old man's dark eyes lit up with amusement upon seeing them. When she had really been married to Nikhil, she and Dada had bonded almost immediately, giving her the comfort of family that she craved.

It was the first time she was really glad she'd agreed to do this.

Even if it was a lie.

She and Nikhil bowed down to touch his feet. Dada placed his hand on their heads in blessing and motioned for them to sit. Nikhil sat in the chair next to his grandfather without so much as glancing at Anita. It was the only chair. Dada steeled Nikhil with a sharp look.

"Beta, let Anita sit. Don't be rude."

Nikhil pressed his lips together and forced a smile as he stood. "Of course."

Anita was unprepared for the pain and sadness that accompanied his anger as he made eye contact with her. He had once looked at her as if she were his entire world. Now he looked at her as if she'd ruined it. Well, maybe she had.

She tore her gaze from Nikhil and smiled at his grandfather as she sat down.

"Ah. That's wonderful." Dada-ji beamed. "Tell me. What are you both doing with your lives these days?"

She leaned toward him, squeezing his hand. "I'm so sorry about Dadi, and I'm sorry I haven't called you. I really have no good excuse."

Dada squeezed her hand back. "Thank you, beti. Your mother-in-law passed on your sympathies."

"You must miss her," Anita said softly.

"That, I do." His voice was rough with grief, and his eyes turned down briefly before he squeezed her hand again and made eye contact. "If she were here, she would want to know why you two haven't given us great-grandchildren."

And there it was. The first of the million times she bet she would hear that question over the next five days.

Nikhil's handsome face darkened. "Come now, Dada. You know better than to bring up such things." He glanced at Anita, his expression unreadable. "Anita and I aren't even—"

"Ready just yet," Anita cut in. "We're busy with our careers." She sharpened her gaze at Nikhil. *Play. Along.*

He narrowed his eyes at her, but nodded to his grandfather.

"Dada," Anita continued brightly, "you know Nikhil published a second book and is getting ready to go on tour for his third." So maybe she'd followed his career. It didn't mean anything. She paused, looking him in the eye.

"Seema told me that you are finishing your second year of law school. And you are working at the local legal aid center. A fantastic way to get started." Whether Dada had noted her glare at her "husband" or not, he dropped the baby subject and beamed at her. "I did something similar when I was a young barrister in India."

Anita saw clear as day the disappointment that flashed across Nikhil's face as Dada made no mention whatsoever of his accomplishments. He covered it quickly, and most people probably didn't notice.

But she did.

Seema-auntie arrived with a plate of food for her father. Anita stood. "Here, let me take that." Nikhil's mother gave her a tight smile and handed her the plate.

"Mom, come with me, I have to show you something in the kitchen." Nikhil glared at his mother.

Anita stood between them, the tension building like waves around them.

"I'm busy just now." She fussed over her father.

"It's really important," Nikhil spoke through gritted teeth and stared his mother down.

"I can sit with Dada—" Anita made eye contact with Nikhil's mother and forced out the next word "—Mom." She hadn't used it in years. She smiled at the older man. "I want to hear his stories."

"Actually, *dear*—" Nikhil narrowed his eyes at her "—it's wedding stuff. I need you both."

Dada, apparently oblivious to the tension, focused on his food. "I'm old. I'm not an invalid. I can eat on my own. Besides, the whole family is here." He gestured with his hand. "Go. Take care of your business."

Anita walked beside Nikhil, the backs of their hands brushing together, electrifying her. He still had that effect on her. She took this opportunity to really look at him. To try to glean from his face and body what he had been up to for the past three years. He towered head and shoulders over her. His cream silk jabho complemented his dark skin, and conformed to his muscles quite nicely. He was bigger than she'd remembered. But they had still been practically children back then. He was clean-shaven, as always, which allowed her to see exactly how hard he was clenching his jaw. He'd need emergency dental work if he kept that up.

Nikhil stopped at the door of his mother's study, opening it to allow them to enter. Anita had always loved this room. She inhaled deeply and the scent of the books lining two of the walls calmed her nerves, if only just a bit. She remembered all of the books she'd read from this library and then discussed later with Nikhil. It had been one of their favorite things to do.

Anita was just about to shut the door when Nikhil's older brother, Rocky, slipped in. He raised his eyebrows at her in surprise, then smiled at her. She smiled back—finally a friendly face. She shut the door and found Nikhil glaring at the two of them. He turned to the room and boomed, "What the hell is going on here?"

Chapter 2

"Language, beta." Nikhil's mother was the picture of calm. Her accent was slight, but still present. She straightened her sari, patted her hair.

Rocky was standing next to Anita, grinning, and Nikhil had an overwhelming urge to punch him for doing so.

"Ma!"

His mother sighed magnificently. "Fine. I would think it was obvious. My father doesn't know you're divorced. So, I asked Anita to come to the wedding and behave as though she was still married to you." She spoke as if Anita wasn't standing right there.

He caught Rocky shaking his head in the periphery. What the hell was he doing here?

He stared at his mother, incredulity seeping into him. He allowed himself a moment to pass his gaze over his ex-wife as if to confirm she was actually there. It quickly returned to his mother as if gazing at Anita had scorched him. Which it had.

"What do you mean they don't know we're divorced?"

His mother shifted uncomfortably. "I couldn't tell them at the time."

From the corner of his eye, Nikhil saw Anita fidget with her wedding rings. The magnitude of his mother's words hit him as the diamonds glinted in the dimly lit room. "Wait, *what*?"

"I knew they would be disappointed, so I kept putting it off. It was humiliating to admit to a divorce in the family. It reflects badly—and could have made it difficult for Tina to get married."

Nikhil clenched his jaw harder. Of course it would be all about how his failed marriage reflected on them.

"Before I knew it, a couple years had passed. Then Dadi passed and Dada had his heart attack." She paused and swallowed. "I just didn't think he could handle it. Now Tina is getting married—and since she's marrying a non-Indian, it's a good thing my father did not know about the divorce."

That didn't sound right. Dada would not have a problem with a non-Indian. But the divorce? Maybe.

She turned away and threw up her arms as she sat down in the large leather seat. "At least Jake is a lawyer. It was the one saving grace."

"Well, that seems to fix everything, doesn't it?" He shot an accusatory look in Anita's direction even as he flushed.

"It'll never work." Rocky wore a cocky smirk.

"Dad would never agree to this," Nikhil shot back.

"Well, he's not here, is he?" His mother's voice softened. "What was I supposed to do, Rakesh? Tell my father that Nikhil was divorced?" His mother spoke to her older son as if Nikhil wasn't even the room.

"What does it matter? Dada doesn't expect Nicky to fall into line. He always does whatever he wants anyway." Rocky knew Nikhil hated the use of that nickname, but he used it anyway—most likely on purpose.

"Your grandfather would be humiliated, knowing there was a divorce in the family," their mother insisted.

"Not if it was Nicky," Rocky said.

They were literally talking about him like he wasn't even in the room. It was choosing colleges all over again. Back then, Nikhil had gone against everything Rocky and his mom had suggested. He had stayed local and attended University of Maryland as an English major.

Nikhil felt himself flush. None of this was anything he hadn't heard before. He was the one who didn't fall in line, or follow the rules, or become a lawyer. Or stay married. He stared straight ahead, as though he could feel Anita's eyes on him.

"And with Tina getting married before him…" She shrugged and finally turned toward Nikhil. "It's just five days."

"What about your friends?" Nikhil asked.

"I only told my closest circle. They know to just go along. Most people think you are still married. Just too busy to attend the parties, et cetera." She glanced at Anita and a small smile came over her face. "It is good to see you, beti."

"She's not your beti anymore," Nikhil snapped.

"Nikhil!"

"It was her choice, Ma." He stared straight ahead at

his mother, but he might as well have reached out and pointed a finger at her. Without turning his head, he knew Anita had lifted her chin in defiance.

His mother waved a dismissive hand. "I honestly did not think Dada's health would allow for him to make it to the wedding, until he called a few days ago to say he could make it after all."

Rocky opened his mouth again. "No way Nicky's going to be able to pull off an act like that. He doesn't have the savvy for it."

Nikhil fired up at his brother. "I have the savvy for it just fine. It's just that it's ridiculous." He turned to his mother. "You're lying to your dad. And you want me to do the same." He leaned toward her. "I'm not doing this. Either you tell him, or I will."

His mother was unfazed. "Nikhil! This is not about me. He's my father and he is close to being on oxygen, for god's sake. A divorce in the family would...*crush* him. He would never get over the humiliation. He would never be able to get over the fact that people were talking ill about you."

"But doesn't the rest of the family know?" This wasn't happening. This kind of thing happened in soap operas, not real life. Besides, the family had been talking about him since he was a child. The middle kid, never quite as good at things as his older brother, the golden child, never quite as accomplished as even his younger sister.

Nikhil had had little interest in grades, preferring to play with his friends, or read books or get in trouble. As he got older, it became apparent that he had no interest in the family business, and that was the last straw.

Rocky lived for the law, and Joshi Family Law would

be his someday. He had also found an amazing woman to marry him. Easha was a brilliant lawyer, abundantly kind, and an all-around lovely person. Nikhil couldn't believe Rocky was lucky enough to meet someone like her.

Out of the corner of his eye—because that's all he could give her—he saw Anita take a step back.

"Well, beta…" His mother continued her confession.

Nikhil froze and scanned the room as if looking for answers. Clarity dawned. Hiral and Sangeeta. And all their other cousins. This wasn't a soap opera; it was a sitcom. Except it wasn't that funny. "You never told *anyone* I was divorced, did you? When you say closest circle, who is that even?" He racked his brain for a moment, recalling their meeting with Dada and coming here to this room. Realization hit him hard. "*No one* was surprised to see her here."

He finally turned to Anita to face her head-on. "You knew about this?" The question burned through him. Looking at her head-on had him slightly off-kilter. Maybe because he hadn't seen her in a while, but even in his mounting anger, she was more beautiful than he remembered.

Anita shook her head, amber eyes ablaze. "Seriously? How could I possibly know what your mother told people?"

He paced the office for a moment to gather himself, before turning back to his family. "No." He shook his head. "I'm going to go tell Dada the truth, that she and I are no longer together." It was too hard to even say her name. "I'll make an announcement. Tell everyone at the same time." *Damn*. It was like getting divorced all over again.

"Subtle," his brother mumbled.

His mother paled. "Please think about what you're proposing to do. You will make a scene."

"What did you think he was going to do, Mom? Nicky always does whatever he damn well pleases." Rocky pursed his lips at him.

Nikhil tried to ignore his brother.

"Think about your sister," his mother implored.

He threw his hand out in a dismissive fashion. "Don't use her against me." She was the only one he would reconsider for, and his mother knew it. "Besides, they'll find out anyway. Our friends know."

"That's like maybe ten people out of the hundreds that will be attending," Anita finally spoke up. "If we get to them first, then it shouldn't be a problem."

Why the hell was she so invested in this? "How did they get you to do this?" He turned to face her again, this time braced for the impact of seeing her. He hadn't seen her in over three years. Maryland law required them to live apart for a year before they filed for divorce. They never tried to see each other during that first year. Things were said, they were who they were and they couldn't be together. She had walked out, and that was the last he'd seen of her.

And sure enough, a year to the day that she had moved out, he was served with papers. Anger had made him sign them and send them off. Any second thoughts he might have had were crumpled up and stored in the back of his mind.

She looked him in the eye, calm and confident. "I could tell you that it was to protect Dada, but that would only be part of the reason." She glanced at his mother, and lifted her chin before turning back to him. "Your mother is helping me with my law school tuition."

Nikhil felt like he'd been punched in the gut; acid and bile churned. Of course. She was one of them. Seeing her in person for the first time in years, that sari hugging her curves just so, her voice with that unnamable soothing quality that he'd always found irresistible, he'd forgotten for a moment who she had turned out to be.

He remembered now.

She had tried to return the engagement and wedding rings to him when she had collected her things, but he didn't want them back. They were hers. And always would be.

"If we get to them first? Are you listening to yourself?"

"What? A group text and it's done. 'Dada doesn't know about the divorce. Pretend Neets and I are still married.' Simple." She froze as she used his nickname for her. Clearly it had not been intended.

He shook his head. "This is crazy. I'm telling him." He stormed out of the study with every intention of finding his grandfather and telling him the truth. Lies never worked. He'd find out eventually. This was real life. Not a sitcom.

His mother's sari rustled softly behind him as she followed as closely as she could without running. Without creating a scene.

He knew Anita was with her because he could smell her perfume. Its familiarity was like drifting into the past. He fought it.

Nikhil found the tabla player and whispered something. The bearded young man handed over his mic.

He caught sight of his mother at the front of the

crowd, gripping his ex-wife's arm. His. *Ex*. Wife. Rocky was on her other side, his mouth smashed together, superiority oozing from every cell in his body. Rocky glanced down at Anita, shaking his head, secure in the knowledge that Nikhil would once again screw things up.

"Hey, everybody! If you'll excuse the interruption, I need a moment of your attention."

A hush fell over the assembled crowd of friends and relatives as everyone gave him their attention. Tina sat stiff and helpless as her brother took center stage.

"I'm Nikhil, one of Tina's brothers, and I just have an announcement to make."

Anita's gaze met his and she gave a slight shake of her head, glancing toward the corner with her eyes. He looked over to see his grandfather sitting next to his cousin Sangeeta. The man was still distinguished at eighty-eight, still a force to be reckoned with. But what Nikhil saw here was a much older, almost delicate version of that powerhouse. He saw an old man—frailer than he remembered—surrounded by his family, beaming with pride as he looked around and chatted with his grandchildren, and even one great-grand. The fruits of his lifetime.

Nikhil caught Anita's eye and something inside him jumped.

Nikhil did not speak for a minute. If he did, the truth would be revealed. Dada really did look frail enough to have another heart attack. And the reality was that his mother was right. Dada would be humiliated that there had been a divorce in the family. Whatever his parents and brother said about him, Nikhil had a special place in his heart for his grandfather, and his grandfather for him. Not to mention, that bond had extended to Anita, and if nothing else, Nikhil knew Anita adored his grandfather.

Damn it.

"The truth…is I didn't think any guy would ever be able to put up with my sister." He turned to Tina and winked as laughter erupted. "And any guy who would want her, wouldn't have been good enough for her anyway." Laughter rang through the house. "But Jake is an incredible person. And you know that's true because I'm saying it and he isn't even here." More laughter. "The important thing is that he loves my sister." He smiled at Tina, his gaze passing over Anita briefly. He turned and whispered to the musicians, who began playing an old Hindi song about brothers and sisters. Nikhil stepped closer to the mic, his eyes on his sister, and began to sing.

Anita fell in love with Nikhil's written words first. Then his chai—hands down, he made the best chai she'd ever had. He had never revealed his secret, but after trying it just once, Anita only drank Nikhil's chai.

But it was his voice that sealed the deal.

His voice was as angsty and rich as she remembered, and a flush hit her cheeks as she recalled the love songs he used to sing to her.

Their first date had come after weeks of getting to know each other, and she remembered that exhilaration, the excitement of finally being able to go out with him. They had gone to dinner, then back to his place. She woke in the morning to the sound of Nikhil singing as he had prepared her breakfast.

He had been singing an old Hindi love song, his voice

soft and unassuming, almost as if he didn't even realize he was singing. Anita couldn't imagine a better sound to wake up to. He had flushed slightly when he found her watching him.

"You sing."

He shrugged. "I don't even notice I'm doing it half the time."

"Your voice is…heart melting." Her heart had raced at showing her vulnerability.

But he had simply handed her a mug of that incredible chai, kissed her and returned to breakfast prep and his singing.

All of that came rushing back to her as she took in his beautiful voice, as he sang a classic Bollywood song about the enduring bond of brothers and sisters.

As he continued singing to his sister, she remembered how she had seen his affection for Tina when they'd first started dating. She'd thought that any guy who loved his sister like that was worth being with. For a moment, she allowed herself to remember how it felt to love and be loved by him.

Once the song was over, his gaze landed on hers and for a brief second, she could have sworn some love shone through, but before she could fully grasp it, his dark eyes hardened, and she clearly remembered why she had left.

She'd had no other choice.

Chapter 3

Tina separated herself from her circle of besties and made her way to her brother, encircling her arms around him, trying not to smush the still-drying mehndi on her hands, now covered in plastic.

She stood on tiptoe and he bent down to her.

"I'm sorry, Nikhil. I had no idea until this morning..."

"It's fine." He pulled back and smiled at her. They were only a year and a bit apart, but he always thought of her as his little sister. "Really. It'll be okay. It's for Dada, right?"

His sister, his rock, nodded. "Dada is the best. And I have always loved that song."

He glanced behind her at Anita.

Tina followed his gaze. "You going to be okay hanging out with her all weekend?"

He shrugged. "It's just five days."

Tina nodded, but concern furrowed her brow. When he and Anita split, Tina had been the one who checked on him every day. Made sure he ate. He'd tried to hide his misery, but Tina had always seen right through him.

"Well," he said, grinning at her, "lucky for me, this is not a dry wedding." He grabbed a drink from a passing waiter and stepped back from his sister. "Don't worry about me. You have bride things to do—whatever they might be." He shooed her back to her friends, and glanced to where Anita stood chatting with Jake's mother and sister.

He grabbed a second drink and walked over to her. Might as well get the show on the road. "Hey…" *Sweetheart. Honey. Neets.* The endearments wouldn't come. He held out the second drink for her. "I got you a drink." He smiled at her, hoping he was convincing. "I see you've met Jake's mother and his sister." Nikhil leaned over and hugged Christi Collins. "Really good to see you Mrs. Collins."

"You too, Nikhil." She smiled warmly at Anita. "You'll meet the rest of the family at the rehearsal dinner tomorrow."

"I look forward to it." Anita smiled at Mrs. Collins as someone else approached her.

She grinned at Nikhil and took the drink. He thought he saw gratitude flit across her features. But it was gone before he could confirm it. "Thanks…" She sipped. "Just what I needed."

"You two are the cutest." His cousin Sangeeta came bounding up to them, drink in hand. She was easily twenty-six years old, but she bubbled over with energy. Sangeeta's mom, Neepa, and Nikhil's mom were sisters. "Ohh! You two should renew your vows on your fifth anniversary—you know, since you never had a whole big wedding thing! That would be such fun."

"Oh no. That's not necessary. Mom had a fabulous reception—" Anita started to say, darting a glance at him.

"But half of us couldn't make it," Sangeeta insisted. "Since you married at city hall and then Seema-masi had a last-minute party." She nearly pouted. "But no worries. I'll plan it with my mom and Seema-masi. We'll even get Deepa-masi to help." She hurried off, leaving Nikhil and Anita alone.

Their fifth anniversary would have been next month. They looked at each other and sipped their drinks, the silence between them thick with unsaid words. Better that way.

Thankfully, his phone buzzed. He grabbed it like a drowning man grabs a life preserver. His publicist, confirming that he was good to go for his launch next week. "I have to take this."

"Sure." Anita shrugged. "Whatever." She stepped away to give him space and was immediately approached by some of his mother's friends.

Nikhil downed his drink and stared after her for a moment, then turned away and opened the text.

Anita sipped her drink and made small talk with the extended family and friends. She remembered most of them and found it surprisingly easy to fill in the gap of the past three years with general answers. The most popular question was about children. Those questions might have been annoying had she been married—seriously, who was she kidding? She wanted children eventually, but even so, the questions about her reproductive state were irritating.

Her former in-laws had excellent taste, and demanded the best in everything, including the liquor they selected, so her Manhattan was incredible. As were her surroundings. She'd always loved this house despite its large size, because she'd imagined it filled with people for parties and gatherings, just like this.

Her parents had enjoyed entertaining, and they had been the type to cook everything at home—no catering in the Virani household. It's how she and her brother learned how to cook. The four of them would plan the menu based on the guest list and then map a plan of execution for the big day.

She missed planning those parties. Her brother, Amar still cooked—it was his job after all. But being in the family kitchen was never the same for her, after... everything. She cooked to feed herself, but ate anywhere but in the kitchen. Her brother basically lived in the kitchen. She gave herself a little shake to bring herself back to the moment, plastering a smile on her face. *Focus, Anita.*

The house she grew up in was hardly at this level, however.

Not only were she and Nikhil staying here, but so were Rocky and Easha, their cousin Hiral and his fiancée, Meeta, Sangeeta, and Seema-auntie's sisters and, of course, Dada.

Nikhil had never particularly enjoyed being here, but they'd had dinner here every Sunday evening as per his mother. It was the one day a week that the whole family sat down together. Nikhil had told her they had been doing it since his father was alive, and his mother didn't see any reason for it to stop just because her children were grown. It was the only time that all devices were nowhere near them, and they talked to each other. It was the one time that JFL was not a priority, if only for an hour or two.

Anita had reveled in the feeling of family, but Nikhil had always been tense and gruff at these dinners, itching to fulfil his duty and leave.

The bourbon warmed her body and relaxed her muscles as it soothed down her throat. She hadn't realized how tense she'd been. It had seemed harmless enough when Auntie had asked her to do this, but now, in Nikhil's presence, and everyone expecting them to be this happily married couple, it became quite real.

Nikhil returned after answering his text, a fresh drink in his hand. He stood next to her, with enough of a gap between them that only the air around them touched. But Anita felt that air solidly.

"Here comes Neepa-masi." She nodded as one of his mother's older sisters approached. She slipped her hand into his and tightened her grip against his instinct to pull back. She put on her best oh-my-god-I'm-happy-to-see-you smile. "Hi, Neepa-masi! It has been too long. You must be so excited about Hiral and Meeta's wedding."

"We are very excited." Neepa-masi's answers were always measured. It had always seemed to Anita that Neepa-masi was not a fan of enthusiasm. "Seema has managed to arrange things beautifully." She drew her gaze around the room. "Even though she claims to be so busy with the business."

Anita nodded and forced a smile. "Well, Mom has always planned beautiful events, even with running JFL." She shouldn't care about the slight. After all,

Seema Joshi was no longer her mother-in-law. But she did care. She was simply playing the part, she told herself. "I would expect every attention to every detail, Neepa-masi. You know how particular Mom can be."

Neepa-masi nodded and glanced at Nikhil, her eyes scanning their clasped hands. She seemed to nod with satisfaction. "So good to see you both here. Law school is so demanding, Anita, but it's good to take a break and spend time with family."

"Of course, Neepa-masi," Anita answered.

"You will be coming to Virginia for Hiral and Meeta's wedding, of course." It was a statement, an order. Anita was struck by the differences in the two sisters. And the similarities.

"Of course, Masi. We wouldn't miss it for anything." Anita couldn't stop herself.

Nikhil squeezed her hand. She was making promises she knew she wouldn't keep. But she couldn't give Neepa-masi the satisfaction of knowing she wouldn't be at Hiral's wedding. Neepa-masi would not miss the opportunity to lord it over her younger sister.

"Well, maybe by then you two will have some good news for us." She gave Anita a meaningful look. "I'm sure my little sister would love to be a dadi."

They both froze for an instant, with no response. Neepa-masi grinned and walked away.

No sooner had Seema turned her back on them than Anita let go of Nikhil's hand. No need to touch him any longer than was necessary. A waiter passed and Nikhil exchanged his empty glass for another. He raised an eyebrow at her.

"Oh hell yes. Please." She placed her empty on the

waiter's tray and Nikhil grabbed her another drink. He took a huge gulp of his.

"Easy there. It's five days." Anita glanced at his bourbon.

"Whatever."

Anita shrugged. "It's your hangover."

That was their first direct interaction with each other.

They walked around together, saying hello to guests as they would have if they had been a real couple. It was actually a relief to be forced to socialize, since Anita had no idea what she would say to Nikhil if they were alone.

Anita was quite surprised Nikhil was going along with the ruse, given how angry he'd been a few hours ago. After an hour or so, they found themselves alone on the patio, everyone having gone in to eat.

Nikhil's phone buzzed and he pulled it out and started typing.

"Wow. Working at your sister's wedding," Anita deadpanned.

Nikhil arched an eyebrow and glanced at her from beneath his shock of black hair. It would have been sexy if it hadn't been accompanied by a grimace. "Work is work. You know that. It's basically the Joshi family motto. Or did you forget?" He went back to his text.

"I didn't forget. I'm just surprised *you* adapted to that particular family motto."

Nikhil stopped typing and turned his full attention on her. "I *am* a member of this family."

Disappointment flooded Anita. "So you are."

Nikhil put his phone away and shrugged. "However, the truth is if you're not a lawyer around here, you have no value."

Anita had noticed that the guests' conversations were primarily directed at her and law school. "At least they aren't bombarding you with the best times to have a baby."

He raised his eyebrows at her. "Says you."

"Shut up, people are telling you when to have a baby?"

He shrugged. "Not exactly. They're wondering how we will make it work when you're in school and so busy as a lawyer." He turned away and mumbled. "As if I didn't exist. As if I couldn't take care of my own child while my wife worked."

"You know we're not really married or considering having a baby, right?"

He side-eyed her.

"So what does it matter what they say?"

He looked at her, his eyes narrowed. "Are you saying it's not getting to you?"

Anita sipped her drink and looked away. It did bother her, but maybe not for the same reasons it annoyed Nikhil. She did want a family one day, and every time people asked, she was reminded of exactly how far from having that family she was. Further now that she had walked out on her marriage.

"Right." He nodded and downed his drink. "That's what I thought."

"Come on, you two. Dinner." Hiral called them in. "Your honeymoon's been over for years. Give it a rest."

Nikhil jutted his chin at his cousin with what Anita clearly read as a forced smile, and motioned Anita into the house by placing his hand at the small of her back. She tensed from the sudden intimacy, and, at her flinch, he pulled his hand away and simply followed Anita through the door.

The enticing aromas of Indian street food circulated

in the air, a backdrop for the laughter, chatter and music of the celebration. A buffet of chaat, frankies and pav bhaji tempted the guests. Hiral introduced Meeta to Anita and handed them each a plate.

Anita grabbed a frankie and scoop of chaat, while chatting with Meeta. The guys filled their plates, and the four of them found a place to sit. Hiral grabbed a bottle of bourbon and some glasses from the bar and brought it to them.

They drank and ate and laughed, and Anita almost felt like she'd never left, except for the fact that Nikhil kept avoiding her gaze, where at one time, making eye contact across a crowded room was their most intimate form of foreplay.

"You know, I have heard so much about you from Hiral and Sangeeta, I feel like I know you. I can't wait for you to come to Virginia for our wedding. I love that you and Tina are so close. We're all going to be like sisters—I just know it!" Meeta pronounced.

Anita smiled and nodded, unable to bring the lie out. She and Tina had been close, but Anita lost her in the divorce. Meeta was amazing, and Anita knew if she had the chance she could be close to her—but she wasn't really part of the family, was she? She had given up her place.

"Well, that would be interesting, wouldn't it?" Tina appeared behind Meeta, passing a hard gaze over Anita.

Meeta grinned, oblivious to the tension. "Yes! It's going to be great!"

Nikhil stood. "Have a seat, Princess Bride. I'll get you some food."

Tina took Nikhil's vacated seat on the sofa, turning her body slightly away from Anita, while she chatted wedding plans with her cousins. She stiffly held out her mehndi-covered hands so as not to ruin the artist's hard work while the paste dried.

"Let's not forget Nikhil and Anita-bhabhi's five-year anniversary party next month." Sangeeta joined them with her plate towering with food. "I mentioned it to Mom, and she thinks it's a great idea. Kind of extending your wedding celebration, Tina."

Tina raised an eyebrow at Anita. "You agreed to this?"

"Why wouldn't she?" Sangeeta asked.

"Bhabs is not really the party type," Tina explained stiffly.

"She doesn't have to be," Sangeeta continued. "She just has to keep loving Nikhil-bhai. I'll do the rest."

Anita shrugged. There was no reining Sangeeta in.

Nikhil arrived with a plateful of food. Anita scooted over to make room for him next to Tina. He sat and held out a frankie sandwich for Tina. She bit into it and groaned.

"Oh my god. Soo good."

Nikhil smiled. "Here—try this." He held out a spoonful of the chaat.

Tina's eyes widened. "Amazing!"

Nikhil continued to feed his sister, all the while calling her a princess, although his love for her was apparent even in his teasing.

"I don't remember this caterer," Tina said.

"Yes, you do." Nikhil rolled his eyes. "We tasted the food."

"Yeah, but this is way better than what we sampled at the tasting." Tina closed her eyes and continued to chew. "No way this is Taj's usual spread."

Anita froze. "Who?"

"Taj. You know—" Nikhil started to say.

"Oh, I know." She widened her eyes at him, and as if the universe hadn't messed with her enough, a familiar and slightly unwelcome voice called to her.

"Anita? Is that you?"

Anita closed her eyes and inhaled before popping up from her seat and going to greet Sonny Pandya before he could come to her. He had on a navy chef's jacket with "Taj" embroidered on the breast and was carrying a small tray of samosas. She had gone on one date with Sonny a month or so ago, and while he was a lovely person, there hadn't been any sparks. Anita simply wasn't interested in him that way. And he wasn't getting the hint.

"Hey, Sonny. What are you doing here?" She walked away from the group.

"Your brother and I are helping Taj with this wedding." He looked over her shoulder. "Isn't that your ex-husband?"

"Yes, well. It's complicated."

"You never answered my texts after our date. I was hoping—"

"Hi, honey." Nikhil came over and dropped his hand on her shoulder and kissed her cheek. She flushed and froze.

"Hi."

"Oh, hi. I'm Nikhil, her husband." Nikhil extended his hand to Sonny.

"You're still married?" Sonny's eyebrows shot up and in the next instant they furrowed. "I'm confused. Amar said you were divorced. And you went out with me…" He looked from Anita to Nikhil and back.

Anita felt Nikhil's body tense next to her. She lowered her voice. "Well, we are divorced. I did not lie to you, Sonny. It's just—"

"We're back together," Nikhil laughed. "And I'm jumping the gun by hoping we'll get—" he cleared his throat "—well, remarried." He squeezed Anita, drawing her closer to him. "Right, honey?" He looked at her. They had never once called each other *honey*. And now he'd said it twice in as many minutes.

"Yep. That's right. Jumping the gun." She nodded at Sonny. "But yes, we are giving it another chance."

"Oh. That's why you didn't respond to my texts."

"Right. And I probably should have just come clean, but you know how it is when you're not sure where something is going…" Anita nodded at him.

"Sure." Sonny nodded, looking slightly sad. "Well, okay then. I should get back to work."

"Um, so, Sonny…" Anita threw a furtive glance at Nikhil. "We don't have to mention this to my brother—"

"Anita?"

She tensed and closed her eyes again, Nikhil withdrew his arm. This voice belonged to her brother.

"What are you doing here?"

"Hey, Amar!" She brightened up as if this was just a funny coincidence. "Imagine seeing you here! Though Sonny here was just telling us how you both were helping Taj with this wedding."

Amar looked from Sonny to Anita, his gaze landing on Nikhil and their proximity to one another.

"Amar, I wish you'd told me they were getting back together," Sonny said.

"What?" Amar's already big brown eyes nearly bugged out.

Anita widened her eyes to her brother to not blow

it. But she was having less and less faith in her eyes' ability to communicate accurately. The universe must have had pity on her in that moment because a tuxedoed waiter approached them.

"Sonny. Boss needs you in the kitchen."

Sonny nodded and turned to Anita. "Good luck to you." He left.

"You two are getting back together?" Amar whispered loudly.

"Well, no. Not exactly," Anita began.

"Not exactly?" Amar's eyes were still bugged out, and a vein at his temple was starting to throb.

She pulled him aside, gesturing for Nikhil to follow. "We're faking being married, but then Nikhil told Sonny we were getting back together, which is actually helpful because he won't stop texting me. So now at least, that's taken care of." Anita spilled out the words quickly and smiled at her brother as if it all made complete sense. *Fake it till you make it.*

He stared at her. "Do I have to ask why you are faking being married?"

"Well, it seems my mother never told anyone we were divorced," Nikhil finally offered, but all the fun had left his voice.

"She *what*?" Amar raised his voice, then immediately lowered it again. "What do you mean?"

"I mean she didn't tell anyone, especially my grandfather. He recently had a heart attack, and she's afraid he's too frail to handle the truth," Nikhil said, his tone flat.

"That's ridiculous! And why is that Anita's problem?"

"Hey. This wasn't my idea. It was all my mom. Trust me, spending five days with my ex-wife isn't really what I'd call fun."

Anita fired up. "It's not a joy for me either."

"Then why are you here?" insisted Amar.

"Because…" She paused, glanced around. "It's like Nikhil said. Dada's health is bad."

"Anita." Amar frowned at her. "Still not your problem. It was hard enough—"

"Don't worry. She'll be fine." Nikhil's voice was bitter. "She's only here for tuition money. It's strictly business."

Amar's eyes bugged out. "Tuition? Anita, what the—"

"Hey, Virani. Boss needs you. Now." A waiter had come to get him.

Amar looked back at the waiter who had called him, then turned back to Anita. "This is not over, little sis."

"Whatever." Anita rolled her eyes. "Just don't tell Sonny."

Amar waved a dismissive hand at her as he walked away.

"Well, that went well, don't you think?" Nikhil said.

Anita threw him a withering look. "Let's just get through the next four days, huh? We don't have to actually like each other or anything—we simply have to act like we do."

"I can do that."

"Fine. Me too." Anita just needed to ignore how good it felt to have his arm around her and have him kiss her cheek.

It was going to be a long five days.

Chapter 4

Nikhil knew Anita's brother had never really been his biggest fan, even when they were married. Amar had always felt that Anita had married him too quickly. Her brother was a fan of taking things slow and steady.

Maybe he was onto something. Maybe if Nikhil and Anita had taken their time, they'd still be married. Or maybe they never would've gotten married to begin with.

He had no idea what had possessed him to tell that guy that he and Anita were back together. He'd had no idea that Anita was dating; maybe that's all it was. It couldn't have been because he was jealous. He'd been on a few dates. No second dates, just a few first dates, during which he either found himself bored or finding fault with the young woman. It was no surprise that he was the one with the problem, so he stopped subjecting perfectly wonderful young women to his unwarranted scrutiny.

He really was dreading the next few days here, pretending to be married to his ex-wife while his sister got married. Especially since it had felt nice to hold Anita for those few minutes. They still fit together, just so. Not to mention she smelled like citrus and flowers. And her skin was soft.

Stop. It was five days and then everyone would go their separate ways.

Frustrated, Nikhil signaled a passing server. He grabbed two cocktails from the woman's tray and handed one to Anita. "You're dating?" What could he say? He was a glutton for punishment.

Anita shrugged, still clearly thinking about her brother. "Not really. Sonny and Amar went to culinary school together. I guess Sonny was interested and asked Amar if I would be. I thought it couldn't hurt. You and I have been—divorced—for almost three years. So I went."

"And?" He couldn't help it—the curiosity was stabbing at him. He quickly gulped his drink.

"And nothing." She looked him in the eye, trying not to smile. "There was absolutely no chemistry." The smile broke through and she chuckled. "We have nothing in common except food—" She shook her head, tossing her ponytail a bit. "He's a very nice guy, but I just couldn't."

Nikhil chuckled along with her, an inexplicable feeling of relief coming over him.

"What about you?" She lifted one sari-draped shoulder. "Date much? Seeing anyone?" She sipped her drink.

He shrugged, looking into her amber eyes. He was going to lie. He knew it even as the words came out. They didn't play games, but they were playing the ultimate game right now, so why not max it out? Why not make it appear as though he had moved on from her? "I do date," he heard himself saying. "Regularly."

Did her face fall? If it did, she masked it pretty quickly. He took a gulp of his very excellent Manhattan.

"Oh. Well, that's great. I'm happy for you." She took a sip of her drink. "Anybody...special?" Anita fidgeted with her rings as she widened her eyes, trying to appear nonchalant. It was her tell. She was nervous asking the question.

Warmth flooded through him, as he held her eyes, and this time he opted for honesty. "No. Not even close."

He thought relief flashed across her face, but his cousin was calling out to them.

"Hey, guys. Outside, impromptu dance party." Hiral came over to get them.

Nikhil chugged his Manhattan. It burned on the way down, tingling his limbs. "Let's do it." He followed Hiral toward the sound of the tabla outside and assumed that Anita followed him.

The live band had been enticed into singing a garba to great applause. Concentric circles were spontaneously formed as each circle did a different step. Garba was basically a line dance done in a circle. The outer circles did easier steps, while Nikhil and Anita always danced in the centermost circle, which featured the most challenging steps. The beat started slow, but steadily increased. The alcohol was starting to hit Nikhil, but he managed.

Then a blur of blue nearly hit his face as Anita's sari flew while she danced next to him. He missed a step, bumping something, and the blue fell into him, falling.

Nikhil caught Anita midfall with one arm around

her waist, before she hit the ground. He pulled her up toward him, her skin soft and cool beneath his hand.

Damn, but she felt great as he wrapped his other arm around her to steady her. Her breath came hard as he held her close, her smart and sexy mouth open as she tried to catch her breath.

She leaned into him, so their bodies touched, her beautiful eyes focused on his mouth.

The rhythm of the tabla faded into the background, and the laughter of the dancers blurred into the night.

There was only Anita in his arms. Things were spinning, and he forced himself to focus.

"Neets?" he whispered. He must have had too much to drink, because the next thing he knew, his lips were on hers and he was kissing her deeply, as if they were still married.

He thought he must really be drunk, because kissing Anita felt like the most natural thing to be doing. Not to mention, she was kissing him back.

And despite the wrongs and mistakes of the past three years, it felt so very, very right.

Nikhil's mouth on hers felt like coming home. Like the thing she'd wanted more than anything, but she didn't even know she'd missed it.

His hands at her waist were strong and warm and she gave in to the feeling of security she'd always had with him.

She kissed him as if the past three years hadn't happened, melting into his arms.

Then all at once, the beat of the tabla and the sounds of celebration rushed back to her, and she pulled away from Nikhil's embrace. Her heart raced as she stared at him, the taste of him still on her lips. What the...?

By the time guests had cleared out, Nikhil was swaying as he stood. Tina had removed the plastic and scraped off the paste, so her hands were free. She helped Anita get Nikhil up to their room.

"You know something?" Nikhil slurred.

"What's that, Bhaiya?" Tina laughed as they made it to the top of the steps.

"I am invisible." He looked at Anita.

Tina laughed. "Jeez, Bhaiya, how much did you drink? I see you just fine."

"But I am. To everyone but you and Dad."

Anita snapped her head to Tina and Nikhil at the mention of their father.

Tina's expression had softened. "You're right. Dad saw everybody."

They reached their room and Tina helped Anita lay Nikhil down in the bed. She removed his shoes. "Thanks, Tina. No way I could've gotten him up here myself."

All the mirth was gone from the young bride. "He's my brother. I wouldn't leave him lying around downstairs, drunk. And just so you know, that kiss outside was fake, for show."

"Of course it was. Did you think I wasn't playing along?" Anita retorted. But it hadn't felt fake, on his part or on hers. It had felt strangely good, right. She had broken off the kiss when she had come to her senses, but the way Nikhil had been looking at her...it didn't matter. Clearly he was intoxicated, and Tina was right. She should remember it was all for show.

Tina stood there for a moment, not quite glaring, not quite kind. "Look, I don't know how Mom got you to come and do this marriage act. Just don't make him fall for you again. He was a mess the last time. I don't think he could stand it again."

Anita's heart fell into her stomach with the reminder of how she had hurt him when she left. She nodded, numbly. "No danger of that. He clearly doesn't want me here. It's all for show. For the family. For Dada."

Nikhil groaned in the bed. Tina glanced at her brother as she left. "Grah shanti at 8:30 a.m."

Another groan.

Anita turned to the form of her ex-husband splayed across the bed. Tousled dark hair, brown skin with a slight five-o'clock shadow on a purposeful square jaw... At six feet tall, he took up almost the whole bed lying diagonally like he was. Say what you wanted about Nikhil Joshi, but there was no denying those classic movie-star good looks.

Anita sighed. *Definitely hot.*

Nikhil groaned again. "Hey." He sat up and looked at her, his voice barely even a drunken whisper. "You look like my wife." He waved a hand. "My ex-wife. Her name was Neets." His words were slurred. "I lost her because she couldn't see me. Because I'm invisible."

"Uh-huh." Anita tried to move him so he wouldn't roll over and have his head hanging over the side. She was barely registering his words.

"You know why she couldn't see me?"

Anita grabbed the empty trash bin and put it next to the bed. Just in case. "Why couldn't she see you?" This was going to be good. She placed electrolyte water on the end table.

"Because I wasn't successful. Because I was never going to be a lawyer, like the rest of my family. Like her. Wonder if she can see me now?"

Anita stared at him, her heart thumping inside her chest. "That's not true." Sadness gripped her as she started arguing with a drunk man.f "I never cared about—"

Before she could finish, he fell back onto the bed and passed out.

PERSUASION

~POWERFUL WOMEN~

and Anita recognized the scent almost before she recognized the woman.

Seema Joshi. Her former mother-in-law. For some reason, tears burned behind her eyes, and she swallowed hard as she stepped back.

"Auntie?" The word sounded foreign to her as she addressed the woman she'd once referred to as *Mom*. Anita had lost her own parents in a car accident, so when her mother-in-law had embraced her as a daughter, Anita had been more than willing to accept her.

"Beti." The word trembled coming off of Seema-auntie's lips.

Anita searched the woman's face for a reason for her sudden appearance. "Auntie—did something happen? Is...he...all right?" It was a reflex. *He* might be her ex, but certainly she wished him no harm.

"Nikhil is just fine," Seema-auntie answered, her mouth going tight and the soft, loving tone she'd just used to address Anita became clipped.

So some things never change. Mother and son had always bashed heads. Probably, because they were so alike. Though neither one could ever see that.

Seema-auntie's eyes widened, and she reached out a comforting hand on Anita's shoulder. Seema Joshi must have been in her late fifties, but good genes and skin care had her looking no older than forty. Truthfully, she could easily pass for thirty-five. She was smartly dressed in white jeans and a floral top with a light sweater. She still carried herself almost regally. Seema Joshi was one of the founders of Joshi Family Law, her late husband being the other. When Vikash Joshi had passed at the age of forty, Seema had taken it over. JFL now the preeminent law firm in the area.

"Do you have a minute?" Seema-auntie's voice was tentative, cautious. Unusual. While Seema Joshi was kind, she was never timid or unsure of herself. She commanded every room she was in. But not this one, today.

"Of course." Anita backed up into the fluorescent-lit classroom and sat down at one of the desks, all of her belongings basically clattering to the floor. She motioned for her former mother-in-law to sit beside her.

"Teaching English as a Second Language, I see." Her smile was achingly similar to her younger son's. "How wonderful."

"I really do enjoy it."

"And being at night, you are free to work for the Herreras' firm," she added, a bit of pride in her voice.

Anita nodded. "Well, I'm only there occasionally now."

"Of course—law school."

At Anita's look of surprise, Seema-auntie quickly added, "I have lunch with Priscilla Herrera on occasion, and she always has wonderful things to say about you and your work."

There was a point to this conversation; Anita was sure of it. She just didn't know what it was, or when it would show itself.

"Let me get to the point, beti."

Anita nodded.

Seema-auntie fidgeted with her bangles (real gold) and rings (real gemstones) for a moment before she finally sighed heavily and looked Anita in the eye. "I need a favor. A huge one, and I hesitated to ask, but I'm worried about Dada's health…"

"What's wrong with Dada?" Anita perked up. Nikhil's grandparents had always been so warm and welcoming to her. Nikhil and Anita had visited them in India after they were married, and whenever Dada and Dadi were stateside, they always made a point to see them. She'd lost touch with Dada after the divorce, but that was to be expected.

"He had a heart attack six months ago." Seema-auntie's lip quivered. "And Dadi passed a year ago."

A heaviness filled Anita's heart to hear of Dadi's passing. She quickly pushed it aside. Those feelings were misplaced. She no longer had a connection to this family. They weren't her family anymore, were they? "Oh, I'm so sorry," she somehow managed to say.

Seema-auntie nodded, tears filling her eyes. Anita took the older woman's hands in her own. She knew how it felt to lose a mother.

"What do you need?" Though Anita could not imagine what she could possibly offer.

Seema-auntie swallowed hard, and cleared her throat, squeezing Anita's hands. "Tina is getting married."

Anita steeled her face to show nothing but happiness. Tina had become one of her closest friends when she'd met Nikhil, almost a sister. Anita lost her in the divorce. She was happy for her former sister-in-law, but there had been a time when Anita would have been among the first to know. Not anymore. "That's fantastic!"

"Thank you. We're very excited." Seema-auntie paused and looked Anita in the eye.

"His name is Jake Collins, and she met him at JFL." A genuine smile came across her auntie's face as she spoke about her future son-in-law. "Not on Tina's team, but he's in line to run the real estate division, while Tina's just doing amazing work in the administrative and regulatory branch of the practice."

Anita nodded, her face still frozen in fake happiness. Still all in the family. Everyone in the immediate family was in the practice. Everyone except for Nikhil, that is.

"The thing is…see…" Seema-auntie continued. "I was never able to… What I mean is… I never told any of our family or friends that you and Nikhil divorced." Her last words came out in a rush.

The fake smile dropped into real astonishment. "What?"

"I just couldn't. My mother died and my father had a heart attack—there was no good time. Plus a divorce in the family would be very humiliating for Papa. I never even told my friends, because I was afraid it would get back to him."

"What do they think? I mean, when Nikhil and I don't come to functions?" She stared straight ahead at her auntie. "What did your sisters and Dada say when we didn't call them when Dadi passed?"

She shrugged. "We called as a family. Dada asked about you—I said you were busy. Our friends understand busy children. So I just say you're both busy. Working. Studying."

Anita's mouth gaped open for a second before she responded, her words firm and commanding. She wasn't this woman's daughter-in-law anymore and this was beyond anything Anita could have imagined. "You have to tell them, Auntie." She couldn't believe this. How was it possible that people—lots of people—thought she was still married to Nikhil? "You have to tell Dada. He'll want to know why I'm not there at Tina's wedding." Her heart pounded in her chest.

Seema Joshi sat straight in her chair and leveled her gaze on Anita.

"Not if you're there." Her former mother-in-law fixed her in her gaze. This was why she was here.

"What does that mean, if I'm there? You can't possibly want me to come to the wedding? How is that even—"

"You'll have to behave as if you and Nikhil are still married." The older woman spit the words out fast.

Anita shook her head while she tried to calm her breathing. "That's not... I mean, that will never work."

"Why not?"

"Because it's a lie." And how could she spend five days with a man she once loved but no longer had? "Besides, Nikhil will never agree." Of this, Anita was certain.

Seema-auntie continued as if she hadn't spoken. "Beti. Listen. It's just five days. I know you're in law school and that you applied for a loan." She stared Anita down. "You put us down as cosigners."

"I needed to be sure I'd get the loan. I'd never ask you to pay—"

"Of course. I understand. I also know your scholarship only covers two-thirds." She paused as only a lawyer can, before speaking with methodical preciseness, as if she was a surgeon wielding a scalpel as opposed to a lawyer wielding her words. "Do this. Spend five days as a part of our family, and I will take care of that remaining third. Imagine, your education will be paid for—you will have no added debt. No other strings attached. That is all. Then I promise not to bother you again."

No one knew about the scholarship except for Anita and the school. And her best friend, Divya. Because Anita hadn't mentioned it. She had been a shoo-in for a full ride, but at the last minute, she got a letter telling her she only got two-thirds. She and her brother, Amar, had the remaining third in their savings, but it was his dream to open his own catering business, and she had already told him to use that money as start-up funding. She had been that sure of the full ride.

"That is crazy." She frowned and shook her head. She'd have to pretend to be married. To her ex-husband. For five whole days. She hadn't even set eyes on him since she'd walked out three years ago. How could she possibly be in the same room as him after all this time?

After the way she had left?

What would her parents have said? She shook her head. That was irrelevant, because chances were she might not have married Nikhil so quickly if her parents had been alive.

It didn't matter. No way. She would just have to take out the loan and pay off the debt after she graduated. Lots of people did it. "No, Auntie. I'm sorry." She started gathering her things. "It's just such a crazy idea—"

"I know, beti. But you have to understand, that's how desperate I am." Her auntie watched her grab her computer bag and purse, with increasing panic on her face. "Please listen. I went to India after my father's heart attack. He was so weak and frail back then. And according to Neepa-masi, he hasn't shown much improvement." She leaned in toward Anita. "You know how crucial the first year after losing a spouse can be. And you know the stigma of divorce in our community."

Anita pressed her lips together. "I am *fully* aware of the stigma of divorce in our community, Auntie." People stared at her at the mandhir, and she heard whisperings from her parents' friends. Divya tried to downplay the whole thing, but even Divya's parents had told Anita that it would be very difficult for her to remarry within the community.

Which was actually fine by Anita, since she had no intention of starting a new relationship right now anyway. She was focused on finishing law school and getting a job. She and Amar were struggling to make the mortgage payments, but it was easier than selling their family home and getting an apartment. Besides, Amar would never leave the house.

Although...not having any school debt might solve her problems. Not having any debt would certainly make her feel more grounded. It was five days out of her whole life. She and Nikhil simply had to put on a show. The computer bag fell from her shoulder.

"Of course you are." Seema-auntie stood. "You're right. This is crazy. I don't know what I was thinking." She walked to the door. "Sorry to have wasted your time. I'll just tell them you have a big case in another city."

"But won't Nikhil tell them?"

"Don't worry about Nikhil." She dismissed him with a wave of her hand and left.

Anita sat back down, stunned, though her mind was whirring away. Seema-auntie had left her card with her cell number on it. Of course she did. Thirty grand for five days. How hard could it be? What was she afraid of, anyway? Nikhil was probably well over her by now. She had no intention of getting back together with him. It might be uncomfortable, but that little bit of discomfort would pay off nicely in the end.

She dug her phone out of her bag and dialed. Auntie picked up on the first ring. "Yes?"

"I don't have clothes for this kind of thing," Anita said.

Seema-auntie appeared in the doorway, relief oozing from her. "I will provide all of your outfits. The mehndi is in five days."

"I haven't said yes yet."

She smiled. "Why else would you call?"

DAY TWO

MORNING OF OBSTACLE REMOVAL

Making way for new things

Chapter 6

Anita woke to a stabbing pain in her hip and a crick in her neck as her payback for being chivalrous and sleeping on the sofa. Not that she'd had a choice, given the way Nikhil had drunkenly sprawled across the bed. Truth was she wouldn't have slept with him on the bed anyway.

Their "room" was a small suite, with an area for the king-size bed and a separate sitting room, and their own private bath. There was also an overlarge walk-in closet that allowed Anita to have 'her' side and Nikhil to have 'his' side. Anita's side had been empty when she had first arrived, so she had unpacked her small suitcase in there. Part of her deal with her former mother-in-law was that she would provide her wedding attire, as Anita had no time—or money—to purchase the nine outfits required in less than five days. At some point yesterday, her closet had been filled with saris, chaniya choli and lehnga, as well as a bridesmaid's gown. Shoes and jewelry were also tucked in there. Seema-auntie had seen to every detail.

On the few occasions that Nikhil and Anita had spent the night when they were married, they had stayed here, in his old room. It smelled of sandalwood and his cologne, and was comfy and familiar and brought back memories long forgotten.

Memories she had spent the last three years trying to squelch.

Her phone dinged. Amar. Her stomach quivered seeing his name. He had been pretty pissed last night when he saw her here.

Tuition money? Seriously, A. It's not worth it. We'll figure it out…

She muted the conversation and turned away from her phone.

No sooner did she shake off the guilt that had washed over her than her phone dinged again. Divya.

How's it going with the butthead?

She had ceased being a fan of Nikhil's after the divorce. No matter that she had thought he was amazing when Anita was married to him. Divya's loyalty was pure.

He's still sleeping off the shock of being fake married to me.

Drunk?

Yep. Get this. Taj is the caterer. So Amar is here.
shocked face emoji

shocked face emoji Good luck. I'm in grocery store hell.

Divya was an incredible pastry chef but her skills
were currently being wasted at a grocery store bakery.
It paid the bills but was far from what she wanted to
do with her life.

She sat up and peeked over at the bed. There was no
movement from Nikhil, save the regular rise and fall
of his fabulous chest.

Anita grabbed her laptop and checked her email.
She glanced at the date and a pang hit her heart. She
tamped it down and turned her focus to her work. A
couple emails from the local law clinic where she volunteered. There was nothing pressing, but one of the
emails hinted at a client of hers possibly facing eviction. She pulled up some paperwork and emailed it over.
Hopefully this would buy them until Monday, when she
could physically go down and talk to someone.

The puja was still a couple hours away, so she got
to work on her homework. Anita started her third year
of law school in a couple months, but they had already
been assigned readings. She washed up, then settled in
to complete an assignment. This wedding would put her
behind on her schedule, but not having any debt would
more than make up for it.

Once she finished the assignment, she showered and
put on her sari.

Well, she did the best she could. She always needed
help with a couple safety pins. Nikhil used to help her.

She was struggling with pinning pleats behind her

left shoulder when Nikhil groaned. She watched him through the mirror as he slowly attempted to sit up in bed. He ended up lying back down, holding his head.

"Electrolytes next to you," she said, finally securing the pin. The sari sagged a bit, but whatever. She'd managed it in the end.

She tried not to look at him. He was ridiculously handsome first thing in the morning. Tousled dark hair and scruff on his chin. The soft, bewildered look in his dark eyes, matched with a slight pout of full lips.

She had always loved waking up next to him. He was sexy and handsome—some mornings, she couldn't believe her good fortune. That *she* was the one who got to wake up next to him every day. That she was the one he loved above all else.

Or so she had thought.

"Electrolytes." She raised her voice a bit. "On the nightstand."

He started at her voice, which only made him moan again. "Neets?"

He really needed to stop calling her that. "Anita," she corrected him as she donned large dangly earrings and a necklace and reached for her matching bangles, desperately trying to ignore how sensual her name sounded in even his dry-throat voice.

"What the hell are you doing in my room?" he croaked at her.

"Right now, it's our room. We're supposed to be married, remember?" Her bangles jingled as she slid them on, the sound reminding her of wedded bliss.

"I'm trying to forget."

Did he remember kissing her? Didn't matter. "You certainly tried to forget last night." She looked at her phone. "You have forty-five minutes to get up and be presentable. The grah shanti starts at eight thirty."

He grunted. She walked over and shook him. He reeked of alcohol.

"What are you doing?" he grumbled, clutching his head in obvious pain.

"Tina's first puja is in forty-five minutes, downstairs, and you need to be there." She handed him the glass of electrolytes. "Though I get paid regardless of whether or not you show. I told your mother I would not be responsible for your attendance."

He sat up and took the glass, looking at it like it might bite him. "I'm sure she drew up the appropriate documents."

"No. I did." She smirked at him.

He scowled at her as he sipped the electrolytes.

"Pithi today too."

The grah shanti would start with a Ganesh puja, to remove all obstacles—spiritual and otherwise—from the upcoming wedding ceremonies and would end with everyone taking turns applying a turmeric and chickpea flour paste, pithi, to all parts of Tina's skin. This part of the ceremony tended to disintegrate into everyone spreading the pithi on everyone else. Almost as if everyone wanted to be cleansed and purified for the wedding. Well, not really. Everyone just wanted to rub paste all over each other because it was fun.

Anita and Nikhil had never done this as they had opted to get married at city hall and forgo all of the traditional celebrations. A big wedding seemed odd, since her parents wouldn't be there, and Amar and Anita couldn't have afforded a big multiday wedding with all the trappings, anyway. The city hall idea had appealed

to Nikhil's rebellious nature. Only his mother, his siblings and Amar and Divya had been at their small ceremony.

Of course, Seema-auntie had still insisted on throwing them a huge wedding reception, which Nikhil had
been opposed to.

"She just wants to showcase us. It's not because she
really cares," Nikhil had argued.

"So what? It's a party to celebrate our marriage.
What's wrong with that? Besides, she seems really excited about it," Anita had countered.

The party had been a mix of both. Yes, Seema-auntie
had wanted to show them off, but she was genuinely
happy for them.

"Yeah. I got it."

Nikhil's sullen voice jarred Anita back to the present.

Silence floated between them and Anita was visited by the thought that they were both thinking about
what they had missed out on by not having a wedding.

Anita found everyone gathered in the large great
room, which encompassed the family room and eat-in
kitchen with a large central island that could seat twelve.

"Jay Shree Krishna, beti." Seema-auntie greeted her
with warmth and praise to god, which felt truly genuine, and not just for show.

"Jay Shree Krishna." Anita returned the greeting.
The comforting scents of chai and coffee mixed with
warm laughter and fond calls of "Hey, Bhabhi," "Anita-
ben" and "beti" filled her heart momentarily with the
joy of family. Until she remembered that they really
weren't her family at all, which was accompanied by a
pang of grief for her parents. It had been close to nine

years since they'd been taken from her, but grief reared its spiky head when she least expected it.

The priest was already there (a good sign for a timely start) and the family was enjoying hot chai and coffee along with breakfast. Anita was catching up with cousins when Nikhil ventured down.

He was wearing a blue cotton tunic with the sleeves rolled up, over the traditional slim-fit bottoms. His hair was still damp, the curls starting to dry. Simple, but he looked amazing. And not even a little bit hungover. How the hell did he do that? He was all smiles and jokes with his cousins, working so hard to not look in her direction, to not acknowledge her, that she knew that he was more than aware of her presence in the room.

Anita had plastered a smile on her face but something of her true feelings of awkwardness and sadness must have shown through because when Dada finally entered, the first thing he did was bark at Nikhil.

"Nikhil! What is your wife doing so far from you? Sit with her. You never know how many days you have left."

The loss of his wife must have hit him hard. Dada furrowed his brow at Nikhil, though he looked well rested and stronger than he had yesterday. The flight must have been rough on him.

Ever the obedient grandson, Nikhil made his way to Anita and stopped at the coffee service. She watched as he put in the exact amount of cream and sugar that she liked, before continuing toward her. So sweet of him to bring her coffee. She reached out her hand for the cup, at the same time he took a sip himself.

"Way to make me look like an ass," he mumbled from the mug as he glanced at her outstretched hand.

"You don't need my help for that." She rolled her

eyes. "How the hell was I supposed to know the coffee wasn't for me?" she mumbled, a smile on her face for the crowd. "You used to bring me coffee all the time."

"We aren't married anymore." He spoke through gritted teeth. "And I used to make you chai all the time." He dropped an ice-cold glare on her. "How soon we forget."

She hadn't forgotten. Though she had insisted on coffee in the morning, it was his chai that got her through the afternoons. She had gone back to mainlining coffee when they divorced.

She grinned for the people watching them. "We're supposed to be married. Just hand it over."

A smack upside his head caused him to spill coffee down his front. He jumped and turned.

"Dada!" Nikhil was dripping hot coffee. "What was that for?"

Anita tried not to smile. She failed.

The old man had moved to the coffee service to make a cup of coffee.

"It's okay, Dada. You don't have to get me another cup," Nikhil said.

"I'm not," the old man grumbled. "This is for your wife."

Anita flushed, mortified that an elder was getting her coffee. She popped up from her chair, meeting Dada halfway. "Oh no. That's okay, Dada. I can get my own coffee."

He handed her the mug and a huge smile. "I know, beti. But how much better it is when given with love." He glared at Nikhil. "Treasure the people you love. There is never enough time."

Nikhil simply stood there, mopping his shirt. His mother passed by, slightly frazzled, a tray of sweets in her arms. She took one look at Nikhil, Anita and her father and barked at Nikhil, "Nikhil, quickly, go change. You and Anita are sitting in the puja."

Nikhil ran up to his room, taking off the wet jabho as he walked. He ran the stain under cold water, then tossed it toward the hamper. It landed next to the hamper. Close enough. His head still pounded; the acetaminophen had yet to take effect.

It was just his damn luck that his sister-in-law didn't feel well enough to sit the puja, so Dada had volunteered him and Anita. They weren't even really a couple! Of course, his grandfather didn't know that.

Last night was something of a blur. He remembered lots of alcohol and joining the dancing outside, but then things got very swimmy. There was the fleeting memory of cool lips on his.

Wait. Did he kiss Anita last night? Did she kiss him back? No. That was the alcohol talking.

He'd have to sit next to Anita for the next few hours as they performed the rites the priest asked of them that would serve to remove obstacles from the wedding of his sister. Didn't bode well. Not that he couldn't sit next to Anita. Of course he could. Her body next to his didn't mean anything anymore, right? It didn't help that his head was pounding.

Did he really kiss her?

His phone rang. What? A glance at the screen revealed that Chantelle was calling again. It must be something huge for her to call two days in a row, because she never called. She preferred email. He glanced at the door. He needed to get downstairs. This wouldn't take long. Nikhil answered.

"Chantelle?"

"Hey, Nikhil—great news! That publisher we are

wild about? The one who can take N. V. Joshi to the next level? They have an editor in your town. This weekend. She's attending a wedding, but she's willing to meet with you on Saturday!"

"What?" Nikhil couldn't believe what he was hearing. This was what he had been waiting for. He didn't even think about it. "Yes. Yes. Schedule it. Uh..."

Saturday was the fourth day of all the festivities. The Indian ceremony would be that day. Which meant he had a small gap in the afternoon for this meeting. Couldn't take more than thirty minutes, right? "Say Saturday afternoon? I'm kind of at a family thing this weekend myself, but I can make myself available for a while."

"I'll let them know and I'll be in touch."

She hung up and Nikhil stood there, trying to take it all in. This was it; this was his time. If he got this publisher to offer him a contract, his family would finally be able to see him as a success. They would finally have to acknowledge that he wasn't a screwup just because he didn't want to be a lawyer.

A pang hit him as he thought about how proud his father would have been of him. Lawyer or not, his dad had always had his back.

Nikhil used to spend hours reading in the den while his father worked. From time to time, Vikash Joshi would look up from his papers and smile proudly at his younger son. "Keep reading, Nikhil. Success is in those books."

Maybe he took it a bit too literally, but those words were always with Nikhil.

Even Anita would have to acknowledge that he was a success. Something he had never been sure she'd believed when they were married.

Laughter from downstairs brought him back to the festivities. He rifled through his closet and found a red silk jabho. That would work for sitting in the puja. He donned the tunic and hurried back downstairs, praying the meds would kick in soon.

The familiar sound of Anita's hearty laugh had him turning toward the priest. There she stood, her mouth open, body relaxed, black hair catching the morning sun, her sari wilting off her shoulder.

Nikhil strode over and he knew the instant she saw him, because the light in her eyes was replaced by apprehension.

"Jay Shree Krishna." He greeted the priest with his hands together. "I need to steal…my wife for a moment." The words came out easier today than yesterday.

The priest nodded his approval and went back to his preparations.

"What's up?" Anita looked up at him, a forced smile on her face. Her eyes betrayed her apprehension around him. For just a moment, he found himself longing to see the relaxed smile and taunting eyes she used to save just for him.

"I, uh." He pointed to her shoulder as he asked permission to touch this woman. This woman whose body there was hardly an inch he hadn't touched at some point. "Your sari is falling… Do you have pins?"

"Oh, yes. I do." She reached into the little purse attached to her sari. "But it's okay. I can just get your mom to—"

"She's busy."

"Well, then Easha-bhabhi…"

"She's throwing up."

Anita grinned, an inquiring yet knowing eyebrow cocked. "Is she?"

"Yes, she's pregnant. She's not past the first trimester, so we're not telling anyone just yet. Rocky wants to keep it quiet." Nikhil looked around. "We'll use Mom's study." He extended his arm for her to lead the way.

He walked behind her to the study, and her floral perfume wafted back to him, conjuring memories of their life together. What was it about certain scents that could make you believe the past was present? That maybe the divorce never happened, and they were still happily married? They were stopped at least four times on the way to greet cousins and friends, some of whom they hadn't seen since their marriage party.

Nikhil placed his hand on Anita's lower back to guide her back to the study. This time, she didn't flinch, but seemed to relax into his touch. It shouldn't please him so much...but it did.

Once in, Nikhil closed the door, shutting out the exuberance of the house and locking in the thick silence between them. Anita handed him the extra safety pins and took out the one on her shoulder. Nikhil watched as she gracefully brought the fabric back and forth, making perfectly even pleats. The sari was half-off, revealing the short blouse beneath, as well as the smooth bronze skin of her toned torso.

Nikhil forced himself to look away.

When she was done, she flipped the pleats around her body and over her shoulder, coming down back to front, toward her torso, and waited for him expectantly. He was trying so hard not to look at her, he didn't move right away.

She cleared her throat. "Nikhil. Safety pin."

"Of course." He leaned over her shoulder to fasten the pleats. His fingers grazed the skin of her back. Goose bumps appeared on her skin. Well, at least he wasn't the only one affected.

She pulled the bottommost pleat free, pulling it across and covering her breasts and torso. Another safety pin was required near her lower back to secure this piece.

"Nikhil." Her voice was soft. She turned her head toward him, their faces were inches from one another. "Back here."

For a moment he forgot they weren't married.

"Hmm." He forced his focus onto the safety pin. She tossed her hair, the soft tresses landing on his hand, obscuring his view.

"Oh sorry," she said.

"No problem." He gently picked up her hair and moved it aside so he could fasten the safety pin. He fastened the pin and turned his head. Mistake. Now their mouths were mere centimeters from each other. A foggy flashback came to him.

"You kissed me last night." It was almost an accusation.

"You kissed me first." She turned and stepped away from him, the moment gone.

So it had *happened.*

"That's not how I remember it." He shrugged.

"Well, I'm surprised you remember anything. Let's just chalk it up to alcohol and forget about it." She checked the rest of her sari and nodded at him.

Kissing her had always been one of his favorite things. In fact they'd made out in this room more than once during their short but intense dating days.

A phone chirp interrupted his wayward thoughts.

Anita reached for her phone from the small purse hooked to her sari. Nikhil saw the name before he could help himself.

Amar. Her brother. Who obviously knew they were actually divorced.

Anita made a face and put her phone away.

"You're not going to answer him?"

"He's still irritated that I'm here." She rolled her eyes. "You know how he gets."

She sighed. Amar had missed the call when the police had phoned to tell them their parents were in the hospital. The officers had called Anita next. Amar had never forgiven himself for missing that call, and he would get worried if Anita didn't respond, automatically assuming the worst. "Fine. I'll send him a text." She quickly texted him and put her phone away.

He patted the area he had secured her safety pin. It wasn't an excuse to touch her again—it wasn't. "Well, at least Mom can't glare at you for not being properly put together. You look amazing."

Anita flushed under his open admiration. "She never glared at me for that—she made eyes at you. Because *you* couldn't bother to be 'properly attired.' Who shows up for family portraits in a T-shirt?" There was laughter in her words, and Nikhil knew she was remembering the admonishment he'd endured from his mother for doing just that. His mother had had no sympathy for his antics, even back then.

Nikhil warmed to the first real smile on her face he'd seen since she arrived. He quickly reminded himself of how she had given up on him all those years ago. How she had hurt him. And how she had left him.

Chapter 7

Anita kept her back stiff and straight during the small ceremony and focused on the pandit. The goal was to avoid touching Nikhil as much as possible as they performed the various rites. From the caution that Nikhil was showing with his hand movements, he clearly had a similar goal.

He never looked at her or reacted to her. It was almost as if she wasn't sitting next to him.

They were both sitting cross-legged on the floor, heads bowed. It was his turn to offer flowers in the ceremony. Nikhil sat, hands clasped together, eyes closed, the epitome of serene. He didn't move. She nudged his elbow with hers. He remained still. The pandit cleared his throat and continued chanting. She nudged him again. His eyes popped open and he looked at her from the corner of his eye. She motioned in front of them with her eyes.

He smiled sheepishly at the pandit. "Oh, sorry," he murmured as he completed the action.

Finally, her eye-based communication was working.

She carefully met Nikhil's eyes and caught him biting his bottom lip, trying to hold in a chuckle. She pressed her lips together to stifle her own laugh. The pandit instructed them to hold a spoon of water. They both reached for the spoon together, fingers grazing each other. Neither of them pulled back.

Shortly after they had married, they held the traditional housewarming ceremony for blessings in their new apartment and invited their friends and relatives. The puja was set for 8:00 a.m. on a Saturday morning. Nikhil and Anita had attended the engagement party of a close friend the night before. Anita may have had more to drink than she should have, because when she woke at 6:00 a.m. the next morning, she was still a bit tipsy. They sat in the puja, and every time they closed their eyes, Anita fell asleep. Nikhil had had to continuously nudge her elbow to get her to pay attention.

She shook her head at him as that memory filled her simultaneously with happiness and melancholy.

The puja finished within the allotted time, and it was time to apply the pithi on Tina. Nikhil's mother was first to apply the yellow paste on her daughter. As the bride's older sister-in-law, Rocky's wife, Easha, was next. Then Anita. Anita dipped the two betel leaves into the paste and approached Tina. Tina avoided looking at her, so Anita simply dabbed Tina's hands and feet with the paste and moved on, an incredible sadness weighing her down.

She found herself sitting next to Dada as the rest of the family and friends took their turn. It was only a matter of time before all the guests were covered in turmeric paste.

"Come, beti. Let's walk." He stood and grabbed his cane. Anita allowed him to lead her outside, noting that he wasn't really using the cane. They walked side by side on the sidewalk. Dada was tall and not even slightly hunched. He might have been thinner than she remembered, but he certainly looked better than last night.

"You're looking more yourself today, Dada," Anita said.

"The flight always makes me nauseous. I feel much better today." He was silent for a time, seemingly lost in thought, though he walked at a good pace. Finally, he spoke. "You and Nikhil. You remind me of me and your dadi." He smiled at her. "She was so like you. Smart. Witty. Beautiful." He shrugged. "Active in the community. Not much of a cook."

He looked at her. "Do you cook?"

She grinned. "Yes, I do. In fact, Nikhil and I used to cook together." Wait, where did that come from? She had almost forgotten. It had been something they looked forward to when their schedules lined up. They even used to cook at the house with Amar, from time to time, helping him with new recipes or spice combinations.

"You don't anymore?"

Uh-oh. "Well, we're so much busier these days, you know. He's busy writing. I'm busy with law school."

The older man grinned with pride. "The family must be thrilled. Another attorney in the family business."

Anita stared at the older man. He had no idea that he had just fallen onto the major reason she and Nikhil were divorced. Nikhil had hated the fact that she wanted to be a lawyer. Better not to say anything.

He patted her hands. "You have been through quite a bit at such a young age. Losing your parents so young. How fortunate that you and Nikhil have each other to lean on."

She had leaned on him. Her parents had been gone a couple years when she'd met Nikhil. She'd been out of college a year or so, was still floundering, trying to find her way. She found work teaching as a substitute teacher during the day. In the evenings she was the assistant to an English professor who taught creative writing. It was how she met Nikhil.

She had still been grieving and lost from the loss of her parents. He had been there for her. Until he wasn't.

"You know, beti. What I have learned these past years is that we are always stronger than we think and that it is never too late for anything."

Anita stared at the old man. If she didn't know better, she would have thought he was trying to get her back with Nikhil.

They had returned to the house, and Anita heard her name being called as they entered.

"There she is! Anita-bhabhi!" The Joshi cousins were nothing if not loud and affectionate.

Nikhil waved her over and bits of dried paste fell from his hands. He had turmeric paste on his cheeks and clothes and hands. Anita covered her mouth with her hands as she walked over and took in Tina. Every inch of the girl's exposed skin was completely covered in turmeric paste. Anita was sure the girl's girlfriends had probably gone under the sari a bit as well. Her hair was caked yellow. She glanced at Nikhil.

He had the audacity to grin with pride. "I did the hair."

"How am I going to get to the shower?" Tina widened her eyes. The thing about turmeric was that it was multifunctional. It was used to cure a sore throat, mend a cut and beautify skin. It also permanently stained just about anything, except skin and metal cooking utensils. But most certainly, it would stain the cream-colored carpet that ran all through the Joshi household.

Anita grabbed a nearby towel, likely set out for just such a purpose, and laid it in front of her. "Walk." When Tina had walked the length of the towel, another friend or cousin would bring one forward and lay it down before her. Pieces of dried turmeric paste fell onto the towels as she walked.

Anita shook her head. "Total princess."

Tina simply humphed and slowly continued her journey to the upstairs bathroom. Anita continued to direct the path from towel to towel, ignoring Tina's curious glances at her. They finally reached the door of Tina's bedroom and Anita opened it. Tina entered, not meeting her eyes.

One of Tina's best friends came up behind Anita. "Hey, Anita! So good to see you!" She pulled Anita into a warm hug.

"Anu!" Anita fell into the young woman's embrace.

"It's been a while." Anu pulled back, beaming.

Anita shrugged. "Well, you know…"

"I know. I heard about the divorce." Anu nodded, glancing quickly at Tina. "But hey, I'm super excited to hear that you and Nikhil are getting back together."

"What?" Both she and Tina chorused their surprise.

"Sonny Pandya? Sonny is like my cousin's cousin on the other side of their family. Anyway, he's here with the caterer and he told me that you told him that you and Nikhil are getting back together."

"That is one hundred percent—" Tina started to say.

"True," Anita interrupted, giving Tina a *look* to just go with it.

Tina's eyes widened and she opened her mouth, but Anita spoke over her. "Nikhil and I are giving each other another chance, and Tina's wedding came up while we were figuring all that out. But hey, do me a favor and don't say anything about any of this. We're trying to put it behind us and move on."

"Um, yes. Sure. Of course. Makes sense," Anu agreed, looking slightly confused. "I already told the girls—we were so excited you were here. Is that okay?"

"Sure. Just let's keep it between us." Anita smiled sweetly at Tina and silently begged her to keep quiet.

Having accepted what Anita said, Anu was talking. "Well, I missed you! We used to have so much fun together."

They had had a lot of fun together. Anita had gotten to know Tina's closest friends while she was married to Nikhil. They had all been on more than one girls' night together.

But when Anita left, she left them all. She really missed that sisterhood.

"I missed you all, too."

"Ooh," Anu squeaked. "Maybe we could all hang out again, you know, since you and Nikhil are a thing again."

Tina cleared her throat. The two women turned to her. She was covered in drying turmeric paste, standing in the middle of the room glaring at Anita. Anu shook her head and started laughing. Anita joined her. At first, Tina remained stoic, but within minutes she, too, was laughing hysterically. She bent over.

"Oh no! Stop!" Anita called out, still giggling. "It'll fall off." She turned to Anu. "You got her?"

"Well," Anu answered, eyeing Tina, "I could use a hand for getting that sari off."

"It's fine, Anu. The two of us can handle it," Tina spoke up, all her mirth gone as she flicked her gaze to Anita.

Anita shrugged as if she didn't care that Tina was angry with her. That was fine. Getting Tina ready was not part of the contract. "No worries, I'll see what they need downstairs." She threw what she hoped was a nonchalant look at the girls and headed for the door.

"Are you kidding?" Anu screeched. "Wait, Anita. With both of us, there'll be less to clean up."

Anita stopped and looked at Tina. Tina pressed her lips together. "Fine."

"Great." Anu grinned. "Let's get her in the bathroom."

Anita and Anu started to unwrap Tina's turmeric-caked sari in the bathtub. Once the sari was off, Tina was able to take over. Anu and Anita left Tina to shower.

Her job done, Anita headed for the door when Anu's phone dinged. "Ugh! I have to go talk to the tabla guy."

"Right now?"

"I'm in charge of the music this weekend, and the tabla guy is having some crisis."

"Well, I'm sure I can take care of that for you, since you're also getting the bride ready." Anita grinned.

"Well, actually, no, you can't." Anu waved her hands at Anita. "I'll go. Besides, you do such a great sari." She was nearly pouting.

"Um, I don't think that's a good idea." She shifted her gaze to the bathroom. She didn't really need to be alone with Tina.

Anu's phone dinged again. She glanced at it as she rushed out the door. "You'll be fine."

"Anu—" It was no use; she was gone. The emergency was probably concocted so she could flirt with him, but either way, Anita was left alone to help with Tina's sari.

Great.

Anita walked around Tina's room while she waited, grateful for a moment where she didn't feel like she was pretending. There was a picture of Anita, Nikhil and Tina from a beach weekend. They looked happy. They *were* happy.

A knock at the door tore her from her reverie and Nikhil's voice called from the other side. "Can I come in?"

"Sure. She's still in the shower," Anita called. She cleared her throat and started to smooth her hair but stopped herself.

Nikhil slowly opened the door, avoiding her eyes. "Just wanted to see how long she'd be." His hair was still damp from his shower and curled a bit at his neck. He had on a fresh, rust-colored kurta shirt and nice jeans, and was paste free.

"Pithi can be hard to take off..."

His gaze bounced around the room. "Thanks for... the puja." He waved an elbow.

Anita shrugged. "Returning the favor. Besides, can't have you falling asleep at a puja. Your family would never let you live that down."

"Especially Rocky," Nikhil agreed.

Silence lay thick with memories between them. Nikhil pointed at the picture Anita was still holding. "I remember when that was taken." He walked over with his hand out. Anita handed him the photo. "It was just after our first anniversary. Tina had tagged along on our beach vacation." He didn't step back, simply gazed at it, the smile on his face fading into a tight-lipped frown.

This close to him, Anita caught the scent of his shower. Clean, fresh, him.

"We were so happy." He met Anita's eyes. "Is Amar still pissed at you?"

"Probably. But he's busy. He's getting overtime to work this wedding, which is fabulous, since he needs to start his own business."

"That's still the goal?" Nikhil smiled.

Anita nodded. "He just has to jump in and do it. Not sure what's holding him back."

Nikhil nodded, not saying anything. Maybe he was thinking about when they used to cook together at her parents' house.

"Oh, and the bridesmaids think we're, uh, well... getting back together." Anita flushed.

"What?"

Anita shook her head. "It's a whole cousin thing, Anu knows Sonny. He told her."

"Yeah. So why are you perpetuating that lie?" Tina emerged turmeric-paste free, makeup done and dressed in her sari blouse and floor-length petticoat.

"So that Anita can let down an admirer softly and not have to tell him she's not interested." Nikhil's jaw was set as he placed the photo back and addressed his sister. "Mom wants to know how long."

Tina glanced at Anita. "Give me thirty minutes and I'll have my hair done, too."

"I'll tell her." Nikhil left without even looking at Anita again.

Anita was left in thick silence with her former sister-in-law. Tina looked around. "Let me guess. Emergency with the tabla guy?"

"You called it. She assumed I would stay and help you with your sari."

"Let's do it then." Tina sighed.

Anita motioned for Tina to turn and sit in front of the large vanity-style mirror. She started rolling sections of Tina's hair in hot rollers.

Bride or no, waves of irritation were flowing off Tina right now, so Anita did not feel the need to fill the silence as she normally might. There had been a time when they had talked about everything, late into the night, grudgingly succumbing to sleep when one (or both) of them fell asleep on the sofa in the apartment Anita had shared with Nikhil.

Understandable, since Anita was her brother's ex-wife, but come on, they had been friends. "Stand up and I'll get the sari."

"She's paying you or something," Tina stated as if they had been having this conversation. Maybe they had.

Anita pressed her lips together. That was between her and Seema-auntie. Tina did not need to know everything. She handed Tina the sari so she could get it started.

"It's ridiculous." Tina shook her head. "Not to mention dangerous." She turned and tucked and then handed the rest to Anita.

"How is it dangerous?"

Tina met Anita's eye in the mirror. Her gaze was hard. "For my brother."

"I'm not going to do anything to him." Anita made the pleats and pinned them. She then wound the sari around Tina, tossing the pleats back and over her left shoulder.

"You were kissing him last night!" Her voice was hard, accusatory.

"He kissed *me*." It was her defense, and she was sticking with it.

"Your being here is enough. And Mom has you in the same bedroom. I tried to get her to at least give you separate bedrooms—it's a recipe for disaster."

"There's no need for you to be concerned. I'm over him. Or I wouldn't have agreed to come." Anita was really getting good at this whole lying thing. "Besides, I slept on the sofa."

Tina narrowed her eyes as Anita turned her away from the mirror to face her and make final adjustments before securing everything with safety pins. "Well, good for you, but Nikhil hasn't been the same since."

Anita paused in her primping. "What do you mean?"

"My brother was a mess after you left him. All he did was sit in that apartment and write all the time. Mom didn't even know if he was eating." Tina spit the words at her.

Anita looked away, heartbreak and shame overcoming her. "I—I had no idea."

"How could you? You never looked back, did you? You just walked away."

Anita forced herself to raise her chin at Tina, even as sorrow filled her with the idea that Tina (or Nikhil) thought she could just walk away. "Not that it's any of your business, but I didn't just walk away. We weren't happy." She swallowed to hide the fact that her voice had cracked. "What was the point of staying together?" Walking away from Nikhil had been one of the hardest things she'd ever had to do. But he hadn't supported her, he hadn't been there for her, so she'd had to go.

A fleeting glimpse of pain in Tina's eyes was quickly replaced by anger. "He told me that you were the one who filed the papers."

Filing those papers had taken every bit of strength she'd had. "That's true." She secured the last safety pin in the sari. Tina looked beautiful, even with the anger in her eyes.

"You be careful around him. Just remember that this whole weekend is pretend. Just because we're acting civil around you doesn't mean that we've forgotten the pain you caused us."

"Us?" Anita asked.

Tina blinked as if she had revealed too much. "The family."

Anita had had no idea that Nikhil had been so distraught, nor did she have an inkling that this weekend would be difficult for Nikhil in any way. He had made it clear at the time how he felt about the law, more specifically, how he felt about Anita going into law. He'd shown very little concern for the fact that being a lawyer was a way for Anita to have that sense of security she had lost when her parents were suddenly taken from her.

Anita became very interested in fussing with the sari, even though it was perfectly put on at this point. She had given up the family when she divorced Nikhil because, well, they were his family, and she was no longer a part of it.

"You're getting married this weekend. Let's focus on that. Nothing is going to happen between me and Nikhil. We had our chance. We blew it. End of story."

Anita sounded more matter-of-fact than she felt, but it was the truth. "Turn."

Tina was gorgeous. Her sari was a light silk of a solid deep pink color with a silver-threaded border and draped beautifully over her curves. Elegant enough for a bride, yet casual enough for the in-between time right now where they would be simply mingling with who-ever stopped by.

"Sit." Tina sat back down in front of the mirror as Anita unrolled the hot rollers and finger-combed her hair. "All set. With five minutes to spare."

"Thank you." Tina's gratitude was softer than Anita had expected. "You still are the best at putting on a sari."

"It's easier on someone else." Anita shrugged. "I—I always need help with the pins."

She had learned from her mother. Anita had spent hours over the years watching her mother don a sari to go out or just dress up. She had started learning as soon as her hands were large enough to make pleats. To this day, Anita could still hear her mother's words of guidance on how to tuck the ends just so, or make the pleats in perfect alignment. She could almost smell her mother's perfume in the air and feel her gentle touch in the silk. When she was married, Anita helped all the women and girls in the family put on their saris. She had thoroughly enjoyed it. Right now, she swallowed the tears that burned at her eyes.

"You should go down. Everyone's waiting for you," Anita said. "I'm just going back to my room to change."

"Remember what I said." Tina arched a perfect eye-brow before leaving the room.

Anita nodded as Tina shut the door. Tina was only

protecting her brother. Anita didn't blame her for that. She would do the same. But she missed that closeness, and Tina's anger only added to the emotional weight on her shoulders.

Anita went to her room and quickly changed into a beaded emerald green salwar kameez she found hanging in the closet. The matching jewelry was on the bureau. Her former mother-in-law had thought of everything.

Tears built hot and insistent behind her eyes as she fastened the dangling earrings. She closed her eyes to fight them, but she failed. Turns out she had missed the family more than she had thought. Especially Tina.

DAY TWO:

REHEARSALS AND PRACTICE

When the past meets your present.

Chapter 8

Nikhil opened the door to the private room in the back of the restaurant to the sounds of laughter and a live band playing background music. Jake's parents were hosting a rehearsal dinner, and everyone was already here after the dress rehearsal.

He searched the crowd. His mother caught his eye and walked to him.

"Nikhil! You missed the rehearsal! The Collinses were asking for you." His mother's admonishment hardly landed.

"My interview ran long. I couldn't very well leave in the middle of it." He inhaled. "It's work. I'll make nice with Jake's parents. I promise." He scanned the room as he spoke.

His mother pressed her lips together, following his gaze. "What is so important you can't focus on what I'm telling you?"

"Nothing." He turned to face his mother. He certainly wasn't looking for his ex-wife.

The restaurant decor was simple and understated, and Jake's father, Michael, had proclaimed the food to be phenomenal. The band was actually quite good, and Nikhil found himself humming the tune to himself.

Anita was in the center of the room, surrounded by his mother's friends, when she caught his gaze. She looked like prey being hunted. She widened her eyes at him and bit her bottom lip. It had always been their unofficial sign for 'get me out of here!' He found himself smiling at her and motioning to the bar. When she nodded, he headed for the bar to grab them drinks. He was waiting for their Manhattans when a familiar voice reached him.

"Nikhil Joshi." The voice was smooth and confident, and it made the hairs on the back of his neck stand up.

Jalissa Sheth. What in the hell was she doing here? And why did his family feel the need to surprise him with every woman he'd had a relationship with? He turned to face her. She was laser focused on him and sauntered closer until she was leaning against the bar next to him. She was wearing a low-cut green cocktail dress, her dark hair cascading around her shoulders.

He narrowed his eyes. "What are you doing here, Jalissa? It's family only."

She shrugged. "I must be family."

"Whatever." Thankfully the bartender put two Manhattans in front of him. Nikhil picked them up and started to walk away from Jalissa.

"It seems talk about your divorce is exaggerated." She nodded in Anita's direction.

Nikhil clenched his jaw. "What do you want, Jalissa?"

"Well, I had hoped to make amends." She stepped closer to him, resting a hand on his chest. "We ended things—poorly."

Nikhil laughed. "Are you serious right now? You dropped me like a hot potato as soon as my family hired you."

"That's an extremely simplistic way of putting it, Nicky."

"No. It's an exact way of putting it." Nikhil stepped back so her hand would drop. "It's Nikhil. And it's over." He turned away from the nightmare that was Jalissa and scanned the room for Anita.

When he finally caught sight of Anita, it was like finding oxygen after talking to Jalissa. She was easily the most beautiful woman in the room, gorgeous in a simple black cocktail dress that skimmed her curves, leaving one shoulder open. Her hair was curly and swept over to one side, revealing her neck and bare shoulder. Nikhil walked over to join her.

She was being given the third degree by some of his mother's friends about why they didn't have children. Neepa-masi was very interested in the topic in particular. "You have been married nearly five years." She smiled as she directed her conversation at Anita. "It is time. You aren't getting any younger."

Before either of them could respond, a squeal at the door grabbed everyone's attention. Nikhil recognized it immediately. Deepa-masi, his mother's middle sister.

Neepa-masi made a beeline for her sister, embracing her and taking her in. "So great you made it!"

"Of course! I wouldn't miss it!"

"You missed the mehndi and grah shanti." Nikhil's mother had approached. "And the rehearsal."

"Good to see you, too, Seema." Deepa-masi rolled

her eyes. "I couldn't get a flight any earlier and traveling from the West Coast takes all day."

Neepa-masi put her arm around her younger sister. "It doesn't matter. You're here now. Come. Papa has been asking about you."

"Of course. Why would it matter to miss the beginning of my daughter's wedding?" his mother mumbled.

The two women swept past Nikhil's mother like she wasn't even there. Dada greeted Deepa with open arms and hugs. That's how it was. Deepa-masi was the middle child; she could do no wrong. Total opposite of his family.

"Some things never change." Jalissa was standing on his other side, her hand on his bicep. Nikhil had been watching his mother and hadn't noticed her coming up to him.

Anita glanced at her, her face darkened as she swept her gaze over Jalissa's hand on him.

"Hi. I'm Anita Joshi." Anita extended her hand to Jalissa.

Nikhil stared at Anita. Even when they were married, she went by Anita Virani. Was she staking a claim right now? Why would she even care?

"Jalissa Sheth." Jalissa let go of his bicep to shake Anita's hand. "I had heard it wasn't Joshi anymore." She smiled in what to anyone else would appear to be a sweet manner. Nikhil saw it for it was. Challenge.

Anita smiled back equally sweetly. "Clearly you heard wrong."

Jalissa took her hand back and glanced at Nikhil. "Clearly. Good seeing you, Nicky." She dragged her fingers over his arm as she walked away.

Anita raised an eyebrow at him. "Nicky?"

He shook his head and grumbled. "Not now."

"Nicky." Rocky came striding over, clearly agitated.

"Nikhil," Anita corrected.

Nikhil did a double-take at her, before facing his brother to see what he had done wrong now. "Rock."

"You totally missed the rehearsal." Rocky was flabbergasted. "How could you do that? You have to know where to stand, and when to walk—"

"How hard is that?" Nikhil dismissed his brother's concerns. "Anyway, I had a work thing that ran long. So, I'm sorry. But that was important. I'd think that you and Mom of all people would understand work being a priority."

"Nicky—"

"Nikhil," Anita stated as she sipped her Manhattan.

"This is family—it's more important than work." Rocky narrowed his eyes as if he were speaking to an idiot.

"Since when?" Nikhil stared at his brother, speechless for a moment. His whole life, he'd heard that work was the most important thing. Anything having to do with JFL always took precedence. "Or maybe because my work isn't associated with JFL it's not as important?"

"No. Mom and I aren't working these few days either."

"You took off for Tina's wedding?" Nikhil couldn't believe what he was hearing.

"Yes. And before you think about it too hard, we all took off when you got married, too," Rocky stated.

"You went in late," Nikhil corrected.

"We were there," Rocky insisted.

"Damn, Rocky, who *are* you?" Nikhil shook his head.

"Me? Who are *you*, Nicky?" Rocky shot back.

"Nikhil." Anita turned to face Rocky. "His name

is Nikhil. How hard is that to remember? He's your brother, for god's sake!" Anita spit out.

Rocky looked like he'd been slapped. Nikhil took the opportunity to take Anita's hand and walk away. "That was awesome. Did you see his face?" Nikhil laughed and squeezed her hand. He snapped his gaze to her when she squeezed it back.

"He's right, though," she whispered when they had made it back to the bar. "It's your sister's wedding. Maybe don't schedule work things."

"I only have one more thing. Saturday afternoon. But it's huge. My agent actually called to tell me about it. This publisher we have been after has finally agreed to meet with me to talk about my potential future with them. This publisher can offer everything I've ever wanted. So it's a big deal."

Anita sipped her drink. "I'm happy for you—honestly—but it's your sister's wedding."

"I thought you'd be all for it. Finally seeing me work." Nikhil smirked at her, all of his gratitude at her for standing up to Rocky gone. "I believe the word *lazy* was used more than once at the end of our marriage."

Anita just stared at him. She shook her head at him, her lips twisted in disgust. "Is that what you got out of it? That's what you remember about the end of our marriage? That I used the word *lazy*?" She inhaled deeply. "You know what? That bitch in the green dress can have you."

"What the hell does that mean? You're leaving this farce?" What was she so mad about? She was the one who left. His next words belied the surge of panic that rushed through him at the thought that she might actually leave. But he bit them out anyway. "Feel free."

He remembered much more than the words she'd

used. What haunted him in those moments that he thought about the divorce were the words he never used. Words like *I'm here for you. Go for it. Do what makes you happy.*

Her eyes hardened. "No. I'm not leaving. Not until this wedding is over."

"Don't you mean not until you get your tuition money?" Until he said it, he didn't realize how much that hurt him. That she was only here for a payoff.

Familiar sadness and pain flickered in her eyes before she hardened them again.

It didn't matter if he spoke or not. He was always hurting her.

Anita turned away from Nikhil. Blood pounded in her ears, her heart raced and she was sure her jaw was clenched so tight it might never open again. Many things were said at the end of their marriage. But that hadn't been the point. Nikhil had been clueless then, and he was clueless now.

She couldn't even look at him right now. Green Dress was watching them from across the room. If Anita stomped off right now, they risked their little ruse being exposed. Or it would just look like a husband and wife having an argument. Though the look on Green Dress Bitch's face said she was on to them anyway. Anita stayed put, not looking at her ass of an ex-husband.

He was right. She had said he was lazy. He had quit a nicely paying job at a local bar so he could concentrate on his writing, while Anita worked two jobs. Which she really did not have a problem with. She knew he would be successful one day. The problem was when she had decided that she wanted to go to law school and he flipped out.

* * *

"Why would you want to be a lawyer?" Nikhil had looked up from his computer to ask this question.

She had gone to him, excitement bubbling out from her. "You should have seen it. This family lost their daughter to DUI. Priscilla Herrera found the driver and prosecuted. The family got closure. I want to do that."

Nikhil had not said much at the time, but over the next few weeks, Anita would come home with information on classes she needed to take, scheduling of the LSAT, which schools were best, and each time she brought it up, he became more and more distant. Until one night she had called him on it.

"What's going on here, Nikhil? I feel like you're not on board with the law school route."

"I'm not. I've seen this my whole life. My mom, my brother, my sister, everything revolves around JFL. They miss everything and anything, if JFL needs something. I can see you going down that road, and it scares me."

"That won't happen. I probably won't even work for JFL—"

"Ha! Like you'll have a choice. The family will get their hooks in you. They already have." Nikhil had dismissed her.

His dismissal of their discussion and her dreams had infuriated her. He was supposed to love her, shouldn't he have been supporting her? "Well, at least I won't be sitting around all day staring at my computer, doing nothing," she had retorted, biting the words out in anger.

"Are you calling me lazy?"

"If the shoe fits."

Not her finest moment.
Not really his either.

Anita watched Jalissa walk around. She was drop-dead gorgeous in a low-cut, curve-hugging cocktail dress. Anita swore the woman was swaying her hips with the knowledge that Nikhil was watching her. A quick glance at Nikhil confirmed that he was.

Well, she couldn't really blame him. The woman was clearly interested in him, and she was beautiful. What Anita could not understand was her urge to gouge the woman's eyes out. Nor did she have an explanation for why she introduced herself as a Joshi. It was like she was marking her territory. Except that he really wasn't her territory at all. And if she had been married to Nikhil for real, she never would have staked her territory anyway. It wasn't her style.

In any case, Nikhil was clearly irritated and didn't want to talk about it, so she dropped it. She sipped her Manhattan.

"I was insensitive." Nikhil faced the bar, next to her. His suit jacket brushed against her bare arm. "I didn't want you to work for JFL." His soft tone surprised her after the words they had just spit at each other.

"I got that. But here you are, doing exactly what you hated your family for doing."

"It's not the same thing." He swirled his drink.

"What do you mean?"

"I mean—"

"Hey, you two! Give Deepa-masi some hugs!"

Deepa-masi was the most fun of the sisters. She was married with a couple children who were still in college. Her husband traveled quite a bit for work, frequently leaving Deepa-masi on her own, which she did not seem to mind.

"Deepa-masi." Nikhil turned to greet her with a hug. "Good to see you."

Deepa-masi glanced at their joined hands. "Here you are! Look at you two. Still honeymooning." She hugged them both. "You haven't made it out west yet. I'm waiting."

"Soon, Masi. I promise," Anita said. There she went again, making promises she knew she wouldn't be keeping.

"Well, I was hoping to come out here for a baby shower." She grinned at Anita.

"Oh, we're not ready for that quite yet," Anita responded.

"She's in law school," Nikhil added. "She wants to focus on that."

"That's nice." Neepa-masi was back. "But keep in mind your priorities."

"Their priorities are just fine," Seema-auntie interjected, coming up behind her sister.

Anita stared at all three sisters. She couldn't remember seeing them all together like this. They must have been for the wedding reception the Joshis had had for them, but Anita met so many people that day, it was hard to remember.

In any case, it was clear to Anita that Neepa-masi and Deepa-masi, the oldest and the middle, were quite close, while Seema seemed to simply tolerate them. Or maybe it was the other way around.

"Come," Seema-auntie spoke to her sisters, "let's get a drink."

Anita simply stared as the sisters walked away. "What the hell was that?" she said, turning to Nikhil, their earlier tensions having subsided with the appearance of the masis. Nikhil had his lips pressed together, trying not to laugh.

"Is this funny for you?" Anita exclaimed. She tried

to sound indignant, but a smile fell across her face as a chuckle escaped Nikhil.

"I mean, come on. Yes." He shook his head. "You're in law school, doing very well, I'm sure. And all they can focus on is when you're planning on having a family. And then they use that as a reason to one-up each other. The best is that now, you're the one getting bent out of shape." He leaned in close to her ear. "And we're not even married."

"Well, they don't know that." She shouldn't, but she leaned into him, his breath sending goose bumps up and down her spine.

They shared a chuckle, before looking at each other again. "Do you think we would have had children by now?" he asked.

Anita twisted her rings. She had thought she might be a mother by now. She shrugged. "Maybe." She looked up at him.

He grinned. "Two boys."

"And a girl." She smiled back. "Maybe two." That had been their plan. She had loved the idea of a big family, an always-full house. They had lain awake some nights, naked and spent, thinking about the children they would have, what they would name them.

Nikhil held her gaze.

"Nikhil." Michael Collins, Jake's father, walked over and offered Nikhil his hand. Nikhil shook it. "Good to see you. Books are doing well." He beamed at him, just as his wife came up to them as well.

"Mr. Collins, so sorry to have missed the rehearsal. I was on an interview that ran long and—"

"Nikhil Joshi, do not worry one bit about it. You can make it up to me with an early copy of your next book." Christi Collins squeezed his hands. "I absolutely love your books. I can't wait for the next one. Bestsellers, all of them!"

Nikhil grinned. "Done! And thank you."

She fixed him in her gaze. "And we would not say no to a song."

"Mrs. Collins—" Nikhil started to protest. But Anita knew it wouldn't take much to convince him to sing. He loved it.

"Christi. And I won't take no for an answer."

"He'd be happy to sing tonight," Anita interjected. "He should. He missed the rehearsal."

"It's all set then." Mrs. Collins cut her eyes to Anita. "Good to see you again, Anita. I've heard so much about you."

"Have you?" Anita asked, glancing at Nikhil. Surely Jake's parents know about the divorce.

Christi pulled Anita into a hug. "I have." She whispered, "Tina always talks so fondly about how close you two were." Christi pulled back, a smile on her face. "You are good to come and do this for Seema. She was quite distraught."

Unexpectedly, tears burned Anita's eyes. "Well, they're a good family. Though I will say, Tina is quite—"

"Don't get me started on Tina," Michael interrupted. "I couldn't ask for a better daughter-in-law."

Christi smiled at her husband and rolled her eyes a bit. "They like to test wits, my husband and Tina, and it literally makes his day."

"Good luck with that, Mr. Collins." Nikhil grinned. "I never win. In fact, no one in my family has."

"Well, they should all know better than to take me on." Tina smiled at the group as she and Jake joined them.

Michael shook his head, grinning. "She's a tough one, Jake."

"Ms. Virani?" A young woman's voice called to her from behind Tina.

Anita shifted her position to see who had called her name. A young woman in a waiter's outfit approached her, an empty tray in hand.

"Yes." Anita could not place the petite woman.

"You may not remember me, but you helped my dad get disability when he was injured on the job. From the law clinic, downtown?"

Anita smiled. "Yes, of course. Megan, isn't it? How's your dad doing now?"

"Much better, thanks. He should be back to work in a week or two." The young woman sighed relief. "Your help with that made all the difference."

"I'm so glad to hear that. Please give him my best." Anita squeezed Megan's hand before she left.

"You work at the law clinic?" Nikhil asked.

Anita nodded. "Well, I'm an unpaid intern. I love the work, and it's great experience. I'm hoping they'll hire me when I graduate."

"Well, if they don't, I'm sure JFL will," Jake said. "We've been trying to get a community division going forever."

"That's generous, but Jake, the firm is not affordable." Anita shrugged, and sipped her drink.

"No, that's the point. We'd all be taking a couple cases basically pro bono to give back to the community, but we need someone to run that. You'd be great," Jake insisted.

Anita beamed. "Really? So I could do all that work for the community and you all would help, and we wouldn't charge?"

"Yep."

"Is that even possible?" Anita was interested, but it had to be real, not just a thought.

"If you're interested, we'll make it possible." Jake beamed.

She glanced at Nikhil. "I'd love that. But I'd have to think about it. I still have a year left and then there's the bar."

Nikhil pressed his lips together. "I'll get us another round."

"Everyone," Christi said, nodding at the group, "we're seating for dinner now."

"Seriously, Rocky?" Nikhil was pissed but trying not to draw attention. "What the hell is Jalissa doing here?" They were at the bar waiting for drinks, while dinner was being served.

"It wasn't my idea." Rocky pressed his lips together.

"Why would I believe you? You're the one who hired her," Nikhil said.

"How was I supposed to know she'd dump you after she got the job?" Rocky sipped his drink and cast his gaze around the room.

"Well, you didn't fire her." And now they were offering Anita a job. Good thing they weren't together anymore.

"You know we couldn't do that. It opened us up to retaliation." Rocky shook his head.

What Nikhil knew was that a woman he thought he loved had used him to get a job in his family's company, then dumped him within six months. Granted they had started dating while she was in law school. The family took her on as an intern and hired her upon graduation, pending passing the bar. She passed the bar, secured her position, and then dumped him. And his family kept her on. He met Anita a few months after that breakup.

He couldn't stop himself from watching Jalissa throughout the night. Something about her presence made him uncomfortable because he couldn't place why she would even want to be here. So it was best to know what the enemy might be up to.

Christi Collins took the mic. "We have a treat tonight. As your dinners are being served, our daughter-in-law-to-be's brother is going to treat us to a song." She smiled in Nikhil's direction, and he raised a glass to her.

Great. What had he agreed to? Actually Anita had volunteered him.

"In any case," Rocky whispered in his ear, "you're supposed to be married, so stop watching her." Rocky looked him in the eye.

Nikhil shook his head at his brother. "I have to sing now." He widened his eyes in mock innocence and went to take the mic from Mrs. Collins. Turning to the crowd, he thought for a moment before speaking.

"This is a song you all know, but it is my wish for my sister and her new husband in their new life together, that they have a love and life that is all these things." He nodded at the band and began.

He sang about new beginnings and reasons for living. Anita stood in the back, next to one of the bridesmaids, watching him with her whole body. She seemed oblivious to whatever was happening around her.

Without realizing it, he was singing to her again. Telling her his hopes and wishes and there was nothing but the two of them.

No divorce. No fake marriage.

No regrets.

Nikhil and Anita said their goodbyes to the Collins family and headed on home, carpooling with Rocky and Easha. Easha was still barely keeping food down, but she was being a trooper, attending whatever events she could.

"You could just stay back and rest," Rocky was saying as he drove.

"Why? I'm going to be sick whether I'm alone or out here celebrating," Easha insisted.

Rocky took her hand and kept the other on the wheel. "If you're sure."

"I'm sure." She smiled at him.

"Okay then." He lifted their joined hands and kissed her hand.

Nikhil and Anita exchanged looks in the back seat. Rocky? Showing PDA? What was going on in the universe?

When they finally got back to their room, they went about getting ready for bed.

"Do you want the bathroom first?" Nikhil asked.

"Um, no, you go ahead." She pulled out her laptop.

Nikhil went into the bathroom and took off his shirt. He popped his head out. "Are you going to work for my family?" Nikhil blurted out.

"What? I don't know." Anita looked up from her computer. "It still matters to you whether I work for them or not? We aren't even together anymore. And you're more of a workaholic than us all."

"Whatever." Nikhil hoped he sounded nonchalant and went back into the bathroom.

"Okay." Anita appeared at the door. "Why? Why is it such a big deal if I work for JFL? They *are* the biggest practice around here. Their reputation is incredible."

"I don't care." He looked at her in the mirror and began brushing his teeth.

Anita folded her arms across her chest, watching him in the mirror. "It sounds like you might."

"Nope."

The way she stared at him in the mirror, there was no way she believed him. "You never could be happy for me, could you? If there was anything to do with your family, you just couldn't stand it." Anita was fired up.

Nikhil finished brushing his teeth, and wiped his mouth, suddenly very aware of the fact that he was shirtless. "That's not true." But it kind of was. Just not how she was saying it.

"Isn't it, though?"

"Do you honestly believe I was unable to be happy for you?" He watched her in the mirror.

"Yes." Her eyes widened and she threw back her shoulders while raising her chin to him. "I wanted to go to law school, actually follow my passion, and you freaked out. Your family was happy for me, and you couldn't be bothered." She was nearly shouting. "Why do you think I left? And now, you're all bent out of shape because I might work for JFL. They're huge, and you don't work there."

"You left because you thought I wasn't happy for you?" He didn't shout back out of confusion. He had not once said he wasn't happy for her.

"You weren't. You didn't want to talk about law school, or me working at the firm, or anything."

He turned to face her. "I heard you." The memory that was never far from the surface came front and center.

"What are you talking about?" Anita's voice was raised in irritation.

"Back then? I heard you talking to my brother. So *grateful*—" Nikhil made air quotes here "—that he understood you, and that he was helping you with the LSAT. I heard you tell him there was no way that I could understand. As if I wasn't even capable of being happy for you and your success. You had already decided." The bathroom wasn't small, but Nikhil had stepped closer to her to make his point.

"You had told me you didn't like that I wanted to go to law school. Every time I came to you excited about something, you clammed up, which was completely unfair. I was looking for stability—for family—and every time I got close to it, you pulled me back. They're your family. You would think that—"

"That what? That I would be happy for you? I was."

"Did you think there was something going on between me and Rocky?"

"Of course not." Nikhil shook his head. "But it was clear to me that you were getting closer to them. That you shared something with them that you did not share with me." He knew where that led. It started out as small conversations, then led to meals, then the meals ran into the meetings until it was all one meeting, one conversation all day long. He'd seen it happen with his siblings to the point where Nikhil was completely invisible. Or it led to her being offered a job and then ditching him anyway.

"So what was wrong with that?" Anita challenged him.

He stared at her, knowing that if she had joined JFL when they were married, he would have lost his connection to her. He froze, unable to voice his fears that he might not be enough for her, unable to form the words that would confirm that he in fact could never be enough for her.

Because the connection to JFL was stronger than

any other connection there was. That was the lesson he'd learned less than one year after his father's death.

Young Nikhil's nose had pulsed with pain from the punch he'd taken from one of the guys. He had been sure it was bleeding, if not broken. The ominous sound of his mother's heels clunking toward him from the hallway filled his stomach with more apprehension than actually facing down the boys he had fought.

The principal looked up from her desk.

"Mrs. Joshi. I'd like to say it's good to see you, but under the circumstances..." She glanced at Nikhil.

His mother turned to look at him and clenched her jaw. She turned back to the principal. "What happened?"

"He was in a fight with at least three other boys."

"He's suspended?"

The principal nodded. "It's the third time this month."

His mother nodded at the principal and had turned to him at that moment. "Get up." She had handed him a handkerchief, which he had mildly registered as being his dad's. She was silent until they got in the car. She pulled out of the lot before she spoke.

"I'm at my wit's end with you, Nikhil. I am fed up with all the fighting. What has gotten into you?"

He opened his mouth.

"I do not want to hear it. I don't even care at this point. Just stop. Just stop fighting. I do not have time to keep leaving the office to come down here and take care of your mishaps. You're suspended for three days this time. You're coming to the office to do scut work. Your dad never believed in it, but I do. And since he's not here anymore to handle you, you'll do things my way!"

Nikhil had actually been excited at the prospect of

going to the office with his mother. Maybe he'd catch her in a good mood and be able to explain his side of the fight.

But when he had gone to the office with her the next day, she had assigned him to an intern and he didn't see her again until it was time to go home.

He said nothing now, nothing to explain himself, his feelings or fears. Though why he cared if Anita worked for JFL now, he had no idea.

Anita fumed, her eyes registering a sudden realization over coming her. "You have got to be kidding me! You let me go because your family *actually liked me*? That is completely ridiculous." She shook her head in disgust. "I can't believe I married you in the first place."

She turned away from him and marched out of the room.

The door slammed and Nikhil was left shirtless and alone, once again.

Chapter 9

Anita marched down to the kitchen and was greeted by the scent of lemon cleaning products, as the staff put finishing touches on the cleanup and prep for tomorrow. She headed for the bar and poured herself a bourbon—the good stuff, neat, screw the ice. She took the drink and collapsed into one of the oversize leather chairs in the family room.

Floor-to-ceiling windows in this room overlooked a small brook. The night sky was clear midnight blue, leaving the backyard to be lit by the crescent moon. The small brook babbled along happily, as if she hadn't just found out that she was divorced because her husband was jealous of his family. She closed her eyes and inhaled. Though that didn't really make any sense to her. He had his issues with his family, sure, but he loved them just the same.

His almost hypnotic singing voice echoed in her ears. She had been completely mesmerized by him earlier that evening. Every time he sang, she felt as though he sang only to her. There really wasn't anything sexier than a man who could sing like that. She shook her head as if to dislodge his voice and her thoughts. More thoughts came in instead. Memories of him singing to her on their first date. She squeezed her eyes shut against those thoughts.

Three more days. That's all she had to endure. Three more days. Maybe some old feelings for Nikhil would pop up. Hell, maybe they'd never left. But she was done for now.

She sipped her bourbon, staring out at the brook, and that last argument came back to her. Anita had needed law school like she needed breath.

Her world had been turned upside down when her parents were killed. Up until that point, she'd led a charmed life. She had a life plan, a loose one, but a plan nonetheless. She would go to college, start her career, fall in love, get married and have children.

Dilip and Varsha Virani were all about their children's dreams. Amar had always had his—he was almost born a chef. Her parents had encouraged her to find her passion, and that was what she had been searching for when they died.

The fact that she would never be able to share her passion with her parents always left her feeling slightly hollow.

The call from the police at the scene of the auto accident had come to her cell phone. Everything had slowed down and sped up all at the same time. Her first call had been to Amar. She remembered meeting him at the hospital and she hadn't even cried yet. It was as if she had shut down a part of herself so she could function. When the doctors confirmed their parents' deaths, Amar had broken down, but she had felt nothing. Maybe she'd been too numb to comprehend what was happening.

There was the house to take care of, bills and so much more. Amar had been so overcome with grief that he had been barely able to function for a day or two, so she had made all the arrangements. After the funeral, Amar seemed better, and they shared the responsibilities. It made sense for them both to live in the house and finish school while they worked. They had sublet their respective apartments and moved back into their childhood home. That was where Anita lived now, with her brother.

It was almost two months after her parents died that the well-wishers had stopped coming by. It was as if they had done their part, and now the rest of the way was up to her and Amar. It was true, in a way. No one could grieve for them. But it left them feeling…not abandoned, exactly. Just…empty.

Not long after, Anita had gone grocery shopping to get some basics, and something she and Amar could use to cook dinner together. It had felt almost normal to be buying fruit, veggies, milk and cereal. She had even gone to the Indian grocery store to replenish spices. She was unloading the groceries and putting them away when it happened. She started talking to her mother, like she used to when she was a teenager helping to put away groceries. She just went on about this new recipe she'd found online and how they should test it before telling Amar about it.

What do you think, Mom? We could add that tan-

door masala instead of what everyone else uses. Amar
would love it. What do you think? Mom?

She had turned away from the fridge where she was
going to put away the milk to see why her mom hadn't
answered. Then she remembered. Her mother was gone,
and she'd never be able to talk to her like that again.

Just like that, the ground beneath her gave way. She
slid down the fridge to the ceramic tile floor, hard and
cold. The room spun and her stomach roiled. Her foundation, her rock, was gone.

She was shaking when her brother found her, still
clutching the milk, unable to get off the kitchen floor.
Everything around her seemed to move in slow motion, only to suddenly speed up to a pace she couldn't
match. That's when the tears finally came. She had
wrenched out sobs in her brother's arms right there on
the kitchen floor. How long they sat there, she had no
idea. But when she was finally drained, she and Amar
had stayed up talking, not finding sleep until the wee
hours of the morning.

They each found a therapist who guided them
through those first months and stages of loss, but Anita
could not shake the feeling that she was floating through
life with no one or nothing to ground her.

When she'd met Nikhil a couple years later, he
seemed so stable, and his family was so wonderful—
she'd missed the closeness of gathering, the intimacy of
family, and they welcomed her with open arms. They'd
even looked into her parents' case, since the driver of
the vehicle had never been found. She had felt like she
had a foundation again.

Shortly after they married, she'd gone to work as a
secretary in a small law firm that was owned by a friend

of the Joshi family. Her mother-in-law had gone to law school with Priscilla Herrera. The money was good and the Herreras were wonderful to her. She helped with research, and one case involved a hit-and-run. Though it hit close to home, the actual work made her feel grounded again, and she knew that this was what she was meant to do. When she had excitedly told Nikhil about it, he had seemed excited, but there had been a reticence about him.

Soft footsteps sounded over the kitchen tile and she turned, expectant. "Nikhil?"

"No. Rocky." Rocky was the same height as Nikhil, but with a slighter build, and the same Bollywood movie-star good looks. Right now, he was in shorts and a T-shirt and carried a glass of bourbon.

"Hey." Disappointment filled her. Huh.

"No need to sound so excited," he joked, sitting down on the sofa beside the chair. He took a gulp of his bourbon and nodded at hers. "What's your excuse?"

Anita glanced around to see if anyone else was wandering around. No one was there. Even the staff had finished up. "I'm sharing a room with my pain-in-the-ass ex-husband. What about you?"

Rocky laughed. "You win. I needed to relax before going to bed. I worry about Easha." He took another gulp. "Let me guess. He doesn't want you to work for the firm."

"How'd you know?"

"I know my little brother. He's had a chip on his shoulder his whole life." Rocky was dismissive. "Not to mention Jalissa."

"Let's not mention Jalissa," Anita nearly snapped. The mere mention of that woman had Anita seeing green.

Rocky raised his eyebrows at her. She shrugged. "Or maybe the chip is because you are a very hard act to follow."

"That is bullshit. Our parents loved us all the same. Nicky—"

"Damn it, Rocky, he's not a kid anymore. You know he hates when you call him Nicky, and you do it all the time."

Rocky held his hands up in surrender. "When he acts grown-up, I'll reconsider. *Nikhil*—" he rolled his eyes at her "—is actually lucky he didn't have to be the first-born. There was never even a question as to whether I would go into law. It was always assumed I would."

"It wasn't the same for Nikhil?" She drank some of the amber liquid, relishing the warmth as it went down.

"I don't know. But what I do know is that Nikhil made it be known, early on, that he had no interest in going to law school. That he was going to follow his heart. It's a luxury in this family, being able to follow your heart." Rocky looked into his drink. "And damn if he didn't do it. Three books in. Already a bestseller." Rocky shrugged and Anita caught some brotherly pride there.

"How's Easha holding up?"

Rocky grinned. "Best she can. She's still nauseous and throwing up. Don't say anything, huh? To anyone outside the immediate family. About the baby."

"Of course." She didn't bother to correct the fact that she wasn't really family at all. Maybe it was pretend, but she could at least enjoy being a pretend part of the family for a few days.

She was pathetic.

He glanced at his watch. "I should get back to her."

He threw back the last of his bourbon. "Listen. Thanks. For doing this for Mom. I know Nicky isn't easy."

"Actually, *Nikhil* is fine." Not sure why she felt the need to defend him, but there it was. "Mom—Seema-auntie," Anita corrected herself, "didn't tell Neepa-masi and Deepa-masi about the divorce?"

"Hell no. They would be the last ones to know." Rocky shook his head.

"Why?"

"It's like she feels like she has to prove to them that she can be good at things." He shrugged. "Like they underestimate her all the time. I think it got worse when Dad died and they couldn't understand why Mom wouldn't just sell JFL and take a salary."

"But she wanted to maintain JFL. I mean, she loved it—she loved the law. She had lost her husband. She didn't want to lose her dreams, too. If anything, she wanted her dreams even more." Anita could completely understand.

"I remember phone arguments over the years with the masis asking her to come to India, and Mom being unable to go for more than a week at a time, because she had to take care of things here. Although, I suspect on some level, she didn't want to have to deal with her sisters." Rocky sighed, sadness coming over his eyes. "When Dadi fell ill, a year ago, she left things to me and went to India for a few weeks. Dadi passed a week after Mom returned home. She'd been with her mother for weeks and still wasn't at her side when she passed, and her sisters were unsympathetic.

"Mom went back to India when Dada had his heart attack six months ago. She stayed for a month to care for him and then returned. Granted, Neepa-masi took the brunt of caregiving, but Mom offered to bring Dada back with her. Neepa-masi wouldn't allow it. She babies Dada. Mom can't stand that."

He stood. "Anyway, that's the abridged version. She won't want them to know about the divorce because it'll make her look like she can't handle her own children. They'll say she allowed shame to come to the family." He shook his head. "She's already hounded me to be able to tell them about the baby. So she can brag about being a dadi. But I can't, not yet."

"Rakesh Joshi, what aren't you telling me?" She looked up at her former brother-in-law, her chin up, jaw set. She was getting an answer.

He sighed. "Easha had a miscarriage a few months ago, and it really tore her up." He paused, and Anita caught tears in his eyes.

"It tore you both up," Anita said softly.

He nodded. "Yes. Well." He cleared his throat and looked at her, his eyes still wet. "We just want to be *sure,* just pass the first trimester before we say anything, you know."

"Sure, Rocky." She stood and hugged him. "It'll be fine. I heard that morning sickness is a good sign."

"Really?"

She shrugged. "I have no idea. But it sounds good." She grinned.

Rocky smiled and hugged her again. "It's great having you around." He glanced once more at the time. "I really have to go. Good luck with Nicky." Rocky wished her good-night and left.

"Nikhil," she corrected him as he ran off. Anita returned to staring out the window and sipping her drink.

"Hey."

This time, she recognized his voice, and it sent a warmth through her. She turned to Nikhil and found him holding two glasses of bourbon. He had changed into shorts and a T-shirt, and his hair was pleasantly tousled. Her insides turned to goo, as held out a glass to her, his voice as smooth as the alcohol he offered. "Peace offering."

She raised her still half-full glass to him, and he shrugged and poured half of the extra drink into her glass, and the other half into his and leaned back against the bar. She swiveled the chair around to face him.

He was calmer, as was she.

Silence floated between them. "I just heard about the miscarriage."

Nikhil nodded and sipped his drink. "Anita… I owe you an explanation. I wasn't jealous of you and the family. It's just—my whole life, everything was about JFL. It was more important than anything."

"What happened with Jalissa?" Anita asked.

He sighed and stared into his glass before looking at her with his response. "We dated while she was in law school, before I met you. Then my family offered her a job at the firm. She took it. Six months later, she dumped me."

Anita knew there was a reason she hadn't liked her on sight. "They couldn't fire her."

He set his jaw. "Well, that's what they said."

"You really loved her?"

"Not like I loved you," he mumbled into his drink and flushed.

"You were afraid I'd leave if I worked for your family." She stood, looked him closely in the eye.

Nikhil shrugged, unable to meet her eyes. "You left anyway, so the joke's on me." He gulped his drink.

"I never actually had any regret over marrying you." She sipped her bourbon. "Remember our city hall ceremony?"

He nodded, this time looking at her.

"Happiest day of my life," she blurted out without thinking.

His eyes never left her. "Mine, too."

"We just—didn't work." She closed her eyes. The pain in his face, just now, was real.

The sliver of moon provided enough light that she could just see him. She stepped closer to him. The bourbon relaxed and warmed her. She was close enough to feel the heat from his body. He was leaning, his back slouched against the bar.

"You really thought you would lose me if I went to law school?"

He nodded, his gaze still fixed on her.

"We had some good times, though, didn't we?" she asked.

His perfect lips curved into a smile. "We did."

"Remember how we used to cook together?" she asked.

He stared at her, his eyes darkening, and she knew he was thinking about the times they would spend the weekend making love, dressing only to make themselves some food, before discarding their clothes and returning to their bed. Or wherever.

She cleared her throat. "I mean when we used to tweak old recipes from our moms and grandmothers."

He nodded, amusement falling across his face. "They didn't technically have recipes…"

"True." She grinned. "But we figured it out, adding things, whatever."

"That was your talent. You were good at figuring out all of that. Must be in the genes—your brother always loved what we came up with." He was smiling full-on right now. Anita loved that smile.

She shook her head. "Nah—I remember you being pretty good yourself."

"We said we would write a cookbook. Like an homage to our moms and grandmoms." He smiled with the memory, and Anita hadn't seen him this relaxed since she had shown up.

She couldn't look away. Maybe it was the moonlight. Maybe it was the apology. She was drawn to him as ever before. Kissing him yesterday had been…an accident. Kissing him now, on purpose, would be a mistake. It would be a really, really good mistake. But a mistake nonetheless. Her heart raced as he pushed away from the bar and moved closer to her. Could she kiss him and still walk away? She tilted her head up to him. She was about to find out.

The lights flicked on in the kitchen. Anita stepped back from Nikhil, squinting to see who had saved her from herself.

Tina.

The bride-to-be stood there in loose shorts and a T-shirt, her hair in a messy bun, her arms folded tightly across her chest, shoulders slumped. "I need you guys to come with me and tell Mom the wedding's off." Then she burst into tears.

Chapter 10

Nikhil wasn't happy to hear his sister sobbing, but she saved him from kissing his ex-wife.

Again.

He and Anita looked at each other and went into action. Nikhil poured his sister a bourbon while Anita tried to get her to sit down.

"I'm not sitting down." She glared at her brother.

"Well, we're not coming with you until we hear what happened." He held out the bourbon to her.

She looked from him to Anita and back. "You two always were a united front." She sighed and sat down as she took the bourbon. "I don't know what happened behind closed doors, but you were a force when you were on the same side."

Nikhil flicked his gaze quickly at Anita, but she was determinedly looking at Tina.

They waited until Tina had a sip. Then Anita spoke first. "What happened?"

Tina's deep inhale spoke of all the drama of a bride unable to come to terms with her groom. "He doesn't want me to change my name."

Nikhil and Anita stared at Tina for a minute in silence and blinked. "But I thought you wanted to keep Joshi as your last name." Anita spoke slowly as if her normal cadence might spook the young bride.

"I do." Tina looked at them like they were the idiots for not understanding.

"Help me out here. I'm just a guy," Nikhil said.

She sighed deeply again and took a sip of her drink. "We were talking about last names. And I said, 'What about hyphenating?'" She looked at Anita, for support it seemed, because Anita nodded and Tina continued, "Like Joshi-Collins."

"Okay." Nikhil had no idea where this was going.

"And he said, 'Why do you want to do that? Just keep Joshi,' and I said, 'Why? Don't you want me to be a Collins?' And he said, 'Why do you want to be a Collins? I thought you were just keeping Joshi.'"

At this point, Nikhil had no idea what was happening, but Anita nodded with deep understanding. "Somebody enlighten me."

Anita pressed her lips together and looked at him like he was a child. "She's upset because she wants him to *want* her to change to Collins, even though he knows that she's keeping Joshi."

Tina frowned and nodded. "So you see? We can't get married."

"I don't see," Nikhil said. "You're getting what you want. He's supporting whatever decision you make. It's your name, and he's in favor of what you want." Maybe he needed another drink.

"God, Bhaiya. You really don't understand anything, do you?" Tina rolled her eyes.

"See, Tina?" Anita grinned. "Sometimes, guys don't get it. Even when you spell it out for them. Nikhil is the perfect example of not getting it."

Hey. Wait a minute. He opened his mouth to protest, but Anita shot him a look that told him to shut it and shut it fast. "It doesn't mean he doesn't love you. Maybe you just need to talk. Weddings are stressful—"

"Tina." Jake's voice came from the front door. "Tina?"

Tina's eyes widened and she turned to face him as he entered the kitchen.

Anita leaned over to Nikhil. "Uh, how did he get in here?" she whispered.

He smiled, whispering back, "You kidding? He's practically been family for ages now. He's had a key and the codes to the house for months." Nikhil rolled his eyes. "He's here more than me."

"Tina. You didn't talk to your mom yet, did you?" Jake was in athletic shorts and a T-shirt and flip-flops and he was slightly out of breath. His hair was tousled and his green eyes held panic. He'd clearly rushed over here as fast as he could.

"Not yet." But Tina's voice was soft and had lost all the angst and determination of five minutes ago.

Jake sighed relief. "Oh thank god. Listen. I would *love* for you to be a Collins, if that is what you want." He walked toward her until he could touch his hand to her face. "It would be an honor to share my name with someone as amazing as you. But it's your name. You do what feels right for you. Either way, you're part of my family, the same way I'm part of yours. My parents will love you, the same way your mom loves me. Regardless of what your last name is. I love you either way. We're family. That's how it is."

"You came all the way out here to tell me that?"

"Well, yes. I want us to be married." He frowned, clearly upset. "Were you—are you—going to call it off?"

Tina fell into his arms.

Nikhil whispered to Anita, "Isn't that what I said?" She shushed him.

Nikhil cleared his throat. "So, everyone, still getting married?"

Tina wrapped an arm around her fiancé, and turned to them, grinning broadly. "Yes." She turned a look of complete adoration on Jake, before turning back to Nikhil and Anita.

"I just wanted it to be like—like the way our family loved her." Tina focused on Nikhil as if Anita suddenly wasn't even there. "Mom loved her like she was one of us."

It was true. Seema Joshi had always treated Anita like she was one of her children, not an in-law. Anita had always felt loved and accepted by the family. She had missed them dearly when she divorced their son.

"They absolutely liked you better than they liked me." Nikhil turned to Anita. "That's for sure, regardless. They still like you better." Nikhil shook his head, a small smile on his face.

"It's true." Tina nodded, finally looking at Anita.

"Well, I have no doubt that the same is true for the Collinses as Jake has said," Anita said. "Though be careful using us as a bar to measure by." Anita elbowed

Nikhil and laughed. "Because in the end, it didn't really work out."

Nikhil's eyes widened. Tina's head snapped up and flicked her gaze between them both. Nikhil seemed horrified, but then broke out into a half smile. "I mean..." He shrugged. "She's not wrong."

Jake joined Anita's laughter. "I'm never letting this one go." He squeezed his fiancée tight.

Tina's eyes widened. She didn't seem to think this was funny. "You two are unbelievable."

Nikhil just stared at Jake. He had let Anita go. Why had he done that? What had been more important than having her in his life? He absolutely couldn't remember.

"Nikhil. Nikhil." Tina was waving a hand in front of his face. "Good night."

He snapped out of it and nodded. "Good night. See you at wedding number one." He forced a smile, still lost in his own thoughts.

Tina and Jake left the kitchen, arm in arm.

"Well, crisis averted," said Anita softly. The two of them were alone, in the now brightly lit kitchen. While Nikhil rinsed out the glasses, he thought about how close they'd come to a near disaster. Maybe it was the moonlight, maybe it was the bourbon or maybe it was the reminiscing, but here in the stark light of the kitchen in the middle of the night, he knew he should not be kissing Anita Virani.

He never should have let her go, so now he certainly did not deserve to have her back. If he kissed her, he wouldn't want to stop.

While Nikhil changed for bed in his ample walk-in closet, Anita was checking email on her phone. When he came out in just his shorts, he found Anita sitting on the bed, staring at her phone, a melancholy look on her face.

"What's up?"

"Nothing." She looked up, her eyes glassy. He glanced at her phone. She had been looking at a picture of her parents. Dilip and Varsha Virani had been a handsome couple. The photo she had pulled up was from her high school graduation. Proud parents on either side of their young grad and big brother towering over them behind her.

"They were already gone for over a year when I graduated from college. Amar was there, and Divya. We weren't even going to take pictures, but Divya insisted." Anita shook her head. "She's good like that."

He donned a T-shirt as he sat down next to her. "Doesn't get easier, does it?" He recalled holding her as she had marked Mother's Day and Father's Day and birthdays and anniversaries without her parents. Just as he had marked many of those days without his own father.

She looked back at the photo. He put his arm around her shoulders and squeezed her to him as he mentally reviewed the date. He chided himself for not remembering sooner. "Your mom's birthday. Jeez, Anita. I'm sorry I didn't remember."

She shook her head, wiping her eyes. "No. It's okay. I couldn't face it today. I just—" She let out a sob. "What kind of daughter does that? I didn't even call my brother today. He called and I ignored it because I didn't want to talk to him about why I'm here."

"Call him now." Nikhil nodded at the phone.

"It's almost midnight."

"So what?"

She stared at her phone for a moment.

"He's your brother. If anyone knows what you're going through, it's him." Nikhil kissed the top of her head without thinking.

She nodded at him and calmed her breathing before tapping his number on her phone. "Hey, Amar."

Nikhil removed his arm from her shoulders to give her privacy. She grabbed his hand before he could stand and motioned for him to stay next to her.

"Sorry I missed your call earlier. I…forgot what day it was. Well, I didn't really forget. I just couldn't…"

She nodded and her eyes filled with tears. Nikhil scribbled something on a sticky note: "Dance while she cooked?" She smiled.

"Remember that time we caught her dancing in the kitchen?" She laugh-sobbed. "Celery!"

She nodded at whatever he was saying, a smile coming through her tears. "No. It was 'I Will Survive,' remember?" She laughed at something he said. "Mom had moves!" She wiped her eyes dry and leaned on Nikhil's shoulder.

"Church and reception tomorrow." She nodded at whatever he was saying. "So a different caterer tomorrow?… Okay… You're working the Indian ceremony and the sangeet-garba reception on Saturday?… So, I'll see you then… Miss you… Will do." She tapped the phone off and looked at him. "Thanks for that. And for sitting with me."

"No problem."

She fidgeted with her phone for a moment before looking at him. "You don't really have to, you know, since we really aren't anything to each other."

Nikhil had no answer for that, so he said nothing about it. "What was the *Will do*?"

She rolled her eyes and shook her head as she sniffled. "He wants me to say hi to Divya if I talk to her."

Nikhil widened his eyes. "Divya, huh?"

Anita turned and sat cross-legged on the bed facing him. "He's got it bad. Though he'll never admit it."

"Did you tell Divya?"

Anita dropped her mouth open in horror. "Sibling code. No way. Besides, he's never actually even admitted it to me."

She glanced at the sticky note in her hand. "Mom was so full of life." She looked at Nikhil. "Too bad you never met her. Or my dad."

"You and Amar used to talk about them so much, I felt like I knew them. Besides, I could never imagine my mother singing and dancing while she cooked, using celery as a mic. She's too stoic."

"Reserved."

"Also—I think the last time she cooked was the night she met you."

"She's a really good cook." Anita turned on the bed to face him. "That can't be the last time she cooked."

Nikhil nodded his head. "And I was surprised even then."

"That was a fun night." Anita grinned.

"Was it, though? Meeting my whole family, all the law talk. And Tina and Rocky arguing. I was surprised you didn't break up with me right then."

"I loved all the law talk. But what I really loved was the loudness and even the arguing. I had missed that sense of family." She paused. "It was nice having it again. Even if it was only for a while." She looked away from him, sadness covering her face again.

"Rocky was pretty pissed when we broke up. Not as angry as Tina, but still." Rocky had bugged his eyes in anger, shaking his head at Nikhil as if he was a complete idiot. *She's the best thing that ever happened to you, schmuck. How could you let her walk? How could you not do everything in your power to keep her?*

His mother had shared the same sentiment. That he was the one at fault for the breakup. It never mattered to them that Anita had been the one who filed for divorce. He had dismissed Rocky's admonition at that time as simply typical Rocky. But he had wondered many times since then if his older brother wasn't right.

Tina had been the only one who seemed to be on his side. The only one who had been angry with Anita. And actually, the only one who still was. His mother and Rocky seemed actually happy that Anita was here, at the wedding. Nikhil had long since passed anger when it came to Anita. He was firmly at longing.

"I think you'd be surprised at what Rocky really thinks of you." She caught his eye.

"I doubt that. He has always made it clear." Nikhil leaned back on to the bed, resting his head on one elbow as he faced Anita.

Anita shrugged. "Has he made it clear that he's proud of you? That he respects you for not falling in line with your parents' expectations?"

Nikhil shook his head in disbelief. "He said that?"

"Maybe you should talk to him yourself." She uncrossed her legs and hopped off the bed. "We should get some sleep. Tomorrow is a long day." She stretched before heading for the bathroom.

He made up the sofa and closed his eyes when he lay down. He heard the water running and imagined her doing her nighttime routine.

He shifted and inhaled deeply, willing sleep to come. It would not. He'd gotten so close to kissing her, but that wasn't all that was keeping him awake. He'd enjoyed their camaraderie in helping Tina, in warding off nosy aunties, in actually making their fake marriage work.

And yes, that almost kiss was definitely keeping him awake.

In a bit, he heard her come out and head toward the sofa. She stopped when she found him there, "asleep." She quietly turned away and he heard her climb into the bed. She always applied lotion before bed, and the clean scent always reminded him of her. It floated to him now, taking him back to when she was his.

DAY THREE:

I DOS AND CHAMPAGNE TOASTS

Make it to the Church on time…

Chapter 11

By the time Anita woke, the sofa was tidy, and Nikhil was not in the room.

Probably on another call. She did not remember him being such a workaholic when they were married. In fact, one of the things she had really loved was his ability to prioritize and know when to work and when to take time off. He seemed to have lost that ability. It was not attractive.

She freshened up and pulled out her laptop and was contemplating coffee when Nikhil entered the room, the aroma of hot chai coming in with him. He had on athletic shorts and a fitted T-shirt, but his hair was still attractively mussed from sleep. He carried two large mugs from which emanated the most luscious aroma. She closed her eyes and inhaled. "That better be your chai, because—"

"You'll only drink my chai in the morning." He grinned at her. "I'm not new."

She nearly grabbed the mug from him and wrapped her hands around it, inhaling and savoring the luxurious aroma of cinnamon, cardamom and clove before she finally indulged in the first life-giving sip. Nikhil really did make the best chai.

She had made chai a few times after the divorce, had even had her brother make it, too. It really wasn't that complicated, but even as a culinary student with a developed sense of taste, he couldn't quite replicate the flavor she remembered. It remained lost to her.

Like so much else she remembered about him...

"Are you ever going to tell me the secret to this chai?" She nearly moaned, closing her eyes.

She opened her eyes to find Nikhil staring at her, his eyes dark. "Nikhil?"

He startled and refocused, a sly grin on his face. "I make my own spice."

Anita widened her eyes. "You mean, you actually grind out the spices and make it yourself?"

"Yes."

"If you had told me that when we were married, I might not have left." She pursed her lips and cocked an eyebrow at him.

He rolled his eyes. "And before you ask, no, I am not going to tell you how I make it, or what I put in it."

"Fine." She took her chai to the desk and sat down in front of her laptop. "I have some work to do before we leave for the church."

"Me too." He pulled out his laptop and made himself comfortable on the sofa.

"We almost kissed last night." Anita tried to keep her tone focused, even businesslike. "Again."

"I know." He looked at her over the top of his laptop.

"That can't happen." Anita was firm.

"Agreed."

"Probably too much alcohol."

"Exactly," Nikhil agreed. "Plus reminiscing…" He waved his hand.

"And we used to be really good together."

Nikhil paused, a slight grin coming over his face. "That is true. We were really good together…" His voice drifted off.

Anita cleared her throat. "Well, it's probably best we don't dwell on that. Nothing good could possibly come of it. Right?"

"Right."

They stared at each other a moment, during which she recalled exactly the good that used to come out of them being together, and she flushed.

She snapped her attention back to her computer. "I need to get this done."

"Okay." He grinned.

They were working in quiet companionship for a while, when her phone buzzed with a text from the clinic. She called in.

"Hey, Marisa."

"Anita, I know you're busy this weekend, but I have Charlotte Montgomery here. She's freaking out about the hardship-stay hearing today. She said the landlord keeps threatening to throw them out on the street."

"Okay. Put her on."

"Hey, Ms. Virani." The young woman's voice was shaky.

"Charlotte, please call me Anita."

"Okay, Ms. Virani."

Anita rolled her eyes. "What's going on?"

"The landlord keeps threatening to throw us out. I told him we're going to court today—but he won't listen. I'm scared and I don't know what to say...and I can't mess this up. My kids and my mom need me." Charlotte's voice cracked, and Anita's heart broke for her. The poor girl probably hadn't even slept in days.

"Okay. I'll be there. Look at the paper—there should be a time on it. Read me the time."

When Charlotte read her the summons, Anita's nerves hummed. She would be cutting it close to the wedding. Still, there was no way she was going to leave her client alone to face an eviction hearing. She'd figure out the timing. "Okay. No problem."

"I'll have to bring the kids," Charlotte said. "There's no one to watch them."

"Even better." Anita grinned. "We'll take them with us."

"Everything okay?" Nikhil asked after she hung up and went straight into her bag for papers.

"Yep. Nothing an email can't handle," she lied. She pressed her lips together, her mind whirring. She had all the paperwork and necessary signatures. She was supposed to be meeting with the landlord on Monday, but he was just being a dick. Finding Charlotte a better place to live was the ultimate goal, but right now, Anita needed to make sure that Charlotte wouldn't be homeless by tomorrow. She could email all the documents, but it really sounded like Charlotte just needed someone by her side to make sure things went smoothly. It was a no-brainer. Anita would simply go down there and attend the hearing with her. And be back in time for the wedding and hope no one noticed.

If she made her hair appointment earlier, and left the dress in the car, she could deliver the papers and be back in time to meet the limo before it left for the church.

She called the hairdresser and changed her time slot. She had been added on to the end at the last minute, so she simply asked to be shifted as early as they could push her. She quickly did her makeup and gathered all her things.

"You're taking the dress to the hair thing?" Nikhil asked.

"Well, sometimes they run late and we want to make sure everyone is ready for pictures. You know." She shrugged, knowing it was a lame excuse.

He studied her closely for a moment, and Anita thought he might be on to her, but he shrugged. "Okay… you better go before you lose your spot in the hair line or whatever is happening over there. The limo is coming here half an hour before the wedding."

"I'll see you then." She grinned and grabbed her bag, which had all her papers and computer in it.

"You're taking that with you?"

She hesitated. She should probably tell him. But didn't she just lecture him on working during the wedding? "It takes time to get hair done. I can get a bit of work done while I sit." She walked out the door, ignoring the pit that was developing in her stomach from her simple lie of omission. Though why it mattered that she was lying to him when they were both being untruthful to a few hundred people this weekend was beyond her. She pushed those thoughts from her mind as she drove to the salon and parked in front.

Only Easha was in the salon with Laila, the hairdresser, when Anita got there. Tina and the other bridesmaids were scheduled for a bit later. Perfect. Anita could get her hair done and sneak out without running into anyone.

Easha had thick dark hair that Laila was teasing and twisting into the same updo they would all have. She hadn't yet put on her makeup, but her brown skin was flawless, except that Easha looked a bit green.

"Can I get you something?" asked Anita. "Ginger tea?"

Easha pointed at the table. "I have some, thanks."

Anita greeted Laila and took a seat. "I'm very excited for you and Rocky. You must be very happy."

Easha nodded. "It's been a long time coming. Just weird timing. The wedding and all that."

"Rocky told me everything," Anita blurted out. "I'm so sorry for your loss."

"Thank you. We're...well, we're excited about this one." She nodded, tears in her eyes. "I'm sorry. I cry all the time. Hormones, I guess." She chuckled through her tears. They sat in awkward silence for a moment. "You know, Nikhil didn't come to Sunday dinner for months after you left."

Easha and Rocky had gotten married a year before Anita and Nikhil. At the time, Anita and Easha were quite friendly, but Easha had been new to JFL and was working all the time. They basically met at Sunday dinners. Anita didn't know what to say with the information Easha was offering her.

"It was Tina who finally dragged him over, and even then, he wouldn't say much and he would leave as soon as possible."

"He used to do that when I was around, too."

Easha shook her head. "No. He was getting better about staying after you two were married for a bit."

"And now?"

Easha shrugged. "Since he's found success in something he loves, he's better. But there's always a loneliness about him." She fixed Anita in her gaze. "I think he misses you."

"But he works all the time now. I mean, I understand working hard, but it's almost like he's scheduling interviews and meetings during the wedding to prove how successful he is."

"Maybe he is. He's always acted like he had something to prove—" Easha met her eyes "—to the people around him. Rocky. You. His mother."

Anita shook her head. "I don't know." That couldn't really be true, could it? "Rocky seems different." Anita changed the subject.

Easha beamed as she nodded. "I think the prospect of becoming parents has changed us both. Like we love our work, but we want to be there for our kids. So we're taking on more associates so we can have some family time."

Anita shook her head. "Who would have thought of Rocky Joshi as a family man? The Rocky I remember was a tough, take-no-bull litigator. It took a while to find his soft side."

"You're telling me." Easha rolled her eyes.

"Even you, Easha-bhabhi. I think you were tougher than him." Anita smiled. How easily Anita called her sister-in-law.

Easha laughed. "I still am tough at work. I've just shifted my priorities." She looked Anita in the eye. "People change."

Anita simply nodded, not taking the bait. Maybe.

Laila finished Easha's hair and motioned Anita to her chair.

Easha gathered her things. "I'm going to carefully lay down and get some rest before the craziness starts." She started for the door and turned back. "You know, neither one of you has ever said that you don't love the other anymore."

Easha's parting words hung in the air while Anita watched her leave. She pulled out her laptop while Laila did her hair and focused on work. She needed to make sure everything was in order for the court hearing today. Laila tugged and twisted Anita's hair into the same updo she'd given Easha.

Hair done, documents gathered, Anita was just leaving when the other bridesmaids all showed up at the same time.

They squealed with delight as they walked in, and literally slammed into her with hugs.

"Oh my god! It's so good to see you," Miki squealed. "Why did you never answer our texts?"

Anita hugged them back. She hadn't seen these ladies since the divorce. "How's the tabla guy?" she teased Anu.

"He's a fantastic kisser. Thank you for asking." Anu grinned, not even trying hide that she'd deceived Anita earlier.

"You didn't have to leave us just because Nikhil was acting like a dick." This was Julie. "Oh, but how cool that you two are getting back together!"

"Yes." Anita nodded. She had forgotten that these ladies thought she and Nikhil were together now but knew that they had been divorced. Hard to keep track

of the lies. "And he wasn't acting like a dick. He was…"
So many things that Anita had not known about. Trying to prove himself. Trying to protect himself. It was too much to think about.

"Well, you'd say that now, anyway. Maybe we'll get to come your wedding soon!" gushed Anu.

Oh god. How was she going to keep all this straight? "Where's Tina?"

"She's on her way."

"Has anyone talked to her today?"

"Why? What's happening?" asked Anu.

"Nothing. I'm fine." Tina's voice from behind them was commanding and joyous, perfectly befitting a bride.

The bridesmaids all squealed like teenagers again as they welcomed the woman of the day. Anita held back, gathering her things. She needed to leave soon if she was going to make it back in time.

"Anita." Tina's voice was soft and without anger.

Anita looked at her. "Congrats. I'm sure all will go well today."

"Thank you for last night." She gave a small smile.

"Of course."

Silence filled the room. "I should go." Anita walked to the door. "I'll see you all at the limo."

Anita parked in front of the courthouse and scanned the area for Charlotte and her children. She got out of the car and saw the young woman, who at twenty-two years old still looked like a teenager, with one toddler on her hip and one by her side. The most adorable, well-behaved twins Anita had ever seen.

Charlotte was a single mom and the only caretaker for her ailing mother. She'd missed a few shifts at her job, because she'd had to accompany her mother to the doctor, so she'd lost several paychecks and as a result was behind on rent. Charlotte's boss was threatening to fire her for not showing up, but Anita would deal with *him* on Monday.

"Hi, Charlotte." Anita grinned and presented her with a coffee and a bagful of bagels that she'd picked up on her way out there. She squinted in the sun, despite her sunglasses, as the humidity threatened her updo.

"Hey, Ms. Virani." Charlotte's face immediately relaxed and she broke out into a huge smile. "Thank you so much for coming."

"Of course." She greeted the children, and they shyly waved to her.

"This is Elizabeth—" she indicated the little girl on her hip "—and Evan," Charlotte said, introducing her children. "Your hair looks nice. You look like you're going to a wedding," commented Charlotte.

"Well, thank you, and I am in fact going to a wedding today. So let's go meet with this judge and secure your apartment. On Monday, we'll talk to your boss."

Charlotte beamed. "Thank you so much." She looked at her kids. "Hear that? Ms. Virani is going to make things all better."

Anita took in the young mother and her two children and butterflies filled her stomach. If this didn't go well, this family would be on the street. She would return to the Joshi mansion and attend her fake sister-in-law's wedding.

What was she thinking? She should have called her boss, let her handle this. But her boss wouldn't have been able to come out like this. She had so many other families just like this who needed her. Anita was Charlotte's only chance.

Anita inhaled deeply and drew up her shoulders, a smile plastered on her face. There simply was no room for a bad outcome here. This family was staying in their apartment while they looked for a more suitable place to live.

"That's right," Anita told the children. "We're not taking no for answer." *Behave like the person you want to be, even if you're not quite there yet, because eventually that's who you will become.* Her father used to say that to her and Amar all the time. Basically, his version of "Fake it till you make it." She certainly did not feel that confident, but there was no alternative.

She took Evan's hand and led the way into the building and found the assigned courtroom. She walked with purpose, as if she did this all the time, when in fact, she had only been here a couple times before. Her dad's voice echoed in her ears. *If you don't believe it, no one else will. So move with purpose and the force of your convictions.* He used to say this to her whenever she was nervous. "No kidding, Dad." She smiled to herself. It was almost as if he was right there with her.

They arrived in the small courtroom just as their case was being called. Charlotte tensed as she pointed out the landlord, a middle-aged man who looked rather unassuming, but who, Charlotte guaranteed Anita, was anything but. Anita reassured her that all would be well and seated the little family next to her.

Anita stepped forward with confidence she hardly felt and raised her chin. She swallowed and cleared her throat and then calmly addressed the court. She barely even noticed that people were watching her. It was nothing like her dance days, because right now, Anita's performance was about Charlotte and her family.

"We request a hardship stay, to give Ms. Charlotte Montgomery extra time to find a place that can accommodate her children and her mother. Ms. Montgomery is hardworking and up until her mother fell ill, she never missed a day of work. As of right now and the foreseeable future, there is no one else to care for Ms. Montgomery's mother. We have a meeting with Ms. Montgomery's employer on Monday, to secure her position as well as come up with a schedule that will allow Ms. Montgomery to care for her mother and provide for her family. I have provided the court with medical records detailing the mother's illness with relevant dates." She passed the paperwork to the bailiff and took her seat.

The judge was a middle-aged black woman whose expression revealed nothing. She eyed Anita and Charlotte and the two children before nodding at the young man who was representing the landlord.

The landlord's attorney stood. "Your Honor, rent has to be paid. You cannot live somewhere for free. Ms. Montgomery is not alone in having hardship. Everyone else manages to pay rent."

Anita stood. She was out of turn, but there was no taking no for an answer. "Ma'am. Charlotte Montgomery is an extremely hardworking young woman. She was unable to finish college when her mother fell ill, as her mother was her primary source of childcare. Her mother's condition worsened, requiring Ms. Montgomery to become the primary caregiver for her mother. She is one year shy of a bachelor's degree. Putting her on the street because of missed rent would be a great disservice to her family and her children, as well as to Ms. Montgomery herself. Not to mention the greater society as well."

"Ms. Virani." The judge turned a frown on Anita. "I am well aware of Ms. Montgomery's situation, as you have provided extremely detailed documentation of the facts."

"Yes, Ma'am. I just wanted—"

"Sit down, Ms. Virani," the judge told her.

Crap. Her heart fell. She shouldn't have opened her mouth. She should apologize to the judge. Anita started to stand.

The judge looked at her and shook her head. "Do not stand. I have made my decision."

Anita sat back down, her back completely straight, and took Charlotte's hand. It seemed an eternity before the judge spoke again.

"Very well, four months' hardship extension ought to do it." She shuffled some papers and called out. "Next."

Anita stood. "Thank you, ma'am. Your Honor. Ma'am."

The judge passed a glare over Anita. "Next!"

Anita nodded and led Charlotte and the children out of the courtroom. Charlotte hugged Anita tight, and beamed. "Thank you so much, Ms. Virani!"

"My pleasure. I will meet you on Monday, and we'll take care of your job, okay?"

"My boss is going to be tougher. It's really hard for me to get in for shift work. I have a neighbor who can sometimes watch the kids, but not always. Mom is too weak to keep two toddlers, and there just isn't enough money for childcare."

Anita looked at Charlotte as an idea dawned on her. "Can you type?"

"Of course."

"Okay. Listen, I have an idea. I'm not sure if it will work or not, so check in with the clinic from time to time this weekend, okay?"

"What—"

"I don't want to say anything until I work out the details. Listen, I have to get to the wedding. Do you need a ride somewhere?" Technically, she wasn't supposed to do that, but she didn't want to leave Charlotte just standing there.

"No. It's just a couple blocks and the kids need to run off some energy before we get to my mom."

"Okay. I'll be in touch."

"Thank you so much, Ms. Virani. Now you better get going if you're going to make that wedding."

Anita ran to the car, elated. *This* was why she wanted to be a lawyer. Charlotte had a place to live until she found something better. It wasn't perfect, but she wasn't on the street. She sent a small thank-you to her parents, started the car and raced to the church.

Chapter 12

Nikhil stood by the limos in front of the house and glanced at the time on his phone again. He was starting to sweat in his tux in the summer sun. He pulled open his bow tie. He'd retie it in the limo. Anita should have been here fifteen minutes ago. The limo would leave in ten minutes, with or without her. Where was she?

He called her. Voicemail again. He left a message.

"She'll be here," Rocky whispered in his ear.

"No doubt," retorted Nikhil. If Anita agreed to something, she was in a hundred percent.

He turned to his sister, the bridesmaids, his mother and Neepa-masi. "Go ahead and get in. I'll find her."

Tina pressed her lips together. His mother squeezed his sister's hand. "Don't worry. She'll show."

"Meeta has been here for half an hour." Neepa-masi pursed her mouth with pride.

Nikhil's mother closed her eyes and inhaled. "Yes,

we know that your daughter-in-law-to-be is wonderful, Neepa. Easha is also here. I'm sure Anita will show any minute now."

Neepa-masi shrugged. It was clear she found it doubtful. She smiled her approval at Meeta. Meeta, for her part, smiled back, but made eye contact with Easha. The two young women rolled their eyes at each other and smiled.

Meeta and Easha were both in floor-length blue gowns, as they were part of the bridal party. The masis were also in floor-length gowns similar to what Nikhil's mother wore, but all three in different colors.

"It's not me that cares, Mom," Tina said. "I told you this was a bad idea. You just should have told Dada—"

"Told Dada what?" Neepa-masi asked.

"Don't worry about that, Neepa," his mother snapped at her sister. "Just get in. Where is Deepa?" She looked around for her other sister.

"I'm here." Deepa-masi came running up. As long as he could remember, Deepa-masi was always running late.

"Where's Papa?" his mother asked her.

"He's coming." Deepa-masi waved her hand behind her.

"Jeez, Deepa. You couldn't wait for him?" Neepa-masi called from the limo.

"He can walk, Neepa," said his mom, with exaggerated patience.

"He's had a heart attack." Neepa-masi glared at her.

"Six months ago, Neepa." Deepa-masi rolled her eyes. "He's a lot stronger than you think."

"Thank you, Deepa." His mother seemed shocked that Deepa-masi had actually taken her side.

"Neepa treats him like an invalid," Deepa-masi said. "Even the doctor says he's fine."

"He still has that cane," Neepa-masi insisted.

"Which I don't think he really needs," said Seema. "Stop babying him."

"Seema, you really don't know anything about it. You're never there," Neepa-masi snapped.

"I have a business to run, and children—"

"The children are grown." Neepa-masi rolled her eyes. "All you ever think about is your business. All these years, all we ever hear about is your business this, your business that. Your father needs you. It's *your* business—why can't you take time off?"

"I did take time off for him, and I am going to take time off when I become a grandmother in six months!" Seema snapped. She immediately pressed her lips together and glanced at Easha, realizing she'd said too much.

"Mom." Easha shook her head, as both masis' eyes popped open. "What are you saying?"

"Seriously?" Rocky raised his voice from next to Nikhil, where he and the other guys were trying to stay away from the sister squabble. "Unbelievable. We specifically asked you *not* to say anything, but no. When it comes to the masis…" He threw his hands up and shook his head.

Neepa-masi and Deepa-masi grinned. "Well, you blew that secret."

"I'm sorry, Easha. It just came out," his mother tried to explain as Easha made her way past her mother-in-law and into the air conditioning of the limo, still shaking her head.

"Why do you let them get to you?" Easha whispered

softly to her mother-in-law before she sat down. Rocky was still glaring at his mother.

She looked away from her older son and turned to her younger son. "Do you know where she is?" His mother looked at him, desperate for an answer.

"Don't worry. Anita would never let you down," Dada said as he finally joined them, looking quite dapper in a tuxedo as well.

Nikhil and his mother turned to the older man. He did not have his cane and he was smiling.

"What do you mean?" Nikhil's mother asked.

"I mean Anita is a good daughter-in-law, and she will be here." Dada smiled at his daughter. "If she is late, there is a good reason. Right, Nikhil?"

"Absolutely true," Nikhil said. She was acting odd when she'd left for her hair appointment. She had made a call…something must have come up at the clinic. She wouldn't risk everything for nothing. "You need to go. Come on, Deepa-masi, Meeta. Get in with Tina and Mom and get to the church. We're right behind you."

Seema Joshi inhaled and closed her eyes as she entered the limo. Nikhil knew she was dreading sitting in there with her sisters.

Nikhil helped his grandfather get into the limousine that was taking the men. Rocky was still fuming and already seated along with Hiral.

"Come on, Nikhil," Rocky called. "Don't make us late."

Nikhil looked around before getting in, hoping to catch sight of Anita's car. The street was still. He checked his watch one more time and climbed in behind Dada.

Anita parked her car in the church parking lot, grabbed her strappy sandals and dress and made a beeline for the bathroom. She had been too late to make the limo, so she came straight to the church. Even so, she saw the limos pulling up as she entered the church. She quickly put on the bridesmaid's dress in the bathroom, a beautiful and elegant strapless baby blue gown that just grazed her curves and trailed an inch on the floor. She freshened up her makeup and checked her hair before finally going out to meet the family. She nearly floated, still excited from the hearing.

She found Nikhil in heavy discussion with his mother and sister.

"I'm telling you, she will be here," Nikhil was saying.

"But where would she go?" Tina asked.

"I think she went to help someone at the law clinic downtown. She said something yesterday about a client being evicted." He shrugged. "But she'll be here. I know it. She won't let you down."

"So, work?" Tina pursed her lips.

"No. Helping someone—I'm sure of it." He was standing up for her. Confident in the fact that Anita would be there as promised. Nikhil had faith in her.

"Hey, everyone!" Anita stepped up as if she'd just gotten there. She squeezed Tina's hand. "You look like a fantasy." She met Seema-auntie's eyes. "Sorry I missed the limo."

"No problem, dear. We're just happy you're here." She looked at Nikhil. "Go. Both of you, take your spots."

"Bridesmaids line up over there." The wedding planner pointed to the door to the chapel. "Groomsmen across from them."

Nikhil took Anita's hand and led her to the lineup. He was very handsome in his perfectly fitted tuxedo, though Nikhil had always cleaned up nicely. He squeezed her hand and she looked at him. He looked at her with a mixture of intimacy and pride that was completely new to her. The old Nikhil had never looked at her this way. Come to think of it, the old Nikhil would have assumed she wasn't coming when she was late.

Not this guy. This version was calm and confident that if she made a commitment, she would stand by it. It was the truth, but his faith in her and the way he was looking at her rendered her almost speechless.

Almost.

She grinned at him, still high from what she'd done that morning. "Wait until you hear where I was." The next instant, the chapel doors were open. She placed her hand in the crook of Nikhil's arm as she had been instructed and they followed Rocky and Easha down the aisle. They separated at the end and turned to watch Tina arrive.

Jake was focused on the door Tina would come through, his excitement almost palatable. His cousin Matthew stood next to him as his best man. A memory popped into Anita's head. She and Tina had been talking about weddings, and Tina had proclaimed that if she should ever get married, Anita would be her maid of honor. Today, Anu stood in the maid of honor position.

Jake's green eyes were bright and the smile on his face was a gateway to his feelings. All of his love for Tina was right there for everyone to see.

She caught Nikhil's eye and caught him watching her. Her stomach actually fluttered in excitement. What had gone wrong between them? Were they just too young at that time? Too selfish? Too immature? She honestly could not remember in this moment.

She hadn't even told him where she was going to be this morning, and yet, he had calmly defended her, knowing she would not abandon either of her responsibilities. He trusted her. This was not the Nikhil she had been married to.

Nor was she the Anita he had been married to.

After the ceremony, the bridal party was whisked off for formal pictures before the reception. Tina had chosen to go to Lake Kittamaqundi in town. The lake sported an outdoor amphitheater and was itself picturesque.

The photographer was quick and efficient, lining them all up in the predetermined poses. Being a "married" couple, she and Nikhil were put together often. A few times, Anita tried to duck out—they certainly did not need Nikhil's fake wife ex-wife in the wedding pictures—but someone would always call her back. Not that she was in any way opposed to having Nikhil's muscular chest pressed against her back—or her front—depending on the pose. And this photographer was a fan of having Nikhil's hand at her waist at almost all times. By the time they were done, Anita didn't know if she was sweating because of the hot Maryland summer sun, or because of the constant touch of her ex-husband.

The smiles on the bride's and groom's faces never dimmed. There was laughter, there were a few emotional tears, but the couple's happiness infected everyone around them. They could not take their eyes off each other.

"Your sister looks really happy," she whispered during one pose when they were facing each other, Anita's chest against his.

Nikhil smiled and his face lit up, taking Anita's breath away for just a second. "Jake's a good guy. They are well matched."

"They really are." She couldn't stop looking at him. "People probably think we're well matched as well."

Nikhil raised an eyebrow at her.

"By the way, thanks for having my back earlier," she whispered as the photographer posed the others.

"Of course. I didn't think you'd bail or even risk being late for no reason." Nikhil's voice was calm and sincere.

"I had to keep a client from being evicted."

Nikhil's eyes popped wide, but the photographer returned before he could say anything.

"Hey, middle brother and the wife. Not your day to make googly eyes at each other. Look at the camera," the photographer admonished.

Nikhil's hand at her waist tightened as he pulled her closer and they shared a quiet laugh as they turned to face the camera.

The group made it to the cocktail hour in time to grab drinks and be seated for the start of the reception. Tina was radiant in her dress, and Jake couldn't keep his eyes off of her.

Nikhil and Anita were seated with Rocky and Easha, as well as Hiral and his fiancée, Meeta, and Miki and her fiancé, Nitin, and of course, Sangeeta. Rocky had put aside his anger with his mother for the time being and doted on Easha, getting her ginger tea and crackers to nibble on. Hiral and Meeta were hilarious, entertaining the group with stories of the over-the-top engagement party Hiral's parents had thrown for them in India.

Miki and Nitin were the youngest of the group and had just gotten engaged a month ago. They could barely keep their hands off of each other.

"So, how did you propose, Nitin?" Anita asked as the salad was being served. She sipped her wine, a crisp summer white that just hit the spot.

"Well, actually, Miki proposed." Nitin kissed her

cheek. "Thank god." He grinned. "I wanted to, and I was hashing a plan, but she beat me to it."

"Wow, Miki. Awesome. How did you do it?"

"Nothing outlandish. We were walking one evening after having a lovely meal with our families, and it felt right. Our parents had introduced us, so I knew they were on board. So I just asked him to marry me." She flushed as she looked at him. "And he said yes. And the next day, we bought a ring." She waggled her ring finger, upon which was a beautiful diamond ring.

"That's such a great story," Easha gushed and took Rocky's hand. "Rocky actually picked out my ring—it was perfect. Then he got down on one knee and everything right in our favorite restaurant. I could barely see the ring through my tears." She laughed and tilted her head toward him. Rocky looked at her with such fondness. Anita had never seen that before. It was touching.

"What about you, Hiral? How did you propose?" Rocky asked.

Hiral and Meeta looked at each other, glanced at Sangeeta and flushed. "We'd rather not say," Meeta mumbled, clearing her throat.

"What, you can't say it because I'm here?" asked Sangeeta.

"Yes. My little sister doesn't need to hear..." He drifted off as Meeta burned red.

Sangeeta rolled her eyes. "You might want to come up with some G-rated version because everyone will ask at your wedding."

The other three couples exchanged raised eyebrows and grins. Meeta finally turned to Anita. "How about you two?"

Tension rent the air for a moment while Anita gathered herself. After all, only Meeta, Hiral and Sangeeta didn't know about the divorce. Besides, she hadn't thought about this in a long time. She then glanced at Nikhil, who also looked lost in the past. He cleared his throat. "Well. We hadn't really known each other long."

"But we were very much in love," Anita added, for Hiral's and Meeta's benefit.

"Of course." Hiral winked at them. "We can still see it."

"Most certainly." Dada's voice reached them as he walked up behind them. He held up a hand as they all turned to look at him. "Continue with the story. I've never heard it. And back in our day, our parents did all of this, so we didn't get to be so romantic until after we got married." He nodded at Anita.

"Well." She turned back to the table. "Nikhil was very romantic. He took me to the beach. The only light that night was a sliver of the moon." She glanced at Nikhil quickly, then back at the group. "He sang to me." Anita smiled at the memory. It really had been wonderfully romantic. The barely crescent moon, the stars in the clear night sky, the empty beach. Most people would think that a full moon would be more romantic, but that crescent sliver suspended in the clear night sky was as mesmerizing as any full moon. The salty scent of the ocean had lingered in the air, the crashing of waves was their playlist and it had felt like they were the only two people on the planet. There was no way to say no. And she hadn't wanted to. Being with Nikhil had steadied her for the first time since her parents had died. And she had wanted that. She had wanted the stability that came from being with someone you loved. That she had thought marriage would offer. She had been mistaken.

Sangeeta had tears in her eyes. "That's so romantic!"

"What was the song?" asked Meeta.

Everything seemed to stop and focus on them. Anita remembered the song but she couldn't look at Nikhil or say the name of the song. "Oh, that's not—"

"'Janam Janam' from *Diwale*," Nikhil answered, his voice soft and low, as if he were sharing an intimate secret. Which he was.

"Perfect." Hiral smiled in admiration.

"Oh! We'll use it for your anniversary party!" Sangeeta made a note in her phone.

"Absolutely," agreed Dada. "*Mera Hoke hamesha hi rehna, Kabhi na kehna alvida.* Beautiful." *Always be mine, Never say goodbye.*

Anita glanced at Nikhil. His jaw was tight and his gaze was focused in front of him. Of course, she had said goodbye. "I toasted you, as well." Nikhil's voice had turned heavy, tight.

She had not forgotten. She nodded, unable to tear her gaze away from him. "With chai."

"What?" Easha exclaimed.

"Um, Nikhil makes the best chai." Anita turned back to the table, forcing a smile on her face. She glanced at him, but his jaw was still tight. "I never could resist his chai."

"I needed a guarantee," Nikhil finally spoke. "The chai was the best way."

"So how did you two meet? Did Seema-masi arrange it?"

Nikhil looked away. Anita took over the answer. "I was assistant teaching a nighttime graduate-level creative writing class that Nikhil was taking at the time." She paused. "I did most of the grading because the professor had been already overtaxed when they assigned her this class. Anyway, Nikhil did not like the grade I gave him on a paper." She smiled at the memory and glanced at Nikhil. He remained silent. "He stayed after class one night to discuss it with me. After that he stayed after every class to discuss something about the lesson. And he always brought a thermos—seriously, a thermos—filled with chai."

"I had to." Nikhil perked up. "I really didn't care about the grade." He looked at her, dark eyes soft, a small smile peeking through on his lips. "I just wanted to spend time with her, but she wouldn't date me because she was kind of my teacher. So I brought chai and we would have chai in Styrofoam cups after class and talk about—" he looked directly at her "—everything."

Anita grinned at the memory. He had been quite persistent when she had refused to go out with him. She needed the money and couldn't afford to lose that job because of a guy. No matter how handsome and charming she had found him.

On the last day of the semester, after grades had already been turned in, Nikhil had waited for her after class as he had been doing. This time without his thermos.

"Where's the chai?" she had asked, quite disappointed that they weren't going to hang out together.

He shrugged. "Last day of class."

She tried to hide her disappointment and nodded. "So, nothing to discuss, I suppose."

"Did you turn the grades in?" he asked.

"I did. But no, I will not tell you your grade." She jutted her chin at him.

He smiled and placed his hand over his heart, moving closer to her. "I expect nothing less."

He was now close enough that she felt his breath on her ear when he bent down and whispered to her, "If grades are in, you're not my teacher anymore."

Goose bumps had covered her body from his proximity. She still remembered the musky scent of the last of his cologne and how she had simply wanted to melt into it. "No," she had whispered back, "I'm not."

"Then today is the best day of my life," he continued in that whisper as he moved yet closer to her.

"Why is that?" She tilted her head up.

"Because today is the first day of you and me." His eyes darkened, and his voice grew gruff. Her body outright tingled in anticipation. "And I'm finally going to get to kiss you." With that, he lowered his mouth to hers, finally closing the distance between them, and kissed her.

He was gentle at first, but she captured his mouth with hers and they kissed each other senseless.

When they stopped to breathe, Nikhil turned his beautiful smile on her again. "I didn't bring the thermos, because I was hoping we might have chai later," his eyes had glinted with mischief, "like first thing in the morning."

As Anita found out, morning chai was even better.

She met Nikhil's gaze and flushed as he met hers. He clearly remembered that night, too.

"So what happened on the last day of class?" Meeta asked.

Nikhil cleared his throat. "I, uh, I asked her out to dinner. And that was our first official date." That was the G-rated version.

"Fantastic," Dada proclaimed. "Worthy of Bollywood." He chuckled. "I must insist the two of you treat us to a performance tomorrow evening at the sangeet-garba reception after the Indian ceremony."

"I'm sure Nikhil is already singing. Aren't you?" Anita asked, panic rising in her.

"Yes, Dada, I am."

"No, beti—a dance. I am sure Anita can dance. Nikhil can sing, Anita can dance," Dada insisted. "I'm an old man. Humor me."

Anita shook her head. "Oh no, Dada. I don't really dance like that—in front of people. Nikhil can sing." She had no problem throwing him under the bus. "That will be great."

"No," Dada insisted. "You two are the picture of love. Maybe Easha and Rocky would like to join you?"

Both Rocky and Easha shook their heads emphatically.

"Very well, just you two then. Just something simple."

"But Dada…" called Anita, but Dada was already in conversation with someone else.

She turned to Nikhil, who still watched her.

"I can't do this." Anita was panicked. "You know how I have stage fright. I'll just freeze."

Nikhil shrugged. "No way out of it. Got to keep Dada happy."

She placed her hand on her belly. Her stomach churned at just the thought of dancing in front of people. She shook her head again.

"I'll be right there with you. I'll be singing, so I can cue you." Nikhil looked her in the eye. "I promise." He smiled and while her belly did not relax, she melted a little under his gaze.

Chapter 13

The table resumed normal chatter after Dada's little visit, so Nikhil relaxed a bit. He should have expected these questions, but he hadn't been prepared for that little trip down memory lane.

Nikhil had taken Anita out to dinner that night, and it was their first official date. He had already fallen for her over the course of their after-class meetings during the semester. His writing had also drastically improved, but he chalked that up to the fact that he wanted to impress her in every way possible.

He wasn't sure exactly when it had happened, but he had fallen for her as they sat and drank chai after class in the classroom. At first they discussed his writing and how to improve it. But that quickly morphed into conversations about anything and everything. She had told him about her parents and how she and Amar were surviving, leaning on each other. Nikhil had been in awe of her strength and positivity.

Nikhil and his siblings had certainly leaned on each other when they lost their father, but they had been much younger. Nikhil and Tina had been there for each other as their mother channeled her grief into JFL, and Rocky pulled back from them, becoming more serious and focused in school.

Where Anita had remained focused and positive, Nikhil had frequently found himself in detention. His method of problem-solving had usually involved fists, which led to more than one suspension.

Before she even went back to his place that night, he knew she was the one. But when she confirmed that she felt the same way, Nikhil felt that his life was turning around. This was the woman he wanted to spend the rest of his life with. He had known it in his soul.

Dinner was served, and Nikhil picked at his food and simply watched Anita. She teased Meeta and kept an eye on Easha. She patted Rocky's hand from time to time, and laughed heartily at Hiral's antics, all the while trying to include Nitin in the craziness. In that instant he was struck with a solid fact. Anita Virani was his family, more than anyone else at this table, more than anyone else in this room. She was his home, and he was the idiot that had let her walk out of his life.

He was still in love with her. Which basically meant he was screwed, because she had been the one to leave, and he had no idea how to get her back.

He had been so caught up in what he might lose, and how he might lose it, he hadn't ever seen what he really had. And what he'd had was this woman's love. Was it still there?

He continued to watch her, and every so often, she turned her head toward him and gave him a smile that weakened him. It was that secret special smile that was just for him, because it said *I'm thinking about you right now.*

Maybe. Maybe it was still there. Though he hardly deserved her.

His phone rang. It was his agent. He tapped Anita's shoulder to indicate he was stepping out to take the call.

It was Chantelle. "Nikhil. Good news. The publisher's representative is excited to meet with you."

"Great. You'd said she was here for a wedding. Do you know where it is?"

She named the hotel, and he couldn't believe his luck. It was the same location as his sister's wedding. For a second, he considered telling her that no, he could not take a meeting *during* his sister's wedding. But then he thought about all the times his mother and brother and father had scheduled meetings during vacations, or even dinners out. And this was one of the most important meetings of his career. No, he was as hard a worker as they were.

He pulled up the wedding schedule. He could fit in a quick drink between the post-wedding ceremony lunch and the reception. Thanks to Dada volunteering them, he really needed that time to practice for his performance with Anita.

Well, how long could a drink take? He'd make it work. "Perfect. Text me the time."

He returned to the table to loud voices, the dominant one of which was Anita's easy tone. Except that she was riled up.

"Who said Nikhil wasn't successful?" Anita demanded, not bothering to lower her voice, despite the guests around them.

His mother stood next to Anita, both of them half-turned away from him. "No one, beti." She sounded surprised. "Of course, Nikhil is successful, in his own way." Her smile was oversweet for the benefit of the others at the table.

Anita pulled herself to her full height and took a step closer to his mother. "Nikhil is successful in *any* way, Mom." This time, she measured her voice, but did not back down. Nikhil's heart leaped.

"He writes books. Fiction." Nikhil's mother shook her head as if writing books was an easy way to gain success. "*You* at least are helping people."

"He has written three books, in the past three years. Two are published and on the market, the third releases in ten days and he is currently working on a fourth." There was pride in her voice. He had never allowed himself to consider that anyone in his family was following his career, least of all Anita. Happiness—and hope—bloomed inside him as she spoke, rattling off titles and the outlets that had reviewed them. "He's on bestseller lists, has had rave reviews and people are talking about his books."

At this, his mother turned all the way to her, giving Anita her full attention. "He makes up stories." She shrugged, that one action making Nikhil's accomplishments completely inconsequential.

"Have you even read his books?" Anita lifted her chin. From where he stood, Nikhil could hear the challenge in her words. "Because I have."

She read his books? After all this time, that little bit

of knowledge had the power to undo even the insult of his mother minimizing his work.

His mother continued to appraise Anita. "Were you impressed?"

"You read them and see if you are impressed," Anita said.

Rocky interrupted, "I've read them."

What?

Anita turned his way and Nikhil could see her profile. She was not surprised.

His mother looked taken aback.

"They're really good, Mom," Rocky confirmed. "Well written and insightful."

"Rocky, you read my books?" Nikhil said as he stepped up to the table. He couldn't stop himself.

Rocky flushed and shrugged. "Well, yes. You are my brother." He flicked his gaze toward their mother. "And you were brave enough to forge your own path."

Nikhil was speechless. Rocky had never given any indication he wanted something other than to dedicate his career to the law.

"Besides, I had to make sure you were good before I acknowledged that N. V. Joshi was my brother." Rocky laughed as he surveyed the group, but landed a serious gaze on Nikhil.

"Hey, how about we toast our little sister and wedded bliss?" Nikhil called out into the silence. "I'll go grab some champagne."

"I'll go with you." Rocky nodded at him.

"Okay."

"Listen, Nikhil." Nikhil turned to his brother. It was the first time he hadn't called him Nicky. "I really am proud of you. I know I don't say it or even act that way.

But you went off and made a name for yourself without relying on the family name. You're braver than I am for sure."

"Are you saying that you don't want to be a lawyer?"

Rocky shook his head. "No. I'm saying I never even considered another possibility. Probably neither did Tina. But you did."

"Only because Mom gave up on me years ago."

"She didn't."

"It doesn't matter." Nikhil shrugged. It mattered. To him.

"Listen, not for nothing, but Anita is *here*. Right now. Making nice with the family. And it can't just be for whatever Mom promised her. Maybe it started that way but that's not what's happening now."

"What are you saying?" His heart lifted. Did Rocky think there was a chance for him and Anita?

"I'm saying she was the best thing that ever happened to you and you're being granted a second chance, so don't screw that up."

"I don't know about that."

"You don't want her back?"

"It's complicated."

The bartender handed over a bottle of champagne and went to get glasses, when someone tapped him on the shoulder. Expecting Anita, he turned around with a huge smile. "Hey, you."

But instead of Anita's beautiful amber eyes, he was met with Jalissa's green contact lenses.

"Jalissa." Nikhil pressed his lips together and nodded to Rocky. "All set?"

Rocky pointed to the champagne bottle and grinned. "Just waiting for glasses."

Nikhil stepped back from her, but she rested her hand on his bicep.

"Nikhil." Her voice was soft. "Have a drink with me."

"Um, not only no, but hell no." He grabbed the bottle, thinking he'd just make Rocky wait for the glasses, but she held on to his arm. "Jalissa, I'm not having a drink with you."

"Nikhil. One drink. I just want to talk. We ended things so badly…"

"We?" His eyebrows shot up. This woman could not be for real.

"Nikhil, come on. For old times' sake. One drink. What's the harm?" She pouted overlipsticked lips at him and Nikhil was struck with the thought that he couldn't for the world imagine why he'd ever had any feelings for this person.

Nikhil sighed. He shouldn't. Jalissa was nothing but trouble. She did nothing without an agenda. She also did not take no for an answer.

"One drink," Nikhil relented.

The glasses arrived and Rocky grabbed them and the champagne. He gave Nikhil a warning look before leaving.

Jalissa grinned and motioned to the bartender for two beers. She grabbed their drinks and sat down at a table close by. Nikhil sat in silence while he waited for her to speak.

"So how are you?" She kept her voice low and soft.

"I'm just fine, Jalissa."

"No, really. You seem happily married." She grinned.

Nikhil stared her down without speaking.

"Or are you?"

"What actual business is it of yours?"

"Just…well…if you're happily married, I'll walk. But if not, then maybe I have a chance."

"A chance at what?"

"At you."

Nikhil could not help the laughter that escaped him. "There's no chance for us." He started to stand.

"You haven't even touched your beer." Jalissa nodded.

"Whatever, Jalissa."

"I know you're divorced and that you're faking for your grandfather." Jalissa sneered at him as she stood, all the softness gone from her voice.

"Get to the point, Jalissa."

She leaned into him, her hand on his. "Another chance. I get it—you're putting on some kind of show with her for this wedding. It's all over in a couple days. Call me next week, and we can pick up where we left off." She placed her hand on his chest and drew her fingers down.

It had been her go-to move when they were together.

But now? Nothing. Nikhil felt absolutely nothing for her, from her.

He placed his hand over hers as she quite literally grabbed his belt. "No, thank you."

She leaned closer so her mouth was inches from his. "I'll call you."

"The hell you will." Anita's voice came from behind him.

Nikhil turned to find Anita staring down Jalissa. Those amber eyes he loved so much were twin lights of heat. If she'd had the power, Anita could have set Jalissa on fire with that look. "What part of *he's married* do you not understand?"

"He's not married—I know you two are divorced." Jalissa had the nerve to sneer.

"Are we, though?" Anita stepped into her face and Jalissa backed off. "Would we do this if we were faking?" She grabbed Nikhil and kissed him full on, on the mouth. He responded to her instantly. He trailed his tongue over her lips, enticing her—no, daring her—to open her mouth. Once she did, there was no returning.

He had no idea how long they kissed each other; he just never wanted to stop. When they broke, he was a bit dizzy and shocked. "What the hell was that?" He stepped away from her, instantly regretting his action.

Her eyes widened as she seemed to realize what she had just done. "I—I…"

Jalissa's smile was victorious. "I knew it." She pursed her lips at Nikhil. "Like I said, call me when you're done with the farce." She walked away.

Chapter 14

Someone had taken over her body. That was really the only explanation she had for kissing Nikhil like that. She had come to find out if he was okay, after he'd overheard Seema-auntie's comments, and saw Jalissa with her hands all over Nikhil. A green haze had come over her.

Who did that woman think she was, touching her husband like that? The fact that Nikhil was not in fact her husband seemed irrelevant and Anita had gone and staked her claim like some alpha dog. She wasn't even thinking; she simply acted.

She was frozen to her spot as Nikhil stared at her in disbelief after kissing her completely senseless and pulling away. Jalissa finally left, but Anita had the feeling that the woman was on to them and their marriage act.

Neither she nor Nikhil moved for what seemed an eternity. Everything appeared to be moving in slow motion. Until all at once, Anita was brought back to her reality.

Damn it! She had kissed Nikhil and he had pushed her away, in front of his ex-girlfriend.

Her hand flew to her mouth where she could still taste him. She was such an idiot. What the hell had possessed her?

"Oh no. I'm sorry." Heat crawled up her neck and into her face. She was sick to her stomach. "I don't know why I did that. I had no idea you were trying to... Never mind. Clearly it was a mistake. I'm sorry. Let's pretend that never happened, okay?"

Nikhil nodded, a glazed look still lingering in his eyes. "Yes. Of course—a mistake. Just probably got carried away with the role."

"Yes." Anita clung to that idea like a lifesaver. "Yes. Of course. We used to be married and we're pretending now, so I just got carried away. Sorry if I messed things up for you."

"What? Oh no. Actually I'm grateful. She was coming on very strong. Doesn't like to take no for an answer." Was he as flustered as she was, or was that just wishful thinking?

"Wait...so you're not trying to get back with her?"

"Oh hell no. I told you. She used me to get a job at JFL. That'll never happen."

"Right." Nikhil would never be with someone who worked for his family. It was actually Jalissa they had to thank for that, damn her.

Stop. Nikhil was not really hers anymore. She needed to remember that.

"Gather around, everyone. Time for Tina and Jake's first dance as a couple," the DJ announced.

Everyone turned to see Jake lead Tina out to the dance floor. They were a beautiful couple. All eyes followed them as they moved in unison.

"I know it may seem cheesy, but now that I see Jake and Tina together, I kind of miss that we never had the big wedding." Nikhil was smiling at her.

Anita had been thinking the same thing. "Well, I suppose it's just as well. Considering how things turned out."

Nikhil nodded, and she thought she caught some sadness flit over that smile. The DJ called for the family couples to join the newlyweds. Nikhil turned to her, his hand extended. "Might as well continue the farce."

She nodded and took his hand, almost eager to be in his arms again, fake or not. It was definitely dangerous for her to dance with him, but if he could do it, so could she.

See? She was fine.

Nikhil led her to the dance floor, where he wrapped one arm around her waist, the other still holding her hand. He held her close, their bodies just touching. The song the couple had chosen was about a man trying to understand his good fortune at being with the woman. He was simply thrilled that this amazing woman loved him.

"You were right to leave me," he said softly as they swayed back and forth.

"Why would you say that?"

"Because it's true. I was too young. Too self-absorbed. Not there for you." He was looking directly at her, not behind her or around the room. She could see the vulnerability on his face, in his eyes.

Anita digested that a moment. "I was also too young, too vulnerable. Too ready to cling to anyone who could stabilize me after my parents' death." She shrugged. "Wrong time for us both, I guess."

She looked up at him. He met her gaze with a small smile and she could swear he was thinking about kissing her again. He shifted his gaze to something behind her, so she took the opportunity to study him. Clean-shaven, but with a just a hint of evening scruff on his brown skin, strong jaw, fabulous mouth. That kiss was still imprinted on her lips. She thought she had been making progress in steeling herself against him. But that kiss had now set her back. Not to mention what dancing in his arms was doing to her. She was enjoying being wrapped up in him just a little too much. She inched closer so now their bodies were pressed against each other.

He looked down at her and smiled. She had forgotten what a heart-melting smile Nikhil had. At least when he had looked at her. She could watch him smile at her forever.

"You know, I never really understood why you were with me in the first place," he said without looking away. "I fell for you after maybe that second time we stayed after class."

"Is that why you kept coming back?"

"I had to. I couldn't be away from you. I wanted to debate with you, listen to you laugh, take the sadness from your eyes." He paused. "You didn't know anything about the family business or wealth—you seemed to like me for me."

"Of course, I did." She shrugged. "I saw your potential as a writer. Your use of words was poetic and seemed to flow so naturally from you. You were tough, but kind and strong." She grinned. "I loved you when you were just a wannabe writer. Now look at you."

"No. Now look at *you*."

Why had he been such an idiot as to let her go? True, that kiss had taken him by surprise. But then she back-tracked so fast, he wasn't sure what to make of it. Had she just pressed against him on purpose?

He led her in a small waltz, even twirling her around. They were in complete sync without so much as a word being spoken between them.

Too soon, the song was over and a faster song started. Anita stepped back and started dancing with him, showing no interest in leaving the floor. When they were married, they couldn't always afford to go out, so they would move the furniture and turn on music and dance in their little apartment.

Nikhil still lived in that apartment, much to the annoyance of his mother. She never could understand why he hadn't let her help them get a bigger place, and after the divorce, she had assumed he would move back into the family house.

His mother had been insistent. "Why are you staying in that tiny little apartment? I understand you and Anita wanted to play house, but now she is gone. Just let it go and move back home."

"We were not playing house. That apartment was our home," Nikhil had stated for the millionth time. He hadn't bothered to explain why he wanted that apartment. It was what he could afford. He didn't want to use her money.

And besides, he felt closer to Anita there.

Miki and Nitin joined them on the dance floor, along with Meeta and Hiral. Anita laughed and the sound filled his heart with a happiness he hadn't felt since they had first been married.

No, he never should have let her go. He took her hand and spun her on the dance floor, bringing her into him when she stopped the spin. She smiled up at him.

"Remember when we used to move the furniture?" She laughed.

"I was just thinking about that. Those were the best times. You would dance in my arms."

"You would sing to me." Her voice was breathless and everything around them fell away. All that existed was her.

"Lovebirds!" Hiral's voice cut through their moment. "Come over here! We're doing shots at the bar!"

Nikhil nodded without looking away from Anita. "We're coming."

Anita broke out in a smile and grabbed his hand. "Come on!"

He trailed after her. Hiral was handing out shots of god-knows-what to everyone. He held his up. "To Tina and Jake!" They clinked glasses and downed the shots.

It burned on the way down. Anita crinkled up her face. "Damn, Hiral. What the hell? At least spring for something that goes down easier." Turning to the bar, she ordered another round for the group. "Try this," she challenged, passing glasses around, then holding hers up in a toast. "To Tina and Jake and their happily-ever-after." They all drank the alcohol.

"Much smoother, Anita-bhabhi. You're right," Hiral conceded.

Hearing Anita called "bhabhi" was like a balm to Nikhil's heart. "We have wedding number two tomorrow," Nikhil reminded them. "Because of course, Tina has to get married twice. So let's do this again tomorrow. But Hiral does not get to pick the shot."

"Anita-bhabhi!" the cousins all chorused.

She flushed as they cheered her, basking in the love. She deserved this. She deserved the love and family and all that.

But he just wasn't sure he was the one to give it to her.

At the end of the night, they crammed into an Uber with Rocky and Easha and Hiral and Meeta.

The laughter was free flowing as was the comfortable conversation.

"Rocky does that all the time! Like, how hard is it to pick up your socks?" Easha was laughing.

"Hiral gets his socks—for him it's the wet towel! I'm like, hang it up so it'll dry." Meeta shook her head at her fiancé.

"Nikhil couldn't get clothes into the hamper. Remember the coffee spill on him yesterday? I get back to the room and it's *next to the hamper*! They play basketball, and can get that ball into a stupid hoop, but they can't get a shirt into the hamper!" Anita laughed and the girls all high fived each other.

Nikhil shook his head along with the guys. "Listen to these women complaining about their husbands." He looked at Anita. "We have no complaints whatsoever about our wives."

"Duh. We're amazing!" Meeta laughed.

Anita met his eyes.

Once home, Nikhil loosened his tie and Anita tugged off her strappy heels and held them in her hand. "Good night, you guys! More wedding tomorrow." He took Anita's hand and they walked to their room together, still hand in hand.

Like a real married couple. And no one was even watching.

Chapter 15

Anita took Nikhil's hand and spun in toward him, landing with her back against his very solid, very muscular chest. He had removed the bow tie, unbuttoned the top of his dress shirt and draped the jacket on the sofa. She was still in her bridesmaid's gown and bare feet. Her hair was slowly falling out of the careful updo Laila had managed this morning. They'd been practicing for their dance tomorrow night for the past couple of hours.

She tilted her head up to him and he met her eyes with his before spinning her out again. The beat carried them the rest of the way through. They ended in each other's arms and the music finished.

"Perfect." Nikhil grinned at her. "I forgot what a natural you are at this. I don't know why you get so nervous."

Anita grimaced. "You know I hate being the center of attention."

"But you did all that bharat natyam dancing when you were growing up. Amar showed me the pictures."

She had done years of classical dance training, but that hadn't cured her of stage fright. "You know, between you and me, I never really enjoyed that kind of dancing."

"But it's such hard work—hours of practice."

She nodded. "It was. But the more I think about it, I was doing it to please my mom. Not that she forced me. I just knew it would make her happy if I did it, so I did."

They were in the sitting room area of their bedroom suite, and Nikhil had insisted on showing her the video of the dance they would be doing the next day.

"Are you sure you want to be a lawyer?" he joked as he sat down on the sofa. "I mean, you'll have to stand up and argue your case in a courtroom."

"It's different." She shrugged. "I did it today. When I was in front of all those people, including a judge, I was focused on being an advocate for my client. So, I wasn't self-conscious. It wasn't about me, so I was able to power through. You know, part of becoming a lawyer was the fact that it was what I really wanted to do with my life. I wasn't doing it to make someone else happy, or fulfil an obligation. It was for me. Still is. Being a lawyer is who I am." Anita stood and stretched.

"I always knew you'd be great."

Anita froze. "You always thought I'd be a great lawyer?"

"Of course." His tone was matter-of-fact.

"You never said that before."

Nikhil frowned. "Didn't I?"

Anita shook her head. "No. You were pretty much against the whole lawyer thing."

Nikhil rubbed his forehead. "I was too young and stupid at the time to realize that it wasn't always about me."

Anita nodded. "Well, we were both *young.*" She caught his eye and smiled.

"Ha-ha." Nikhil grinned at her and her belly did a small flip.

Silence wafted between them.

"Thanks for standing up for me tonight," Nikhil said.

Anita shrugged. "Of course. You should stand up for yourself. Your mother is not going to know what you do if you do not include her."

"You know, Rocky said he was actually proud of me."

"Well, he should be." Anita widened her eyes. "Though you should be proud, regardless."

Nikhil nodded. "Tina is the only one who ever came to my book launches."

"Did you ever ask your mom or Rocky to come?"

"I stopped asking my mom to come to things a long time ago." He shrugged.

"Maybe they don't come because you don't ask," Anita suggested as she gathered her things and went into the bathroom. "Try them again. People change."

Anita undressed and hopped into the shower, trying not to think about how naked she was with Nikhil mere feet away. She had thought he would be angry with her for cutting it so close this morning, but instead, he had been supportive and understanding.

Huh.

She shook her head. If she was having warm and fuzzy thoughts about Nikhil, it was only because they had taken that trip down memory lane. Which is probably why she kissed him. Not because she was jealous. Or she was trying to stake some claim on him so Jalissa would back down.

After the first couple after-class chai meetings, Anita had gone from being irritated with them to looking forward to them. Nikhil was funny, charming and forging his own path.

By the time she had finally been able to kiss him and he had invited her to stay for morning-after chai, she was already in love with him. She hadn't even known about JFL or his family's wealth until the day he brought her home to meet his family, because their relationship had had such tunnel vision.

Nikhil had been so sure of his path, and his family had been so welcoming, it was no wonder that Anita fell for him and for them.

She toweled off and came out of the bathroom to find Nikhil shirtless and doing push-ups on the bedroom floor.

Damn, but the man was beautiful. His bronzed skin was touchably smooth as she watched the muscles of his back contract and relax as he moved down, then up. Down, then up. A small, tiny part of her brain tried to tell her to stop watching, but the rest of her brain and her body insisted she continue. Majority rules.

"Bathroom's open."

He grunted.

"You're doing push-ups." She bit her bottom lip.

He stopped his push-ups and stood. His skin shone with just a shimmer of sweat from his activity. "Just waiting for you to get out of the shower." He raked his gaze over her from the towel on top of her head to her feet and back up again until he caught her eyes with an intensity she hadn't expected. He might as well have touched her.

Her breath caught. "You didn't have to wait." This was not wise. Yet she couldn't stop the words.

His eyes darkened and he shook his head. But he did not move.

Anita stepped toward him, close enough that the only thing between his hard muscles and her skin was the towel.

"This is not a good idea." His voice was husky, and he hadn't torn his eyes from her or moved.

"It's not," she agreed.

"I was a mess when you left." He leaned into her. Heat from his body emanated through the towel.

"So was I," she whispered, barely able to get the words out.

The way he was looking at her, though. Hooded eyes, full, parted lips.

"Terrible idea." He brought a finger to her shoulder and ran it across and up her neck, goose bumps in its wake. He rested his hand gently on her face.

She couldn't make a coherent thought right now if you paid her. Nikhil leaned down and gently touched his lips to her shoulder. It was just the whisper of a kiss, and yet her whole body responded instantly.

The towel was in her way.

She brought his face to hers and pressed her lips against his, properly kissing him, demanding that he open his mouth to her. Demanding that he kiss her back. He obliged, taking over just as he had earlier, deepening their kiss. This time, Anita pressed closer, drawing her fingers lightly over those muscles on his back, reveling in his moan of pleasure.

He continued to kiss her and brought his other hand gently across her shoulder and down her collarbone, gripping the towel in front of her chest. She might have moaned or maybe he did, but he tugged on the towel and finally she was free of it. The towel slipped to the floor and, exposed, Anita sighed as his skin touched hers.

This was not the plan. There were maybe a hundred reasons not to do this, but she couldn't think of any of them right now. She couldn't think right now, and she didn't want to. She just wanted to feel.

Anita groaned into his mouth, wrapping her arms around his shoulders to pull him yet closer to her.

They eventually broke for air. "Anita?" Nikhil's voice was husky and soft.

She just looked at him, unable to speak. She loved him. Damn it. She had never stopped. She had simply squished all those feelings down into a small, locked box in her heart, and they had just burst open. Being with Nikhil tonight was going to set her back, but right now, she could not think of one good reason not to be with him.

Just this one last time.

Nikhil searched her face. He was looking for her doubt.

He wouldn't find it.

"Yes?"

"Want to take another shower?" Nikhil's grin was delightfully devilish.

She stepped back from him and grabbed his hand, leading him back to the bathroom.

DAY FOUR:

DROPPING THE WHITE CLOTH

AND DANCES

Two Souls Becoming One...

Chapter 16

Nikhil's eyes fluttered open in the darkness to find Anita curled up into him, their legs entwined. A quick glance through the skylight showed him the moon high in the sky, so there was plenty of night still left. He shifted slightly, trying not to wake her.

"Nikhil?" Her voice was groggy with sleep.

"Hey. Sorry. I didn't mean to wake you," he whispered.

"It's okay." She shifted closer to him.

He wrapped his arm around her and pulled her closer and wished this night could last forever.

"Nikhil?" Her voice was soft in the darkness, but no longer laced with sleep.

"Hmm."

"How did you finally start writing?"

Of all the questions… He half smiled to himself. She wanted to know how he finally got moving.

He had had the hardest time getting started on his dream when they were married. He had taken some writing classes, and then had quit his one paying job as a bartender to pursue his writing. Which basically consisted of him staring at his computer for hours on end. While Anita worked.

He really had been a complete ass. He wondered again why she had ever married him to begin with. Though why she had left was becoming increasingly more clear.

"Why did you ever even marry me?" Nikhil countered.

"I asked first."

"I know."

Silence. The sound of Anita's deep, resigned sigh reached him through the darkness. "I was in love with you. You were sweet and charming, and you could have followed in your family's expected path, but you wanted to find your own way. I thought that was admirable. Especially since I was—lost."

"Lost? You were so busy when we met. Substitute teaching during the day, assisting professors at night and helping Amar with recipes in between. You had almost no downtime."

"That's how I wanted it. I didn't want to think about my parents being gone—I couldn't handle that sense of floating I felt when I thought about them being gone. I was looking for solid ground." She paused. "I clung to you. That was completely unfair."

"Well, I was truly a selfish bastard. I was too caught up in myself to even see what you were going through. I'd let my mother's expectations—or lack thereof—control my decisions for so long, I was truly blind to the good relationships in my life. Like you. Rocky."

"You didn't answer my question. How did you finally start writing?"

He drew his fingers gently down her spine. She wiggled closer to him. "Are you trying to distract me?"

"Is it working?" He grinned into the dark and pulled her gently on top of him.

Her hair tumbled forward, grazing his chest. "It is."

Nikhil never wanted to leave this room. He was conscious of this before his eyes opened to the early-morning light pouring in from the skylight. He patted the space next to him and felt a jolt of disappointment when he found the bed empty. The shower was running and he smiled to himself as he left the bed to join his wife in the shower—again.

His ex-wife.

What the *hell* was he doing?

He stared at the bathroom door. It was ajar. She left it open for him. The water turned off and he listened to her hum while she toweled off. Just as he decided he was doing what he wanted, and what he wanted to do right now was her, she walked out, a towel wrapped around her, hair damp.

"Isn't this how we started all this?" he asked as he went to her.

She shrugged and dropped her towel just as their bedroom door opened.

"Bhaiya— Ah! What is happening?" Tina shrieked, squeezing her eyes shut and turning away.

"Oh s—!" Anita muttered a curse, quickly reached down and grabbed her towel before fleeing into the bathroom.

Nikhil quickly grabbed at his shorts, which happened to be on the floor. "Knock much, Tina?"

"Well, how was I supposed to know—you two are divorced!" Tina screeched.

"Still," Nikhil growled. He found a T-shirt and put it on. "What do you want?"

Tina slowly turned around, opening only one eye at first, checking if it was safe.

Anita slammed the door to the bathroom shut and leaned against it, her heart racing. She looked down at herself and quickly wrapped the towel around her tighter as if Tina could still see her.

What the hell was happening? And she didn't mean just Tina barging in. Last night had been incredible with Nikhil. But— Loud voices from outside the bathroom interrupted her thoughts.

"What is the matter with you, Bhaiya?" Tina was whisper-shouting. "Don't you remember how you were when she left the last time? She broke your heart. Just because she's here doing something nice, it doesn't mean that she's going to stay." Tina softened. "Unless she is?"

Anita may have imagined it, but there seemed to be a flicker of hope in Tina's softened voice.

"Maybe." Nikhil's voice was heavy. "No. I don't know."

Anita's heart fell. She couldn't explain why. She was a grown woman. She knew that one night of sex did not equal a relationship. No matter what her feelings for him were. If he didn't know if he wanted her, then that was that.

"All I'm saying is, be careful with your heart. She's only bound to us for a few more days."

"Us?"

"You. I meant you."

"No, you meant us." Nikhil's voice gentled.

Anita couldn't believe what she was hearing. When she divorced Nikhil, she left the whole family. Even Tina. She had thought about reaching out a few times via text, but at the last minute, she never did.

"Well, I couldn't very well go on seeing her when the mere mention of her name had you either in a rage or moping," Tina countered.

"Well, all that is past now. You can, and should, do whatever you want."

Anita wanted to rush out and hug her. Tina had been like a sister to her, and she had missed her terribly. But Tina was right: Anita was leaving in two days. There was no point in renewing bonds that were bound to be broken again.

Maybe she should have thought about that last night instead of giving in to her feelings.

"This isn't about me, Nikhil. It's about you. And her."

"Aren't you getting married again today?" Nikhil had forced humor in his voice. He was done talking to his sister.

"Nikhil…"

"Tina…" Nikhil sighed. "I'm a grown man. I can take care of myself."

"Mmm-hmm."

"Why are you even here?" Nikhil asked, feigning irritation.

"I just…wanted to see you before I got married." Anita heard muffled sounds and smiled to herself, realizing Nikhil was hugging his little sister.

"Good luck today. You're a lucky girl. Jake's amazing."

"Wait. Aren't you supposed to tell me how lucky Jake is, to get someone as amazing as me?"

"Why would I say that?" The amusement in his voice made Anita shake her head. "Jake made his choice. He's stuck with you. You were born into this family— I had no choice."

"You're the worst," she admonished, but the laughter in her voice was just as clear. "I'm sure Rocky will be nicer than you."

"Little Sis, if you're waiting for Rakesh Joshi to be nicer than me, you have a long wait."

"Ha-ha."

"Go. Go make yourself into a beautiful bride."

Anita heard the door open. "Love you," Nikhil called.

"Love you, too, Bhaiya."

Anita heard the door shut. She stared at the bathroom doorknob, waiting to see if Nikhil would try it, to pick up where they had left off or not. She wasn't sure what she would do if he tried the knob. Would she throw caution—and her heart—to the wind and open it?

She stared at the knob for a few minutes.

"Anita?" he called from the other side of the door.

She opened the door.

"You heard?"

She nodded. "Probably best if we didn't—" It seemed the safest thing to do.

He nodded. "Yeah, probably right."

"Last night was—" she started to say.

"Amazing."

The way he was looking at her, she was going to melt into him again, her heart be damned. Time to back it up. She used her best nonchalant tone. "I was going to say *expected*. I mean we were married. We always enjoyed each other. We're grown, consenting adults, we were bound to sleep together since we were in close proximity."

"Grown, consenting adults." Nikhil stared at her a moment, then shook his head, stepping back from her. "Of course."

Silence hung in the air, during which Anita tried to convince herself that her words were true.

"I'm going to get dressed. Be out in a minute."

"We need to practice." He spoke after a moment.

"Can we just forget about the dance?" Anita pleaded.

"Um, no. We promised Dada."

"Well, I have hair and makeup in an hour, so we can practice until then." She smiled gamely. "We certainly wouldn't want to disappoint your grandfather."

Anita was stiff in his arms as they practiced, not anywhere near as relaxed as she had been last night. But who was he kidding? He was keeping his physical distance as well. Tina was right. He couldn't afford to forget that he and Anita had had their chance and it hadn't worked out.

Besides, what had Anita said? *Grown, consenting adults.* It was just sex. She didn't have any real feelings for him. Though as much as he had been trying to deny his feelings for Anita, they were there, and had probably never left. He had simply gotten used to dealing with them.

Or maybe he had hoped that one day, he would be able to get her back.

"I'm definitely going to need your cues to get through this," Anita said as they finished up.

"Of course." Cues. That's what he was good for. He

reminded himself that Anita was here for a reason. To put on a show and get her tuition paid.

"I'm just going to put on my sari and get going for hair and makeup."

"Sure."

The distance between them seemed larger today for some reason. They were extra polite.

She went into the bathroom to change into the sari blouse and the slip. Nikhil sighed—just as well. Not six hours ago, they had been naked together.

She came out and stood in front of the long mirror in her heels, floor-length sari slip and short sari blouse. She turned on a YouTube video on her phone and put it in front of her as she started to put on the sari. Curious that the sari master was going to the internet for help, Nikhil peeked over her shoulder.

"Um." He reached out to touch the sari. "Can I?" he asked the woman he had been married to. Who he'd just had his hands—and mouth—all over.

"Oh. Yeah. We're supposed to wear it mermaid style, which is cute, but—"

"Here. You just need someone to hold this." He held the sari in place while she wrapped and made pleats. Once she had everything secure, she handed him a safety pin and he pinned the sari in place.

He looked at her in the mirror. The sari was the same color blue as the bridesmaid's dress she had worn yesterday. Tina had picked a simple chiffon sari with a thick silver beaded border, which was perfect for the way Anita had wrapped it. The border drew a long line across her body from shoulder to calf, the rest of the sari hugging her curves tight. Hence the term *mermaid*.

But Anita didn't need the sari to make her beautiful. Nikhil studied her in the mirror as she made final adjustments. She was beautiful in a way he had never noticed before. "You look different."

"Do I?" She turned her face to him.

"What were you just thinking about?"

"Oh," she said, then hesitated, still looking at him. "I was thinking about my case yesterday and how I still have to take care of things, but I think I have a solution."

"Yeah? What is it? Tell me." He took her hand and sat down on the bed.

She bit her bottom lip. "I don't want to jinx it before I've gotten it, you know?"

"Of course." But he desperately wanted her to share her thoughts. It was not lost on him that had he listened to her while they were married, they might still be married.

She took back her hand and he felt slightly empty. He sat as she gathered her things and made to leave.

And just like that, Anita was out the door.

Chapter 17

Anita needed to get away from Nikhil and all the warm, fuzzy feelings she was having for him. Having him help her put on her sari, just like old times, had all those feelings buzzing inside her again. Not to mention that incredible night, the hours they'd spent in each other's arms.

She had been thinking about *him* when he asked. So, of course she lied and told him that she was thinking about work. If not, who knew what she might say—or god forbid—do? They'd had their chance and it was over. Only a fool would go down the same road twice. And she was done being a fool.

She might no longer be the person she was back then, and he might be different, too. But that didn't mean they should be together. No matter how good the sex was.

She made a detour at the house before leaving for the hotel, so she could talk to Seema-auntie. She knocked on Seema-auntie's study door, knowing there was no way she was still in bed. She was likely answering emails, or setting up a brief before things got going here today. But no answer. She cracked the door and found the room empty. Hmph.

"Can I help you with something, beti?" Seema-auntie's voice came from behind her.

Anita spun around, startled. "I was actually looking for you. I assumed you had work to do." She indicated the study.

Seema-auntie chuckled. "My daughter is getting married. I am not working at all this weekend. I have the associates to handle any emergencies that come up."

Anita was stunned.

Seema-auntie continued to grin at her. "People change, beti."

Apparently.

"What can I help you with?"

"Let's talk in the study."

Seema-auntie nodded and led the way in. She shut the door and turned to Anita.

"I was wondering if we could change the terms of our agreement." Anita got right to it.

"Oh?"

"I'll keep my end, of course. I'm not trying to leave." Although, it might be easier to move on from Nikhil if she left now. "But I was wondering if instead of tuition money for me, you would be willing to hire a young woman who is a client of mine. She's hardworking and a quick learner. The caveat is she needs childcare, as well."

Seema-auntie stared at her. "You want to forfeit your tuition to get this young woman a job?"

Anita continued as if Seema-auntie hadn't spoken. "I know you have childcare on the premises. She could earn a decent living and her children would be taken care of. Every so often, she might need to work from home, as she has an ailing mother. But I looked it up, you *are* looking for secretarial help, and she'd be perfect. Maybe a bit of training, but I know she'd be an asset to JFL."

Seema-auntie eyed her carefully. "Why are you helping this girl?"

"She's a client. Her mother is ill and needs care. She wants to move her mother in with her, but she's currently working shift work for an hourly rate and can't afford a bigger place. She's barely making rent on her current place. She also has two small children."

"You're trying to ground her, give her something solid she can believe in."

"I suppose I am. But I also know she has potential. She won't be a secretary forever." Anita smiled.

"I thought you wanted to be debt free."

"I'll manage. I'll be fine. Just give this young woman the job and we'll be even. Anything beyond that is up to her." Anita found she wasn't even exaggerating. She was fine taking a loan. Debt wasn't the end of the world. It was one year's tuition. She'd been through worse. She would find a way to handle it. But Charlotte was stuck, and this was a way to help her.

"What if she's not as good as you say?"

Anita shrugged. "Fire her. By then, the wedding will be over—you'll have gotten your end. I'm only asking you give her a chance."

Seema-auntie studied her a moment, then held out her hand. "Done. I'll make the changes."

Anita shook her hand, but then went in to hug her. "Thank you so much! You won't be sorry."

"I'm not worried."

"I better go." Anita smiled. "Hair and makeup."

Her heart was light as she drove to the hotel where the wedding would be. Charlotte would be taken care of at JFL as long as she worked hard.

Anita arrived in the bridal suite expecting to see all the girls, but instead found only Tina, her hair and makeup done. She tried not to think about how Tina had caught her naked with Nikhil that morning.

Too late, she felt the flush rise up her face. "Oh." She looked around as if maybe the other girls were hiding. "I thought we were all meeting here today."

"We are. The others are running late." Tina shrugged as if she'd expected it and didn't make eye contact. "I think they're hungover. Anu went to get chai. She'll be back in a minute." Tina motioned for Anita to sit.

"Sure." Anita looked at Tina. Her hair had been done in a beautiful updo that left some strands free. Flowers sat in almost a crown around the updo. Her makeup was natural, her jewelry, simple gold. All in all, she was a beautiful bride. "Need help with the sari?"

Tina nodded. Anita stood and retrieved the sari from the closet. "This is a beautiful panetar," gushed Anita. It was the traditional white sari with a thick red border. It had simple bead work and sparse design, but the material was exquisite. They stood in front of the full-length mirror and Anita started wrapping the red-and-white bridal sari.

"Yours looks good," Tina said, making eye contact in the mirror.

Anita cleared her throat. "Nikhil helped me."

Tina pressed her lips together, her body stiff. "You're messing with my brother's heart. I warned—"

Anita tensed and looked Tina in the eye through the mirror. "I most certainly am not."

Tina pursed her lips. "That's not what I saw this morning."

"What you saw is really none of your business," Anita snapped, despite the flush she felt rise to her face. "Knock next time."

"Lock the door," Tina retorted.

"I would have if I had thought— It wasn't *planned*..." Anita slowed down and inhaled deeply. "Not the point. The point is whatever happens or doesn't happen between Nikhil and me is between us."

"Until I have to pick up the pieces. Again," Tina spit back.

"There will be no pieces." Nikhil would have to have real feelings for her for him to break into pieces. But he had agreed that they were simply consenting adults with a past, who were good together in bed. So...no pieces. "Nikhil and I are adults. We know what we're doing." Ha. *Good one, Anita!*

"Whatever." Tina rolled her eyes. "It's not just him, you know. You left us all."

"You mean you." Anita softened her voice.

"Yes. I mean me. You were the closest thing to a sister that I had. We confided in each other, and just like that you're gone." She snapped her fingers.

"What was I supposed to do—have coffee and lunch with my ex-husband's sister?" Anita defended herself.

"No, you were supposed to be my friend."

"Well, I couldn't." Anita tried to concentrate on making pleats.

"Why not?" Tina was nothing if not challenging.

"Because it would have been awkward and weird. And I thought he might need you. He's closer to you than anyone else in the family." It was true. That was a part of it.

"Sure, it might have been in the beginning. But it wasn't like he was coming with us. I reached out to you. And you ignored me."

Anita let silence flow in the air. Tina was getting married today; they didn't need to get into all that now.

"So you're not going to say anything?" Tina insisted.

"It's your wedding day." Anita tried to remain calm, focused. She restarted the pleats. They weren't working today.

"So what?" Tina snapped.

"What do you want me to say?" Anita dropped the pleats again but didn't bother to pick them up. The sari pooled in a mound of red, white and gold at their feet. "That I ignored your texts because it was too hard to see you? Because seeing you would remind me of him? And I missed him so damn much, some days it was all I could do to not call him or, worse, show up at the apartment and beg him to give our marriage a second chance?" Anita was shouting into the mirror now, close to tears. That was the truth of it. She *had* ignored Tina's texts because she knew Nikhil needed his sister. But the whole truth was that Anita could not have anything to do with anyone who was part of Nikhil. It was too hard.

"You're angry because I hurt your brother and stopped talking to you. I'm sorry I hurt you. But I lost *all* of you when I left." And after losing her parents a few years before, the loss of the Joshi family... It was too much. It had been easier to simply cut everyone off at the time.

Tina gazed at her in the mirror. "You still love Nikhil."

Anita shook her head as she fought back the tears that burned at her eyes. "No. Don't be ridiculous."

Tina turned away from the mirror and looked at Anita head-on. "I'm not." A sad smile came across her face. "I don't know why I didn't see it before. You *are* still in love with him. And he's still in love with you."

Anita's traitorous heart fluttered at the thought that Nikhil might still be in love with her. After last night, she'd hoped for just a second, but she didn't really think they had a chance. She was in law school. She might actually work for JFL one day, if what Jake had said actually panned out. Maybe Jalissa had screwed him, but Anita wasn't about to spend her whole life convincing Nikhil that she wasn't Jalissa. It didn't really matter how they felt. She ignored it. Tina didn't know what she was talking about.

She shook her head. "Not true. Any of it. Me. Nikhil." Apparently she could no longer make sentences either.

"I know you. I know my brother. And you're not here just to help my mom or Dada or for tuition money. You're in love with him. And you're afraid of what that means."

No. That wasn't true.

Except that it was.

Chapter 18

Nikhil was just donning his blue sherwani for the wedding when Rocky texted him.

Meet in Mom's study ASAP. It's Jalissa.

Nikhil didn't bother with the buttons on his sherwani, instead racing down to his mother's study with his jacket half open. He barged into the study, to find Rocky and Jalissa waiting for him. Rocky was fuming. Jalissa looked cool as a cucumber, already dressed for the wedding, a vicious smirk on her face. "What the hell is going on?"

Rocky answered. "Jalissa here wants the community division we're starting up."

"That's Anita's," Nikhil blurted out as if it were a fact. It was, as far as he was concerned. From the look on his brother's face, Rocky thought so, too. "Absolutely not."

Jalissa grinned her answer. "If I don't get the community division, I'll tell your grandfather about your divorce."

"You're bluffing," Nikhil said.

"Am I?"

"Yes. If you tell Dada about my divorce, you'll be fired. There's no way you would risk your job." He glanced at Rocky, an eyebrow raised. Rocky nodded his agreement. Felt nice to be on the same page as his brother for once.

Jalissa shrugged. "I'm not risking it. You all have been falling over yourselves to save face in front of him. Not to mention, that as the associate bringing in the highest amount of revenue, I seriously doubt you'll fire me."

"Don't flatter yourself, Jalissa." Rocky's mouth was twisted in disgust. "It doesn't matter how much you bring in if you're screwing with the family."

Panic flashed across her contact-lens-green eyes, but Jalissa quickly rallied and gave a one-shouldered shrug. She hadn't counted on money not being the most important thing at JFL. "I'm not concerned."

"She clearly has something else already lined up, Rock," Nikhil said as he walked over to his brother. "I say we fire her."

Rocky pursed his lips to hide a smile as he nodded. "I concur. You forgot that the practice is called Joshi *Family* Law," Rocky said as he turned to Jalissa. "Not only do you not get the community division, you are also fired from JFL as of right now. I'm changing your access to all files. Go take the other position, Jalissa, if indeed you have one. JFL doesn't bow to blackmail, and we stand by family. Also, leave this wedding. You never should have been here to begin with."

"You don't even have that authority. Only your mom can fire me." Jalissa's words were firm, but Nikhil caught her eye flick. She didn't know anything.

"Try me." Rocky stared her down for a minute.

"You're making a huge mistake," Jalissa nearly hissed on her way out.

"No. The mistake was letting you stay on after you treated my brother badly. We're a family firm. And he's my family," Rocky barked at her.

Jalissa left in a huff. Nikhil watched her huff away, a pang of unease settling into his stomach. This wasn't over yet.

"Thanks, Rocky," Nikhil said, still staring at the door. "We should just end this farce ourselves and tell Dada the truth."

"Let's just get through today. Let Tina have her day." Rocky was already on his phone. "Don't thank me yet. It takes a minute to lock her out of the files." He barked orders into his phone.

"Hey!" The door to the bridal suite opened. "I have chai for the bride!" Anu's singsong voice reached them along with the aroma of spiced chai. The girl was perceptive, however, and sensed something was up right away. "What happened?"

"Bhabs is in love with Nikhil." Tina sounded happy. Anita's heart ached at the sound of the shortened version of *bhabhi* that Tina had always used for her. "Which is great, because I know Nikhil still loves her."

Anu's eyes widened. "Well, duh. They're getting back together, or at least trying it out, right?"

Anita shook her head. "Yes. No. I don't know." She picked up the sari and handed it to Anu. "You can finish putting on her sari. I need to go." She stepped around a shocked Anu. "And don't call me Bhabs," she called without turning around. "I'm not your sister-in-law."

She thought maybe Tina had called out to her, but it didn't matter. This whole thing had been a mistake. How had she thought this was going to work? Did she really think that she could be in Nikhil's presence and protect her heart? Ridiculous. She needed to just leave. If she stayed, she'd only fall harder. It would be so easy to believe Tina and give in to her feelings. But the reality was that people didn't really change. Nikhil would never believe she loved him for him. And she wouldn't spend her life proving that to him.

Tears blurred her eyes as she left the bridal suite and made her way down the spiral stairs and toward the front where she had parked her car. She was moving toward the back entrance as fast as her pointy heels would carry her, wiping her eyes, when she remembered the new deal she had made with Auntie just that morning.

Charlotte's job in exchange for her presence.

She had to stay. She had no choice. It wasn't just about her anymore. Her heart heavy, she turned back and bumped into something very solid.

She stepped back, catching her balance. "Oh sorry."

"I'm sorry!"

As they apologized in unison, Anita realized that male voice was very familiar.

"Amar?"

"Anita?" He stepped back from her. He was wearing chef's whites with "Taj" embroidered over the left breast. "Have you been crying? What did Nikhil do?"

His face filled with anger with a velocity Anita had not known was possible.

"Nothing, Amar. It's fine."

"It's fine, is it? You pretending to be married to your ex-husband for tuition money?"

"Well, not when you say it like that." He made it sound slightly sordid.

"And what's this about you getting back together with him? That better not be true."

She shook her head. "It's not. I was just trying to let Sonny down gently."

"Talk to me, Anita. What's happening?" Amar's voice was gentle.

She shook her head. "Not now. I just need to get through this day."

"I actually texted you a few times. I need help," Amar said.

"I must have silenced my phone during the reception last night. Sorry. What's up?"

"The pastry chef is sick."

"What does that mean? No cake?"

"No. The cake is started, and her team can finish that, but I need someone to do the desserts. Mini gulab jamun, rose truffles…"

Anita already had her phone out and was texting.

"Who are you texting?"

"Divya." Duh.

Amar's eyes widened in panic. "Divya? No, don't text *her*. I don't want her to come. I was thinking one of her pastry school friends. What was that one woman's name, who used to come over with her? Who made that whimsical cake? Emily?"

Anita rolled her eyes. "Divya is the one who taught

Emily how to make that cake. And they did not go to pastry school together. Emily is a nurse." Anita looked at her brother like he was crazy. Of course he had no real idea who Emily was because when Divya was around, she was the only person he noticed. "Divya's great, she works fast and you're desperate."

"She has no experience."

"Not true. She has a ton of experience. And once again, you're desperate."

Amar threw his gaze all over the foyer for a couple minutes, as if a pastry chef would emerge from the walls. Finally, he looked back at Anita, his mouth in a line. "Fine. Text her. But she better be good."

"She is." Anita hit Send. And Divya responded almost immediately.

Will I get paid?

"She gets paid, right?"

"Of course."

Anita sent off another text, then grinned when the reply popped up. "Then she'll be here in thirty minutes."

"Thank you." Amar's gratitude was genuine, but she could see he was preoccupied by the fact that he would be working side by side with Divya.

Another catering employee walked by. "Hey, something's up in the kitchen. Boss needs you."

Amar shook his head. "I have to go." He started to walk away, and turned back. "Can you tell her to come to the back entrance?"

Anita texted him Divya's number. "Tell her yourself."

Amar threw her an irritated look. Whatever. She

couldn't be his go-between right now. He was a grown man. He'd figure it out.

Anita nodded. She didn't want to go back to the girls. So she found a bathroom to freshen up in. Her phone rang. Divya.

"Hey, Divya, aren't you supposed to be on your way here?"

"I am. I'm driving. You're on speaker." Divya paused. "Did Amar ask for me, specifically?"

"No. He thought your friend Emily was a pastry chef." Anita laughed.

"Oh."

Was it her imagination, or did her friend sound slightly disappointed?

Then Divya laughed. "Ha. Whatever. How's it going with Nikhil?"

Sudden tears choked her throat so she couldn't talk.

"Anita? Are you crying?"

"No." She sniffled.

"Aw. You just realized you were still in love with Nikhil."

"What? No. How did you know?"

"Um, duh. I'm your best friend. I know things."

"Then why didn't you stop me from agreeing to this whole arrangement?"

"Like that was even possible. And besides, when is the last time you didn't just do what you wanted?" Divya said.

There wasn't one.

"You actually never stopped loving him, in case you didn't know. You didn't leave because you stopped loving him—you left because he didn't support you." Divya was very wise.

"But it's been years—"

"Do you love him? Isn't that why you're crying?"

"Maybe."

"Did you sleep with him?"

"Maybe?"

"Oh jeez. Then what happened?"

"Tina caught us."

Divya laughed. "I wish I could have seen your face!"

"Do you, though?"

"Okay, maybe not." She quieted her laughter. "Did you talk to him?"

"About what?"

"Anita, come on. Did you tell him how you feel?"

"No."

"You need to talk to him."

"I can't tell him I'm in love with him when I'm the one who left. It's not fair." She finished touching up her makeup and walked out of the bathroom while Divya spoke.

"It's not about being fair. It's about you and him. People change, Anita. You've grown and changed. In fact, you started when you left the marriage. That was you learning to stand on your own two feet. That was you learning to live without your parents or anyone else to save you. You saved yourself. And look at you now."

Before she could completely digest what Divya had said, a familiar voice called out to her.

"Anita," Rocky asked her, "you got a minute? The shit has hit the fan."

The look on Rocky's face made her heart drop into her belly. "Divya. Amar says go to the back entrance when you get here. I've got to go." She tapped her phone off and turned to Rocky. "What happened?"

Rocky filled her in on Jalissa's threat. "Just a heads-up in case you come across her. She should be gone, but you never know. Also let's keep this from Tina for now, let her enjoy her day."

"Yeah, sure. Shouldn't we just come clean to Dada, though?"

"That's exactly what Nikhil wants to do." Rocky studied her a moment, amusement flitting across his features. "But we're going to wait until after today." Rocky became all business again. "Let's get through the celebration and then we can face the music."

"Sure." Anita nodded her agreement with the plan. "It's a risk. But it makes sense." She'd find a way to make it through the day.

After that run-in with Jalissa, Nikhil drove to the wedding hotel, checked into his hotel room and went upstairs to write for a while. It was a five-star hotel, and he and Anita were in a suite that had a small office area. He wrote words then deleted them. Wrote more and deleted. The words weren't coming, and they hadn't been for almost a month. He had a deadline and for the first time in several years, he didn't think he was going to make it.

All he could think about was Anita. And if he was honest, he had been thinking about her long before she showed up here three days ago. He had never really stopped thinking about her. She was always there, in the scent of her perfume on a passing stranger, when he made a recipe she had tweaked or watched a Bolly-wood film he knew she would enjoy.

His family had been in wedding-planning mode for the past three months, since Tina and Jake's timeline required they move fast. Tina had been working the administrative, regulatory and business counseling division and had recently been promoted, as her expertise in this area had expedited a business opening for a big client of theirs. She wanted to get married before things got super busy at the office.

They had hired a planner, but of course, weddings made Nikhil think of divorce. Specifically his. But Tina was his little sister, so he sucked it up and helped wherever he had been needed. So, by the time he had found Anita standing next to his mother three days ago, Nikhil had already had a brain full of thoughts about her.

He had been trying to figure where they had gone wrong, wondering if there was any way to fix it, when she'd shown up. Almost like he'd conjured her from his heart and brought her to him. The ultimate Accio spell.

Even though he was not making any real progress, he lost track of the time. Nikhil arrived downstairs at the wedding hall later than he had intended. He had wanted to dance with the jaan, the groom's procession, but he seemed to have missed it. Hopefully no one noticed.

Nikhil followed the sounds of the pandit's chanting to find the wedding hall. Had they actually started on time?

His brother greeted him at the door to the wedding hall. "You're late. I've been texting you."

"Phone's on silent." Nikhil looked at his watch. "I was working, got carried away with an idea."

"You're an hour late. You missed the jaan, so you weren't here to greet the groom. Everyone is inside. Go take your seat. Tina's procession will start in a few minutes." His brother was thoroughly annoyed with him. "Mom was asking where you were."

"How was I supposed to know you'd start on time?" He was completely bummed he missed the jaan. Not to mention, he completely sounded like a child. "I'm sorry. The time just got away from me."

"It's our sister's wedding," Rocky insisted. "Why are you working?"

"Where's my real brother and what did you do with him?" Nikhil deadpanned.

"Shut up." Rocky shook his head, softening. "I'm going to be a dad soon. And I want to make sure I'm there for my kid. I don't want to miss things, like Mom and Dad did. I mean they were building a business—I get it. But I want to watch my kids play sports or dance or whatever."

"Wow. That's a change."

"It really isn't. We just don't talk like that in our family. Whether you see it or not, you have that Joshi family crazy work ethic."

"No, I do not. I would go to my kid's things," Nikhil insisted.

"It's not just kid things, Nikhil. It's everything. It's life. Yes, work hard. But don't miss out on life because you were working the whole time. You just spent two hours in your room trying to work. You could have been hanging out with the cousins, meeting friends or even just being with Anita. Not to mention you missed the rehearsal the other day. And we had fun, which you missed out on. I bet you have something scheduled this afternoon."

Nikhil opened his mouth to protest, but nothing came out.

"Uh-huh. That's what I thought." Rocky shook his head. "What are you trying to prove?"

He wasn't trying to prove anything, was he? Nikhil

was aghast but followed his brother to the mandap, where his mother was performing a ceremony with Jake before Tina arrived. Jake's parents sat on either side of their son, watching.

Maybe he was working too much. He'd reconsider his priorities after the big meeting this afternoon.

The pandit finished the welcoming-the-groom puja and excused Nikhil's mother. Michael and Christi had their seats moved back behind Jake in preparation for Tina's arrival.

Two of Jake's friends held up the antarpat. This decorated white cloth was held between the bride and groom until the bride arrived in the mandap, at which time the antarpat would be dropped. This hearkened back to olden times when the bride and groom would see each other for the very first time when the antarpat was dropped. The separation was symbolic of their individual lives, so dropping the antarpat symbolized the two souls becoming one.

The DJ started the music and everyone stood to watch the bride enter. Deepa-masi and Neepa-masi and her family were Tina's escorts today. But before them came Tina's bridal party. Anita was part of this procession.

Nikhil never even saw his sister enter with their masis because he could not take his eyes off Anita. He'd just seen her a few hours ago, but it wasn't the hair and makeup that made her so irresistible. There was something else about her. She glowed. That was all there was to it.

Tina floated into the mandap and stood, staring at the white cloth. Jake stared at the cloth from his side. He inhaled deeply and nodded to his friends. They dropped the cloth, allowing bride and groom to finally see each other. Tina and Jake each radiated the other's love. The pandit invited Tina to sit, and the ceremony began.

Nikhil watched Anita as she took her seat behind his sister. He thought his heart might burst in that moment with longing and love for Anita. It was exactly then that he realized that he was desperately in love with her. The antarpat was down, and he was looking at the woman he loved. And that changed everything.

Chapter 19

The ceremony finished to cheering and the throwing of flower petals. His sister was finally married to the love of her life, and she had never looked more radiant. Family pictures followed, during which he noticed Anita went missing. Some of the bridesmaids went to find her, but to no avail.

She was avoiding being in the pictures, because she knew she would be leaving the family tomorrow, and the charade would be over. Smart girl. Though it put a pang in his heart.

Just as well—Nikhil didn't think he could stand being so close to her like yesterday's pictures. Not knowing for sure that she would be gone.

Nikhil went to the bar at the allotted time to meet with the representative from his publishing house. Within minutes a woman in a black dress suit and slick high ponytail approached.

"Hi, I'm Mehgna Sura with ADS Publishing." She held out her hand.

Nikhil shook it and sneaked a peek at his watch. How long was this going to take? "Nikhil Joshi."

"Of course. Thank you so much for taking the time to meet with me, during a wedding."

"Aren't you here for a wedding as well?" On second glance Mehgna wasn't wearing a dress suit as much as she had donned a blazer over a cocktail dress. "Wait, are we here for the same one? There's only one here today."

"I am. I'm on the groom's side. That's so funny."

He hesitated. "I'm with the bride."

"Oh, nice. My husband went to college with Jake. How do you know the bride?"

"She's my sister."

Mehgna did a double-take at him. "Your sister? And you let them schedule this meeting?"

"I was told it was important. And that you were here."

"Well, it is. I'm just surprised to have found someone as crazy as me willing to work during a family wedding." She pulled out her laptop.

Nikhil stared at the laptop. "I thought we were just having a drink, getting to know each other."

"We are. But I want to map out your next few projects as well." She stared him down. "Is that a problem?"

"No." He shook his head. Work was work, right? Though Rocky's voice echoed in his head. "Let's get to it."

Mehgna was in no hurry and took her time to discuss his future with their publishing house. He should have been thrilled; it was everything he'd been working for. Mehgna's plan would take him from a bestselling author to a blockbuster author, with his books becoming movies or even television shows.

His focus was not as strong as usual. All he could do was keep glancing at the time on her computer. Thirty minutes became forty-five became sixty. The reception had started. He missed practice time with Anita, but he needed to go if he was to make it in time for the performance. He still needed to be miked so he could sing.

He was just considering apologizing to Mehgna and leaving, when Sangeeta came running up. "Nikhil-bhai! Come on, your dance. What are you doing here?"

His cousin literally grabbed him by the arm and started to drag him toward the reception hall. "I'm sorry, Mehgna. I need to go. Let's pick this up on Monday? I'll come to you."

Mehgna did not look thrilled, but Nikhil allowed Sangeeta to drag him to the reception hall.

"What the hell were you doing?" Sangeeta admonished. "Anita is waiting for you."

She was probably pissed. He had missed practice and now he was late for the actual performance. After all the promises he'd made. But work was work.

Or was it?

He grimaced. "Well then, let's not keep her waiting."

The music was just starting when he entered the hall and Sangeeta shouted, "I have Nikhil."

Nikhil jogged to the dance floor in the dimmed reception hall and waited while his brother miked him. "Where the hell have you been?" Rocky mumbled. "I was about to dance for you."

"I had a meeting."

Rocky's glare could have cut diamonds, and he was a bit more aggressive with the portable microphone than was absolutely necessary. However irritated Rocky was, it was nothing compared to the pained fury in Anita's eyes.

She might have forgiven him for missing their practice, if he had actually shown up on time for the performance. Anita had tried to start without Nikhil, with his brother gamely filling in for the guy's part, but the crowd was cheering and she froze, as she usually did, without the cues they'd worked out the night before.

As soon as Nikhil got there and was miked, he began singing, cueing her as he had in practice, but she was angry and already flustered, so she was a step off the beat.

Anita finally started dancing, but she knew her moves were stiff. All of her discomfort about dancing in front of crowds came rushing back to her. She reached for Nikhil as they had practiced, but instead of taking her hand, he barely grasped her fingers, and she forgot the next step. She tried to catch up with him, but instead, bumped into him. Nikhil raised an eyebrow at her and extended his hand out to her. Seriously? He was going to question *her* with that eyebrow? She bypassed his hand and they both missed the next step, bumping into each other. She glared at him. He glared right back.

They were a disaster. People were chuckling, a few people even outright laughing! They probably thought it was a comedy bit.

Anita glanced at Tina and Jake, who were seated front and center. Jake was chuckling, and Tina had plastered a smile to her face, but the horror shone through in her eyes. The music continued, never seeming to end, but not before Anita tripped, nearly falling. She was saved by Nikhil's firm grasp, though it had been his foot she tripped over.

She stood up in his arms, ready to push him away, when a hush fell over the room. Anita looked out into the audience and found everyone looking at their phones, and then looking up at them. What was going on? She glanced at Nikhil just as she heard her brother's voice booming through the speakers.

"It's fine, is it? You pretending to be married to your ex-husband for tuition money?"

"Well, not when you say it like that." She sounded pathetic.

"And what's this about you getting back together with him? That better not be true."

She shook her head. *"It's not. I was just trying to let Sonny down gently."*

She pulled herself free of Nikhil's grasp and looked behind him at the big screen that was going to be used for the photo slideshow of the newlyweds. But instead of the slideshow, there was a video clip playing of her and Amar in the hallway that morning. Amar in his catering uniform, and her in tears. It kept replaying those few lines, and an image of Tina and Jake's wedding app was stamped in the corner of the screen. She pulled out her phone from the small pouch hooked to her sari and opened the app to confirm what she already feared. She didn't even need to scroll through the pictures. Confirmation hit her like a punch to the belly. A picture of her and Nikhil's signatures on their divorce papers.

She put her phone back in the pouch and stomped to the computer that was showing the slideshow. She typed a few things and the video stopped, silence resonating throughout the hall.

She marched out of the hall, oblivious to the stares and murmurs that followed her. All she registered was that Nikhil was at her heels. She continued walking up and down the hallway.

She saw Sonny from the corner of her eye. He looked terrible, stricken. She couldn't blame him. She would apologize to him, but first—

"What are you doing?" Nikhil asked from behind her.

"Looking for *her*," she spit out from between her teeth.

"Anita—"

And then there she was. Anita knew she would stick around to gloat. There was no point to doing all of that if she couldn't watch. And that was her mistake. Every villain made one, and this was Jalissa's.

Anita ripped off the rings from all her fingers and thrust them at Nikhil. "Hold these."

The bitch didn't even move as Anita approached her, sari hiked up so she could take long strides.

Anita didn't even speak. She didn't even stop moving. She marched right up to Jalissa and punched her. Jalissa's hand went to her face, where the punch had landed, her mouth opened in a horrified O. She looked for a moment as if she wanted to retaliate, but whether it was the look on Anita's face or the fact that Nikhil was fuming next to her or that Dada called out at just that moment, Jalissa took off without even looking back.

Anita turned at the sound of Dada's voice and marched back, Nikhil still at her heels. She'd never raised a hand to anyone in her whole life. She'd never really wanted to. Her hand was really going to hurt in the morning.

Rocky was guiding Dada into a small meeting room off the hallway, Seema-auntie and her sisters close behind. And with a stab of guilt, she realized they'd seen everything.

"Nikhil Vikash Joshi."

"Yes, Dada." Nikhil tugged at the mic that was clipped to him, disconnecting it.

"Start talking." His grandfather's tone was stiffer than he'd ever heard.

"Well, Dada. Anita and I are divorced."

"That is apparent." He nodded at Rocky's phone. "Why?"

Nikhil deflated. "Because Dada, she walked out. And I let her go." He did not look at Anita; he simply focused on Dada.

"So," Dada stated, sounding for all the world as if he were addressing a courtroom, "my youngest grandson is an idiot." Dada arched a white eyebrow.

"Yes, sir."

"Disappointing." His arched eyebrow spoke volumes. Disappointment was only the beginning. Nikhil saw anger and frustration, and when he looked into his grandfather's eyes, he saw sadness as well.

Nikhil's heart broke.

"And why are you pretending to be married?" Dada's laser focus never waned, and despite his grand discomfort, and his elder's obvious disappointment, Nikhil noted that Dada was looking and sounding quite like his old self. Certainly not frail or weak.

Nikhil squirmed under that scrutiny and flicked his

gaze to his mother. "Well, we didn't want to disappoint you, and then your health—"

His mother stepped forward. "That was my doing, Papa."

Dada's eyebrow again. "Why am I not surprised?"

Nikhil's masis made noises of agreement from behind her.

His mother turned to face them. "Oh shut up, you two! I don't know why I spend so much time trying to fit in with you two. You're both basically suck-ups to Papa."

Their looks of complete indignation were a sight to behold.

Seema-auntie swallowed. "They ended their marriage after two years. I didn't want you to suffer the humiliation of a divorce in the family, so I put off telling you. Then Ma passed and you had your heart attack. You were weak and I was afraid news like this might give you another heart attack. So when Tina's wedding came up, I asked Anita to come and pretend to be married to Nikhil for the duration. She agreed."

"You are paying her." Dada's voice dripped with sadness.

"In a sense." She could barely look her father in the eye. Nikhil noticed the masis were wide-eyed and gaping. No sign of sneering or that air of superiority they carried around his mother.

"What do you mean, in a sense?" Nikhil fired up. "You can't go back on your deal. She's counting on the money."

Seema-auntie turned to her younger son. "We amended the details this morning. I will give a job to one of her clients instead."

Nikhil snapped around to Anita. But she avoided his gaze.

Dada turned to Anita, then Nikhil. "You two..." His voice cracked.

"How could you do this to Papa?" demanded Neepa-masi. "Keeping secrets, lying. You never change, Seema."

"You didn't even tell us. We're your sisters, for god's sake!" Deepa-masi added.

"Sisters? Ha!" Seema-auntie stood and faced them. "You have never once treated me like your sister. You always have your little secrets and you have never even supported my career. When Vikash passed, I ran JFL while I raised three children. The fact that you didn't help was one thing, but then you would get upset when I couldn't drop everything and come running for whatever was happening. I am a lawyer. And a damn good one, too. And if I had told you about the divorce you would have gone running to Papa and Ma and told them how I screwed up again. And I refuse to let Papa suffer more humiliation."

"Was it really Dada who would have been humiliated by Nikhil's divorce?" Rocky spoke up. "Or was it you, Mom?"

"I was not humiliated... Nikhil is my son. I felt bad that things didn't work out for him."

"Then how come *no one* knows, even here, in town?" Rocky continued. "Face it. It was easier to tell the lie that they were still together, because you could save face. You have always underestimated Nikhil, and you continue to do so, by not telling the truth."

"No. That's not true." Seema-auntie worried the end of her sari in defiance.

"Isn't it, Mom?" Nikhil finally spoke, a sadness in his voice.

"Nikhil... I..."

"Never mind, Mom. It's fine." He shrugged.

She shook her head at Nikhil and turned to Rocky. "Rakesh Joshi, you should have come to me with Jalissa's demands."

"Why? You would have given in."

"Damn right I would have." His mother shrugged. "It would have saved us this drama at your sister's wedding."

"What would have saved the drama, Mom, was not inviting Jalissa to begin with, or even better, being honest about Nikhil's divorce. I fired Jalissa rather than let her blackmail our family."

"On whose authority—"

"On *mine*, Mom. I run the day-to-day. And you have no room to talk right now, the way you told everyone about the baby when Easha and I specifically—"

"So what if they know? You worry too much."

"Not your call, Mom. You can't just go around controlling everyone, rewriting the narrative when you don't like it. Like this whole thing with Nikhil and Anita. You didn't even warn Nikhil that Anita was coming! No more, Mom. You have issues with your family. That's on you. Nikhil, Tina and I aren't playing anymore."

His mother stood there, speechless. No one had ever spoken to her like this, least of all her golden child, Rocky.

She deflated. "You know, my whole life I have raced to keep up with my sisters. They always did everything so perfect. And I was just...overlooked. I suppose I simply wanted to be seen and seen as successful and competent and—"

"Perfect?" said Nikhil.

She nodded, tears in her eyes.

"Welcome to the club," Nikhil spoke softly.

"I always focused on how you three reflected upon me. I was a single mother, and I wanted—no, needed—to prove that I was capable of doing it all myself. Any mess up of yours indicated that I was a failure. And you, Nikhil, being on your own, unknown path since the minute you were born, were a source of stress for me always. I should have embraced your spirit, but instead, I tried to push it into a mold of my making. And look what happened. You're working at your sister's wedding. Missing once-in-a-lifetime events to prove you are successful, worthy. I blame myself."

Nikhil couldn't believe what he was hearing. And a quick glance at Rocky told him his brother did not either. Their mother had always been a formidable force in their lives, more intimidating and demanding after their father had died. He couldn't reconcile that with the vulnerable woman who was confessing her fears to them right now. "Well, I didn't exactly make it easy."

She grinned. "No, you did not." She shook her head. "I have always seen so much of me in you. Your sense of independence, not wanting to follow the crowd." She cut her eyes to her sisters. "But I never once suspected that you felt that need to prove yourself, like I did." Her face fell. "I suppose I should have, seeing as how that's how I spent my life, but... I didn't." She stood. "I am proud of you, and I always have been. Even before you became a bestselling author. I was proud of your spirit and the man I watched you become. That is success."

She smiled at her father, who nodded at her. "And don't let anyone tell you otherwise. Even me."

She went to her father and lifted her chin and looked him in the eye. "Nikhil and Anita are divorced. I asked Anita to come and pretend to be married to Nikhil so I didn't have to tell you. News of your failing health was much exaggerated—" she cut her eyes to her older sister "—but even when I saw that you were fine, I continued with the charade because Nikhil being divorced meant that *I* had failed *him* somehow. And I did not want to face that I had actually failed one of my children, even though I knew it was true."

Dada looked at her, his face expressionless for a moment. "As parents, we all fail our children, somehow, even with the best of intentions." He grinned at her. "Me included." He wrapped his arms around her. "Beti. You did the best you could, as we all did. The rest is up to them. And stop competing with your sisters. It's tiresome after fifty years, and no one will ever win. I have three strong, independent, highly opinionated daughters. Each of you has unique strengths and weaknesses and I love you all equally." Nikhil's mother pulled back, and he saw tears in her eyes.

Dada, however, had a twinkle in his eye. "My grandchildren will always beat you three out." He chuckled. "Anita?" He turned toward her. "Did you just punch Jalissa?"

"Yes, Dada. I did," Anita answered tight-lipped, but with her chin in defiance.

Dada grinned from ear to ear. "She's my favorite."

Chapter 20

"**W**here were you?" Anita fired at him as they stood in the hall. They'd left Nikhil's mother with her father and sisters and Rocky to figure how to best handle the uproar Jalissa's bombshell had caused.

"I'm sorry. I had a meeting with a publisher and it ran long—"

"I *knew* it. You were working."

"If you knew it, why are you so mad?" He said it as if it were a completely normal thing to do.

"So you weren't there for me, when I specifically asked you to cue me, because you were working?" Her voice went up an octave.

"It was just a dance. The meeting was with that big publisher I've been telling you about. It was important." The words sounded hollow, however, even to him.

"Just a dance? In front of like four hundred people.

At your sister's wedding! The person you say is your most favorite person in the world and you were *working*!" They ended up alone in front of the elevators. People were coming and going; the elevator ding was constant. Anita stopped walking in a corner where the activity was minimal.

"What do you care? You're leaving tomorrow anyway. You won't see any of these people ever again," Nikhil argued.

She opened her mouth to retort, but changed her mind. "You know what? You're right. But why wait until tomorrow? This farce is over." She shook her head at him. "You have changed. I always knew you wanted to be a successful writer, but working and chasing success is what has become most important to you. Maybe your mom is right, and you're doing that to prove something. Although what that something is, I have no idea. You never were like this when we were married. What happened to you?"

"Nothing happened to me. I'm just trying to be a success. Like the rest of my family. Like I have been told my whole life. My whole family has always worked and put work ahead of anything else. I'm just doing what I'm supposed to be doing." Nikhil paused.

He was serious. Anita shook her head at him. "I married you when you had nothing. I left because you did not support my dreams and goals, even though I fully supported yours. I was looking for purpose like I needed air, and when I found it, *you*, the person who claimed to love me most, did not stand by me. I had no choice but to leave. I had to take care of myself, because you taught me that no one else would," Anita said.

Silence permeated the space in between them. Anita

got onto an elevator and pushed the button for their floor. In minutes, they were on the floor and walking into their room.

"Listen to us. Listen to me." Anita leaned against the door when it shut. "Pissed off at you for not cueing me—in a dance. I'm not five." She shook her head. "To be honest, I barely even bothered to learn the steps." She shrugged. "I just figured I'd lean on you." Her voice softened.

"Anita, I'm sorry."

"It's not you. Sure, you should have shown up—but it's not all on you. I'm responsible for my part in this whole fiasco." She sighed. "I married you because I fell in love with your creativity and spirit. But I was also looking for stable ground. When my parents died, my whole life turned upside down. I was privileged and taken care of. But in an instant, I was forced to take care of myself. Like really take care of myself. No parental money or support. It was just me and Amar." She looked at him. "I thought marrying you would ground me. That it would somehow take away that lost feeling I had after losing my parents."

"Did it?"

She shrugged. "For a time, maybe. But it was wrong of me to put that burden on you—and you didn't even know."

"Did you…did you even love me?" His voice shook like her answer could change the world.

The hesitation in his voice was heartbreaking. But she had no trouble answering with the truth. "That is the one thing I know for sure. I did love you when I married you." It was all she could say.

She couldn't ask if he'd loved her. She was afraid of the answer. Either way.

She started taking off her jewelry and putting it in the small boxes that had already been laid out for her. It was time for her to leave. This marriage act they'd put on was done. She'd just run to the house while everyone was still here and pick up the rest of her few things.

Her overnight bag had magically arrived from the house, with a change of clothes. Perfect. She started to remove her sari as Nikhil watched her.

"I never answered your question," he said, watching her. "From the other night."

"It's okay. It doesn't matter." She folded the sari and started to pull pins from her hair.

"You had asked what started me finally writing. The short answer is, you left."

Anita stopped moving for a moment to turn and look at him. He was telling the truth. "I don't understand."

"Well, you left. And I found myself flailing. I had failed at marriage. I had failed you. So, I locked myself in my apartment and sat myself in front of my computer. And I forced the words out. At first just five hundred words. Then a thousand. Then a chapter."

"So? You started writing when I was no longer in your life." She harrumphed. "Proof we should not be together."

"I started writing *because* you were no longer in my life. I thought that if I was successful, like the rest of my family, you might want to come back. I didn't realize how incredibly wrong I was until now." He sat in the armchair, with his elbows on his knees, and rubbed his face, before looking at her again. "You didn't leave because I was not successful. You left because you needed me and I wasn't there for you. Because you wanted to follow your passion, and instead of supporting you, I let all my insecurities rule me and I shut you down. Just like tonight. We'd rehearsed for this, I promised I'd cue you, but again, I allowed myself to get caught up in impressing you and my family with how busy and successful I am, when in fact, all I did was piss off my brother and sister and worst of all, let you down—again." He stood. "That is unforgivable. No matter how much I love you."

Anita let his words sink in to every part of her. He loved her. *He loved her.* A lightness started to move through her. She halted it.

"You have been successful for a while now." Her voice was heavy as realization set in. "You didn't reach out to me."

"That's the problem, isn't it? A little part of me always knew…that I…would never be enough, no matter how successful, because the reality is that I know that I don't deserve you."

Sadness weighed down his words and Nikhil Joshi unceremoniously turned and left her life.

Chapter 21

"What are you doing home?" Amar asked as he rolled in after midnight.

Anita was on the sofa in leggings and a T-shirt, blanket covering her, watching old home movies and eating ice cream from the carton. She was a cliché. Whatever, just add it to the pile. She shrugged. "Like you didn't hear."

"Everyone heard." He glanced at the TV and sat down. They watched a clip of one of their birthday parties. Their parents looked so young.

"How much trouble are you in at work?" Anita finally asked.

"Enough. Apparently, yelling at your sister, while not a good big-brother thing to do, is not a fireable offense in the catering industry."

"Good to know."

"Changing the recipe for three of the side dishes is."

"You did what?" Anita sat up and looked at him.

"I improved those dishes. They were bland and boring. I didn't do an overhaul—I just made a small adjustment when no one was looking."

"Small, like…?"

"Like I added some of Mom's special masala to them!"

"Wait—you know how to make the special masala?" Anita sat up straight.

"Well, it's not perfect, but I'm close." Amar grinned.

"And you used it tonight?"

"Yes, but then Ranjit, the head chef, tasted it and figured out what happened."

"How did he know?"

Amar was suddenly interested in his fingernails. "It might not have been the first time I did that."

"You're fired?"

"Looks that way." He looked sheepish.

Anita nodded. "You know I forfeited the money?"

"Yes. But who is Charlotte?"

Anita told him the whole story. "So, you have no job, and I have to take out a loan for my last year of school. We're quite the pair, you and I."

"You did the right thing, Anita." He took the spoon from her and pointed it at her. "Don't worry." He scooped up some ice cream and tasted it. "What's this? It's amazing. Cardamom, vanilla, a hint of orange."

"A Divya concoction. Seriously, that girl is going to have me the size of a house at the rate she's trying new things. How was she tonight?"

Her brother's face lit up for a moment, Anita noticed, before he realized it and masked his face. "She was good."

"That's it? She was good?"

"She was great. What do you want? She did the job."
Anita rolled her eyes.

Amar took another spoonful.

"Hey, get your own ice cream. My life just—"

"Just what?"

"Imploded."

Her big brother turned and looked at her. "You're in
love with him again."

"Wrong." She snatched back the spoon.

"Oh, I don't think I'm—"

Anita put a huge spoonful of ice cream in her mouth
and spoke around it. "I never really stopped loving him."

"Does he love you?"

"Yes." She couldn't deny it. When she thought about
all that happened over the four days, she knew it in her
heart that he was in love with her. Which made the truth
sting even more. "He just doesn't think he deserves me.
And it's not my job to convince him."

It was well past midnight by the time Nikhil finally
made it back to his hotel room. His cousins had questions, his uncles, their parents' friends—not to mention
that this had been Tina's wedding reception.

He and Rocky had taken over the reception, seen to
it that there was still a celebration for their sister and
new husband and that all the guests were fed. If they
learned nothing from their mother, it was that no one
came to an Indian wedding and left without being properly fed. They took to the dance floor in celebration,
but the talk was all about Nikhil and Anita. Every time
he heard her name, his heart broke just a little bit more.
He simply smiled and moved on.

"So, I guess no fifth-anniversary party, huh?" asked Sangeeta.

"Seeing as how we are divorced…"

"You could have called us anytime, bhai." Hiral had slapped him on the shoulder and given him a hug. "But I have to say, she really didn't seem like she was faking while she was here."

"Thanks." Nikhil refused to allow himself the hope that she might actually be in love with him.

His mother remained reserved, quietly thanking the guests, and not commenting on much more. Dada was just as quiet, as were his masis.

The night finally ended and Nikhil was forced to make his way up to his very empty hotel room. He checked his email. There was one from Chantelle, telling him that the publisher's representative was appalled that he left in the middle of a meeting. Not to mention, she was there for all the family drama. The publisher felt that he should not have scheduled a meeting during a time when he had other priorities. They were questioning his professionalism, and strongly reconsidering whether they wanted to work with him. Chantelle was trying to smooth things over.

He was numb. That publisher had been everything he'd wanted from his writing career. Being with them would have put him on a trajectory he'd only dreamed of.

He hadn't committed to his family. He hadn't committed to his job. The only thing he really cared about was Anita. And he would never have her.

He was just getting out of the shower when there was a knock at the door. His heart leaped for a minute thinking it might be Anita. But he squelched that thought by the time he answered it.

"Hey." Rocky was still in his suit, tie draped around his neck, two cold beers in his hand.

"Hey." Nikhil left the door open and walked back in. "Don't you have a pregnant wife to dote upon?"

"She's sleeping." Rocky came in and shut the door behind him, handing Nikhil a beer. He held his out, and Nikhil tapped it. "Nicely done today, little brother. Who needs a wedding planner?"

"She took off fast, didn't she?"

"Apparently even we do not pay her enough for all that drama." Rocky took a swig of his beer. "Tina was happy in the end. That's all that mattered."

"True that." Nikhil smiled. "They're good together, her and Jake."

"She's pregnant."

"What the hell?" Nikhil sat up straight in his armchair, his heart racing, spilling some beer. "Does Mom know?"

Rocky started laughing. "Gotcha!"

Nikhil threw a pillow at his brother. "Jackass." He settled back into the chair. "Give me a goddamn heart attack. Forget about Dada, you're going to put *me* in the hospital."

Rocky had a few chuckles left inside him. "Your face, though."

"Why are you here, Rock?" Nikhil sipped his beer. He had no idea how much he'd wanted it until the bitter, cool, fizzy liquid hit his tongue.

"What happened?"

Nikhil knew what he meant. They were brothers, after all.

"She left. Packed her bags. Probably stopped by at the house, grabbed her stuff and left." He picked at the label on the bottle before taking a healthy swallow.

"And what? You let her walk?"

"Yes."

"You're going after her tomorrow? Just giving her time to cool off?"

"She was cool when she left."

"Then what's the plan?"

"There's no plan, Rock. We're done. We were done three years ago." He rubbed his brow. "After the way I treated her back then? Of course we're staying divorced."

"What?"

"That's pretty much why she left. She was trying to stand on her own two feet, and I couldn't be bothered to see that. I was so caught up in the idea that she would leave me—either figuratively or literally— once she went to work for JFL, that I didn't see what she wanted."

"Which was?"

"Just for me to support her, like married couples do."

"So tell her." Rocky sat up in the chair.

"I did." Nikhil sunk further into his.

"Did you ask her to come back?"

"No."

"Why not?"

"Because."

"Because *what*? You're clearly in love with her. After you got over the initial shock of her being here, I haven't seen you that happy since you guys were married."

"Just let it go, Rocky."

"Why?"

"Look, I appreciate you doing the whole big-brother

thing, but you've done your part, you can feel good about coming here and talking to me, but I'm done."

"I didn't come here to play a part. I *am* your big brother, damn it. Take a minute and remember that. We used to be close. Remember?"

Nikhil did remember. Their parents had left the three of them with a nanny more than once as children, but it was always Rocky that Nikhil and Tina had looked to. Though Rocky had become more intense after their father died, and less the fun big brother. He'd had more rules, which had not gone over well with young Nikhil.

Nikhil looked at his brother. "I guess you didn't really feel like a kid after Dad died."

Rocky shrugged. "Tell me why you can't go after the one woman you've always loved."

Nikhil shrugged. "I just can't."

"What's stopping you?"

Nikhil shook his head.

"Nikhil!" Rocky raised his voice. "What is the matter with you?"

"I don't deserve her!" Nikhil shouted back.

"What?"

"You heard me. I do not deserve her." He slumped his shoulders in admission. It cost him to reveal his fears to Rocky. "She was everything to me. She gave me her heart. And I did not hesitate to break it because I was selfish, caught up in my own fears. I'm a cliché, Rock. Didn't know what I had until she was gone." He shook his head. "She's better off without me."

"You really believe that?" Rocky asked.

"I do." Nikhil's heart sat heavy in his chest.

"Okay. Maybe you're right. She's smart, fun, gorgeous—she'll find someone new in no time."

"Sure." Nikhil nodded, his stomach churning.

"You'll find someone soon, too," Rocky said, relaxing back into the armchair. "Oh!" He sat up. "Easha told me Mom got a few offers tonight after your divorce was revealed. You'll be fine." His brother's sarcasm was not lost on him.

Nikhil shrugged. The idea of someone new for him was not appealing. Though the idea of someone new for Anita was even worse.

They drank their beers in silence for a moment.

"Answer me this." Rocky pointed his bottle at Nikhil. "Are you the same man you were when you were married to her?"

"What is this BS?"

"Just answer the question," insisted Rocky.

"No. Of course not. I was young, insecure, had a chip on my shoulder the size of your ego." Nikhil frowned and sipped his beer.

"And now?"

Nikhil stayed silent instead of throwing out the retort he had ready to go. To his credit, Rocky remained silent while Nikhil mulled. "Now… I guess now I don't have that chip on my shoulder."

"Why?"

"Because I found my own way, on my own terms."

"Exactly. You're a different man than you were back then. A better man, even. You let the Jalissa thing eat at you, when that woman simply used you from the get go. She never had any real feelings for you at all."

"What kind of idiot falls for that?" Nikhil was still a bit disgusted with himself.

"The good kind." Rocky's voice softened. "That's the part of yourself you need to come to terms with.

That good, kind soul. You always rooted for the under-
dog. You always stood up for people, regardless of what
would happen to you. But you didn't care about *winning*—you cared about people, about what was right."
Rocky paused, quieted his voice. "I know you fought
those jerks in high school because they were bullying
that boy with the turban."

"How do you know that?"

"I heard Mom talking to his parents. They had called
to thank her for what you did. The boy was too scared
to come forward, so you were suspended. Why do you
think Mom never punished you?"

"I thought she was too busy and couldn't be bothered." Nikhil shrugged.

Rocky was silent for a moment. "In all seriousness,
do you for one second believe that Anita would screw
you over the way Jalissa did?"

He didn't. He knew there had been a time when he
did fear that. But that was based on his fears, as opposed to anything real that Anita had ever done. "No.
Not anymore."

"Then that's your answer. You made a mistake. People make mistakes. You grow and change. Anita loves
you. You deserve that. You deserve to at least try."

"You think she still loves me?"

"I know she does." Rocky finished his beer and
tapped the bottle down. "Why do you think she punched
Jalissa? Anita is willing to fight for you." He tipped his
head at Nikhil. "Pretty hot."

Nikhil could not stop his grin. It was pretty damn hot.

DAY FIVE:

EGGS, ROTLI, AND THE NEWSPAPER

Brunch Off Site…

Chapter 22

Nikhil woke with a pit in his stomach and a defined feeling of loss.

Anita.

Interesting because the last time she left, he only felt anger and defiance. He closed his eyes and tried to fall back asleep. He might have dreamed about her, and he'd rather go back to that than face today's postwedding brunch with the whole family.

Sleep would not come.

He sat up in bed and inhaled. Maybe he would get used to not having her around as time went on.

Except that he didn't want to. He wanted to blow off the brunch and go find her. His conversation with Rocky was still fresh in his head as he finished showering when there was a banging at his door.

Again, his entire body lightened in the hope that it was Anita. "I'm coming."

He opened the door to find Dada standing there, dressed and ready for the day. "Dada?"

So not Anita.

"Get dressed. I need you to take me somewhere."

"Where?"

"Don't ask questions. Just hurry up before your masis wake up."

Nikhil held the door open. "Okay, sit down. I just need five minutes."

Ten minutes later they were in Nikhil's car, having sneaked out the back way to avoid running into any family members. Nikhil had no idea what his grandfather was up to, and the older man wasn't giving any clues.

"Okay, drive," Dada commanded as he fastened his seat belt.

"Where am I going?"

"Pull out of this massive driveway and I will tell you," Dada ordered. "And quickly before my daughters see us. They never let me do what I want."

Nikhil pulled the car down the long driveway and then Dada pulled out a piece of paper and directed him.

"Can I see the paper?"

"No. Just drive."

After a few turns they got on the highway for two exits, and then a couple more turns into an older upper-middle-class residential neighborhood. It was too familiar to Nikhil.

He looked at his grandfather as realization set in. "Seriously, Dada?"

"What? I want brunch." Now all of a sudden, the old man was innocent and pleasant.

Nikhil rolled his eyes. "Mom has brunch at home."

Dada actually winked at him. "True. But she does not have Anita."

* * *

Anita and Amar had stayed up too late talking and planning, but Anita was awake early anyway. Amar had helped her wrap her hand after icing it for a bit. She flexed her fingers. Stiff with bruising.

She couldn't sleep. Every time she closed her eyes, images of Nikhil bombarded her. She was debating going for a run to clear her head when the doorbell rang. She bolted for the door before it could ring again, so that her brother could sleep in.

She opened the door and her heart lifted before she could control it. Nikhil stood next to his grandfather, looking sheepish and ridiculously handsome.

"I'm sorry to bother you like this." He looked at his grandfather. "He just told me to drive, I had no idea—"

"Stop apologizing, boy. She is happy to see you," Dada interrupted.

"Come in, please. It's fine, really." She focused on Dada. It was too much to look at Nikhil. She stepped aside to allow them in. "Amar is still sleeping."

"No problem. We do not need him right now," Dada announced as he looked around her house.

"What can I do for you?" Anita asked.

"Brunch," Dada stated simply as if it was obvious.

Anita furrowed her brow and finally made eye contact with Nikhil, who shook his head, put his hands out and shrugged.

"Isn't there a wedding brunch at your place?" Anita spoke slowly.

"I have not lost my mind, children. I know that there is a meal at my daughter's house. But I want brunch *here*. And I want you two to make it." He was firm, and with that, he walked into Anita's house and sat himself at the large island in her kitchen.

Anita stared at Nikhil, her eyes wide.

"Stop staring at each other and get to work. I know that both of you were raised properly, so I know that when an elder asks for something—especially food—you comply. Honestly, it is the very minimum you could do for an old man after lying to him for four days."

With huge sighs of compliance as well as some chagrin, both Nikhil and Anita made their way to the kitchen.

"Okay." Nikhil sighed, glancing at Anita for confirmation.

Anita nodded her agreement, but she couldn't really look at him.

"Well, don't just stand there. Anita has told me that you are both excellent cooks. So? Let's see what you can do," Dada commanded.

"You told him we could cook?" Nikhil said, slightly irritated, as he grabbed two aprons from a drawer and handed her one.

Anita took the apron. *He remembered which drawer.* They'd cooked here a few times with Amar. But that was ages ago. In spite of herself, she was impressed.

"Well, we used to cook together. *I* can still cook well. Not sure about you," Anita shot back.

"Oh, I can cook just fine, *Neets*."

Anita froze in the middle of tying her apron, then looked at him. Amusement danced in his eyes; he had said her nickname on purpose. "Bring it then, *Nicky*." That was why Nikhil hated when Rocky called him Nicky, because it was what she used to call him when it was just the two of them.

They both turned to Dada and spoke at the same time. "Dada, what would you like for brunch?" They glanced at each other.

"What kind of question is that? Just make brunch. But add an Indian kick." Dada had found Anita's newspaper and was rifling through it. He had made himself completely at home. As if he was at his grandchild's home. Anita smiled.

"Okay, then." She went to the fridge and bumped into Nikhil, who was doing same thing. She shot him a look and he stepped back as she opened the door. She reached in to grab the eggs, just as Nikhil did the same.

"I got the eggs," Anita called out.

"Fine." Nikhil reached for the milk, just as Anita did with her empty hand. She backed away and Nikhil picked up the milk.

Anita put the eggs on the island and went back to get vegetables from the fridge.

"I got the vegetables." Nikhil put bell peppers, zucchini and jalapenos on the island.

"Fine." She grabbed the butter.

"Just get the—"

She put the butter on the island.

"—butter."

Anita raised an eyebrow at him. "I know we need butter."

He held his hands up in surrender.

"Why don't you get—"

But Nikhil already had his hands on the stainless steel container that held leftover rotli. "The rotli?" he asked, both eyebrows raised at her.

Anita made a face. "And the athanu." She headed back to the fridge for cilantro and tomatoes. She noticed that Nikhil went to the pantry and came out with onions, garlic and the jar of spicy mango pickle she'd asked for. They assembled their ingredients and considered them.

"How about some chai?" Dada asked from the other end of the island. He seemed quite content, if not extremely amused.

Anita gave a one-armed shrug with a small smile and glanced at Nikhil. "Well, that's his area of expertise." She turned to him. "But of course I don't have your secret masala here."

Nikhil shrugged. "Worth a try, anyway."

"Or you could just make the masala here." Anita pursed her lips. "I promise not to look."

Nikhil chuckled. "Nice try. But I'll make do with whatever you have."

"I have the one Divya makes for us." She reached into a cupboard and handed him a jar.

"Not a problem." Nikhil grabbed the saucepan and Anita placed the milk next to the stove, along with fresh ginger root and some leaves of fresh mint she plucked from the plant in the windowsill.

Meanwhile, Nikhil gathered the loose tea and filled the pot with water, setting it on the stove to boil.

Anita pulled out two cutting boards and two knives and set about chopping onions on hers. Nikhil peeled a few cloves of garlic and set them next to her cutting board. He set about chopping up the jalapenos and bell pepper.

"What happened with that publisher meeting?" Anita asked as she started chopping garlic.

"They were pissed. They questioned my priorities for scheduling a work meeting when I clearly had other obligations." He side-eyed her, but Anita did not hide her grimace of satisfaction. "They were ready to pull the offer. Chantelle smoothed things over and they offered to reschedule."

"I guess that's good for you." Anita kept chopping.

"I told them no."

Anita stopped chopping and looked up at him. "You did what?"

Nikhil sliced the bell pepper thinly, the long way. He did not look up from his task. "I told her no."

"But I thought that's what you wanted. That publisher was going to give you everything you dreamed of."

He flicked his gaze up at her for a brief second before returning to his task. "Not everything."

Anita watched him work for a moment. "Oh." She returned to her chopping. "So now what?"

Nikhil moved the sliced bell pepper to a bowl and started on the jalapeno. "So now we check out the other offers."

"There are other offers?"

"There will be."

"Okay. Well, that's good then."

"What about you? Will you take out a loan?"

"Most likely. Amar got fired last night."

Nikhil's turn to be surprised. "So a fabulous night for all."

"He literally got fired for improving a dish." Anita shook her head. "He used our mom's masala."

Nikhil stopped chopping and looked at her. "Seriously? He can make that?"

"Just about. Maybe now, he'll consider starting the catering business he's always talked about."

"Good for him." Nikhil moved to the stove to tend to the chai. Anita started chopping the cilantro on the other side of the stove, while she sautéed the onions and peppers.

Nikhil poured three mugs of chai and they stopped for a few moments to enjoy it with Dada. Anita inhaled the aroma of happiness before she took a sip. "This is always amazing, Nicky. Even without your special masala today."

"She is correct. Excellent chai." Dada sipped his and placed it back on the island. "You know what I heard? I heard that Nikhil had Rocky fire Jalissa that day."

Nikhil threw a furtive glance at Dada, then Anita. "Where did you hear that?"

"I'm an old man. People underestimate my ability to hear things." Dada held out his hands and shrugged.

"Is that true, Nikhil? You're the one who pissed her off?" Anita gently put down her mug and turned to him.

"Well, she was trying to blackmail JFL." Nikhil squirmed. "And while I may not be an employee of JFL, I certainly won't stand for blackmail."

"What did she want?" Anita furrowed her brow. She knew what Jalissa wanted. Nikhil. But if she was blackmailing them, she wanted more.

Nikhil pressed his lips together like he didn't want to tell her.

"What's the big deal? Just tell me," Anita insisted.

"She wanted the community division that Jake had mentioned."

Anita just looked at him.

"What? That's yours."

"I haven't even graduated yet."

"One year. And you'll easily pass the bar. You would be perfect for starting that up, and you know it. There's no way Jalissa was getting that."

"You had to know she'd retaliate. I mean, I only met her two days ago and even I could see that about her."

Nikhil shrugged. "I didn't care. And Rocky agreed with me. We don't cave in to blackmail. She should have been gone a long time ago." He smirked at her. "Anyway, *I* wasn't the one who punched her." He nodded at her wrapped hand.

Anita pressed her lips together. "Well, she deserved that, too."

"That she did," Dada agreed. Nikhil laughed and Anita joined him.

"I wasn't planning on taking it," Anita finally said as they got back to cooking.

"What do you mean?" Nikhil beat an egg and poured it over some of the bell-pepper-and-onion mixture in the pan. "The job? But why?"

"Well, we're not really together, are we?" Anita answered as she shredded some cheese.

"What does that have to do with working for JFL?"

"It would be too hard—awkward. They're your family…"

"You could do it. It might be awkward at first—but I shouldn't be getting in the way of things that are good for you."

Anita had to stop and stare at him. Who was this Nikhil? They continued to work in silence. She placed a rotli on top of the flat egg mixture and flipped it over. She added the shredded cheese and rolled it up.

"Nice." Nikhil grinned at her.

"I saw it on Instagram."

"You're amazing," Nikhil whispered.

Anita flushed. "I know." They made a few more roll-ups, potatoes and pancakes, all the while chatting as if they'd been doing this forever. By the time they got out plates, Dada was no longer at the island.

"He's asleep," Anita called from the living room. "On the sofa." She shook her head. "Let him sleep. We'll wake him after we eat."

Nikhil filled plates for them while Anita made mimosas. "What's brunch without a mimosa?"

They sat next to each other and started to eat, the conversation never stopping.

"I'm sorry, Anita." Nikhil's voice went quiet and serious.

"For what?" She took a bite of her eggs. Funny, she'd had no appetite an hour ago.

"For everything. For the way I treated you when we were married, and everything you were put through this week. You deserve better than that." He looked around and motioned with his hands. "You deserve *this*. Good chai, good food, people who love you."

Anita's heart raced. Was he saying what she thought he was? "Dada does love me."

"Yes. He does." Nikhil was looking at her with such intensity. He moved closer.

"You know what else I deserve? Someone who loves me enough to bring me fresh chai when I'm working. Someone who knows I would never cut out without a good reason. Someone who wants what is best for me, even if it isn't what's best for them." Anita moved closer to him. "Know anyone like that?"

"Hey! What smells so good?" Amar bounded into the kitchen. "Nikhil? What are you doing here? And did you two make all this?" He ran his gaze over the food. "Looks amazing."

"Nikhil!" Dada called from the living room. "Time to go."

"You didn't even eat, Dada," Anita chided him.

"Eat?" Dada furrowed his brow. "Ah well. Maybe next time, eh, beti? We need to go before my daughters send the police looking for me."

Anita exchanged a glance with Nikhil, both of them smiling. Dada's motives for brunch were clear. "Sure, Dada. Next time."

Chapter 23

Nikhil stood in the doorway of her classroom. He watched Anita pack up her bags like he had so many times before. Computer bag, purse, coffee mug, bag with snacks. He'd learned what every bag was for when he would hang out with her after class.

He hadn't seen her for a few days. He told himself it was because he had his launch, and he was hanging out with a few cousins who had stayed a few extra days. But the truth was, he had been building up his courage.

His mother had informed him that Charlotte Montgomery was a lovely young woman with a lot on her plate, and that she was happy to give her a job.

"I also offered to pay that last year of tuition, but Anita said a deal was a deal, and that she would be fine," his mother had told him as she cooked dinner for the family.

Nikhil shook his head and smiled. Of course she did.

"Maybe she'll listen to you. Talk to her. She won't have to take the loan." She was chopping cilantro, and the fresh woodsy aroma filled the kitchen.

Nikhil laughed. "It's like you don't even know her, Mom. Or me."

She waved a hand and sighed. "I knew you wouldn't ask her. But I had to try."

"It's not even Sunday, Mom, and you're cooking."

His mother shrugged. "It's time I cut back a bit from JFL. Rocky can handle things. I want to spend time with my family. Especially once the baby comes."

Nikhil watched his mother bustle around in the kitchen. The air between them felt lighter, warmer since the wedding.

"Don't just stand there. Chop onions." She pointed her knife at the onions in front of him. He suppressed a smile and started chopping.

They worked in silence for a moment. "I guess we're more alike than I thought," Nikhil offered.

His mother grinned up at him as she pulled out ginger from the fridge. "I guess we are."

"Why don't you come to the launch tomorrow night?"

"I was thinking to come to your launch tomorrow."

They spoke in unison. Then smiled at each other.

"Sounds good," they both said together.

"Maybe go see Anita," his mother suggested.

"Mom."

She held up her hands in surrender. "It's a suggestion."

Nikhil had enjoyed a delicious meal with his mother and Rocky and Easha. They had opened a bottle of wine and FaceTimed with Tina and Jake.

The only thing missing was Anita.

Nikhil leaned against the doorframe and watched her. Her hair was down, silky and straight. She tucked a piece behind her ear as she balanced the bags on her shoulders and reached for her coffee mug. It wasn't just that he found her to be the most beautiful woman he knew. It wasn't the fact that every cell in his body was propelling him forward to her. It wasn't the fact that his heart raced like he was a teenager in love when he looked at her.

It was simply that he wanted to be the one she shared her life with. He wanted to be at her side while she changed the world.

"I do know someone like that," he said as he entered the classroom.

She jumped at the sound of his voice, nearly dropping all her things.

Nikhil stood just inside the doorway of her classroom, like he had so many times before.

She hadn't seen him since brunch, but then she wasn't sure that she would. She hadn't gone to his launch because, well, frankly, it was too painful. She might have to reconsider going to work for JFL when she graduated.

He was in jeans and a plain navy blue T-shirt that fit him and all his muscles perfectly. The exact clothes she always imagined him in, when she imagined him, which was all the time. He was clean-shaven; his wavy hair was tamed back. But what put her heart and body on alert was the way he was looking at her. He carried himself with an air of confidence she'd never seen before. And he was looking at her like she was the only thing before him. Like there was nothing he'd rather do than just stand there and drink her in.

She had just gathered her many bags and coffee mug and was ready to leave for the evening. Seeing him, hearing his voice, she stopped, and everything clattered to the ground.

"Someone like what?" She knew exactly what he was talking about, but she needed to hear him say it. Her heart pounded in her chest.

"Someone who would bring you chai when you're working. Someone who knows that you would never cut out without a good reason." He was taking small, slow steps toward her, the look in his dark eyes devastating in its intensity. Nikhil's mouth when he smiled at her was a glorious thing. "Someone who wants what is best for you even if it's not best for him."

"Oh yeah?" Anita tried to put some sass in her voice, but the words came out breathy and soft.

"You also deserve someone who will stand by your side no matter what. Someone who understands your silent eye communication." He raised an eyebrow, standing in front of her now, looking at her with no amusement at all. "Someone who will hold you when you're sad. Someone who wants to kiss you senseless all the time." His eyes darkened. "Someone who knows you love them, no matter what. Someone who won't break your heart." He paused and now he was close enough for their bodies to touch. Too close. His next words came out in a husky whisper. "Someone who will love you with everything he has."

Anita swallowed hard. She could feel the heat from his body, smell his cologne. "You say you know someone like that?" She widened her eyes at him.

"I do."

The way he looked at her, that smile, the love in his eyes. "I love you. Only you." He spread his arms wide and let them drop. "I have always been yours even when I thought I wasn't. And I always will be, whether you'll have me or not." He paused and seemed to gather courage. "But I'm really hoping that you'll have me."

She reached up and kissed him, slowly at first. His response was immediate, but tentative. She relaxed and gave into her feelings for him in the same instant he kissed her with abandon. Almost as if he didn't care if she knew how intensely he loved her, because it was unchanging.

She held nothing back from him in that kiss, and neither did he.

When they parted, she lightly smacked him on the shoulder. "I knew you understood my eye communication."

He laughed. "Is that all you have to say?"

She shook her head. "I would love some chai."

"Now?" His eyes darkened and his voice thickened in anticipation of her response.

"No." She snuggled closer to him and whispered, "Tomorrow morning."

ALL THE REST OF THE DAYS—

HAPPILY EVER AFTER

Epilogue

Nikhil fidgeted in the groom's chair in the mandap staring at the white cloth in front of him. Two separate lives, two separate souls, becoming one.

The music cued him that Anita was on the way. Easha would walk first, then Tina. Amar was doing the puja that parents usually do. Divya would escort her down the aisle. He tried to peek around the cloth, and took a kick to the ankle from Rocky, who was holding the antarpat in front of him, his new brother-in-law Jake supporting the other side.

Her sari rustled and her anklets jingled as she entered the mandap and the music died down. Nikhil couldn't remember the last time he'd felt so at peace.

On just the other side of this cloth was a woman he loved with not just his heart, but his whole self—and who returned his love. A woman he could never be without. A woman he loved from the depths of his soul, to the ends of the universe. A woman he had once lost, but would never let go of again.

On the other side of this cloth was the rest of his life.

Rocky glanced at Jake, and then both men looked at him. Nikhil inhaled deeply and nodded. They dropped the cloth.

Anita stood before him resplendent and beautiful in her red-and-white bridal sari, unabashedly smiling at him, love emanating from her very being.

Nikhil's heart raced. He had no explanation for it, other than the knowledge that he had finally embraced his good fortune that Anita had returned to his life.

She met his gaze and silently told him she loved him. A tear in her eye told him that she missed having her parents here. He let his smile and eyes tell her that he loved her, and she smiled again.

When she was ready, she sat down across from him, her gaze never leaving his, and the rest of their lives began.

* * * * *

HARLEQUIN
PLUS

Try the best multimedia subscription service for romance readers like you!

Read, Watch and Play.

Experience the easiest way to get the romance content you crave.

Start your **FREE TRIAL** at
<u>www.harlequinplus.com/freetrial</u>.